THIRTTENE FRIENDS

THIRTTENE FRIENDS

ELFDREAMS OF PARALLAN
ALBTRÄUME

BENJAMIN TOWE

authorHOUSE®

AuthorHouse™
1663 Liberty Drive
Bloomington, IN 47403
www.authorhouse.com
Phone: 1 (800) 839-8640

Published by AuthorHouse 10/10/2016

ISBN: 978-1-5246-4480-2 (sc)
ISBN: 978-1-5246-4478-9 (hc)
ISBN: 978-1-5246-4479-6 (e)

Library of Congress Control Number: 2016916847

Print information available on the last page.

CONTENTS

Ǿ ∞ Ǿ
I, II, III, IV, V, VI, VII, VIII, IX, X, XI, XII, XIII
∞ Ǿ ∞

The Thirttene Friends

Ǿ ∞ Ǿ
I, II, III, IV, V, VI, VII, VIII, IX, X, XI, XII, XIII
∞ Ǿ ∞

Wisps…
Threads…
Threads of Magick…
Threads of fate…
Threads of time…
Threads connecting worlds …
Dreams connecting worlds …
Dreams of Magick…
The Magick of Dreams…
Magick connecting dreams…
Magick connecting worlds…
Dream raiders…
Elf pressure…
Albtraum…
Albträume, elf dreams, nightmares…

Ǿ ∞ Ǿ

Albträume...

In the words of the Teacher of the Drelves on the occasion of harvesting enhancing root tubers in Green Vale in the World of the Three Suns...

"The plants on the hill in the center are the *Thirttene Friends*. All plants are our friends, but like the enhancing plant, the circle of exceptional trees of various shapes and sizes that occupy the top of the knoll are special. The Thirttene *are* Magick. Even when we are without a Spellweaver, we are not without the Thirttene. Their gifts have saved us many times. But we must reserve their fruits for times of need. The Thirttene Friends and the geyser that gives them life predate our spoken and recorded histories. Legend holds the Thirttene are older than the Lone Oak. The waters of the geyser are Magick. You should respect, but not fear Magick."

CHAPTER 1

The First Sorcerer of Sagain

Nature long ruled the ancient world of Magick Sagain, night less World of Three Suns Parallan, primitive Donothor, and a simple beautiful blue, cloud-covered world. Ultimately fate and Magick entangled the four worlds.

The great gray sun ignored Nature's laws, meandered through space and time, drew near worlds, and bathed them with grayness. Magick flourished in the Gray Wanderer's light. Gray stardust fell from the wondrous sun and filtered through even the densest atmosphere to the surface of fortuitous worlds. Each miniscule piece of the gray sun maintained the properties of the whole and emitted the telltale gray light.

Nature's pawn, an iron rogue remnant of a world doomed by a supernova explosion, hurdled through space and slammed into the Gray Wanderer. The cosmic wallop in the depths of space obliterated the rogue. Fragments of the massive gray sun flew into the void of space and carried the Gray Sun's essence. One such irregular three by five-foot fragment of Grayness came under the gravitational influence of a binary system. Binary systems were common in Nature's galaxies. These two suns struggled for ascendancy like sibling rivals, produced titanic forces, and directed the gray fragment toward the fourth planet in the binary system. The twin suns appeared two twinkling points in the daytime sky of the distant world. Nature gave the planet the light of two distant suns that produced titanic forces.

This unexceptional little planet Sagain had given birth to a rustic civilization. Diverse creatures walked its surface, swam in its seas, and flew in its skies. Preternatural creatures and Nature enjoyed dominion and little resistance to their laws in the little world. The Old Ones were existent on Sagain long before the dawn of Magick. The preternatural creatures provided the old world vestiges of Magick. Winged and horned creatures, beings fleet and silent, wyverns, Baxcats, lee cats, Leicats, griffons, griffins, griphins, gryphons, hamadryads, humming birds, pi rannas, leprechauns, Manticores, medusas, dragons of various colors, nagas, troglodytes, Pegasi of various colors, satyrs, dryads, Minotaurs, pixies, sasquatch, trolls, wyrms, wyverns, sirens, huldra, chimeras, sphinxes, banshee, boogie men, bogeymen, brownies, centaurs, hippogriffs, Dobies, Efreet, fauns, fawns, foans, sprites, adherers, shape changers, doppelgangers, Rocs, Elementals, Xorn, Windwalkers, Night Hags, Devils, Djinn, and other strange beings resisted the forces of Nature and the inexorable march and challenge of time. Few people had seen or heard the Old Ones. Encounters with the subtle creatures for the most part had left the unfortunate who stumbled upon them thinking he had awakened from a disturbing dream. On occasion a fetching female wearing a marvelous white robe and bearing a distaff briefly appeared. Observers fought the urge to run to her and throw themselves down at her feet. No man of Sagain had ever been able to reject the charisma of the Spinner, the Allotter, and the Unturning. The Moirae, the Fates, were the most powerful of the Old Ones and said to be the daughters of night and the wind. The trio sought dominion over the primitive world. The white robed sisters were architects of the destinies of humble mortal men and known by many names, including Nona, Decima, and Mors. Commonly called the Spinner, the Allotter, and the Unturning, the uninvited threesome came calling during the ninth month of pregnancy and again three nights after a child's birth. The Spinner spun the thin precious thread of life over her distaff. The Allotter measured the length of the narrow thread with a mysterious red rod. The Unturning, the inevitable for those mortal, chose the manner of the individual's death and cut the thin thread with her dreaded shears. Nature and time only gently opposed the efforts of the Fates. Magick, like unlit tinder, lay dormant in the inconsequential world. The spark that ignited the tinder came from the far away recesses of space. Sagain's binary star system influenced the course of an irregular three by five-foot fragment of Grayness that streaked through the enormity of space.

The gray fragment first appeared in the sky of the fourth planet as little more than a speck in the sky and went unnoticed by most that lived in the simple mundane world. Until...

The Klarje family scratched a living from the savannah near the Bald Mountains. Young Cydney Klarje took his turn watching his family's herd of Blue Nus, Red Machis, and Purple Enigmas on this cooler than average night. His father had seen a pack of Raptors in the valley near the river, and the gaggle of winged predators posed a real threat to the herd. The hard-working Cydney gave up a night of exchanging stories with his friends in the village tavern. Instead young Cydney was spending the night listening to the gentle lowing of the cloven beasts that had provided his family a livelihood for generations.

Cydney was a good son, who followed his father's instructions to the tee, enjoyed his lot in life, and gladly took his shifts. The young herdsman looked up into the clear evening sky. The thought-provoking new object was moving ever closer. Watchmen had reported the tiny light only recently. Many oldsters warned that it was an omen of sorts, but most elders felt it was simply another passing visitor to the night sky. Transient lights frequented the skies of Sagain. The powerful twin suns bullied cosmic travelers and often altered their courses. As a result, comets, meteors, shooting stars were commonplace. But this object behaved differently, moved purposefully, and drew nearer. Odd grayness surrounded the approaching object.

Cydney sighed, pulled his arms inward, snuggled in his hand-knit palaca sweater, and tried to keep warm while he kept vigil on the restless beasts. A rumbling sound in the distance alarmed the young shepherd. The shepherd took a quick look around and saw no evidence of the feared Raptors. If the opportunistic predators sensed the presence of a herder, the gangly waist high beasts probably wouldn't attack the herd. Still Cydney readied his bow. He was, after all, the best marksman in the whole region.

The sound grew ominously louder. It was not the hunting call of a predator!

Impossible! Even though the hour was late, shadow gave way to illumination, but not the normal light of day. Grayness surrounded Cydney Klarje! He looked to the sky and saw it!

Fire!

A ball of great fire roared toward the ground! Cydney watched in horror as the fireball struck far to the southeast of where he stood. A great explosion shook the ground. Flames and heat roared across the savannah. People within ten leagues of the impact site had no time to scream. Death claimed every person who stood within a circle of radius from the point of impact and the place where Cydney Klarje stood. All life departed the lands in the propinquity of the cataclysm. Hundreds of square miles lay devastated. Great wind emanated from the impact site, swept across the plain with pyroclastic flow, and approached Cydney. He inhaled deeply and prepared for death. A minute fragment of the gray wanderer from deep space struck Cydney's chin. Intense gray light bathed, surrounded, and remained around him. The mighty wind picked up and carried the horrified Cydney toward the distant Bald Mountains and left him in an area of desolation. Cydney crashed to the ground far from the impact. The shepherd inexplicably survived. A heart-shaped, cherry-red mark appeared on Cydney's chin where the tiny gray fragment struck him. Consciousness left him, and the herdsman entered a deep sleep. Young Cydney dreamed of his simple home and loving family.

Shapeless grayness entered his dreams.

Wisps...
Threads...
Threads of Magick...
Threads of fate...
Threads of time...
Threads connecting worlds ...
Dreams connecting worlds ...
Dreams of Magick...
The Magick of Dreams...
Magick connecting dreams...
Magick connecting worlds...
Grayness...

Words formed in Cydney's mind. "Accept the gift of grayness for your people."
The sleeping Cydney managed, "Am I dead? Is all hope lost?"

The intimidating voice replied, "No, my servant. You have found new hope."

Cydney replied, "In my mind I see words, phrases, thoughts that are new to me and without meaning."

Speaking in a dream…
Interacting with one's dream…
Hearing one's dreams and responding…
Speaking and hearing one's dreams respond…

The voice answered, "You will understand when you awaken."

Cydney asked, "Who are you?"

The shapeless form answered, "You are visited by the grayness of Andreas. You may call me Xenn."

Cydney said, "You are only a dream. You are not real."

The voice answered, "In time you will understand. Even now, it will become clearer when you awaken."

The grayness left his dreams. Cydney's mind drifted through memories both good and bad. Then Cydney Klarje awakened bruised and battered. Odd phrases milled about in his mind. Uttering the phrases produced simple Magick. Cydney found one combination of phrases accompanied by simple movements of his hands enabled him to *affect normal fires*. A fire as small as a torch increased to a bonfire or reduced to match light. Reducing the fire cut fuel consumption and increasing the fire burned the fuel more quickly. Initially Cydney's ability did not increase or reduce heat produced by the fire. When he slept thereafter, new Magick appeared in his mind. He learned phrases to produce jets of searing heat from his fingertips. In order to produce the effect Cydney touched his thumbs together and fanned the fingers of both hands whilst uttering phrases that appeared in his dreams. The *burning hands* effect did little damage to enemies and was mainly defensive, but it did ignite flammable materials. The incantation for Hold Portal and its reverse Knock appeared next in the erstwhile shepherd's mind. The spells enabled Cydney Klarje to bar entry and open locked doors with simple spoken phrases. Over time the incantations grew more complex and oft required materials to bring about their effects. Cydney's dreams told him the ingredients necessary for the dweomers. The misty grayness and voice often accompanied the new spell incantations. Sometimes phrases simply appeared. The young transformed shepherd began construction on a cottage on the site the maelstrom deposited him.

After an exhausting day of work, another dream…

Cydney finished another day of construction and retired to his rest chamber. His thoughts returned to his simple life before the cataclysm. Finally, he found sleep and dreamed of simpler times. Then…

Shapeless grayness again entered his dreams.

Wisps…
Threads…
Threads of Magick…
Threads of fate…
Threads of time…
Threads connecting worlds …
Dreams connecting worlds …
Dreams of Magick…
The Magick of Dreams…
Magick connecting dreams…
Magick connecting worlds…
Grayness…

Cydney shivered in his sleep.

The voice said, "You learn well. Your knowledge must be passed forward. Heed these letters and form them into written words. You'll find gifts when you awaken."

Phrases formed in Cydney's mind and imprinted in his memory the letters of an ancient alphabet and the knowledge of a *Comprehend Languages Spell*. When he awakened, Cydney discovered a thick vellum lying upon a rather plain rucksack with a tie closure. Cydney rubbed sleep from his eyes and inspected the large book. Runes written in his newfound language spelled *Chronicle of the Family Klarje* on the dark purple soft cover. Cydney carefully opened the book and flipped through the blank light purple pages. A writing implement appeared in his left hand. He touched the tip of the pen to the first page and with painstakingly smooth strokes recounted his experiences on the night of the cataclysm. The quill pen never ran out of ink. When he finished writing, he closed the tome. The pen disappeared. When he reopened the tome, the pen reappeared in his hand. Cydney turned his attention to the rucksack. The book was larger, but when he touched the volume to the opening in the sack, the opening expanded and accepted the book. The book shrank once within the bag of holding and the weight of the bag did not appreciably increase with the large heavy book inside. Cydney used the sack to store spell components and valuables. The wondrous rucksack enabled Cydney to store and categorize his ever increasing stock of spell components and items of Magick.

Cydney Klarje became the first sorcerer of Sagain and outlived all those of his generation and many thereafter. His third son and second daughter shared the cherry-red, heart-shaped mark on their chins. The cataclysm robbed the simple shepherd of his immediate family and loved ones. The steady march of time robbed the shepherd-turned sorcerer of other family and loved ones. The gray light spared and imparted him the mixed blessing of longevity. Time, Nature, and the gray light were in cahoots. In his loneliest times, Cydney wrote of his pain in the Chronicle of the Klarjes. His slowly dimming vision and imperceptible aging were poor compensation for his lost loved ones.

The great Fire in the Sky forever changed Sagain. Magick emerged from Nature's shadow. The rare, exceptional, and legendary Old Ones had long existed in the primitive world and resisted change. The area of impact remained desolate and lifeless. The impact affected the entire planet and changed its lands forever. Thick gray clouds choked out much of the planet's fauna and flora. Red rain fell from dense clouds. Widespread extinctions followed the cataclysm. To the southeast buttes replaced flat land. Grayness surrounded the area.

At the impact site, a stone table rock rose from the sand and created a lifeless plateau that became known as the Lonely Cliffs. Fine red lines meandered from the Lonely Cliffs through the hot sand. Nothing grew within ten leagues of the Lonely Cliffs.

Time slowly healed the land's wounds, and Nature recouped losses.

The gray storm expanded the Cydney Klarje's vision, redefined his essence, and toughened his constitution. The herdsman passed these changes along his line. Descendants often bore a cherry-red, heart-shaped birthmark on their chin. Cydney Klarje finished his home and founded a community at the site the wind placed him. The community grew, flourished, and become the great city of Thynna. Its citizenry attained long life. Exceptional men and women descended from survivors closest the bizarre impact and touched by red rain. Cydney Klarje and his progeny were most the most extraordinary. Runes and lettering of written language appeared in the changing shepherd's thoughts. He taught the runes to his children. His family etched their genealogy into the Klarje Family Tome. Cydney recorded the story of his family on the purple vellum in Chronicle of the Klarjes. He recorded from memory the names and stories his grandfather told by the fireside. Prior to Cydney's writing, the shepherds of Cydney's family and ilk were not privy to written word. Instead the elders passed down their history in stories by campfires and by the hearths.

Dreams troubled Cydney Klarje the rest of his days.

CHAPTER 2

The Rise of Thynna

Thynna grew in stature, quickly became known as the Center of Magick. The burgeoning conurbation drew extraordinary people touched by grayness and red rain like a beacon drew a wayward vessel tossed by the sea. The Klarjes taught the written language. Fledgling spell casters flocked to study with older wizards. Living in Thynna became synonymous with wealth and stature. Curiosity brought others to the growing community… and drew the attention of arcane forces.

The wizards of Thynna became endowed by progressively greater longevity. With longer lives individual sorcerers gained more knowledge and power. Spell levels became more complex. Enterprising merchants and hunters capitalized on competition for material spell components. This newfound market demanded skins, scales, ichors, and bones of many species of Sagain.

The elders of Thynna erected a great wall around the city. The outer curtain defended against the growing hostility of the outside world. The increasing number of sorcerers within the city became more and more insecure and restricted entry and migration from other areas. Travelers who arrived at Thynna were invariably less powerful and unable to contest the will of the citizenry of Thynna. The leadership of Thynna withdrew behind a second fortified wall, built great edifices, and used Protective Magick to secure the towers. The inner curtain was thicker than the outer wall, and surrounded the opulent inner ward. Each edifice was built greater than its predecessor. The greater the house, the greater its occupant… became the allusion. Wealth brought with it fear and paranoia. The leaders hired mercenaries and recruited legions of guards. The heavily armed legions of Thynna set up outposts beyond the walls of the city and commandeered much of the surrounding countryside. This infringed upon the grazing grounds of the herds of the nomadic peoples of the Great Plains, and restricted the trade of the roughened miners of the nearby mountains. Great resentment and conflict developed.

The city flourished for thirty generations. The leaders of Thynna greeted newcomers with suspicion and contempt and made unwelcome the Old Ones of Sagain. The Old Ones were rarely seen. The area around the Lonely Cliffs remained unexplored.

The most powerful wizards were born in the propinquity of Thynna, or more specifically in the flat terrain to the south and west of the burgeoning conurbation. Rhiann Klarje, the first born of two prominent sorcerers Caye Klarje and Kurth Marsh, was quite exceptional. Caye Klarje descended from the first sorcerer Cydney. Caye's father Thomas Bayard Klarje and his fraternal twin brother Mayard were the oldest children of PT Fleckinghauser Klarje. Caye's Grandfather PT Fleckinghauser served as Lord President of the Council of Thynna, the ruling body of the city of Magick. PT was the oldest sibling in his family and heir to the Chronicle of the Klarjes. He passed the tome to Caye's father, who was the older twin by seven minutes. Thomas Bayard followed his father in serving the Council of Thynna. He worked on many committees and worked in Thynna's inner circle. He rose to the position of High Chancellor. Thomas Bayard's life-mate and Caye's mother Ciera Leftbridge was the daughter of Stewart Leftbridge, the castellan, the city's highest law enforcement official and the third highest position after Lord President and High Chancellor. Thomas and Ciera's marriage was celebrated by both families and all of Thynna and bedecked by much pomp and circumstance. Thynna's inner circle was greatly surprised when the newly wedded couple chose to live outside the inner ward and beyond the inner curtain in the less affluent areas of the outer ward of the city.

Mayard Klarje followed a different path. The younger of the twins never took interest in the affairs of the city. His first love was Magick. Mayard gathered rare spell components and mastered new dweomers. He strengthened the Magick defenses of the city and advanced Magick further than any sorcerer since the first sorcerer, his ancestor Cydney.

Mayard befriended Old Ones and studied their ways. Mayard was often at odds with the ruling Council of Thynna. Mayard Klarje felt their policies toward immigrants and the Old Ones were unfair, iniquitous, and unwarranted.

The council even further restricted entry to Thynna. Newcomers were strictly vetted, and the Old Ones were constrained entry to the city. Ruling sorcerers feared the preternatural residents of Sagain. The Old Ones predated the Dawn of Magick and the cataclysm hat transformed Sagain to a world of Magick.

Mayard rejected the Council of Thynna's decisions to isolate the city from the Old Ones and restrict entry to the city. Cydney Klarje had welcomed newcomers and endeavored to teach them the newfangled ways of Magick. Mayard shared the first sorcerer's view that Magick belonged to all Sagain and should thusly be shared. Mayard oft left on walkabouts and returned with more treasures for the common coffers of Thynna. His contributions earned Mayard Klarje great recognition and led to construction of many edifices to him. A great statue of his likeness stood in the inner ward near the main school. Mayard left on walkabout after the marriage of Caye Klarje and Kurth Marsh.

To the chagrin of the council, Caye and Kurth had also chosen to live in the outer ward and work outside the inner circle. Kurth reluctantly accepted a position on the council following his father's untimely death. Two years after their wedding Caye and Kurth welcomed their first child, a son Rhiann. Rhiann arrived with a cherry-red, heart-shaped birthmark on his little chin. Two years later a second son Arthur Seigh arrived. Mayard Klarje remained away from Thynna.

In Sagain children began formal schooling shortly after their sixth birthday. Ages six to twelve attended an ornate school in the inner ward of Thynna and shared classes. They were not separated by age. Studies included reading, writing, arithmetic, spelling, conjuration, spell materials, and history.

Constructing the school was financed through the efforts of Mayard Klarje, who returned to Thynna with priceless jewels and spell components. His most valuable addition was the Gem Bush, which was planted in the courtyard near the Great Hall of Thynna, the assembly place of the Council of Thynna and the city of Magick's center of government. The Gem Bush was a gift from the Old Ones of the

Hanging Gardens, specifically the Three Sisters, the Spinner, Allotter, and the Unturning. The Gem Bush was thought unique; it was certainly the only one known in all of Sagain. It grew after the impact that created the cataclysm and never increased beyond its current size. The bush was thirteen feet tall. Its diameter was thirteen inchworm lengths. The tree had thirteen limbs, thirteen leaves on each limb, thirteen veins on each leaf, and drew nourishment through thirteen roots. Each limb bore one gem of thirteen different colors, including one ultra-rare red diamond. Only one gem of a given color could be removed every thirteen years. A second gem could not be removed, even with the power of a Limited Wish or Alter Reality Spell. The Three Sisters entrusted the plant to Mayard Klarje and hoped it would improve relations between Thynna and the Old Ones community. Suspicion and greed overrode the gesture and the Council of Thynna accepted the gift, but more restrictions were placed on entry and approach to the city by the preternatural Old Ones. Mayard protested to no avail. Nevertheless, he painstakingly planted the Gem Bush in the Great Hall's courtyard.

Mayard mastered and shared with other sorcerers the spells Stone Shape and Transmute Rock to Mud and its reversal Mud to Rock. Clay and sand brought from the Green River basin were the material components of the spell. The school sat over what had been a marshy area. Mayard's spells hardened the ground and he used hardened mud in the construction. He filled the school's library with tomes and items from faraway places to further the education of Thynna's youth. Not since the founder Cydney Klarje had one sorcerer given so much to the community. The wayfaring Mayard did not stick around to receive gratitude and praise and went off on further journeys.

CHAPTER 3

Mayard Klarje's Sojourns

Mayard Klarje struggled with sleeplessness. The old wayfaring sorcerer had left Thynna a fortnight earlier and spent most of that time wandering the foothills of the Copper Mountains. Mayard pursued and subdued highwaymen Big Boy and Tiny and brought them to Gnome-town to the waiting and grateful hands of Burgomaster Altus Stillwater Darktop. Altus had nineteen given names to go with his family name Stillwater. Gnomes added monikers relating to their accomplishments and adventures. His unusually dark hair had earned him the moniker Darktop. Burgomaster Stillwater now added "Big Boy" as his twentieth given name. The grateful burgomaster had granted Mayard a room in his manor. Mayard had mixed feelings about the reward. The comfortable bedding, brew master's wonderful ale, and wonderful feast prepared by the burgomaster's spouse Enid were offset by relentless pestering by the burgomaster's incorrigible son Norman. If the Gnome-kin didn't get his way, he pitched a veritable fit. His father Altus Twenty-names Big Boy Stillwater termed the outbursts "Norman storms." Mayard Klarje dubbed the little Gnome Storming Norman and the moniker stuck. The little bloke shared his father's dark hair. Storming Norman Darktop now had three names. But Mayard Klarje received more than hospitality and nourishment from the grateful burgomaster. Gnomes, Dwarves, and men worked alongside one another in the mines in the extensive catacombs beneath the mountains. The economy of Gnome-town and success of the industrious Gnomish entrepreneurs depended upon successful harvesting the riches of the Copper Mountains and transporting them to the townships. The Highwaymen Big Boy Brown and Tiny Anderson had disrupted trade and commerce and taken the lives of several miners and citizens of Gnome-town and Dry Creek, the small community nearest the extensive Copper Mountain mines.

Miners had found an odd piece of grayish red ore. The ore was discovered in the depths of the world at precisely a point of impact of a visitor from deep space that produced the cataclysm that forever changed Sagain and heralded the Dawn of Magick. The miners and alchemists had been unable to determine the nature of the ore and brought it under heavy guard to Gnome-town and the care of the burgomaster. Gnomish and Dwarfish gem masters extensively studied the irregular rock, which periodically gave off gray auras. Rarely thick red liquid oozed from the odd stone. By all accounts the ore was unique to Sagain. Burgomaster Altus Twenty-names Big Boy Stillwater Darktop presented the bizarre object to Mayard at dinner. Mayard had no idea of the nature of the artifact but accepted the Gnome's gift. As a general rule it was best not to decline a gift from a Gnome. Likewise respect for the Burgomaster kept Mayard from complaining about the rambunctious Gnome-kin Storming Norman.

Many years passed.

Mayard Klarje continued his sojourns. The old sorcerer much preferred exploring and learning the ways of the world to hobnobbing and enduring the petty social affairs of the inner ward of Thynna. Mayard hazarded visits to the Hanging Gardens in the Veldt. The Hanging Gardens were the stronghold of Sagain's preternatural beings the Old Ones. The old sorcerer enjoyed a special relationship with Nona, one the three Fates. His most recent visit to the Hanging Gardens was not a social visit. Mayard had barely escaped sentries of the closely guarded Amazon Temple of Artemis and got away by the skin of his teeth with an Amazon's arrow impaled in his butt. The Siren Maranna carried the wounded sorcerer to the Hanging Gardens. Healers removed the arrow and Nona used thread spun from her distaff to sew up the wound of Mayard's butt. He dragged his sore tail to bed and sought sleep. Per usual he tucked his knapsack under his head. Mayard always kept the knapsack close at hand. Dimension Door Spells transformed the blue nu hide pouch to a Bag of Holding. Mayard Klarje kept his prized possessions in the fantastic bag which was much larger on the inside. The Magick sack now also held the lump of odd ore from the Copper Mountains and the amazon's arrow that Nona's healers had extracted from his buttock. A few glasses of Jove's nectar eased his pain and brought drowsiness. The old sorcerer uttered a simple "Soften" spell that transformed the knapsack to a fluffy pillow. Soon he slept.

Mayard's long life had seen many adventures and he oft relived them in his dreams. This night was no exception. He dreamed of his early life in Thynna and first disagreements with the Council of Thynna. Mayard bore the mark of the Klarjes, a heart-shaped, cherry-red birthmark on the left side of his chin. He shared this trait with the first sorcerer of Sagain Cydney Klarje. Early in childhood Mayard endured teasing from other children. He and his twin brother Bayard were nigh indistinguishable, save the birthmark on Mayard's face. His sleep continued and he next dreamed of his escapades with Nona, and the moment she gave him her greatest gift. The dream warmed the old sorcerer. The pleasing images faded, and grayness entered his dreams.

Wisps...
Threads...
Threads of Magick...
Threads of fate...
Threads of time...
Threads connecting worlds ...
Dreams connecting worlds ...
Dreams of Magick...
The Magick of Dreams...
Magick connecting dreams...
Magick connecting worlds...
Grayness...

Sorcerers dreamed of grayness and awakened afterward with incantations of new spells etched in their minds. On this occasion however the grayness coalesced into the visage of a young powerful female warrior. Her muscular arms held a replica of the gray-red rock from the Copper Mountains and a second small red heart-shaped stone about the size and color of a matater. Mayard had eaten his share of the red starchy tubers that were a staple of the plains dwellers' diets. In his dream the female warrior wore well-made leather armor that accentuated her curves and a flaming red tunic underneath her armor. She had deep blue eyes and dark brown hair that fell over her armor to the midpoint of her back. All-in-all she was rather pleasant to look upon and the dreaming sorcerer enjoyed the visage.

The warrior spoke, "Mayard Klarje, you have received great gifts and bear greater responsibilities. The time has come to pass that you must make use of these gifts. Grayness has deemed you the steward of Magick. The stone from the Copper Mountain depths is a fragment of the source of Magick. Grayness gives it a purpose. It is a sword stone. A swordsmith of ample and adequate skill now labors in the mines north of Dry Creek and Gnome-town. Carry the sword stone to the Copper Mountains and deliver it to the hand of the dwarf Roswell Kirkey. Take me with you."

Mayard spoke in his dream, "You live only in my dream."

She replied, "I am like you, Mayard Klarje, of grayness. I am the spirit... the heart of the sword. My essence lies within the heartstone."

Mayard said, "I do not possess such a stone. The Copper Mountain ore lies within my reach."

She chuckled and said, "I will be yours when you awaken. Touch the heartstone to the wound on the swordstone. Heal and make it whole."

Mayard queried, "The wound?"

She replied, "The site from which the stone's blood flows. First taste the flowing liquid and then touch the heartstone to the site. Then carry me to the Copper Mountains."

Mayard curiously asked, "What is your name?"

The warrior's face softened and she said, "I was Exeter. I am now a sister of Grayness and the spirit of the sword."

Mayard said, "I don't understand. The Gnomes and miners spoke of the bleeding rock. It has not bled since I possessed it."

Exeter said, "Sleep well, Mayard Klarje. You still have many roads to travel. My race is nearing its end. My goal is in sight. You shan't fulfill everything Grayness asks of you. Others will follow. They will bear the mark of the Klarjes. You must teach them well."

The visage faded.

Formless grayness lingered. A more familiar voice said, "Seal the spirit of Exeter within the swordstone. The swordstone and heartstone must never separate." The voice of grayness known to Mayard as Xenn continued, "Heed her words, son of Grayness. Now know these words, the incantation of the Permanence Spell. You must use the spell after you seal the spirit of the heartstone in the swordstone."

Grayness faded. Mayard Klarje awakened. Gray auras emanated from the knapsack beneath his head. A fist-sized red heart-shaped stone lay on the foot of his bed. The sorcerer picked up the stone. It began to synchronously pulse with his beating heart. Mayard removed the Copper Mountain stone from the Bag of Holding. True to his dream visitor's word red fluid oozed from a single sight on the gray-red rock. Mayard placed his lips onto the stone and drank deeply. He found the taste slightly bitter but pleasant. Mayard felt warm, flushed, and suffered a slight headache. The symptoms soon passed. The rich red fluid satisfied his thirst and hunger.

Mayard placed the heartstone to the site from which the liquid flowed. Intense purple and gray auras filled the room. The larger Copper Mountain stone absorbed the smaller stone. The auras briefly changed to red and then grayness filled the room. Mayard Klarje uttered the incantation of the Permanence Spell and touched the site where the stones came together. The auras ended.

Mayard's wound healed. All soreness left his backside. The precious threads from Nona's distaff fell from his skin to the bedding. Mayard gathered them and placed the threads in his bag of holding.

Over Nona's objections he old sorcerer left the Hanging Gardens and made his way to Gnome-town, where he was greeted by young recently acclaimed Burgomaster Storming Norman Twenty-four names Darktop. He then made his way through the community Dry Creek. The sorcerer stopped off at Jack Taylor's way station and continued on to the Copper Mountain mines and sought the swordsmith Roswell Kirkey. The miners' foreman Haird Daull led Mayard to the forge.

A stout dwarf labored over the forge in the oppressively hot room. Mayard asked, "Are you Roswell Kirkey?"

The dwarf hammered away at a hot piece of metal and said, "The one and only. I've been waiting for you, Mayard Klarje."

Mayard surprised said, "Uh… how'd you know my name?"

The dwarf dipped the hot metal in oil and gingerly placed it on an anvil. He turned and faced the taller sorcerer and said, "I dream too, sorcerer. I've seen you in my dreams. Mind you, I'd rather dream of beautiful Dwarfish and Gnomish females, but I've dreamed of your old a** and the lump of stone you are carrying."

Mayard replied, "Well… yes, I do carry a lump of ore and thus a job for you. I can pay well."

Roswell Kirkey answered, "I don't want your money, sorcerer. I'm honored to work the priceless ore. The longsword I create will be my gift to the world. It will be my legacy. I'll begin the work immediately… but it'll take a long time."

Mayard removed the grayish red ore and held it in his hand. A pleasing feminine voice appeared in his thoughts, "Mayard Klarje, I thank you for bringing me home. Your deed will serve many future bearers. Regarding the future… one of your own in Thynna has need of your tutelage. The mark has appeared."

The old sorcerer recognized the voice of the spirit of Grayness Exeter from his dream in the Hanging Gardens. Mayard extended the ore to the waiting hands of the dwarf and said, "I'll leave you to your work. I've business in Thynna. Family business."

CHAPTER 4

Caye Klarje's Concerns

Caye Klarje Marsh rarely spoke to her children about her adventuresome uncle. She hoped they'd trek more along the paths of her father Bayard Klarje and life-mate Kurth Marsh. The time for starting school approached for young Rhiann.

Caye Klarje Marsh was very active in community affairs and maintained close friendships with many other young sorcerers. She preferred to leave the hobnobbing and political dealing to Rhiann's father Kurth Marsh. Caye joined fathers and mothers with their children in parks and playgrounds. Caye entertained children with harmless spells like Fairie Fire, Dancing Lights, and Speak with Animals. Faerie Fire Spells produced blue, green, and violet outlines to persons and things Caye outlined with her fingers. She was fond of putting purple auras on the little sorcerers' noses and ears. The spells always produced laughter from the little ones. Dancing Lights produced glowing spheres of light of varying colors. Children considered them Magick balloons. Rhiann and other toddlers enjoyed the sparkling colors her spells produced and her conversations with dawgs and cats. As Rhiann grew older Caye allowed him to spend time in supervised play areas in the bustling conurbation. Teenage sorcerers and sorceresses watched over the little ones whilst they played. Thynna's outer ward was a very secure area. The city's walls and security forces kept danger from without at bay so Caye and other mothers and fathers had no concern about the children's' safety. However, the tyke bore the brunt of teasing from older and boisterous children. A bigger child named Jethro never let a play period pass without at least once approaching little Rhiann and maliciously tugging at the red birthmark on his chin. Jethro was two years older and also hassled Rhiann about his speech and size. As their speech developed, Jethro and two cohorts named Bo and Dean developed monikers for Rhiann, including "heart-face," "chicken-heart," and "little heart." Jethro tied Rhiann's shoelaces together, oft pulled his robe over his head, and threw his cap into a well. Jethro placed an Illusion Spell on Rhiann and produced a long furry tail on the tyke's posterior. Rhiann ran all the way home and sought out his mother. Caye cast a Dispel Magick Spell which eliminated the illusion. Rhiann lamented to his father, but Kurth urged him to be strong and reassured him that the children were only trying to be friends. Caye was not so sure. Jethro's mother Pearl had always been envious of the Klarje family's tradition, and Caye had endured some of the same mischief on the playground. Caye gently prodded Rhiann to continue to go to the play areas and try to get along with the other youngsters. Rhiann did so and put up with Jethro's pranks. Jethro used skunk cabbage, conjured up a Stinking Cloud Spell, claimed that Rhiann soiled his clothes, and sent the tyke back home in a rush. Over time, Jethro's insults grew more vicious. The little sorcerers mastered only simple spells, but Bo placed a Push Spell on Rhiann's back and knocked the smaller Rhiann to his knees. Rhiann scraped his knees and ripped his favorite purple robe, which had been a gift from his wayfaring Uncle Mayard. Bo denied casting the spell, and Dean and Jethro made sure there was no evidence of the powdered brass Bo had used as material component for the spell. Dean mastered Ventriloquism and threw his voice onto rocks and other inanimate objects. Once in the play area near the statue honoring Mayard Klarje, Dean threw his voice onto a rock, saying, "Rhiann Klarje, you must throw me through the merchant Elliott's window."

Little Rhiann said, "I cannot. I'll get in trouble."

Dean fought laughter and continued, "Throw me. If you do not, I'll rise up from the ground and fly into the statue of your Uncle Mayard and knock off his nose."

Rhiann answered, "Rocks can't throw themselves!"

The mischievous Dean replied through the stone, "I'm a Magick rock."

Rhiann quickly countered, "Then throw yourself throw the window!"

The rock (Dean) replied, "I'm going to count to seven and then I'm going to break off your Uncle's nose!"

Rhiann said, "No!"

The rock said, "One, two, three…"

Rhiann screamed, "Don't get to unlucky seven!"

Rhiann picked up the stone and threw it through the gruff old merchant's paned elaborate window, which shattered into countless pieces and brought the angry merchant into the street. Jethro, Bo, and Dean beat a hasty retreat, leaving Rhiann to face Elliott's wrath. The merchant escorted the youth home and complained bitterly to Caye. Kurth reimbursed the merchant for his loss. Caye and Kurth listened to Rhiann's version of the tale and suspected he had been a victim of mischief, but there was no way to prove their suspicions. Caye gently told her son the statue of Uncle Mayard was carved from Mount Airie granite, hardened further by Magick, and nigh impossible to damage.

On another occasion, Jethro used a Write Spell to silently write "Kick me" on Rhiann's robe. Rhiann endured six boots to his little rear end before a mother saw the script on his back and kindly removed the cloak.

Most preschool activities saw some mischief fomented by Jethro, Bo, and Dean. The threesome grew adept at sneakiness and were seldom caught. Most of their taunts related to Rhiann's mark on his chin.

Rhiann attempted to cover the bright red mark with his mother's cleansing mud. Jethro waited until Rhiann reached the area around Mayard's statue and cast a Fairie Fire Spell on Rhiann. Flames flickered on Rhiann's back. Bo screamed, "Fire! He's on fire!"

The merchant Elliott rushed out of his store with a large bucket of water and threw it on Rhiann. Jethro dispelled the harmless Fairie Fire Spell. The water washed the mud from Rhiann's face and the cherry-red, heart-shaped birthmark reappeared in all its glory.

Rhiann once again endured the wrath of the merchant.

Elliott fumed, "You, again! Boy, what have you got against me getting in an uninterrupted day's work?'

Jethro guffawed and said, "Answer him, heart-face?"

Elliott gathered his bucket and reentered his shop. Soaked and dejected Rhiann made his way back home for dry clothes. Caye sympathetically listened to her son's lament and made him a snack of tetraberry waffles. From that point forward unless an adult accompanied young Rhiann, the ornery merchant Elliott shooed the boy away from his store.

For that and many other reasons Rhiann enjoyed sojourns into the inner ward with his mother and little brother Arthur Seigh. Jethro, Bo, and Dean kept their distance and usually were on their best behavior when they approached. Caye was a prominent member of the community and spent many hours nurturing the Gem Bush and other plants in the courtyard. Even old Elliott welcomed her, but the merchant kept an eye on little Rhiann. Jethro made it a point to bring refreshments to Caye and her children and offered to carry her bundles.

On their way home Caye commented, "Jethro is such a polite young sorcerer. He's only two years older than you, Rhiann, and he's developed so many social skills. I want you to emulate his behavior when you are around others."

Rhiann shrugged and remained silent. He caught a sly smile on Jethro's face and the suspicious gaze from old Elliott after Caye turned away. Jethro made mocking motions and traced a heart shape on his chin as Rhiann looked back. Bo and Dean chuckled. Rhiann suffered in silence.

Rhiann tried to avoid solo trips into the inner ward, but Caye oft insisted he leave the house and join other children in play. The boy preferred the walks with his mother. Older cousins sometimes accompanied him. Jethro, Bo, and Dean tempered down their teasing whenever Rhiann had back-up. The last days of the warm season passed and soon the time for school neared. There was an unsuccessful attempt by thieves to enter the inner ward which had everyone talking and mothers a bit hesitant to send younger children out. Soon all was well and normal activities resumed. For Rhiann it meant solo trips to the playgrounds and renewed teasing from the three sorcerer-teers.

In Sagain children began formal schooling shortly after their sixth birthday. Ages six to twelve attended an ornate school in the inner ward of Thynna and shared classes. They were not separated by age. Studies included reading, writing, arithmetic, spelling, conjuration, spell materials, and history.

Constructing the school was financed through the efforts of Mayard Klarje, who often returned to Thynna with priceless jewels and spell components. His most valuable addition was the Gem Bush, which was planted in the courtyard near the Great Hall of Thynna, the assembly place of the Council of Thynna and the city of Magick's center of government. The Gem Bush was a gift from the Old Ones of the Hanging Gardens, specifically the Three Sisters, the Spinner, Allotter, and the Unturning. The Gem Bush was thought unique; it was certainly the only one known in all of Sagain. It grew after the impact that created the cataclysm and never increased beyond its current size. The bush was thirteen feet tall. Its diameter was thirteen inchworm lengths. The tree had thirteen limbs, thirteen leaves on each limb, thirteen veins on each leaf, and drew nourishment through thirteen roots. Each limb bore one gem of thirteen different colors, including one ultra-rare red diamond. Only one gem of a given color could be removed every thirteen years. A second gem could not be removed, even with the power of a Limited Wish or Alter Reality Spell. The Three Sisters entrusted the plant to Mayard Klarje and hoped it would improve relations between Thynna and the Old Ones community. The Council of Thynna accepted the gift, but motivated by suspicion and greed, placed more restrictions on entry and approach to the city by the preternatural Old Ones. Mayard protested to no avail. Nevertheless, he painstakingly planted the Gem Bush in the Great Hall's courtyard.

Mayard mastered and shared with other sorcerers the spells Stone Shape and Transmute Rock to Mud and its reversal Mud to Rock. Clay and sand brought from the Green River basin were the material components of the spell. The school sat over what had been a marshy area. Mayard's spells hardened the ground, and he used hardened mud in the construction. He filled the school's library with tomes and items from faraway places to further the education of Thynna's youth. Not since the founder Cydney Klarje had one sorcerer given so much to the community. The wayfaring Mayard did not stick around to receive gratitude and praise and went off on further journeys.

Caye rarely spoke to her children about her adventuresome uncle. She hoped they'd trek more along the paths of her father and life-mate. The time for starting school approached for young Rhiann, who spent as much time as possible in his room.

Rhiann's room was his refuge from outside stressors. His little brother Arthur Seigh Klarje lived in the nursery. Rhiann enjoyed childhood heirlooms that had belonged to his parents and other ancestors. His favorite toys were a set of building blocks that stuck together until he wanted them to fall apart, a jack-in-the-box that produced a different visage each time it opened, and a horse-of-a-different-color that was a different color each morning when he awakened. His bed was stuffed with moongoose down and he slept on a pillow filled with rare lullaby bird feathers. When he lay down on the pillow, the soft pillow emitted gently melodies that helped him to fall asleep. His chest of drawers was made of durable semper fi tree wood that grew on Wombat Mountain to the south of Thynna. A bluewood desk sat against the wall. His chair was made of flexible fibers from a living morphing bush that grew as Rhiann did. He had to water the chair once a week with nutrient rich water. The mirror that hang on his wall was named ICU. A painting of a rambling bramble bush decorated his wall. The painting was in a different location every morning.

Rhiann sat on the edge of his bed and mumbled. He then bade the mirror, "Good night, ICU."

The mirror soothingly named, "Good night, Rhiann. I see you, too. I hope you rest well. Tomorrow is a big day."

CHAPTER 5

First Day of School

Caye Klarje gently urged her son, "You don't want to be late for the first day of school. Your breakfast is ready. I made your favorite, blue blooter eggs and tetraberry waffles. It's getting cold!"

Rhiann Klarje stretched, rubbed sleep from his eyes, and hopped out of his comfy bed. The six-year-old sorcerer hurried to the ornate looking glass that hung on his bedchamber wall. His heart sank. The little bloke sighed and moaned, "Oh, no, it's still there. So much for wishing! I'm doomed."

The child glowered at his reflection. The heart-shaped cherry-red birthmark remained on his chin. Not even the thought of the bright blue eggs and four-colored waffles lifted his spirits.

ICU's feminine voice soothingly flowed from the mirror, "Young Rhiann, what did you expect?"

The boy grumbled, "I'd wished it'd be gone, but it's still there."

The voice from the mirror responded, "Rhiann, you are young, but even you should know that limited wishes are rare, and true wishes are rarest of all. Furthermore, idly wishing…"

Rhiann interrupted, "Who asked you? You haven't had to put up with this birthmark! I hear about it every time I go to the playground. The three 'sorcerer-teers' give me constant grief. Now I'll be starting school with them! The great wizards! Jethro, Bo, and Dean! Jethro has a two-year head start on me. Even my mother thinks he's a prince! Bo and Dean have been there a year! They are never apart and always ready to hassle me! Last week Bo used an Entangle Spell to bind my shoelaces together and I fell flat on my face. Two days ago Dean rubbed grayberry juice on my shoes. I kept checking to see if I'd stepped in… well, you know, excrement! Just last week they used Pattern Spells and painted little hearts all over my favorite cloak. I hid it from mother."

The mirror's voice countered, "She found it in your Bag of Holding and cleaned it. Their red dye was no match for her Dispel Magick and Cleansing Spells. Don't you have other friends?"

Rhiann rubbed his chin vigorously and answered, "Most stay clear of me for fear of incurring the attention of the terrific trio. It's more than just the kids. Fingers point toward me everywhere I go in Thynna. I'm marked!"

Caye Klarje's voice reiterated, "Rhiann! School! Come down!"

The mirror said compassionately, "Best get moving! We'll talk when you get home."

Rhiann slipped on his tunic and robe and grumbled, "If I get home!"

The youngster reluctantly trudged down the stair to the cozy kitchen. Caye happily scurried around the table and put the finishing touches on the meal. Rhiann's father Kurth Marsh finished his passionless fruit juice and sipped on dark coffee.

Kurth muttered, "I thought you'd be excited about school. Rumor has it there will be new teachers. If you master your lessons, there'll be time for spell studies."

Rhiann sat down and politely replied, "Yes, Father, I'm looking forward to all the classes."

Kurth finished his coffee, stood, and said, "Then you can tell me all about it tonight. Caye, I may be late. The Elders have called another meeting of the Council of Thynna. More restrictions to entry to Thynna and strengthening of the walls are on the agenda."

Caye sighed and said, "How much more power does the Council desire? How many more restrictions can they add? It was not the intention of our ancestors to restrict knowledge and citizenship. They intended all touched by Magick to feel welcome. The elders are little better than the barbarians to the north. Their attitudes drove my Uncle Mayard from the city."

Kurth answered, "They are concerned about the safety of the Gem Bush among other things. The guards intercepted mercenaries from the

Veldt. They disguised themselves as merchants and almost made it to the inner curtain."

Caye said, "The inner curtain! They'd have been near the school. How'd they get so close?"

Kurth replied, "Some think they had inside help."

Caye continued, "I'd rather Uncle Mayard and the emissaries to the Hanging Gardens had left the Gem Bush where it was. The Three Sisters really just got rid of a headache and dumped it on Thynna. Baubles and trinkets! Who cares about them?"

Kurth answered, "Many folks both within and outside Thynna's walls treasure gems. Every insalubrious bloke on Sagain would love to steal the Gem Bush. Successfully stealing the Gem Bush would give them a replenishing supply. Besides, how could the elders refuse a gift from the Spinner, Allotter, and Unturning?"

Caye answered, "Most thieves are poor orchardists and horticulturalists. Keeping plants healthy is a lot of work. Caring for the Gem Bush is one of many tasks entrusted to my gardening group. One must know the nutrients and spell components needed to keep the Gem Bush healthy. The bush is the pride of the Council of Thynna! Protecting and nurturing it has become their top priority. Harvested gems adorn the garb of the council members. New gems replace those harvested by the council. Greed is greed, whether from a thief from the Veldt or a Council member from the inner ward of Thynna."

Kurth replied, "I share your opinion, Caye, but bear in mind your legacy entitles us to live in the inner ward. You… uh, we chose to live in the outer ward."

Caye quickly entered, "Yes, away from the snobs!"

Kurth suppressed a chuckle and said, "Now you sound like your Uncle Mayard."

Rhiann excitedly commented, "Where did Great Uncle Mayard go? I often hear elders speak of him. There are monuments to him throughout the city. What can you tell me about him?"

Caye Klarje answered, "You have heard some stories. Mayard is my father Thomas Bayard Klarje's twin brother. Uncle Mayard made many contributions to Magick and Thynna. My grandfather FT Fleckinghauser Klarje headed the Council of Thynna. My father and Uncle were his youngest children. The twins were not identical.

Uncle Mayard is the most innovative and inquisitive sorcerers of his generation. He sought rare spell components and discovered a cache of fossilized shypoke eggshells which he bequeathed to the city's coffers. Uncle Mayard created more spells than any sorcerer, save the founder of Thynna, our ancestor Cydney Klarje. Ultimately Mayard tired of the council's constant bickering and selfishness. He left Thynna in the company of a siren and Manticore and has not returned in many years."

Rhiann nibbled on his blue blooter eggs and said, "A siren! Manticore? Old Ones? Really"

Caye said, "Yes, Rhiann. Mayard never took a life-mate. His first love had always been Magick. He spent a lot of time at the Hanging Gardens. Is the stubbornness and selfishness of the Council of Thynna going to cost us more well-meaning minds, Kurth?"

Kurth replied, "You know my feelings on the matter. Magick should be shared by all. Barbarians and outsiders do pose threats. There's been more sightings of Old Ones. The elders fear the preternatural residents of Sagain."

Caye replied, "Only because they don't understand the Old Ones. Old Ones are already forbidden entry to the city. We are bypassing a great source of knowledge. I'll be meeting with my sisterhood. We have issues to take before the elders. After all, there are more female than male sorcerers!"

Rhiann said, "Old Ones! Have people seen Old Ones? Jethro, Bo, and Dean say their parents say the Old Ones are but legend and stories of them are told to silence unruly children."

Kurth answered, "The Old Ones are as real as Magick, son, and they deserve our respect. Uncle Mayard frequently associated with Sagain's oldest denizens. Not everyone shares our feelings. We'll talk more tonight. Good luck with school."

Rhiann answered, "Yes, Father. Will you tell me more about Old Ones tonight?"

Kurth answered, "I can only relay legends. I've never encountered an Old One. But I'll tell you the stories my father told me. He knew Caye's Uncle Mayard very well. Mayard had traveled to the Hanging Gardens and met the Three Sisters. His efforts bought the Gem Bush to Thynna. Now I must go."

Caye said, "Be on your way! Rhiann, are you ready?"

Rhiann said, "Do I have to go, mother? I'm learning many things here at home. I'd rather hear more stories of Uncle Mayard and the Old Ones. Even the three sorcerer-teers speak respectfully of Mayard Klarje."

Caye answered, "You'll learn so much more and make friends. Why don't you want to go to school?"

Rhiann planted his left index finger firmly onto his chin at the site of his birthmark and said, "This!"

Caye exclaimed, "Your birthmark! Many of my family have borne such a mark!"

Rhiann said, "Well, it makes me different, and the three sorcerer-teers never let me see any peace about it!"

Caye lovingly rubbed his reddish locks and said, "Being different makes you beautiful!"

His mother's comments did not console Rhiann. He rubbed the birthmark and evermore dreaded walking to school. His mind escaped to thoughts of his Uncle Mayard. Rhiann asked, "Did Uncle Mayard really know a siren?"

Caye smiled and answered, "Uncle Mayard constantly sought adventure. He left Thynna when I was just a girl about your age. He's returned briefly from time to time and usually quickly away again. I don't remember much about him. Stories of his escapades have been embellished in all likelihood, but oldsters say everything is true. What's certain are Uncle Mayard's contributions to Magick and Thynna. He dealt directly with the Three Sisters at the Hanging Gardens, a sanctuary of the Old Ones where folk of Thynna have seldom been welcomed. He brought the Gem Bush to Thynna, transplanted it, and taught us how to care for it. Mayard shied away from attention and refused leadership of the council. My father Thomas Bayard Klarje served in his stead. As for the Siren story, I can't confirm it. However, I can confirm that you are going to be late for school. Finish your breakfast."

Rhiann munched on a waffle containing blue, red, green, and orange tetraberries and said, "I'm almost finished. Mother, will you tell me more about Uncle Mayard and the Old Ones?"

Caye reassuringly answered, "Yes, provided you tell me all about your first day of school.

Caye walked with Rhiann to the gate leading to the inner ward. From there it was a short walk to the school. Rhiann still dreaded the short trek, but he made his way past the Gem Bush's courtyard and avoided merchant Elliott, who still blamed Rhiann for the mischief involving his store window, and the three sorcerer-teers, Jethro, Bo, and Dean. He made his way to the school's main amphitheater where the new teacher was scheduled to give the first class, a lecture on the history of Thynna, Magick, and Sagain. Rumors were circulating about the new teacher. Older boys talked of her beauty. Rhiann quietly made his way to a seat on the unpopular first row, where the youths were in clear view of their instructors and were unable to foment trouble. Jethro, Bo, and Dean entered together and made their way to seats in the popular upper rows. A young sorceress named Tiffany Turner sat beside Rhiann. In a few moments the anticipation ended when a woman entered the amphitheater. She wore a maroon teacher's robe and stood about the height of Rhiann's mother. She had auburn hair had fell down her back and haunting green eyes that stared down each student in the large room. Around seventy students in their first three years of schooling were required to attend the lecture.

The attractive woman said, "I am Matron Hiatt. I'm here to tell you about the dawn of Magick and the founding of Thynna."

Matron Hiatt turned to write on the chalkboard.

Dean whispered an incantation and placed a Ventriloquism Spell on Rhiann. The words came from Rhiann's mouth, "The Teacher is a troll." Matron Hiatt turned and asked, "Who said that?"

Bo quickly volunteered, "It came from the first row."

Tiffany Turner quite innocently said, "Rhiann said it."

Jethro energetically added, "Yes. Teacher, it was heart-face!"

The entire class burst into laughter.

Matron Hiatt looked squarely at Rhiann and asked, "Did you call me a troll?"

Rhiann trembled and replied, "The words came from me, but I didn't say them."

The class then laughed again. The teacher turned to the blackboard and began writing through movements of her extended left index finger. The words "The History of Thynna" appeared on the board.

Bo took some ground brass, whispered an incantation, ad sent a Push Spell into Rhiann's back. The power of the seven-year old's spell was minimal, but the spell was strong enough to send Rhiann sprawling onto the floor. He knocked his inkwell to the floor and spilled dark ink. The class burst into laughter.

The teacher turned and calmly asked, "More problems, Rhiann?" Jethro chuckled and added, "Heart-face must have gotten into his father's mead!"

More laugher ensued. Matron Hiatt pointed toward the spilled ink and uttered a few phrases. The inkwell righted and the ink flowed from the floor back into the inkwell. Rhiann picked up the inkwell and placed it on his desk.

The Teacher asked, "Are you injured, Rhiann?"

Jethro guffawed and added, "Only your pride, right, heart-face?"

Rhiann meekly answered, "No, Teacher, I am fine."

The Teacher began to recount the story of the Dawn of Magick. Jethro cast a Write Spell. The words "The Teacher is a troll" appeared on the chalkboard. The class laughed boisterously. Matron Hiatt turned and looked at the board.

Dean again used Ventriloquism to have Rhiann appear to say, "It was me."

The amphitheater again erupted in loud laughter.

The school's elderly Headmaster Lennard rushed into the classroom and queried, "Is there a problem?"

The young teacher answered, "No, Headmaster, here's no problem. My hearing is excellent. I can readily recognize, Ventriloquism, Push, and Write Spell incantations. Am I not correct, young Jethro, Bo, and Dean?"

Jethro, Bo, and Dean blushed.

Headmaster Lennard said firmly, "Elaborate."

Matron Hiatt looked directly at Jethro. He stared back at her green eyes.

The teacher asked, "Why did you do it, Jethro?"

Jethro protested, "No, it was heart-face. Tiffany heard him say it."

Matron Hiatt said, "Now, Jethro, I heard your incantation. The words came from Rhiann, but you put them there. I will commend you on the effectiveness of your spell. You fooled Tiffany. She's only six years old. I'm a bit older. Why do you call Rhiann, heart-face?"

Jethro harrumphed, "Just look at the ridiculous red heart on his face. It shines like new money."

The young matron stood quietly for a moment and then muttered a few phrases. Her visage shimmered many colors. She briefly faded from sight and reappeared as an old man who held his left hand over his chin.

The old man removed his left hand from his chin and said, "Do you refer to the mark that looks like this?" The old man bore a cherry-red, heart-shaped birthmark on his chin. The mark was identical to Rhiann's.

The Headmaster gasped, "Mayard! Mayard Klarje! You have returned!"

The old man replied, "Yes, Lennard, I have returned."

Jethro marveled, "Mayard Klarje! You are the greatest sorcerer since the founder of Thynna. I've heard my grandfather speak of your deeds. But you have one of those marks on your face!"

Mayard Klarje answered, "Yes, young rascal, I do. I bear the mark of Grayness, the mark of the Klarjes. I proudly share this mark with Cydney Klarje the founder of Thynna and young Rhiann Klarje, my great-nephew. Now, if we are finished with the tomfoolery, I'll get on with the lecture."

Mayard Klarje's bright green eyes sparkled as he began, "Look to the sky. I always find it peaceful… blues, greens, grays, clouds and two twinkling points of light. These are our twin suns. Each tries to dominate the other like brothers seeking their father's attention or approval. Our twin suns send life-giving light and great energies to our world. We are the fourth planet in our system. With a powerful looking glass on a clear night you can see the other three. Before the dawn of Magick our little planet had given birth to a rustic civilization. Diverse creatures walked its surface, swam in its seas, and flew in its skies. Preternatural creatures and Nature enjoyed dominion and little resistance to their laws in the little world. My ancestor Cydney Klarje made the first written record of our world in the Chronicle of the Klarje Family. The Chronicle of the Klarjes and my wide exploration of the world are the sources of my knowledge."

Mayard proceeded to relay the story of Cydney Klarje.

Throughout the amphitheater the youths at mesmerized with all eyes fixed on the worn gaunt sorcerer standing before them. The Headmaster knew most of what Mayard had recounted, but even he stood glued to every word. To hear the account as written in the Chronicle of the Klarjes set the old educator aback as well.

Mayard Klarje removed his large rucksack from his back. He scanned the amphitheater and counted the number of eager students and then removed a leather bag from the rucksack. The wayfaring sorcerer muttered an incantation and auras surrounded the little bag. The bag enlarged.

Mayard said, "There's a few more of you than I expected. Not to fear. It's nothing a Rock to Mud, Enlarge, and Stone Shape Spell won't remedy. Mayard said then, "I'll be right back." The old sorcerer briefly exited and returned with an irregular rock from the courtyard. He used a small piece of clay and a bit of water, uttered a gruff conjuration, and softened the rock. He then took a pinch of powdered iron, uttered another incantation, and cast an Enlarge Spell, He followed with a Stone Shape Spell and formed seventy-five small objects, the exact number of students watching the class. Mayard took a piece of string from his rucksack and replicated it. He made odd motions with his hands, uttered more odd phrases, and moved his hands over the little pieces of clay. The old sorcerer then said a single word, "red." Now seventy-five little red objects rested in front of him. Mayard said, "Join." The strings combined with the little red objects. Mayard said "rise" and seventy-five amulets slowly rose from the stone floor and levitated about three feet above the floor. Mayard said, "A memento of my visit! There should be one for each of you. Rhiann, take one please."

Rhiann stood and approached his uncle.

Mayard said, "Don't be shy. It won't hurt you. In fact, it's an amulet of protection. It'll serve you as long as you stay true to Magick and use it thoughtfully. Look closely, Rhiann."

Rhiann took and held the near weightless object. The little cherry-red, heart-shaped stone was precisely the size, shape, and color of the birthmarks on Rhiann and Mayard's chins. Mayard's tale asserted the mark graced the chin of the first sorcerer of Sagain Cydney Klarje.

Mayard said again, "One for everyone. Tomorrow I'll tell you of Cydney Klarje's first spells."

One by one the young sorcerers descended the amphitheater steps and took a levitating amulet. Jethro, Bo, and Dean tarried in their seats.

Mayard motioned for the threesome to approach. They were the last three to accept the prizes.

The wandering Sorcerer Mayard Klarje addressed Jethro, "Jethro, do you have a problem with the red mark on my face?"

Jethro stammered, "Uh…no, Sorcerer Mayard. Why would anyone have a problem with the greatest sorcerer in the history of Magick! Is it true you have the power to turn people into toads?"

Mayard said, "It's been known to happen, but only if they really deserved it. Why do you tease Rhiann?"

Jethro dejectedly said, "I'll start learning to croak so I can be a better toad than sorcerer."

Mayard fought back laughter and struggled to keep a straight face and followed, "That may not be necessary, Jethro. Touch the red mark of my face."

Jethro stammered, "Uh… why, Teacher?"

Mayard calmly replied, "Touch it. It won't hurt you."

Jethro gingerly extended his right index finger and touched the red mark. He youth sighed with relief when nothing happened.

Mayard continued, "Now touch Rhiann's mark."

Jethro hesitated briefly and then did so.

Mayard followed, "Now touch your face."

Once again young Jethro did as the sorcerer asked.

Mayard asked, "What did you feel when you touched our faces?"

Jethro answered. "Just skin, teacher."

Mayard answered, "Did you feel any difference in the red skin on Rhiann's and my face?"

Jethro replied, "No, Teacher, it just felt like skin."

Mayard Klarje said, "Jethro. If someone looks different, it doesn't mean they are less important and lack feelings. Magick is not to be used frivolously, young sorcerers. Think about the consequences of your actions. Always let your hearts guide your deeds."

Jethro humbly said, "Yes, Teacher."

Mayard Klarje reached into his tattered rucksack and removed a small jacket and handed it to Jethro. Jethro accepted the doll-sized garment but said, "Thank you, Teacher. But it's too small for me. It should fit my sister's doll. I'll give it to her."

Mayard smiled and answered, "Your education continues. Place your left hand in the sleeve."

Jethro did not question the famed wizard and stuck his hand into the small sleeve. The fabric expanded and the coat slipped over his body and became a perfect fit.

Jethro marveled, "It feels wonderful. The fabric is warm and cool at the same time."

Mayard smiled and said, "It's made of Sagain silk. The fibers are produced by silkworms that live in the Semper Fi trees on Wombat Mountain. The coat is water resistant and will grow as you do. By the way… it's also fire and cold resistant."

Jethro beamed, "Thank you, Teacher. Receiving a gift from you is an honor! And you've given me two!"

Mayard again smiled and said, "Just remember what you've learned today."

Jethro, Bo, and Dean left the amphitheater. Headmaster Lennard gave Mayard a quizzical glance and then left also. Rhiann helped his great uncle gather his materials and store them in the marvelous rucksack, which maintained its weight and outer dimensions. Rhiann mimicked the Headmaster's quizzical look.

The youngster said, "Uncle Mayard, why did you reward Jethro? He's been very mean to me. You witnessed it. Today was mild compared to other things he's done. I can't go near the merchant Elliott's store. He thinks I'm a troublemaker."

Mayard kept stuffing thinks in the rucksack and said, "Well, I could have changed him to a toad. I really have done it before. Or would you rather have had me place a barbed tail on his backside?"

Rhiann sighed and answered, "Not a bad idea. Uncle Mayard. I might have considered it."

Mayard chuckled, "I thought about it, too. But, Rhiann, if we treat him like he has treated you, are we any better than him? Vengeance is not best served cold. It's best not served at all. Two wrongs do not make a right. You can catch more flies with honey than vinegar. I can recite many more adages if you like."

Rhiann remained perplexed and asked, "Why'd you want to catch flies at all, Uncle Mayard? Mother hates seeing them in the kitchen. I know she'd hate seeing them in the blue bee honey."

Mayard finished his tasks and laughed, "I'd imagine she would! I just meant to say its easier to be nice to people. I try to treat people like I like to be treated."

Rhiann countered, "In the inner ward I've often heard people say 'Do unto others before they do unto you,' 'if I don't do it, somebody else will,' and such."

Mayard said solemnly, "That's a bad attitude. Walk with me. Show me around the inner ward."

Rhiann said, "Uncle Mayard, there are statues of you erected all over Thynna."

Mayard said, "Can't understand the fuss. It's a nice afternoon. Let's walk."

Rhiann and Mayard exited the amphitheater and walked to the Gem Bush.

Rhiann said, "The Gem Bush is very pretty. My mother and her friends spent lots of time nurturing and caring for it. But its fruits are not edible and I don't see any practical value for it."

The old sorcerer smiled when he saw the care that had been given the tree. He said, "It's important to preserve rarities, Rhiann. Once we lose plants or animals to extinction, we cannot get them back. After the Dawn of Magick, little dragon-like beasts called shypokes flourished. Unfortunately, they were rather defenseless and easy to catch. Compound this by the facts that they tasted good and their bones and eggshells were valued as spell material components, the little blighters were driven to extinction. Sagain lost many species as a result of the cataclysm that awakened Magick. However, we gained others. Greedy and short-sighted folks have led to our losing many again. Plans, trees, animals, and the defenseless need our protection."

Rhiann cringed when he saw the merchant Elliott exit his store and move toward them. He mumbled, "Merchant Elliott is the one that doesn't like me."

Mayard acknowledged the comment. The gaunt merchant approached and said, "Sorcerer Mayard Klarje. Rumor had it that you were in Thynna. Would you honor me by visiting my store?"

Mayard said, "I told no one I was coming to Thynna. I just revealed my presence in the school. How'd you know I was here?"

Elliott answered, "Some of the lads told me. I believe they were friends of this young fellow. How are you today?"

Rhiann flabbergasted answered, "I... I'm fine, said, "I'd like some licorice. Let's visit."

Rhiann followed the adults. Elliott drifted a couple of paces behind Mayard Klarje and reached into his coat. Something glinted in the light. The merchant moved his left hand toward Mayard's back.

Mayard Klarje relished the thought of some locally made licorice. His austere diet on his travels lacked such luxury. He heard a young voice mutter a brief incantation and heard a clanking sound on the floor. He turned to see Elliott reaching for his dagger. Mayard uttered a single phase. Elliott froze. Mayard uttered another incantation. The frozen figure of the merchant shimmered and changed to a formless biped. Several citizens heard the ruckus and rushed into the store.

Mayard mumbled. "Shapechanger! Old fool that I am! Let down my guard. Rhiann, did I hear you cast a Fumble Spell?"

Rhiann answered, "Yes, Uncle Mayard."

Mayard continued, "Why?"

Rhiann replied, "I saw the knife in his hand. He was approaching your back. Also... Elliott does not like me. He was entirely too friendly. What was the word you said?"

Mayard answered, "I hope it's a spell you won't have to use. Power Word Stun usually stops an opponent. The Dispel Magick Spell revealed his true colors. Of course the ability to change their appearance is intrinsic for Shapechangers. It's not a spell, but it's still Magick and can be dispelled."

Rhiann asked, "Why'd he want to harm you?"

Mayard answered, "It's a long story Rhiann. I am not very popular with Shapechangers. Many hire out as mercenaries. There is a price on my head, courtesy of their leader. I oft travel in disguise. I returned in the guise of a new school marm. I'm told there have been attempts to steal the Gem Bush. Many of the Council of Thynna think the thieves have had inside help. I fear the real Merchant Elliott has met with foul play. It's good you picked up on the Shapechanger's treachery. You saved my life."

Rhiann said, "There's something else, Uncle Mayard."

Mayard responded, "Yes, Rhiann."

Rhiann said, "I'm not exactly sure how to say this... but... my birthmark... itched."

Mayard confided, "Yes, Great-nephew. It often does."

By now, the courtyard was filled. Security guards took the befuddled Shapechanger into custody. The ill-tempered merchant Elliott was found unharmed locked in his storeroom. The assumption was the Shapechanger needed his coerced help to continue the ruse. Crowds cheered. Several older boys lifted Rhiann onto their shoulders and carried him through the courtyard. Voices rang out heralding Rhiann Klarje as a hero. The loudest praise came from Jethro, Bo, and Dean.

CHAPTER 6

In the City of Magick

Interrogating the Shapechanger was tricky business. The captive had a nasty habit of mimicking his interrogators. The creature was rather impervious to pain and Mayard opposed torturing him. Others of the Council of Thynna were not so temperate. Eventually Spirit Wrack Spells broke him. Security detained a disgruntled former council member who helped the Shapechanger get into Thynna. The Council voted to place a death sentence on the Shapechanger, but Mayard interceded and came up with an alternative. He placed a Magick Mouth Spell on the creature. The spell was set to activate if the Shapechanger tried to reenter Thynna. The Magick Mouth would loudly announce "The sneaky bloke is back." Only a sorcerer of greater ability than Mayard Klarje could dispel the Magick Mouth and at this point in time there was not one of such stature.

Mayard Klarje remained in Thynna for a time. The learned sorcerer was in great demand. He taught several classes in the school named for him and strengthened the inner and outer curtains through Magick. Whenever possible Mayard spent time with young Rhiann. Rhiann enjoyed his time with his great uncle more than his studies. This brought Mayard into conflict with Caye and Kurth and he'd sulk away on a walkabout for a while. Rhiann studied the Chronicle of the Klarjes and an old tattered spell book entrusted to him by Mayard whenever Mayard was away. The mirror ICU quizzed Rhiann about his studies.

Mayard badgered his niece to allow Rhiann to accompany him on short excursions. Caye vehemently objected, but Mayard occasionally sneaked Rhiann outside the city's walls just to give the lad a taste of the outside world. At night Mayard built little campfires in open areas in the outer ward and told Rhiann stories of his travels in Sagain. Other youths oft joined them. Jethro became a staunch friend and stood up for Rhiann should any older or bigger kid pick on him. On Rhiann's tenth birthday his mother allowed Rhiann to take a short journey with Mayard outside Thynna's walls. They visited small villages and farms in the countryside. The area around the city was populated by many folks who had been denied entrance to Thynna proper. Rhiann and Mayard encountered some resentment, but it was widely known that Mayard Klarje opposed the exclusivity advocated by the Council of Thynna and more often they encountered people seeking audience with the wayfaring sorcerer to plead their cases for entry to the city. Mayard was called away to the Samm Hills far to the east of Thynna. He was absent for four years. During the time Rhiann flourished and learned the dweomers in the old spell book. He could recite the Chronicle of the Klarjes. He excelled at school and developed strong friendships with Jethro, Bo, Dean, and Tiffany Turner. Mayard returned to the usual welcomes but none were more enthusiastic than that he received from his fourteen-year-old great nephew Rhiann. Mayard attended a general session of the council of Thynna, underwent the usual social hobnobbing, and taught a seminar at the school. Once responsibilities were met Mayard went about his preferred task of educating his inquisitive great nephew. The traveling sorcerer returned with many material components needed to cast the more complicated spells and he showered Rhiann with a bountiful supply of most.

Rhiann eagerly awaited their sessions and asked, "Uncle Mayard, you have always returned with treasures for the general coffers and gifts for the Council of Thynna. Shouldn't these materials go into the city's supplies?"

Mayard answered, "Some things are not meant for sharing and general knowledge, Rhiann. The Council of Thynna disdains or ignores much of what I hold dear and value of Sagain. The Council belittles the Old Ones and restricts them access to Thynna. Young sorcerers could learn so many things from our preternatural colleagues. The Hanging Gardens are evermore separated from us. I thought the gift of the Gem Bush would soften the Council members' hearts and improve relations with the Three Sisters and other Old Ones."

Rhiann said, "How so, Uncle?"

Mayard said, "The Council of Thynna treasures baubles and bling. They equate material wealth with power. The two are synonymous in their minds. The cataclysm awakened Magick in our world. On the other hand, the tragedy cost Sagain many plant and animal species. Many Old Ones died. Our ancestor Cydney Klarje channeled Magick in the right direction. The Council of Thynna has deviated from Cydney's path. He valued the input of the Old Ones and related to the Three Sisters. The destruction from the impact extended to the outskirts of the Hanging Gardens. A bit further and more would have been lost."

Rhiann interrupted, "You brought the Gem Bush from the Hanging Gardens."

Mayard answered, "Yes, Rhiann. And I want to take you there. Someone must continue the narrow thread of communication between Thynna and the Hanging Gardens. The longevity that comes with living in Thynna distances us from the Three Sisters."

Rhiann requested, "Please tell me of the Three Sisters."

Mayard rubbed the cherry-red birthmark on his chin and pondered a bit. He sighed and answered, "The Moirae, the Fates, are the most powerful of the Old Ones. They are said to be the daughters of night and the wind. the trio have long sought dominion over the primitive world. Architects of the destinies of humble mortal men, the white robed sisters were known by many names, including Nona, Decima, and Mors. Commonly called the Spinner, the Allotter, and the Unturning, the uninvited threesome come calling during the ninth month of pregnancy and again three nights after a child's birth. The Spinner spins the thin precious thread of life over her distaff. The Allotter measures the length of the narrow thread with a mysterious red rod. The Unturning, the inevitable for those mortal, chooses the manner of the individual's death and cuts the thin thread with her dreaded shears. Nature and time only gently opposed the efforts of the Fates. Magick changed everything. The Fates have little influence now on the folk of Thynna, but common folk in Sagain still feel their influence"

Rhiann asked, "Do the Fates affect everyone outside Sagain?"

Mayard replied, "Good question, Rhiann, I think the best answer is that the Thee Sisters influence whomever they choose."

Rhiann continued, "I've not met Old Ones. I'd like to meet the Three Sisters."

Mayard smiled and answered, "I hoped you'd say so. You've studied well. I think it's time."

Rhiann said, "Should I ask my Mother and Father?"

Mayard said, "Best not. Meet me near the outer gate near dusk. Bring your cloak, fill a flask with water, and wear walking boots."

Rhiann asked, "Why don't we just use the Fly Spell?"

Mayard answered, "Traveling the great distance to the gardens in such a way would be dangerous and foolhardy. It's best to use fly spells for only short distances."

CHAPTER 7

Leaving Thynna

Rhiann said, "Uncle Mayard, by orders of the Council of Thynna the outer gate is Wizard Locked at nightfall. None came pass through without disabling the spell. The guards are carefully chosen and given Gems of Seeing to detect Magick and Invisible Creatures. Rings of Protection make the guards unsusceptible to spells such as Sleep, Death, and Stun. Every night a sorcerer places Protection from Magick Spells on the oncoming shift. The outer curtain is made of Stone of Ooranth, dark black stone impervious to most forces and nigh as hard as red diamonds. The wall stands thirty feet high. Guards on the allure have an unobstructed view of the ground in front of the wall. The bartizans rise another thirty feet and are positioned so that guards see several hundred yards. Continual Light Spells placed on Semper Fi Wood poles illuminate the area on the outside of the wall."

Mayard stopped him and said, "Young Nephew, twas I who designed the outer defenses of Thynna. Our ancestor Cydney hoped the community would become an oasis for knowledge and sharing, but time and the exclusionary policies of the Council of Thynna changed all that. Outsiders envy what the Council hoards. The impenetrable wall became necessary to protect children and older citizens and preserve the history of Magick. The inner curtain further strengthens the defenses, but only the elite live in the inner ward. I share your parents' idea of preferred living in the outer ward."

Rhiann countered, "Uncle Mayard, you seldom stay in Thynna for any length of time."

Mayard answered, "I really don't relish being inside walls. Again, meet me near the outer gate at dusk. The guards are accustomed to seeing young sorcerers there to watch the changing of the guard and the placing of the Protection Spell. Depending on who's casting the spell, the recipients are bathed in brilliant colors. The Sorceress Lauper is casting the spell tonight. She creates a rainbow effect."

Mayard headed off to make his own preparations. Rhiann returned home and enjoyed an afternoon snack of warm mulled berries and pinanas. He chatted briefly with his mother Caye and they went up to his room. He answered ICU's questions deviously and gathered up his pack and what he considered his essentials. Rhiann sneaked downstairs and evaded his mother. The young sorcerer made his way through the bustling outer ward and approached the heavily guarded gate. A small crowd gathered as a red-haired sorceress painstakingly uttered Protection from Magick Spells and touched the guards coming on duty. Colors danced on the spell recipients. The youths in the crowd cheered. Sorceress Lauper entertained the youths with Dancing Light Spells. Soon the festivities ended and Rhiann stood alone. He fidgeted and caught the glance of the guards who simply doffed their head cover and went about their business. Soon Mayard Klarje arrived. He led Rhiann into a small alleyway between two now closed shops. They stood beyond sight of the guards, who didn't concern themselves with goings on I the quadrangle.

Mayard extended his left hand and suggested, "Put these in your ears."

Rhiann saw the wriggling bugs in his uncle's hands and muttered, "Yuck! Earplugs! Must we?"

"Yes, you'll understand," Mayard uttered.

A wonderfully melodic feminine voice added, "They won't harm you, Rhiann, and neither will I."

A feminine person joined them. The lovely longhaired creature was so stunning that he had to catch his breath. She overwhelmed all his senses with her looks, voice, and pheromones. Long reddish-orange locks flowed down her neck and crossed over to the front of her chest, falling far below her curvaceous perfect breasts. There was radiance to each beautiful hair, as though every strand lived separately. Her voice was beyond description. His mother's words had always soothed the pangs of scrapes and abrasions, which he had suffered during his play. But what he heard now was beyond the comfort of Caye's most tender words. The youth would amble off a cliff should she request it. Her beauty differed from his mother. She had...soft feathered wings had sprouted naturally from the small of her back. Her wings extended almost involuntarily, and a soft plush tail swished gently behind her as she talked. Rhiann felt heretofore unexperienced stirrings in his essence. Siren... Rhiann Klarje's first encounter with the Old Ones...

Rhiann found speaking difficult. The Siren flashed a coy smile, pushed her soft chest against him, and gently rubbed the cherry-red, heart-shaped birthmark on his face. Her beautiful wings answered the question "how'd she get into Thynna?" Still... the guards should have seen her! Nature's flying beasts usually avoided the skies over the city of Magick. The donjon towered over the inner ward and provided views of the city for archers stationed on its pinnacle. Numerous structures rose above the height of the bartizans in the outer ward. The Fly Spell was rather common knowledge. Usually at least one sorcerer patrolled the skies over Thynna using the power of the dweomer. Of course "Flying" required the sorcerer's undivided Magick attention and fairly quickly exhausted the spell caster. Arms were not wings! The Fly Spell had little utility outside Thynna's friendly confines. Flying wasn't worth the risk of becoming a meal for airborne predators like Rocs, dragons, wyverns, Hippogriffs, Manticores, three-eyed Roc-eaters, Pteranodons, Pterodactyls, Windwalkers, Djinn, Efreet, Devils, Pegasi, and Condors. One touch from the dreaded Tuscon meant sudden death!

Mayard said, "The walls of Thynna did not bar entry to my winged female friend Maranna. Maranna simply flies over the wall unnoticed. She is like a great cat in the dark, and then she is the darkness. She is like a great bird in flight, if she is noticed at all."

The Siren warbled, "My goodness, Mayard, he shares your mark. Finally, another sorcerer of worth comes to Thynna. Perhaps I'll have more luck with this young one, no?"

Mayard replied, "Maranna, I'll, ask that you behave. He's young and unable to withstand your... shall we say... treasures. But thank you for helping us through the gate. With recent transgressions by Shapechangers and efforts by outsiders to gain entry to Thynna, the Council has shored up the defenses. They requested citizenry stay within the city after dark and avoid putting any extra pressure on the defensive forces. I'm reluctant to use Magick and…"

The Siren interrupted, "You may dispense with the noble pretense with me, Mayard Klarje. I know you enjoy the thrill of adventure and evading the Council's measures. That's your motivation!"

Mayard blushed and said, "Guilty as charged! I want Rhiann to see more of the world and learn of the Old Ones. What better way to begin his education than to see you in action, Maranna?"

Maranna smiled coyly again and cooed, "Flattery will get you everywhere! Don't you want him to hear me sing as well?"

Mayard chuckled, "Not even I could withstand your charm. Now let's get to it. Nightfall approaches. I don't relish the flight to the Hanging Gardens even in the light of day."

Maranna puffed her sweet breath onto Rhiann's face. The young sorcerer broke into a sweat. The siren said, "Better put in the ear plugs. You won't hear anything once they are in place, so make your plans."

Mayard said, "We've already talked it over. We'll wait here till the guard goes to the gate. Then we'll follow."

Maranna smiled and said, "Good-bye."

The siren faded from view. Rhiann's eyes lamented her disappearance. He managed, "So she's also a sorcerer."

Mayard said, "No, nephew, it's an innate ability. Put in the ear plugs. Otherwise you'll never want anything more from life than to gaze upon her and do her will… until she releases you. And I've never known one of them to do so."

An invisible Maranna responded, "Now, be fair. I'll release the guards when you are finished playing."

Rhiann relished every word spoken by the unseen siren and chagrinned when quiet footsteps heralded her departure. Mayard and Rhiann placed earplugs near their ears. The warm, fuzzy, squirming little creatures snuggled into their ear canals and effectively deafened the two sorcerers. The duo peeked around the corner. Then the winged woman appeared near the guards at the gate. Her exquisite lips began to move. Before the guards had time to react, they fell under some type of spell.

"She's a real asset," the young sorcerer asserted. His comments fell on Mayard's deafened ears. The gently undulating winged female sang and mesmerized the guards. Rhiann and Mayard Klarje saw her lips moving but could not hear the siren's sweet song. Maranna smiled and winked as they joined her. The guard uttered the command to remove the Wizard Lock and the three walked effortlessly through the gate and across the illuminated area before Thynna's Great Wall. Mayard and Rhiann removed the earplugs.

The winged female smugly furthered, "Works every time."

CHAPTER 8

Cloudmares

Maranna flapped her beautiful wings gracefully, ascended, and flew away. Mayard led Rhiann across the cleared area and into the nearby woods. They came upon the merchant *Elliott* who held three large misty gunmetal gray equines by ornate bridles. The beasts' three huge eyes were the reddest things Rhiann had beheld in his young life. The three eyes sparkled like red diamonds, the rarest of Sagain's jewels. Mayard said the middle or third eye was blind. Rhiann found gazing upon the intriguing beasts pleasant and touched the nearest shadowy creature. Surprisingly his fingers met resistance from the ghostly equine form.

Rhiann asked, "Is that the Shapechanger who attacked you in Elliott's store?"

Mayard answered, "One and the same. He's become a steadfast ally. Of the many facades he might project, he figured looking like old Elliott might worry you the least. He's getting along with the Cloudmares. I've procured the services of these three flying steeds."

Rhiann commented, "Elliott is not fond of me. Looking at a facsimile of him isn't exactly comforting. Those beasts lack wings. I though you said we'd fly to the Hanging Gardens."

Mayard answered, "Cloudmares don't need wings. They blend in well with the clouds. Urra, Shyrra, and Syrrth are Maranna's friends. They graze near her home Cragmore. They have agreed to carry us to the Hanging Gardens and allow the bridles to help us hold on."

Rhiann asked, "Are we really going to the Hanging Gardens. I've read such wondrous stories of them."

Mayard answered, "Fruits and flowers...waterfalls...gardens hanging from the palace terraces...exotic animals... overrun with all manner of Old Ones. This is the picture of the Hanging Gardens in most people's minds."

The beast Urra knelt. Rhiann Klarje sat gingerly upon her, flinched, and expected that he would pass through her hazy form and fall indignantly to the ground. However, the cloudmare's surprisingly firm back felt as comfortable as the smooth cushions of an overstuffed chair. Rhiann remarked, "Not sure I'd ever get used to the feel of her back."

Mayard replied, "You probably won't remember whether or not you did. Cloudmare's have an innate Forget Me Spell that results in observers' sensing they always meet them for the first time. Only when she feels comfortable does the misty mare refrain from using the spell. Urra deals with the Shapechanger Elliott only because of his association with me. Old Ones know I am sympathetic to them. We'd best get started. It's a long flight. We'll camp at Redcreek's source. There's a settlement called Low Gap that sits on the fringes of the Veldt near the source of Redcreek."

Redcreek flowed from its source in the mountains that rimmed the northernmost Veldt. Mineral deposits gave the waters deep red coloration at the creek's headwaters. Sagain's hardiest lots inhabited Low Gap, which was the last settlement before entering the wide expanse of grasslands and desert. Redcreek meandered from the foothills through sparsely populated areas. Its nourishing waters allowed patches of greenness and life in the otherwise arid lands. Redcreek predated the cataclysm. Its waters had long nourished the Hanging Gardens. In antiquity the three ageless sisters supervised the construction of the ancient wonder of Sagain and diverted waters from Redcreek. Tributaries of Redcreek circumvented the site and continued further southward to the Great Pyramid of Deception and on to the distant Eastern Sea.

The three Cloudmares carried Mayard, Rhiann, and the Shapechanger Elliott away from Thynna. They passed fuzzy Wombat Mountain. Semper fi trees stood densely on Wombat Mountain and gave the peak its appearance from the air. They crossed widespread desolation left by the cataclysm. Odd buttes rose from the red sands south of the mountain. Much of the barren land remained unexplored. Most travelers bypassed the impact area and took the long way around.

The Cloudmares blended into the clouds and easily avoided the rare flying beasts the small group encountered. They reached Low Gap by early evening. Mayard cautioned against dealing with the Low Gap merchants, who had close ties with Thynna. Instead the small group hunkered down in the woods a short way from the village. Mayard created an Illusory Terrain Spell to hide their camp and used Fire Magick to keep them warm. *p-Elliott* produced trail mix and dried meats and fruit. Mayard relayed stories of his travels. Rhiann and *p-Elliott* relished every word.

Rhiann queried, "As we travel further south the lands get more arid and unforgiving. How can such soil support the Hanging Gardens?"

Mayard answered, "The waters of Redcreek circle the gardens. At many points the waters flow upward into the gardens. Following the cataclysm upward flowing water was common. Resourceful sorcerers used Magick to influence the flow of streams and provide irrigation to crop growing areas. Redcreek's waters flowed upward before the Dawn of Magick. The Three Sisters are powerful and charismatic."

Rhiann found it hard to sleep in anticipation of seeing the Hanging Gardens and meeting the Fates. *p-Elliott* and Mayard's snoring didn't help. He welcomed morning and some hot breakfast. *p-Elliott* lacked his mother Caye's cooking skills, but in the setting of the woods the meal was excellent. Soon they were on their way and the small party arrived at the beautiful Hanging Gardens after a two-day flight. Accounts of the wondrous home of the Three Sisters failed to accurately describe the area's wonder.

the Hanging Gardens

The approach to the garden sloped like a hillside and several parts of the structure rose from one another tier on tier…on all this, the earth had been piled…and was thickly planted with trees of every kind that, by their great size and other charm, gave pleasure to the beholder…the water machines [raised] the water in great abundance from the river, although no one outside could see it.

"The Garden is quadrangular, and each side is four plethora long. It consists of arched vaults, which are located on checkered cube-like foundations. The ascent of the uppermost terrace-roofs is made by a stairway…"

"The Hanging Garden has plants cultivated above ground level, and the roots of the trees are embedded in an upper terrace rather than in the earth. The whole mass is supported on stone columns…"

"Streams of water emerging from elevated sources flow down sloping channels…these channels irrigate the whole garden saturating the roots of plants and keeping the whole area moist. Hence the grass is permanently green and the leaves of trees grow firmly attached to supple branches…this is a work of art of royal luxury and its most striking feature is that the labor of cultivation is suspended above the heads of the spectators.

With Mayard aboard, Syrrth eased to the ground. Urra with Rhiann and Shyrra with the Shapechanger- *p-Elliott* followed. Three armed centaurs greeted the Cloudmares and their riders. The largest stood centrally and bore the visage of a man's' torso attached to the body of a horse at the withers, where the horse's neck would be; others of his type stood heavily armed a few paces behind the greeting group. The powerful gray male carried a huge halberd. To his left stood a male centaur with a human body and legs joined at the waist with the hindquarters of a horse. This palomino colored male carried a longsword. A third centaur, a beautiful strawberry roan female. had human forelegs terminating in hooves. Her pinkish flowing hair closely matched her hindquarter coloration. She carried a wicked scimitar. Two snow-white winged centaurs hovered above the threesome and carried longbows with nocked arrows. Excepting their beautiful wings, the flying centaurs resembled the large male with the halberd. A blue Pegasus flew between the snow-white winged centaurs. He carried no weapon and looked back toward the walled edifice surrounding the Hanging Gardens.

Mayard Klarje approached the large gray with the halberd and said, "Why the show of force, Chiron? Does an old friend deserve such a greeting?"

The centaur lowered his halberd and addressed the approaching sorcerer, "Oh, it is you, Mayard. Our Cloudmare friends have never borne enemies to our gates, but I wasn't sure we were seeing Cloudmares approach. Ill winds blow from Thynna. The Three Sisters have tightened the guard to protect the Gardens. Your young companion bears the mark of the Klarjes. Your family has always respected Old Ones, and the Sisters have always appreciated it. Most of Thynna's folk don't share your feelings. My winged colleagues fear flying over the city."

Mayard answered, "As well they should, Chiron. My pleading has largely fallen on deaf ears. Please meet my great nephew Rhiann, the son of my niece Caye. My purpose is twofold. I want young Rhiann to make the acquaintance of the Sisters and also to check their feelings."

Chiron added, "I can't read your other comrade. Something's not right about him!"

Mayard acknowledged Chiron's suspicions, "You haven't lost your touch old friend. *p-Elliott* is, indeed, a Shapechanger. Before you raise your weapons, he is beholding to me, and I might add, been a better ally than most sorcerers. Even early on, at least I knew he wanted to do me in. Now I trust him more than anybody, save young Rhiann here and his mother my niece Caye. My once insalubrious colleague has worn the visage so long that he has become accustomed to the moniker *p-Elliott*. It suits him."

Chiron scoffed, "I can't allow a Shapechanger into the Gardens. Many of my comrades within the walls would consider him just a snack. Young Rhiann bears the mark of the Klarjes, so I'll certainly trust him."

Mayard replied, "*p-Elliott* recognizes the dangers he'd face and will gladly remain outside. He, and I, hope your archers refrain from using him for target practice."

Chiron smirked and smugly replied, "I guess the old boy will just have to take his chances."

The Shapechanger *p-Elliott* shimmered briefly and changed his image to a snow-white Centaur foal. Mayard and Chiron laughed. Mayard added, "He has a better chance now."

Rhiann watched intently and remained respectfully silent while his great uncle and the magnificent centaur conversed. *P-Centaur Elliott* whinnied and scampered between the Cloudmares Urra and Syrrth. The flying centaurs overhead eyed him suspiciously. Chiron turned toward the Gardens and bade Rhiann and Mayard follow him. All accounts of the Hanging Gardens of Red Creek underestimated their beauty.

Chiron and a small entourage of centaurs led Mayard and Rhiann to the water's edge. The reddish-orange water flowed quickly before them. Redcreek was over a hundred feet across at this point. Rhiann pondered how they'd cross and why such a robust body of flowing water wasn't called Red River. Winged and horned creatures, beings fleet and silent. Pegasi, Sirens, Dragons, Rocs, Dryads, Gnomes, Elementals, Xorn, Windwalkers, Night Hags, Devils, Djinn, Efreet, and other strange beings filled the area on the opposite side of the river. Chiron reached the water's edge and continued forward. Mayard walked beside him without hesitation onto the invisible bridge.

Mayard whispered, "Walk behind me. The bridge is sturdy."

Rhiann asked, "How'd you know...?"

Mayard said, "Where to walk? I've been here many times."

The group walked across the bridge. Rhiann hazarded a glance downward into the water beneath the invisible bridge. Large sinuous sea creatures shadowed their movement.

Rhiann asked, "What?"

Chiron answered, "Sea knuckers. They won't come out of the water, but they'll devour anything attempting to cross the water uninvited... or invited for that matter."

They reached the far side and walked onto a grassy area. All manner of Old Ones meandered about including many without wings that were effortlessly positioned about thirty feet in the air.

Mayard said, "They are standing on the allure."

Chiron moved forward, whinnied, and stamped his forefoot. A grating sound followed.

The centaur said, "Follow me."

Rhiann and Mayard followed. Mayard commented, "An invisible wall surrounds the gardens. The Three Sisters do not want to obscure the view."

Rhiann asked, "Why is the wall so high?

Mayard answered, "Giants!"

Rhiann queried, "Won't enemies simply fly over it?"

Mayard answered, "Most things that fly are allied with the sisters."

Chiron lead Mayard and Rhiann across an expanse of green grass. The wondrous gardens loomed ahead. The terracing exposed the diverse flora. Every plant in the world was well represented. Rainbow colors intertwined with lush greens. Wonderful fragrances filled the air. Simply inhaling the air invigorated visitors to the Hanging Gardens.

Mayard commented, "I've never seen so many Old Ones here."

Chiron answered, "The Three Sisters have called for support. The Giants have sent scouts deeply into the Veldt. To this point none have braved the entire trek to the Gardens, but the threat is real. These are uncertain times in our world, my old friend. We'd hoped you'd have more influence in Thynna."

Mayard nodded and answered, "As did I, Chiron, but the council grows more secretive and isolationist. Giants are not welcomed in Thynna."

Rhiann tugged on his uncle's robe and asked, "No Old Ones are welcomed in Thynna, Uncle Mayard. Why would giants be any different?"

Mayard answered, "Nephew, Giants are not old Ones. Giants are merely big men. History has shown many alliances between men and giants. The council of Thynna has sent emissaries to the giant kings of Hinderburgh. Sorcerers brought giants from Hinderburgh to quarry large stones from the mountains to the west of Thynna to assist in the construction of the city's defenses. The council tempts the giants and wild men of the north and west with bling and booty."

Chiron added, "Giants are quite chaotic. Getting them to work together takes some skill. When the going gets tough, any given giant will look after number one."

Rhiann asked, "Meaning?"

Mayard chuckled, "Giants put themselves ahead of all others. The old adage 'everybody's got to serve somebody' doesn't apply very well to the big blokes. Some members of the Council of Thynna feel they can buy the giants' loyalty. I think they will ultimately be wrong."

Gently sloping stairs bisected the terraces and led upward to a rotunda, a building with a circular ground plan. A dome covered the structure. The diameter of the rotunda was 144 feet and the domed roof was 89 feet high. A renowned architect named Jefferson Thomas designed and supervised the construction of the Hanging Gardens rotunda. He hoped his design represented the "authority of nature and power of reason." The Three Sisters used the building for formal affairs and living quarters. The rarest plants grew around the rotunda in rich soil collected from Sagain's most fertile lands. The nourishing waters of Redcreek sustained the sumptuous growth. Heavily armed Djinn stood on either side of hefty doors leading into the rotunda. The Djinn held halberds crossed before the door. When Chiron approached the pair snapped the weapons down to their side and stepped aside. Chiron announced his presence and a soft feminine voice bade him enter. The noble centaur opened the door. Mayard and Rhiann followed him inside.

CHAPTER 9

The Three Sisters

A fetching female wearing a marvelous white robe and bearing a distaff opened the door. Her distaff held the unspun fibers of many colors and kept them untangled to ease the spinning process. Fiber was wrapped around the distaff, and tied in place with a piece of golden ribbon. Another white-robed woman stood near the center of the circular room and carried a red rod. A third similarly clad lady sat upon a plush chair and toyed with an ornate cutting shears. The woman nearest the door said, "Welcome back, Mayard Klarje, friend of Nature. What brings you to our home?"

Mayard bowed politely and replied, "Thank you, Nona, I come to seek audience and to acquaint my nephew Rhiann with your wonderful gardens. It's my burden to relay to you events in Thynna."

Nona said, "Young Rhiann has already caught my eye. He bears the mark of the Klarjes and shares your wisdom. From your manner of speaking and the look upon your face, I take it our gift of the Gem Bush did not soften the Council of Thynna's feelings toward us. You must be weary after your travels. Sit and join us for nourishment."

The Moirae, the Fates, were the most powerful of the Old Ones. Said to be the daughters of night and the wind, the trio sought dominion over the primitive world. Architects of the destinies of humble mortal men, the white robed sisters were known by many names, including Nona, Decima, and Mors. Commonly called the Spinner, the Allotter, and the Unturning, the uninvited threesome came calling during the ninth month of pregnancy and again three nights after a child's birth. The Spinner spun the thin precious thread of life over her distaff. The

Allotter measured the length of the narrow thread with a mysterious red rod. The Unturning, the inevitable for those mortal, chose the manner of the individual's death and cut the thin thread with her dreaded shears. All the stories and lore of the Spinner, the Allotter, and the Unturning or Inexorable rushed through Rhiann's mind. A fetching Dryad brought exotic fruits and refreshing beverages. Rhiann's eyes met the serving girls briefly. Mayard's grasp broke up the charming effect of her gaze.

Mayard said, "You must stay on your guard. The dryad almost charmed you. Follow my lead."

Nona gave the lovely dryad a brief reproach.

Mayard began, "My words to the Council of Thynna have fallen on deaf ears. The Council grows ever more hostile to Old Ones and the old ways. Sorcerers resent the hold the Three Sisters have over common men."

Mors the Unturning snipped the air with her shears and argued, "We seldom interfere in the affairs of Thynna. Magick resists the effects of our implements. Thynna's walls and sorcerers' spells exclude us! We sacrificed the Gem Bush for naught. It doesn't dent their greed."

Nona said, "No, sister, we have enjoyed dominion for... a long time. We conceded Thynna's sphere of influence, Mayard. We remain in our Gardens. No one is kept here against their will. We are the Fates. We are who we are and do what we do. We will not allow sorcerers from Thynna to dictate our roles. We... and all Old Ones were here long before the first sorcerers. We'll yield no more of our realm. The Veldt and seven wonders belong to all of Sagain and shall not be compromised. We accept that the Council bans Old Ones from the city of Magick. We'll not concede them quarter should they encroach on the Veldt and threaten that which we hold dear."

Mayard replied, "I'd not except you should, but know the council considers you threats and uses this as a means to bias opinion against you. Untimely deaths are blamed on the three of you. Perhaps a gesture... a commitment to stay clear of the lands north of the Veldt. That would include not using your implements, as you refer to the distaff, rod, and shears."

Mors interjected, "Our last gesture went for naught. The Gem Bush is a priceless relic. It bought us nothing."

Nona added, "Mayard, let us not spend all our time together talking of things we can do nothing about. Sit with me. Tell me of your travels."

Decima playfully tapped the red rod she held against her exposed right thigh. The Three Sisters shared ageless beauty, but Decima appeared younger than Nona and Mors. She flashed a glance at Rhiann and said, "Come to me, pretty one."

Rhiann cleared his throat and asked, "Did you say you want me to…?"

Decima purred, "Yes, sit by me." She patted the luxurious cushion on the settee.

Rhiann walked to her. Decima stood and took his hand. She then planted a soft lingering kiss against his lips. Rhiann felt every nerve ending in his body exploding and felt sensations of manhood that were new to him. When Decima pulled her lips away, he gasped. She queried, "What's wrong? Didn't you like it?"

Rhiann flushed, stammered, and managed, "Oh, no, it was… pleasant. Very pleasant! It's just… I've never kissed a woman before."

Mayard chuckled, "You still haven't kissed a mere woman, nephew."

Decima kept her hands resting on Rhiann's' shoulders and looked into the young sorcerer's eyes. She gently touched his cherry-red, heart-shaped birthmark and then curled a thick strand of his long red hair on her finger. She touched his hair, forehead, and then birth mark with her infamous red rod. The youthful Fate said, "Sister, might I have a length of fiber from your distaff?"

Nona said, "Sister, I am relaxing. But I will honor your request." Nona took a spinning wheel and drew forth a length of multicolored thread. Mors snipped the thread with her shears and carried it to Decima, who kept her face about three inches from Rhiann and enticed him ever more with her sweet breath. The young sorcerer's fingers and toes tingled with excitement. Decima took a strand of her long platinum hair and twisted it around the thread of Rhiann's red hair wrapped around her finger and bound the pair of threads with the fiber that Mors snipped from Nona's distaff. Scintillating lights surrounded Rhiann and the beautiful Fate. Decima gently stretched and braided the interwoven strand. The interwoven hair and fiber grew ever longer and surrounded Decima and Rhiann. She smiled alluringly, gave Rhiann another kiss, and stepped away from him. Mors deftly snipped the strand of hair where it left Decima's head. Rhiann's locks shimmered briefly and then resumed their red color. The long strand he received from Decima meld with his hair and the fiber from Nona's distaff.

Decima purred, "My gift to you, young one. May you walk long in your Uncle Mayard's steps. I hope you visit the gardens often, Rhiann Klarje."

Rhiann regained his composure and sat beside Decima the Allotter. Calmness came over him. Dryads brought more refreshments. Mayard talked with Nona and Mors. The discussions became whispered and brow furrowing. Decima sat by Rhiann and said little. She'd extend her hand and gently massage the tips of Rhiann's fingers and then sip on the nectars brought by the dryads.

Decima suggested, "Let's walk in the gardens, Rhiann."

Rhiann stood and looked to his uncle and Mayard nodded approval. The elder Klarje's discussions with Nona grew more intense. Decima took Rhiann's hand and led him from the rotunda to an adjacent gazebo and a path that led into the lovely flora. They passed the supposedly unique Snowberry Bush, treasured for its white berries that chilled drinks. A yourna bird sang on a dewberry bush. Decima swiped another soft kiss. Twilight enhanced both the gardens and Fate's beauty. Leaving such a beautiful place and woman challenged reason. Rhiann and Decima walked along a meandering path in the opulent gardens. Decima placed her hands on Rhiann's shoulders are looked into his eyes. She raised her left index finger to his face and rubbed the heart-shaped birthmark. She gently kissed first the birthmark and then planted a lingering kiss on his lips. Rhiann awkwardly placed his arms around her waist and held her. Long platinum hair fell over his arms and gave the sensation of a thousand tiny legs running across his skin. Goosebumps covered him.

Decima purred, "Would you like to visit my chamber?"

Rhiann nervously replied, "I... it's beautiful in the gardens. Shouldn't we stay here?"

Decima coyly answered, "There's much more to discover, young sorcerer. I wonder... have you never been with a woman?"

Rhiann blushed and said, "Well, I'm with you, now. I've spent lots of time with my mother. I suppose my mirror ICU doesn't count."

Decima giggled, "No, the mirror doesn't count. Walk with me."

Decima took his hand and gently pulled him toward a small flower-covered cottage near the rotunda. When they neared the door, both heard the sound of fluttering wings. A lovely siren landed by Rhiann.

Decima said coolly, "Maranna, why are you here?"

The Siren Maranna answered just as nippily, "Mayard Klarje tasked me with watching over his nephew and protecting him from dangerous beasts and misadventures. Looks like I was just in time to save him from both. Hello, Rhiann."

Rhiann blushed and dropped Decima's hand, and blurted. "Hello, Maranna."

Decima said, "Its unnecessary for you to snoop around, my winged friend. Rhiann's not in danger."

Maranna answered, "Doesn't look like it to me. Rhiann, looks are deceiving. Do you have any idea how old she is?"

Before Rhiann could answer Decima said tersely, "I'm younger than you. Mind you own business. Why don't you just flutter away the way you came?"

Maranna answered, "In due time, but I'd rather stay with Rhiann."

Decima snipped, "So you can sing to and seduce him. I know your methods, siren!"

Maranna replied curtly, "Now Rhiann should return to his Uncle Mayard in the rotunda. Rhiann, I hope I've neither offended nor embarrassed you. I will wait with Urra, Syrrth, and Shyrra."

Maranna abruptly flew away. Decima grabbed Rhiann's hand and suggested, "Let's not allow her to disrupt our evening."

Rhiann allowed, "It is getting late. I am tired, and Uncle Mayard will be missing me."

Decima sighed, and replied, "Oh, all right. No telling who or what else is going to drop in on us. I just saw a Manticore fly over."

The twin suns had long descended in the west when Mayard stretched and allowed fatigue was getting the better of him. Rhiann and Decima returned to the rotunda. After gracious goodnights, dryads led Mayard and Rhiann down a spiraling stairwell to an opulent guest room. Braziers provided light and burning incenses saturated the air with smoky floral essences. The old sorcerer said little as they prepared to retire. Rhiann sensed his great uncle's preoccupation. The youth's thoughts returned to the pleasantness of Decima's touch and her wonderful kisses. He stood before a looking glass, peered at his reflection in the dim light, and held the unusually long strand of braided hair in his hand. Decima's hair and the flax woven from Nona's distaff were indistinguishable now from his own flaming red hair that was intermingled with them. Decima had adroitly braided the hair and paced a barrette made of translucent ribbon at its tip.

Mayard mumbled, "Don't ever cut that hair."

Rhiann asked, "Will I die if I cut it?"

Mayard chuckled, "Not unless you use a very dangerous shears. Decima gave you her greatest gift."

The old sorcerer removed the weathered pointed hat that seldom left his head and allowed a long strand of graying hair fall to the floor. Mayard continued, "Nona shared with me in my youth, just as did her sister Mors with the first sorcerer, our ancestor Cydney Klarje. Cydney welcomed Old Ones, associated freely with them, and learned many of their ways. I've tried to follow his path. In all the sorcerers of the past several generations, only you and your mother Caye have any inkling of Cydney's attitudes. Only you bear the mark of the Klarjes. The Three Sisters recognize this too.?

Rhiann asked, "Uncle Mayard, did you ask the siren Maranna to watch after me?"

Mayard mumbled, "I might have said something about your safety in passing. Maranna is a great friend and ally. No one tells her what to do. You'd never know that she's around. Invisibility is one of her innate abilities. She will only intervene to protect you. Sirens generally avoid getting involved in the world's affairs. Furthermore, Maranna doesn't spend much time at the Hanging Gardens. Some sort of rivalry with the Three Sisters. It's an Old One thing. I've heard talk of a 'green monster' named jealousy but haven't seen one. Outran a green dragon once, though. I'm very tired now and need to turn in. We have much to discuss on the morrow."

Mayard fell asleep quickly, but Rhiann struggled to join him. His thoughts raced from his encounter with lovely Decima, his uncle's plans, and the Magick that welled up in his mind. The encounter with the Siren in the gardens perplexed the young sorcerer. He did not understand the enmity between Decima and Maranna. It clearly predated his involvement. The wondrous females' eyes exchanged virtual daggers of contempt. Mayard spoke of a "green monster." His mother talked of a "green monster" when discussing quarrels among sorcerers. Decima had mentioned seeing a Manticore. But he'd heard Manticores were red, not green. The mysterious siren's gaze and voice engrossed him as powerfully as did Decima's touch. He pondered Decima's cozy cottage. Should he have gone with her? Decima accused Maranna of wanting to sing. Everyone knew the lore of the siren's song. Mayard trusted the wondrous winged female. He rather trusted the Shapechanger Elliott. Sometimes Rhiann questioned his Uncle Mayard's choice of friends and allies. Just about everyone in Thynna did as well, particularly the Council of Thynna. Was he becoming no better than the narrow minded leaders of the city of Magick! Curse him for doubting his uncle! The young sorcerer's head was spinning. He'd felt emotions and stirrings heretofore unknown to him. Mayard's gentle snoring made Rhiann long for sleep and regret he hadn't mastered the Sleep Spell. Finding a cricket needed for the incantation would be easy in the gardens. He'd heard them chirping all night. Then he heard the call of a night bird. The song grew sweeter and more soothing. Then the warbling changed to soft calming words. Heartening, comforting, gentle words... words... from a bird! Rhiann's eyes grew heavier. His doubts and worries left him. He never felt so warm and comforted. He slept. Once she was sure the young sorcerer had found sleep, the invisible siren eased through the window. Centuries had passed since she last used her lullaby song. Giving the young sorcerer a night's sleep was well worth the effort. Getting his mind off the sultry Decima was gravy.

The next morning Mayard awakened Rhiann with some vigorous shaking and said, "The relationship with Thynna and the Three Sisters continues to deteriorate. Neither will budge. The Sisters are content to leave things the way they are but the Council grows ever power hungry and seeks dominion over the Veldt and its Seven Wonders. The Three Sisters feel the Wonders belong to all of Sagain and should remain under stewardship of the Old Ones. I fear for the safety of the Hanging Gardens and the Sisters themselves. Magick is for everyone. Our family bears great responsibility to assure it is used properly. Your mother Caye is a voice of reason as is your father Kurth... most of the time. Sometimes he thinks too much 'for the good of Thynna.' Are you willing to follow me?"

Rhiann felt his head spinning but managed, "Yes, Uncle Mayard, that's why I'm here. I want to learn everything I can from you. I look forward to our time together."

Mayard sighed, "Young Rhiann, that's what I'm getting to. I must remain at the Hanging Gardens. All I love of Sagain is in jeopardy. Nona has asked me to help shore up the defenses of the gardens. For all their power, Old Ones have little in the realm of Magick. I shall continue my efforts to create peace but I'll work from this end. In my dreams I've seen you far exceeding me in Magick. You must return to Thynna in my stead."

Rhiann queried, "But Uncle Mayard, are the Three Sisters not immortal and ageless?"

Mayard replied, "The Three Sisters do not fear time. When I first encountered Nona, she had fallen victim to a blue magoo. Her charisma has little effect on hungry predators. The blue magoo was about to finish her off. Her life's blood poured from her veins. I smote the beast, bound her wounds, and nursed her back to health in the Veldt's wilderness. Our friendship grew from that encounter. The ripping jaws of a blue magoo and crushing blow from a giant's club are just as lethal go the Three Sisters and any Old Ones as to us. Not long I… uh, saved her from a bewildebeest."

Rhiann said, "But they are the Fates1 Are you saying they don't control their own destiny?"

Mayard chuckled, "Let's just say they are better at it than most of us."

Rhiann continued, "Uncle Mayard, your voice is one of few that opposes the oppression of the Council of Thynna. Your presence is Thynna curtails the Council's actions. You are needed in Thynna."

Mayard said, "Magick has changed Sagain. Our family, the Klarjes are the stewards of Magick. Grayness has spoken to me in my dreams."

Rhiann allowed, "I also have dreams. When I awaken I am aware of new spells. But it's the same with other sorcerers. Everything gains Magick while sleeping. Why are we different?"

Mayard answered, "Because Cydney Klarje was the first sorcerer, and we have received perks. I'm going to bequeath an artifact to you that my grandfather passed to me. He received it after a visit from Grayness."

Mayard reached into his raiment and produced a small nondescript gray stone.

A single rune appeared on the rock and persisted for thirteen heartbeats.

Ω

Then the single letter faded, and three runes appeared on the surface of the rock, which briefly emitted gray light.

Ǿ ∞ Ǿ

The runes faded after 21 heartbeats and the single rune reappeared. The pattern repeated three times. Three runes appeared on the stones surface.

Ǿ ∞ Ǿ

Mayard said, "This is an Omega Stone. It's priceless. You must hold it precious. Keep it with you at all times. It seeks its fellows. It came to our ancestor after a dream. I don't know exactly what it does. It gives me a sense of direction. Nona held it and it made her feel stronger."

Rhiann took the little rock and held the stone in his hand. A single rune appeared on the rock and persisted for thirteen heartbeats.

Ω

Then the single letter faded, and three runes appeared on the surface of the rock, which briefly emitted gray light.

Ǿ ∞ Ǿ

The runes faded after 21 heartbeats and the single rune reappeared. The pattern repeated three times.

The stone warmed, softened, and meld to his flesh. He released the little rock and it resumed its shape. Rhiann said, "It feels good in my hand. It gives me a sense of protection, but I don't feel stronger. Nor do I get a sense of direction."

Mayard said, "The runes always follow the same pattern. It gives different holders different feelings. Different strokes for different folks."

Rhiann said, "Are you sure it's safe?"

Mayard continued, "It passed along the Klarje family line to me. Cydney Klarje received the stone after a dream. Keep it safe. In all the years I carried it, it's only reacted like you just saw and given different feelings to those who hold it. Perhaps one day you'll learn its purpose. I have an important unfulfilled task. You must complete it for me. Its completion entails trekking to the Copper Mountains, which lie north and west of Thynna and treating with the Dwarfish sword master Roswell Kirkey. He works with the miners and is making something for me."

Rhiann said, "I know of the Copper Mountain folk. They are despised in Thynna as being mundane and outsiders. They are forbidden entry."

Mayard said "Thynna's merchants covet the copper and other minerals the miners bring out of the ground, but they have no regard for the miners who risk life and limb entering the dark depths of the world. I have a great working relationship with the miners and have bartered with them. I placed Continual Light Spells on several devices and helped the miners in their excursions deeper into the earth. In exchange for my light-giving Magick, they have given me artifacts and raw materials. I have acted as a go-between for them in their trade with the merchants of Thynna. The miners of the Copper Mountains found a parcel of unique ore deep beneath the surface. The material was a reddish malleable material. The miners bequeathed the red ore to the Burgomaster of Gnome-town. I helped bring two highwaymen named Big Boy and Tiny to justice. The grateful Burgomaster gave me the ore. I made arrangements to have the Dwarfish armorer Roswell forge the ore into a blade. Roswell's meticulous work was also going to take some time, so I returned to Thynna. You saved me from the Shapechanger. I committed to return and give the Copper Mountain miners more lights, but I haven't had the chance to return. Roswell should be finished now. I want you to go in my stead."

Rhiann asked, "Uncle Mayard, the miners don't know me. They trust you, not me. I'm sure the stories told in Thynna of the miners' ruthlessness are embellished, but it's safe to assume they won't trust an outsider. The Council of Thynna respects you. My voice means nothing to them."

Mayard replied, "By the way, the Council does not respect me. It fears reprisals for not following my requests. Don't underestimate your importance. You bear the mark of the Klarjes. Anyway, I'll be with you."

Rhiann said, "But you said you'd remain in the Hanging Gardens to assist the Three Sisters."

Mayard answered, "That I did."

Rhiann returned, "You are speaking in riddles. You are a great sorcerer but not even you can be in two places at once."

Mayard replied, "Very astute, Rhiann, I cannot. But *p-Elliott* will be with you."

Rhiann queried, "The Shapechanger?"

Mayard replied, "His version of me is as good as his copy of the merchant Elliott. He'll pass for me in Thynna and the Copper Mountains."

Rhiann argued, "But he's not a spell caster! He can't create Continual Light Spells. He can't stand before the Council."

Mayard said, "You can cast spells."

Rhiann was taken aback and stammered, "Sure... but... but the miners will know I'm casting the spells."

Mayard answered with a wink, "Not if you are creative. Make it look like *p-Elliott* is throwing the spell. Throw your voice. That doesn't even require Magick!"

Rhiann said, "I don't know the way."

Mayard answered, "p-*Elliott* does."

Rhiann said matter-of-factly, "You trust the Shapechanger, Uncle Mayard. I'm not sure that I do."

Mayard winked again and said, "We'll tell him that I'm me looking like you and I want him to look like me. I'll say I don't trust the miners. Show him the stone. He knows I'm never without it... and he may think it will curse him if he turns against me. I don't fully trust him either. He has seen the runes on the stone. I am ashamed to say that I told him he'd irreversibly turn into a toad if he wronged me or refused my direction."

Rhiann said, "You lied to him."

Mayard confessed, "Yes."

Rhiann said, "Sounds complicated. Why can I wait in the Hanging Gardens with you. I can help, and I'd like to get to know Decima better."

Mayard said, "In my dreams, I've seen the power of the artifact that the dwarf Roswell is creating. The spirit of the stone has spoken to me.

It can't fall into the wrong hands. And someone has to be a voice of reason in Thynna."

Rhiann said, "So *p-Elliott* is going to look like you and think I am you looking like me. The miners will think he is you and I'll secretly cast your spells. The Council of Thynna will think *p-Elliott* is you. The chances of success are slim and none. Shouldn't *p-Elliott* know the truth?"

Mayard replied, "Plausible deniability!"

Rhiann asked, "What does that mean?"

Mayard said, "Plausible deniability is the ability for persons to deny knowledge of or responsibility for any damnable actions committed by others because of a lack of evidence that can confirm their participation. Political leaders use it all the timed. If *p-Elliott* doesn't know our secret, he can't give it away."

Rhiann said, "I'll do as you ask. When should I leave?"

Mayard said, "This day. Oh, and get accustomed to wearing a hat. I'm never without mine."

Rhiann managed a smile and said, "I'm supposed to be you looking like me. I'll go as far as a cowl."

Rhiann and Mayard joined the Three Sisters for breakfast. Mayard confided his plans to Nona. Decima presented Rhiann with a luxurious dark robe with a cowl. The Captain of the Hanging Gardens guard the noble Centaur Chiron still refused the Shapechanger entry to the gardens. *p-Elliott* had been well attended in the perimeter and was no worse for the wear. Mayard Klarje muttered a conjuration. His visage changed to mimic his young nephew Rhiann. The two Rhianns exited the gardens with Chiron and approached the bewildered Shapechanger. The Rhianns shook hands and Mayard (looking like Rhiann) reentered the Hanging Gardens.

CHAPTER 10

Deception
p-Mayard

Pretending to be Mayard, Rhiann said, "*Rhiann* is going to stay behind at the gardens. I'm going to procced to the Copper Mountains and conclude my business with the miners."

p-Elliott asked, "Why do you look like your nephew, Boss? You even sound like him!"

Rhiann said, "I shall appear as my nephew in order to better monitor events in Thynna. It's a ruse. I want you to look like me. I'll look like Rhiann. The miners and Council of Thynna won't know."

The Shapechanger said, "All right, you're the boss. Your actions never surprise me. I'm surprised you're going back though. Last time I wasn't sure we'd get out of there with our hides. You said it was because they thought I was a merchant from Thynna, but their mistrust of sorcerers was very evident. Here goes!"

p-Elliott became p-Mayard.

The innate ability of Shapechangers was not Magick and produced no auras. It just happened. The ersatz Mayard and true Rhiann made their way to the waiting Cloudmares.

The Shapechanger *p-Mayard* said, "You look like Rhiann and I look like you. Syrrth will expect to carry me and you should ride Urra. I suppose you'll want to remain with Syrrth. Urra carried Rhiann before. Shyrra has no *p-Elliott* to carry. Wait!"

Beautiful Syrrth abruptly flew away.

p-Mayard mused, "Why'd Syrrth leave and Shyrra stay? Guess it doesn't really matter. We ought to get going. We should try to get to Low Gap before dark."

The Cloudmare Urra sent a silent message to Rhiann, "I'll continue to carry you, young sorcerer. Your ruse is wasted on me. I see into your mind. Mayard's business is his own, and I learned long ago not to question your uncle's actions. *Think* what you want to say to me."

Urra with Rhiann and Shyrra with the Shapechanger-formerly *p-Elliott* -now *p-Mayard* flew away from the Hanging Gardens. Rhiann snuggled into Urra's soft plush hide and held on tightly.

Urra sent another silent message, "Are you going to follow us to Thynna?"

The invisible siren Maranna silently replied, "Yes, Urra. Mayard has asked me to watch over him. He is powerful, but very inexperienced."

Urra sent back the message, "Maranna, what sort of experience do you plan to offer him?"

Maranna replied, "I don't appreciate what you are implying, my friend. I only have his best interest in mind. I maneuver easily in Thynna. Most sorcerers don't oft employ Detect Invisibility spells."

Urra continued, "Mayard's plans oft perplex me. I'll bear the youth back to Thynna, but the Copper Mountain folk will not welcome my sort. Our presence will be counterproductive to Mayard's plan."

Maranna said, "All these years, Urra, and I still don't understand telepathy. How does young Rhiann not 'hear' us?"

Urra said matter-of-factly, "I'm not thinking to or about him. He hears my thoughts only when I want him to do so."

Maranna said silently, "I'll remain some distance behind you. He may be able to detect invisible creatures. Do you trust the Shapechanger, Urra?"

Urra said silently, "Not fully."

Maranna replied, "Neither do I."

The Shapechanger as Mayard urged his flying steed Shyrra nearer Urra and addressed Rhiann, whom he thought was Mayard, "Mayard... I can't shake the feeling like I'm talking to myself. After we rest up at Low Gap and then get to Thynna, how long will we wait to proceed to the Copper Mountains?"

Rhiann as Mayard said, "I'll address the Council of Thynna and deliver Nona's ultimatum. The forces of Thynna are to remain outside the Veldt. Visitation to the Seven Wonders will remain at the discretion of each shrine's stewards."

The Shapechanger answered, "Boss, even I can tell you the Council isn't going to go for that s**t." The time of the Old Ones is past. The Three Sisters can't hold on forever."

Rhiann replied, "I know. How long will the trek to the Copper Mountains take?"

The Shapechanger said, "Huh? Are you serious, Boss? You've traveled with me to deal with the miners eight times. How fast we get there depends on how good our transportation is. When you had purple enigmas pulling the carts from Thynna the trip took two weeks. Blue nus and red machis are stronger and faster. Purple enigmas are hard to figure out and harder still to predict. If we are carrying finished goods to the miners, I'd suggest we get phi gamms to pull the wagons. They're strongest. Of course, it be nicer if you just used a Teleportation Spell to get us to the mountains or else reconsider the decision about the Cloudmares."

Rhiann dug into his knowledge gained from his great uncle and remarked, "Sorcerers easily learn low-level Teleportation Spells. Teleportation only works over short distances and enables the caster to carry nothing. The caster arrives at his destination nude and defenseless, and this presents problems. Word of Return Spells only permit returning to one's sanctuary, though this valuable dweomer allows some encumbrance; that is, the caster can carry some of his stuff with him! Teleportation and Word of Return enable escape and little else."

Shapechanger-Mayard conceded, "Arriving naked wouldn't impress the miners."

Rhiann added, "As you well know the miners are suspicious of Old Ones and particularly beings like our Cloudmare friends. It's important to stand on solid ground with them. The armorer Roswell has been working on a project for me. I have some special gifts for him along with something I want him to include in his construction."

Urra and Shyrra carried the sorcerer and Shapechanger to the earlier campsite near Low Gap. Rhiann declined the ersatz Mayard's suggestion of a trip into the settlement to sample the wares of the tavern. Urra and Shyrra found bountiful nourishment among the flora around Red Creek. Rhiann warmed the austere camp with a small Magick fire. He and pseudo-Mayard shared victuals sent from the Hanging Gardens. The Siren Maranna lingered near the camp and stood guard through the night. When the twin suns peaked over the mountains, the road weary young sorcerer and Shapechanger *p-Mayard* broke camp and continued on toward Thynna. Urra and Shyrra dropped them off in the woods near their departure point. Rhiann and *pseudo-Mayard* then approached Thynna's formidable outer curtain and its guards. The gatehouse outside the outer curtain bustled with activity, and guards on the wall walk peered down on everyone who approached the city.

p-Mayard asked, "How are we going to get in, Boss?"

Rhiann answered, "You are Mayard Klarje, benefactor of Magick and Thynna. They won't refuse you entry."

p-Mayard replied, "Actually, you are Mayard Klarje. I'm just a likeness. What do I do if they ask me to cast a spell?"

Rhiann replied, "Just wave your hands about and move your lips."

The duo stood before the outer curtain. The Sergeant of the Guard on the allure shouted, "What business have you in the City Thynna?"

p-Mayard said, "Open the gate! I have business with the council."

The guard laughed, "Old timer, lots of blokes want to speak to the council. Dressing up like a sorcerer isn't enough to get you inside the city."

Rhiann said impatiently, "Sergeant, know that you are addressing Mayard Klarje, the foremost sorcerer of this and most any generation. I'd suggest you let us in before he grows impatient and turns you into blue nu crap!"

The burly sergeant barked, "Listen young whipper-snapper! We have strict guidelines on who gets in or out. For all I know you blokes are a couple of Shapechangers! Everyone in Thynna knows of the great Mayard Klarje and his propensity for going on walkabouts. It's also common knowledge that his young nephew Rhiann left with him. You blokes have copied them all the way down to the red marks on your faces."

Rhiann walked to the heavy bluewood gate, uttered an incantation, and pecked on the door. Nothing happened. P-Mayard mumbled and made gestures. Again nothing happened.

The sergeant said, "You fellows having some trouble. Takes more than gestures to undo a Wizard Lock."

Rhiann muttered under his breath, "Idiot that I am! I cast a Knock Spell. Undoing the Wizard Lock requires Dispel Magick! I just hope the sorcerer that placed the spell isn't more powerful than I am."

p-Mayard stood close by and heard Rhiann's rumblings. "Boss, why aren't you opening the door?"

Rhiann said, "It has to look like you do it. Start talking and touch the door."

p-Mayard obliged.

Rhiann concentrated. The phrases of the Dispel Magick incantation flowed flawlessly from his lips for the first time. He furtively touched the door. The massive gate swung noiselessly open. The sorcerers entered Thynna. A squad of armed guards met and surrounded them. The Sergeant of the Guard Regan descended the wall stairs and approached the sorcerers.

Sergeant Regan addressed Rhiann and the Shapechanger in Mayard's visage, "Removing the Wizard Lock proves Magick touches you. I'm not convinced you are who you say you are. I must interrogate you before you enter the city proper."

p-Mayard muttered, "This is outrageous! I'm insulted! I'm not going to honor your questions by answering them. You'll have to talk to my nephew!"

Sergeant Regan said, "Now… that comment puts me in mind of Mayard Klarje. So be it! If you are Rhiann Klarje, you should be able to answer some questions."

Thus Rhiann did most of the talking and passed all the tests of identity given him. Actually, it was easy in that he was really Rhiann.

Sergeant Regan concluded, "You are cleared to enter the city. It's good to have you back, Sorcerer Mayard."

Rhiann and *p-Mayard* meandered along the busy streets and received many greetings. Folk in the outer ward did not share the Council of Thynna's contempt and had great regard for the older Klarje.

p-Mayard said, "Boss, I'm impressed! You even had me convinced that you are your nephew! You handled that well."

Rhiann replied, "You weren't much help!"

The Shapechanger answered, "Well, duh! I'm not you, Mayard! It was best I kept quiet."

Rhiann wanted to spend time with his mother Caye and father Kurth, but his uncle stressed the import of delivering the Fates' answer and then going to the Copper Mountains. The duo passed through the inner curtain and entered the inner ward. They passed the Gem Bush and the statue of Mayard in the courtyard and entered the Council of Thynna's chambers. Rhiann turned *to p-Mayard* and said, "It's your turn now. Just go in there and tell them that Nona demands Thynna not extend its influence into the Veldt."

p-Mayard muttered, "I'm not much of a public speaker, Boss. Couldn't you just be yourself and address them yourself."

Rhiann replied, "My... Rhiann's voice means nothing to the Council."

p-Mayard said, "They aren't going to like what I say. Do you see a quick way out?"

Rhiann said, "The Council of Thynna isn't known for shooting the messenger. Just state your peace and we'll gather goods for our trek to the Copper Mountains."

The Shapechanger grumbled, "My folk don't feel the same about the council."

Rhiann replied, "If you recall, you haven't exactly been a model citizen."

p-Mayard harrumphed, stepped to the podium and delivered Nona's message verbatim. The council erupted in discord. The Shapechanger mimicked Mayard's voice perfectly, spoke succinctly, and moved away. Kurth Marsh approached his son and queried regarding his plans. Rhiann relayed his need to leave Thynna immediately for the Copper Mountains.

Kurth said, "Your mother will be disappointed. She's been quite worried about you. For all your experience, Mayard, you oft lack good judgment. You should have asked Caye and me before leaving with our son. Relations between Thynna and the miners are little better than those between us and the Three Sisters. The miners feel their ores have been undervalued. I'm not sure it's safe for you to travel there. We should seek the counsel of your mother, Rhiann."

p-Mayard replied, "Caye will continue to shelter him! He bears the mark of the Klarjes! His growth as a sorcerer and negotiator will benefit from dealing with the miners!"

Kurth countered, "Yes, he bears the mark and it makes him a target! He needs more time!"

Rhiann said, "How could I be in better hands than with Uncle Mayard?"

Kurth demanded, "We will discuss this with your mother. I'll try to calm some frayed nerves in the Council and then meet you at home shortly. Mayard, I could use your help."

p-Mayard answered, "I've my own affairs to attend. I'll leave holding the Council's hands to you, Kurth. I'm going to make ready."

Rhiann and *p-Mayard* left the Council chamber.

The Shapechanger said, "Wow, you were convincing, boss. Even I thought you were really Rhiann. I bet that young rascal's getting along fine at the Hanging Gardens. The centaurs were rambling about Decima getting sweet on your nephew. Lucky dawg! How'd I do?"

Rhiann struggled with his father's demands but managed, "You did fine. You make a good Mayard. It's going to take my father quite a while to sort out the mess we left with the Council of Thynna. We need to gather materials for our trip. What do you suggest?"

p-Mayard replied, "Are you serious, Boss? Why are you asking me? I'm much better at stealing stuff than negotiating with merchants. Last time I checked my pockets were empty. Merchants like coins and bling."

Rhiann quickly answered, "Oh, I was just testing you. I have money." Rhiann remembered the Shapechangers earlier comments and continued, "Let's hire a sturdy wagon and a team, a brace of phi gamms. With purple enigmas pulling the carts from Thynna the trip took two weeks. Blue nus and red machis are stronger and faster. Purple enigmas are hard to figure out and harder still to predict. We are carrying finished goods to the miners and will get phi gamms to pull the wagons. They're strongest."

p-Mayard confessed, "In my less illustrious days, when I impersonated the old buzzard Elliott, I learned the livery stable run by Chad Hailstone features top of the line phi gamms and heavy wagons. Elliott's store stocks most of the dry goods the miners need. Of course they covet the light furnished by your Magick more than anything, Boss. Do you like my plan?"

Rhiann scanned the area. Commotion and loud voices still emanated from the council room. There was no sign of his father Kurth Marsh.

He said, "Great ideas. Here's a sack of coins. Make the purchases. I'm going to gather a gem from the Gem Bush. We need to make haste."

Rhiann sent the Shapechanger to the livery and approached the Gem Bush. Curious citizens watched the young sorcerer approach the prized gift from the Three Sisters. Rhiann's reputation had been enhanced when he saved his Uncle Mayard and the cantankerous merchant Elliott. Rhiann muttered an incantation and bathed the area with Fairie Fire. Bright lights danced around the courtyard and entertained young and old. The sorcerer used the diversion to pluck a sizeable red diamond and aquamarine emerald from the bush. Clear stones formed immediately at the points he had taken the lovely gems from. In time the clear stones would replace the red diamond and blue-green emerald. Rhiann cast Dancing Lights and Speak with Animals. Two dawgs sang *the Theme song of the Council of Thynna*. Rhiann excused himself and joined *p-Mayard* at Elliott's store. The Shapechanger had done an admirable job of spending the what-he-thought-was-true-Mayard's money. *p-Mayard* had procured a large heavy wagon with two massive phi gamms named Helene and Curtis and was loading the wagon with bountiful dry goods and kegs of ale. The merchant Elliott stood nearby with a broad smile on his face. *p-Mayard* concluded the transactions, and Rhiann joined him on the wagon. The Shapechanger urged the massive phi gamms forward and the wagon lumbered toward the outer curtain. The guards presented no problem and the sorcerers exited Thynna. Kurth Marsh rushed home and found Caye alone. Rhiann's mother allowed a few tears to escape before beginning a tirade about Mayard's irresponsibility and Rhiann's gullibility.

As they exited the city *p-Mayard* said, "If weather's good, we should make it in two or three days."

Rhiann commented, "If we make it at all… Uncle Mayard speaks of highwaymen and brigands looking for easy marks."

The Shapechanger replied, "I'm familiar with such blokes. Most aren't willing to mess with a sorcerer, Boss. Nice you are staying in role as Rhiann and talking about your Uncle Mayard. Mayard Klarje has nothing to worry about, if you ask me."

Rhiann said with relief, "And you look like Mayard Klarje."

The pseudo-Mayard quickly replied, "But more importantly, you *are* Mayard Klarje. Mind you, I'd rather be in young Rhiann's shoes and soaking in the plushness of the Hanging Gardens and the closeness of beautiful Decima. I managed to pick out two good phi gamms to pull the wagon. Helene and Curtis… the stable master named after his spouse's parents. The miners will have to like the goods we brought them. How much do you trust that dwarf Roswell?"

Rhiann replied, "More than I trust the Council of Thynna. He's working on something my family has been seeking since the time of the first sorcerer Cydney Klarje. Cydney dreamed of an artifact buried deep in the Copper Mountains. Mayard… uh, I heard of the miners' discovery in my youth. Finally talked old Forty-niner to part with it. It's going to cost me these gems from the Gem Bush. He wants them for his daughter Clementine."

p-Mayard said, "I wouldn't cross Forty-niner. He's meaner than Clifton Clowers, the chieftain of the wild tribe that inhabits Wolverine Mountain."

Rhiann said, "It's my intention to treat him fairly."

The Shapechanger replied, "I'm hoping he returns the favor."

The duo rode on in silence for a time. The phi gamms tirelessly trudged forward. Streams crossed the plain north of Thynna and provided ample water sources for the big bovines. Plants growing in the water served as nourishment for the beasts of burden. The weather held and they made good time.

p-Mayard said, "With any luck we'll make Gnome-town before dark. I could use a good ale."

CHAPTER 11

Gnome-town

Rhiann looked nervously around and replied, "I'm still worried about the highwaymen. We've passed lots of bends in the road that'd give them good cover."

The Shapechanger said, "Are you all right, Boss? The road between Thynna and Gnome has always been pretty safe. Brigands won't risk riling the council of Thynna and Storming Norman, the Burgomaster of Gnome-town. He's the orneriest little bloke I've run across. Good for us that you are on such good terms with him. He'll be expecting to wet his beak. Hope you brought some extra gems."

Rhiann quickly replied, "I'll let you do all the talking. You are the one that looks like May… uh, me." Rhiann already had one slip of the tongue when he had spoken of *Uncle Mayard* when they were leaving Thynna. The Shapechanger accepted it as good role playing.

p-Mayard laughed, "Good idea! Just as long as one of us doesn't look or act like a Kobold, we'll be OK. Also, we can't try to fool the Gnomes on the value of a stone. They are expert craftsmen, but you know that. Did anybody ever tell you why they named their town Gnome-town?"

Rhiann answered, "It's been called Gnome-town as long as anyone remembers. Legend has it the little blokes couldn't agree on a name. After several rounds of ale, one of them said 'since Gnomes live here, why not call it Gnome-town' and the name stuck. Gnomes and Kobolds have mutual enmity. We won't bring up Kobolds. We're mainly looking for a safe place to stay."

Gnomes were expert diggers and equally comfortable under and above ground. Two mounds of earth flanked the entrance to Gnome-town along the main road. Small wooden doors in sturdy frames were set into the mounds of dirt. Thick green moss covered the mounds and little chimneys protruded from the tops of the mounds. When the phi gamms neared the entrance to town, Gnomes came through the doors in the earthen works. The Gnome on the right walked with the spring of youth in his step whilst the old bloke that came through the left door assisted his gait with a blackthorn cudgel. The older Gnome sported a long gray beard and went by the name Longbeard. Gnomes received a given and family name at birth and added other monikers as their lives played out. As a result, Gnomes had very long names by the time they reached Longbeard's age. Longbeard had nineteen components to his moniker. Burgomaster Storming Norman had 24.

Longbeard said, "Mayard Klarje, a sight for sore eyes!"

Rhiann mutter under his breath, "Uh-oh! Trouble!"

However, Mayard's doppelganger said, "Longbeard Nineteen Names… how have you been?" Per plan *p-Mayard* did most of the talking.

The Gnome answered, "To be honest, bored a bit. The Burgomaster demands we watch this road but nothing ever happens. Highwaymen aren't going to risk running afoul of us and Thynna's security forces. They are more interested in couriers and miners returning from the mountains laden with raw ore and untraceable stones. I'd rather pursue the perpetrators to their lairs. Groups of Kobolds have infested the foothills, and the fearsome foursome, the highwaymen Waymore, Red-headed Stranger, Straight Arrow, and their leader the Man in Black openly brag of their thievery."

The Shapechanger said, "You'd best stay out of the foothills, Longbeard. Dangerous!"

Longbeard replied, "They'd be the ones in danger. Norman has doubled the guards on caravans to the mountains. That leaves fewer of us to do this ****. Don't suppose you'd have a bit of that nectar from the Hanging Gardens on you? I've gotten a dry throat from this guard duty."

p-Mayard said, "If only I did. But I'll treat you a few rounds at Sparty's. I'm a bit thirsty too."

Longbeard said, "Sounds good. Huey, Dewey, and Louie are due to relieve us soon. Why don't you go on to the livery and quarter your team? Your companion looks a bit young for the tavern. The lads in the livery ought to have some sarsaparilla that he could drink. We bottle it here and harvest the plants from the hillsides above town. Gnome-town sarsaparilla will make your muscles strong and your beard grow long!"

Pseudo-Mayard puffed, "He… uh, he's a lot older than he looks. Rhiann has seen… uh, 300 springs. Sorcerers look young for a long time."

Longbeard Nineteen Names observed, "Ah, I see that he bears the mark of the Klarjes, so must be related to you."

Mayard's doppelganger answered, "That's my great nephew Rhiann. He's the son of my niece Caye. He's my apprentice and can hold his own."

Rhiann added, "Yes, I've read every book in every library in Thynna. I've been sneaking out with Uncle Mayard for most of my life. Just recently we went to the Hanging Gardens."

Longbeard said, "If you trust him, that's good enough for me. However, if Madam Darktop hears of anyone under age being served in the tavern, she'll have everyone's hide. Even if he's 300 years old, he still looks like a kid. Storming Norman Darktop, even with his twenty-four names, only thinks he wears the pants in his family and leads this conurbation. Your nephew had best wait in the livery."

Rhiann said, "I don't mind Uncle Mayard. Mother wouldn't want me imbibing strong spirits."

p-Mayard still thought Rhiann was Mayard and thought getting him into the cozy tavern's confines constituted a favor and said, "So be it, Boss, uh, Rhiann. I thought lying about Rhiann's age might help. It's been a long time since your 300th spring. You'll be missing fine ale and mead."

Rhiann muttered, "Sometimes I…uh. Rhiann feels like he's been stumbling around Thynna for 300 years. However, it's only been 16."

p-Mayard said, "Bummer. But now he's lounging around in the Hanging Gardens with Decima. And you at least look young, Boss."

The Shapechanger urged the bovines forward and headed toward the center of the walled town and the stables. Gnomes busily attended their affairs all about. Mayard's doppelganger maneuvered the wagon and its team to a position within the main complex. Attendants helped guide the big bovines toward the wall. Gnomish farriers tended the beasts in the stables with expertise and compassion. Blue nus, red machis, and a single phi gamm rested in stalls. Various equines munched on carefully prepared trail mix. Particular attention was given to stout little halvsies, the favorite steeds of the Gnomish folk. Halvsies were not unexpectedly about half the size of the large workhorses that shared the well-kept livery stalls. Farriers unhitched the team of phi gamms and left them to a large pen socked with an ample supply of grasses. Rhiann and the Shapechanger stood awkwardly by the heavily loaded wagon.

An older Gnomish farrier said matter-of-factly, "You can leave it. Gnomes don't steal."

p-Mayard quickly replied, "We know it's safe. We're waiting for Longbeard Nineteen Names. We will pay well for the care of our animals.

The old Gnome said, "Your reputation precedes you, Sorcerer Mayard Klarje. I, Rutie Twenty-names Bager, will attend your goods."

The Shapechanger gratefully answered, "Ah, Rutie Twenty-names. Though I've not before had the pleasure of your acquaintance, I also know your story. Only you have the tenure and tenacity to challenge Storming Norman."

Rhiann was inwardly relieved. *p-Mayard* remained convinced he traveled with Mayard in Rhiann-guise and was quite convincing in his role as the elder sorcerer. So far Rhiann's little slips had not blown his cover. p-Mayard had traveled extensively with Mayard Klarje and knew many of the older Gnomes, though he had met them in his shopkeeper Elliot guise. The Shapechanger struck up conversations and relayed stories of the Hanging Gardens and the Seven Wonders of the Veldt. His stories mesmerized the hard-working farriers and stable boys. Younger Gnomes prodded p-Mayard for demonstrations of Magick, but the wily Shapechanger deftly dodged the requests. Rhiann kept a wary eye on the wagon laden with goods from Thynna, which were dedicated for the miners. True to Rudie's word, no one approached the wagon. In a little while a booming voice heralded the arrival of Longbeard Nineteen-names. Longbeard broke into a long conversation with *p-Mayard*.

The Shapechanger with subtlety approached Rhiann and asked, "Boss, are you sure you are all right with this arrangement? I mean, I hate for you to miss out on the brewmaster's wares and know how much you enjoy having a pint or two or three. The Gnomes are convinced you are young Rhiann and I'm not really sure I understand why the deception remains necessary, but I'm pretty sure I can keep them fooled. I hate to leave you here with this horse s***."

Rhiann in character quipped, "I'd rather deal with horse s*** than the Council of Thynna."

p-Mayard guffawed, "Ah, now I know it's you in that visage, Boss. You've said a couple of things that perplexed me since we left Thynna. Once you spoke of your Uncle Mayard. Made me wonder."

Rhiann quickly responded, "I'm just getting settled in my role. Changing my visage doesn't come naturally to me. It's been a long time since I was young."

p-Mayard returned, "That's how Magick seems to me. Must you continuously concentrate on the spell that changes you to your nephew's visage? If so, what happens should you need to cast another spell?"

Rhiann answered, "Cancelling my spell and removing my visage requires either a Dispel Magick by a sorcerer more powerful than I am or my willfully removing it. If I must, I'll use Magick. To be honest I've kept sulfur within my reach since we left Thynna in case we needed protection."

p-Mayard laughed again and said, "You crack me up, Boss. Those highwaymen are lucky we stuck to the main road and they stayed away, otherwise, you'd have singed their asses."

Rhiann said, "I'll be all right without a night of drinking. You'd best get back in role. Longbeard Nineteen-names is headed this way. There's a very young lad with him. He's nigh as tall as Longbeard. Definitely not Gnomish."

Nineteen-names boomed, "Mayard, if you have finished entertaining your nephew, I'm thirsty. Young Klarje, this is Iyaca Vassi. He'll get you sarsaparilla, summer sausage, honeydew, or anything we have that you desire."

Iyaca Vassi was a dark-haired, clean-faced youth. He couldn't have been more than eight or nine years old and was not Gnomish. Young Gnomes had beards from age three. He wore tattered clothes and had a pleasant herbal scent. *p-Mayard* and Longbeard Nineteen-names headed out for the tavern. The Gnome blurted an insulting joke about Kobolds and *p-Mayard* countered just as offensive a jab demeaning the guards of Thynna. Soon their laughter faded.

Rhiann studied the youth and said, "Iyaca, how did you come to live in Gnome-town?"

Iyaca Vassi shuffled his feet and hesitated. Finally, he replied, "Do you want a sarsaparilla? My main task is crushing the plant stuff that makes the base of the beverage. People come from near and far to taste Gnome-town's sarsaparilla."

Rhiann said, "I am thirsty. That'd be fine."

Iyaca Vassi hurried away and soon returned with a frosty mug. Rhiann took a sip and said, "It's very good. How long have you been in Gnome-town?"

Iyaca was again evasive and said, "Would you like a pastry? Madam Darktop's Gnomish waybread will keep you filled up all day. And it tastes good too!"

Rhiann answered, "Fine."

The youth again scurried away and soon returned with warm, buttery slices of bread. Rhiann sampled it. Flavors of honey, byneberries, and ginger dominated the taste. Iyaca beamed as he watched Rhiann enjoy the repast. Rhiann nodded his appreciation, and Iyaca was clearly pleased with his efforts.

Rhiann said, "My name is Rhiann Klarje. I'm a sorcerer from Thynna. I'm following in my uncle's footsteps. I'm sixteen years old. My Uncle Mayard and I are on a quest to the Copper Mountains. I'm grateful for the sarsaparilla and waybread."

Iyaca sat on a bale of hay, chewed on a thick piece of straw, and said, "As Longbeard said, my name is Iyaca Vassi. I'm 8 years old. I live with Burgomaster Darktop's servants. The Gnomes took me in two years ago after highwaymen ambushed a merchant caravan that my parents and I were traveling with. The highwaymen killed everyone but me. They laughed about doing me in. The biggest one was called the Man in Black. He stopped the meanest one Straight Arrow from cutting my throat. My parents were sorcerers like you. Well, they weren't powerful, but Magick touched them."

Rhiann said, "I'm sorry about your parents, Iyaca. I've traveled with my uncle a lot and have been away from Thynna. I remember hearing of the attack. The Council of Thynna sent guards to investigate and try to recover the stolen merchandise. The guards failed to capture the highwaymen and some were killed by arrows from snipers. It was believed the Fearsome Foursome fomented the deed."

Iyaca interrupted, "I hate the Fearsome Foursome. The Council of Thynna denied us entry to the city of Magick. I hate them more!"

Rhiann asked, "Understandably so. What is your talent, Iyaca?"

Iyaca said, "Talent?"

Rhiann said, "Magick. What can you do?"

Iyaca said, "Magick. So far there's no sign it touches me."

Rhiann continued, "You said Magick does not touch you, but most everyone on Sagain has a talent of some sort.?"

Iyaca answered, "The Darktops say I'm good with words and letters. I enjoy reading and writing. I came to my parents late in their lives. Both had lived long. So I suppose I'm long-winded and probably long-living, provided I don't run into a highwayman's blade."

Rhiann said, "I surely hope you avoid that fate."

Rhiann's seasons were limited but he knew well many of Mayard's stories and relayed many to the youth. Daylight faded. Farriers bedded down the livestock and activity ebbed in the livery. Mayard and Longbeard Nineteen-lives remained away.

A voice boomed, "Where is Mayard Klarje? I hear he is in town, but he has not sought audience with me. Has he placed me on the pay-no-mind list?"

Iyaca Vassi jumped up and said, "Burgomaster! Sorcerer Klarje is not here!"

Rhiann reflexively jumped up also.

Burgomaster Storming Norman Twenty-four-names Darktop peered at Rhiann and said, "Oh, yet I see the mark of the Klarjes. Isn't stable work a bit demeaning for a sorcerer of your caliber, young Klarje?"

Rhiann stammered, "Sir, your lordship, I'm Rhiann Klarje. Mayard is my great uncle. I've been enjoying the company of Iyaca and your excellent sarsaparilla and waybread. My uncle stepped out with Longbeard Nineteen-names."

Norman bellowed, "Yeah, I'm sure they stepped away to the tavern. Mayard promised me some gems from the Gem Bush and a souvenir from one of the Seven Wonders of the Veldt. The bugger had best not try to hoodwink me."

Rhiann reached into his pocket and removed a thick blue nu hide pouch. The hidden Omega Stone warmed at his touch. Faint gray auras surrounded the sack. Touching the stone inexplicably reassured the young sorcerer. He probed the pouch and removed an exquisite emerald and large chuck of deep blue lapis lazuli. The young sorcerer said, "We'd never dream of shortchanging you, Burgomaster Darktop. Your hospitality reigns supreme. My uncle is … uh, negotiating for companions to accompany us to the Copper Mountains. We have business with the armorer Roswell."

Rhiann extended the emerald and lapis lazuli to the stout Gnome's strong hand. Storming Norman was only a finger length shorter than Rhiann. He towered over five feet tall and was easily twice Rhiann's girth. His arms bulged with muscles. A long thick red beard extended nigh to his hidden navel. He wore well-made leather armor and carried a heavy Warhammer. He was seldom without the weapon. Norman projected a charismatic aura and exuded confidence.

The Burgomaster said, "Ah, you have your uncle's gift of gab and share his ability to kiss ass. The mark on your chin has a proper resting place. Young Klarje, your uncle has aided me many times, as I have oft abetted him. He is wise to recruit guards. The way to the mines remains perilous. It's only two years since the Fearsome Foursome smote young Iyaca's parents. Iyaca's parents hailed from a little hamlet called Plano, near the northernmost fringes of the Veldt and not far from Low Gap. The Vassis were sorcerers of modest ability. They went to Thynna to hope to learn more and better themselves through further knowledge of Magick. The Council of Thynna denied them entry. They and their son Iyaca found passage with a merchant caravan headed for the Samm Hills. The caravan stopped off here for a bit. The Fearsome Foursome's lot fell upon the caravan and killed everyone but young Iyaca. They toyed with his life. Eventually they left him alive and orphaned. Miners returning from the Copper Mountains found the boy and brought him to me. I've put a big price on the Fearsome Foursome's heads in hopes some of their own might turn against them, but Waymore, Red-headed Stranger, Straight Arrow, and their leader the man in black have too much of a stranglehold on the brigands' world. Scumbags all! Young Iyaca is a fine page. He learns quickly and serves well. I'd prefer he be with his own folk, but we seldom see sorcerers, other than your wayfaring Uncle Mayard. He certainly isn't a good option for caring for a youth, present company excepted, of course."

Rhiann politely answered, "I am aware that Thynna has sent no caravans northward since the tragedy two years ago. Word reached Thynna that no one survived the attack."

Norman said, "That's why the miners and Gnome-town appreciate Mayard's visits. Were it not for Mayard's visits, we'd receive none of Thynna's fine wares. Most of our trade goes to towns to the north and east."

Rhiann said, "Missing out on your sarsaparilla and waybread is Thynna's loss."

Storming Norman Twenty-four names boomed again, "Hot dawg! You are an excellent ass kisser! But for Mayard's wagon trips, getting the miners' ores to Thynna falls on them and they'd have less time for mining. The Council of Thynna evermore ignores and indeed abandons the outside world. Quite frankly, we Gnomes in Gnome-town get by fine without Thynna. We accept our position. Many outside Thynna grow more resentful of the Council of Thynna's attitude, just as they resent the meddling of the Fates."

Rhiann said, "My uncle has spoken of such things."

Storming Norman said, "Well, we'll be here sharing a stall with the phi gamms all night if we wait for Mayard and Longbeard Nineteen-names to come back from the tavern. Iyaca, my spouse has promised roasted blooter for supper. Let's escort young Klarje to my manor. You're staying with me tonight, Rhiann. Your Uncle Mayard can fend for himself once he drags himself out of the tavern. I'm still expecting my tribute."

Rhiann asked, "Shouldn't I stay with the wagon?"

Burgomaster Storming Norman Twenty-four names Darktop gloated, "Nary a speck of road grime on that wagon will be disturbed, young Klarje. At least three of my folk with at least seven names attend the livery at night. Furthermore, Gnomes don't steal!"

Rhiann said, "Right!"

Norman twenty-four-names Darktop, Rhiann Klarje, and Iyaca Vassi left the livery and made the short walk to the Burgomaster's manor. For Gnome-town it was an opulent dwelling, and it compared to the better homes in Thynna's outer ward. Most of the Burgomaster's dwelling was above ground, but his bedchamber was cut out of an earthen mound with a thick blackthorn growth over it. Gnomes, even Burgomasters, felt more comfortable sleeping underground. Before dinner Rhiann treated himself to a warm bath in a hot spring and donned fresh raiment. True to Twenty-four names' word Madam Darktop had prepared a succulent feast. Fruits of the forest and various and sundry tubers joined the roasted blooter on the oversized table. After dinner Rhiann exchanged stories with the Burgomaster and his life-mate.

CHAPTER 12

The Burgomaster's Tale
Mayard and Bailiwick

Burgomaster Storming Norman asked, "Rhiann, what do you know about the sorcerer Bailiwick?"

Rhiann answered, "My mother and father sometimes speak of him, but the conversations are usually hushed. In school we were told of his misdeeds. Bailiwick exemplifies what is bad about Magick and is the kind of sorcerer who should not be venerated."

Norman asked, "What does your Uncle Mayard say of Bailiwick?"

Rhiann answered, "Uncle Mayard never speaks of him, but I've heard stories that Uncle Mayard pursued him unsuccessfully."

Burgomaster Darktop continued, "It's probably a sore subject for old Mayard. You see, Mayard trained Bailiwick. I understand many in Thynna held Mayard responsible to some degree for Bailiwick's ill deeds. You are not the first apprentice to come to Gnome-town with Mayard Klarje. Many years ago Bailiwick came with him as his apprentice. Mayard bartered with my father, and Bailiwick and I became pretty good friends. All in all, he wasn't a bad bloke. We went hunting together. In fact, I earned my seventh name, Deerslayer, after a successful hunt with young Bailiwick. Bailiwick knew the simple Hold Spell. The simple spell merely requires a command and no material component. Unfortunately, it often doesn't work. He attempted to stop a bear and an angry Kobold with his spell, and he failed both times. We barely got away from the bear."

Norman stopped for a moment and laughed, "Barely got away from the bear! Get it?"

Rhiann respectfully said, "Yes, Burgomaster. I'm glad you got away."

Norman followed, "Folks in Thynna might not agree with you. Mayard later told me that young Bailiwick became obsessed with the spell, after his return to Thynna and convinced materials in the vault of Thynna's inner ward might help him do so. Rare spell components are stored there. I'm told large stores of sulfur and even shypoke eggshells are inside the vault. Bailiwick dreamed of strengthening the spell. He used his Hold Spell to try to gain entry to the inner vault. Guards thought they stopped him. But later it was discovered that a cache of Tuscon feathers and a number of rare metal nails were missing. Nails are needed to cast the more powerful version of the Hold Spell. Two sorcerers died trying to work with the Tuscon feathers. The Council of Thynna ordered the feathers wrapped and stored for safe keeping. They are just too dangerous to work with. Simply touching the feathers has proven lethal. Anyway, Bailiwick was captured. He attempted a Mass Charm Spell on the guards that apprehended him but the spell failed. While awaiting trial he escaped by pulling nails from the wall and placing a more potent Hold Spell on the guard that brought him his dinner. Before other guards discovered he was missing, Bailiwick somehow managed to get through the gate. Guards on duty had no memory of his passing, so it's thought he used a spell of sort. Mayard Klarje felt responsible in some way and pursued Bailiwick. Mayard found him in league with a group of Kobolds. An intense battle ensued that left the Kobolds dead, Mayard exhausted, and Bailiwick missing. Mayard recovered at Gnome-town. Bailiwick remained at large. Perhaps he cast lots with highwaymen in the area."

Rhiann said, "I may understand why Uncle Mayard doesn't talk about him. The Council of Thynna has strengthened the security of the outer curtain and gates since Bailiwick's escape. It's much tougher to entry and leave the city now."

Storming Norman said, "Let me tell you of my greatest adventure with your Uncle Mayard. I had just been promoted to Captain of the Guard, a position Longbeard Nineteen-names holds today. Rhiann, Kobolds are chaotic. They are evil and look out for number one. Getting them to work together isn't easy. A chieftain named Narg united Kobolds. Mayard and my guards never stopped looking for the renegade sorcerer Bailiwick. Mayard, Longbeard, and I learned he had joined Narg and their forces planned a full scale assault on Gnome-town. We fell on their camp and disrupted their plans. Gnomish guards easily overpowered Kobolds. Mayard smote Narg with a Magick Missile. The angered Kobolds dropped other battles and flew into Mayard. Longbeard and I tried to help, but Bailiwick and Kobold reinforcements arrived. The sorcerer held nails in his hands, conjured, and stopped me and Longbeard with his newfangled Hold Spell. It felt like he was driving that confounded nail into my feet and holding me still! Mayard was too busy fending off Kobolds to help us. I thought we'd had it! unbeknownst to us, my sweetheart Cecelia Kirkey had come to Gnome-town from Flat Rock and followed us. She arrived in a nick of time with several Gnomish and Dwarfish fighters. She hit old Bailiwick in the arm with an arrow and interrupted his spell. The sorcerer broke from the battle and ran. The reinforcements routed the remaining Kobolds. Mayard removed the effect of Bailiwick's spells and we made it back to Gnome-town. I picked up my name Nargsbane after the battle."

Rhiann said, "I thought you said Uncle Mayard killed the Kobolds' leader?"

Burgomaster Storming Norman Twenty-four names Darktop smiled and answered, "Well. He didn't need another name."

Rhiann remained on the edge of his seat. His educators in Thynna rarely spoke of sorcerers that fell from favor. Young Iyaca scurried about and did the High Gnome's bidding. Rhiann rather enjoyed the informality of the affair.

Madam Darktop smiled and said, "It's lucky for you that your sweetheart arrived and saved you, Norman."

The Burgomaster blushed and said, "Uh, yes...dear."

Madam Darktop yawned and said, "I'm tired. Iyaca, I know our guest must be weary. We'll have time for more stories tomorrow. Please take Rhiann to the guest room that looks out onto the plaza. It's a nice view."

Iyaca led Rhiann to a guest room that looked out over the now empty plaza of the village. The accommodation lacked the lavishness of the chamber Rhiann used during his stay at the Hanging Gardens, but the bed was as comfortable as anything Rhiann had slept in Thynna. Young Klarje slept well. On the morrow Rhiann joined the Burgomaster for a delicious breakfast. Madam Darktop's tetraberry pancakes rivaled Rhiann's mother's.

Storming Norman asked, "Young Klarje, Iyaca's parents came from Plano, a hamlet near Flat Rock. Do you know what sorcerers are called in Plano?'

Rhiann said, "Uh… no, Burgomaster."

Norman said, "Just plain ole sorcerers."

The hulking Gnome shook with laughter. He continued, "Young Klarje, why can't my nose be 12 inchworm lengths long?"

Rhiann carefully declined to answer, fearing he'd insult the haughty Gnome.

Storming Norman said, "Tell him, Iyaca!"

Iyaca said, "Cause then it'd be a foot."

Iyaca laughed and gently nudged Rhiann. Rhiann suffered a chuckle. Iyaca whispered, "It's good to laugh at his jokes, no matter how bad they are."

Rhiann whispered, "And how bad his timing is."

The doorman entered and announced visitors. A rather haggard *p-Mayard* and Longbeard Nineteen-names entered. Even a Shapechanger had difficulty disguising the effects of a hangover and spending a night on a straw bed in Nineteen names' austere quarters.

Burgomaster Norman said, "Now look what the wampus cat drug in! You two look like Kobolds' trash!"

p-Mayard noted the feast being enjoyed by *Mayard-Rhiann who was really Rhiann* and puffed, "I've enjoyed about as much of Longbeard Nineteen name's' hospitality as I can stand. Can't say much for his lodging! Madam Darktop, you are as lovely as ever. No one can cook like you. Burgomaster Norman sure runs a tight ship! Your hospitality and security in this wild land is greatly appreciated. Here is a token of my and Rhiann's appreciation."

p-Mayard extended a dark blue arrow with dark red fletching.

Storming Norman said, "By the Seven Wonders of the Veldt, is that an Amazon's arrow?"

p-Mayard gloated, "In the flesh! Comes straight from the Temple of Artemis. Not easy picking, but you are deserving of such a gift, Burgomaster. It's made of bluewood and nigh unbreakable. The fletching is a red condor feather. Amazons raise the big birds like chickens. The arrow is my gift to you."

Storming Norman was duly impressed and said, "Mayard Klarje, you are one of a kind. Now I'd like to see some Magick. Make old Longbeard look pretty. Nah! That'd take a True Wish!"

Then the Burgomaster guffawed.

p-Mayard thought quickly and said, "Now, my friends, you know my feelings about frivolously using Magick. But my nephew Rhiann does need some practice and you have been a wonderful host. How about some entertainment, Rhiann? Maybe a Dancing Lights or Fairie Fire Spell?"

Rhiann smiled, stood up, conjured, and uttered a few phrases. Harmless Magick Fire danced off the Gnomes' beards and around the room. Both Norman and his spouse laughed and then invited p-Mayard and Nineteen names to join the repast. Mayard's doppelganger and the Gnomes exchanged many stories, much to the delight of Rhiann and Iyaca. From that moment negotiations were easy. Burgomaster Norman Twenty-four names insisted on providing an armed escort to accompany Rhiann and p-Mayard to the Copper Mountain mines. Longbeard Nineteen-names volunteered to lead the Gnomish guards. Volunteering facilitated his escape from the boring guard duty at the perimeter.

CHAPTER 13

Albie Kirkey

Mayard and Rhiann spent another day in Gnome-town whilst Longbeard Nineteen-names gathered and equipped his most trusted sentries. Madam Darktop's meals again were the highlight of the day, though Storming Norman, Longbeard, and *p-Mayard* sneaked away to the tavern for a few rounds before bed. Madam Darktop was wise to their escapades and summoned Rhiann to the sitting room, where he met a fellow traveler, a Dwarfish nobleman named Albie Kirkey.

Madam Cecelia Twenty-one-names Darktop said, "Thank you for joining us, young Klarje. I was wondering if you'd entertain my guest Baron Kirkey with some Magick. My no-account spouse has sauntered off to the tavern with Longbeard and your wayfaring Uncle Mayard. Mayard Klarje has contributed to Gnome-town's coffers many times, but I swear he is a bad influence on Norman. Admittedly Norman and Longbeard have accumulated a number of their names whilst adventuring with Mayard. I've picked up a few of mine as well. Baron Kirkey arrived from just after they left."

Albie Kirkey was a bit taller than the Gnomes scurrying about the manor and also sported a wee bit broader chest. He carried an elaborate short sword by his side and wore well-made chain-link armor. His beard was deep red and longer than Madam Darktop's. Rhiann noticed the Burgomaster's spouse was also a might taller and her beard was also longer than the other female Gnomes in the room. Albie shared Cecelia Darktop's deep blue sparkling eyes.

Rhiann answered, "I'd be honored, Madam Darktop. For your enjoyment, Baron Kirkey."

Rhiann conjured and muttered phrases. He spoke to dawgs and cats in the room. He cast the ever popular Dancing Lights and Fairie Fire Spells. He placed Invisibility on Iyaca Vassi, but removed the spell when the youth became distressed. Rhiann concluded and Madam Darktop and Baron Kirkey applauded loudly.

Albie Kirkey said, "Outstanding show, Sister. Your household is never lacking excitement. Though I'd have preferred to exact my business with my brother-in-law the Burgomaster and make my way back to Flat Rock, this show has been well worth it."

Rhiann said, "Thank you, Baron. Did I hear you say you were from Flat Rock? And did you say the Burgomaster is your brother-in-law?"

Albie answered, "Yes, young Klarje, Cecelia Darktop is the Baroness Kirkey. She is my sister. I hail from Flat Rock."

Rhiann said, "Madam Darktop, then you are the sweetheart that saved the Burgomaster and my uncle in their battle with the sorcerer and Kobolds."

Cecelia smiled and said, "That'd be me."

Rhiann continued, "Flat Rock. I've heard Uncle Mayard speak of this Dwarfish community. You and Madam Darktop are dwarves. Your lordship, what is the difference between a dwarf and gnome?"

Albie Kirkey smiled wryly and answered, "About two inches in height and a lot of common sense."

Cecelia Darktop said, "Now, be nice brother."

Albie said, "For you, sister, and out of respect for the mark of the Klarjes. Our father opposed the marriage of my sister and the Burgomaster. However, it was politically correct and stopped not-so-friendly competition between our communities. Our cooperation has enabled us to make the roads between Gnome-town and Flat Rock safer."

Rhiann said, "Safer... but I see you are armed and well armored. I might add your sword and armor are far superior to anything I've seen in Thynna."

Albie proudly added, "You won't see this workmanship in Thynna. My sword was forged by my brother Roswell from ores taken deep from Copper Mountain. Armorers in flat Rock created my armor. It's second to none."

Rhiann said, "Roswell."

Madam Darktop said, "Yes, Roswell Kirkey, the armorer of Copper Mountain is our older brother. We've not seen him for a while. Word has it that he is embroiled in some special secret project."

Rhiann said, "My Uncle Mayard and I are in route to the Copper Mountain mines. Uncle Mayard has business with your brother Roswell."

Albie Kirkey replied, "Figured as much. Mayard and Roswell go back a long way. Only Mayard's voice speaks for the miners in Thynna."

Rhiann countered, "Not everyone in Thynna is callous. Admittedly, many are."

Baron Albie Kirkey said, "Not all voices in Flat Rock and Gnome-town speak for peace and good relations with Thynna. Our mutual enmity for Kobolds and the need to defend against lawlessness unites Gnomes and Dwarves more than kindred spirit. The highwaymen remain a threat. The Fearsome Foursome grows more brazen. In fact, I come to Gnome-town to obtain more support from the Burgomaster in my fight against them. We must step up patrols. I also have an order to send to my brother in the mines. My sentries require more swords and axes."

Rhiann talked with Baron Kirkey until the hour grew late. Madam Darktop brought nightcaps and suggested they turn in. She allowed her spouse would be in no shape for meaningful discussion. The Burgomaster and Mayard Klarje's escapades were the stuff of legend. Iyaca Vassi helped Baron Kirkey to his room. Albie Kirkey preferred the solarium where he could look up at the stars. His favorite night visage was a distal nebulous object oldsters called the Milky Way galaxy because of the thick number f stars at its center. Rhiann returned to his comfortable room that looked out onto the plaza. Sleep evaded the young sorcerer. Rhiann's thoughts returned to the tragic story of Iyaca Vassi's parents and the highwaymen. But for a glimmer of mercy in the outlaws' leader the Man in Black's heart young Iyaca would have shared his parents' fate.

Loud noise from the plaza startled Rhiann.

Voices rang out from the courtyard. Burgomaster Storming Norman Darktop, Longbeard nineteen-names, and Mayard Klarje's doppelganger were returning from a night of too many rounds at the tavern. Madam Darktop met them at the door and administered a rather severe scolding. She ushered the inebriated Burgomaster off to bed and chastised p-Mayard for his bad influence on the Burgomaster. Then she turned her attention to Longbeard nineteen-names, who endured an appropriate tongue-lashing and slinked away to his abode. *p-Mayard* endured a few higher octaves of berating and then stumbled to a guest room near Rhiann's.

CHAPTER 14

Dream in Gnome-town

With *p-Mayard's* return, Rhiann nestled under the covers and fell asleep. He dreamed of his earlier days in Thynna when he endured teasing from his now-friends Bo, Jethro, and Dean. As they entered adolescence the young threesome became more studious and accepting of Rhiann. However, the pressures of living in Thynna's inner ward prevented the youths from fully following Rhiann's path. Fact was… Rhiann's legacy and relationship with his great uncle Mayard created a unique position for him. When he was not away with Mayard on some walkabout, he oft joined Bo, Jethro, and Dean in the libraries of Thynna. In 16 years' calendar time Rhiann absorbed 300 years of knowledge… in terms of the world outside Thynna. Rhiann then dreamed of his mother Caye Klarje and her playful spellcasting in playgrounds of the outer ward of Thynna. Less advantaged children enjoyed her Magick shows.

Then…

Grayness entered his dreams.

Wisps…

Threads…

Threads of Magick…

Threads of fate…

Threads of time…

Threads connecting worlds …

Dreams connecting worlds …

Dreams of Magick…

The Magick of Dreams…
Magick connecting dreams…
Magick connecting worlds…
Grayness…

Grayness oft preceded the appearance of new spell incantations.
Dreams…

A female warrior appeared in his dream. All sorcerers dreamed of
Grayness and afterward awakened with new incantations etched in their
minds. Seeing a visage was unusual. The matron's firmness contrasted
to the softness of his mother.

The woman spoke, "Rhiann, you are so like your Uncle Mayard.
His legacy lies in your hands. The swordsmith's work is completed. I
am ready for your hand. Proceed with haste."

Rhiann tried to speak but the visage faded. Phrases appeared in his
mind. Rhiann awakened refreshed and went downstairs. Baron Albie
Kirkey's entourage was just departing. Cecelia Darktop bade her brother
good-bye and returned to the kitchen. *p-Mayard* and Burgomaster
Storming Norman twenty-four names Darktop sipped coffee and tried
to avoid the still censuring gaze of Madam Darktop. Rhiann enjoyed
breakfast. In a little while Longbeard nineteen-names arrived with a
contingent of armed Gnomes. Cecelia Darktop returned with a basket
of waybread. She was dressed in chainmail and carried a stout axe across
her back.

Storming Norman said, "What is the meaning of this?"

Cecelia replied, "I haven't seen my brother Roswell in a long while. I
need supplies from the mines. Furthermore, I don't need your permission
to go, Norman. You have plenty of work to do here and had better make
good on your commitment to Baron Albie. It's in everyone's best interest
to make safe the road between Gnome-town and Flat Rock."

Norman glared at *p-Mayard* and said, "You've done it again! I can't
stay out of trouble whenever you are around. Cecelia, if you must go,
be sure to take the ruby slippers. They could get you out of a tight jam."

Cecelia Darktop lifted her tunic and exposed her dark red shoes
and said, "I never leave home without them, but I'm not going to leave
Rhiann and Mayard in a bad spot."

Norman turned to Rhiann and said, "I have a gift for you."

Rhiann politely answered, "Your hospitality has been gift enough, Burgomaster."

Burgomaster Storming Norman twenty-four names Darktop said, "My gift is Iyaca. It's best for him to be with his own folk. Iyaca get your things. Stay by Madam Darktop till this journey's end and then I want you to remain with Rhiann Klarje."

At the same moment Rhiann and Mayard's doppelganger said, "But… Burgomaster… I…"

Norman firmly said, "It's settled! Now, last night's ale is talking to me. You'd better get going. It's a hard day's travel to Dry Creek even if you aren't attacked by highwaymen. By the way… there is a huge reward for the Fearsome Foursome. When you pass Jack's Refuge, remind the proprietor Jack Taylor that he owes me a tribute. He owes me a visit, too. It's been quite a while since we downed a few rounds at the tavern."

Madam Darktop snipped, "You get into enough trouble with Mayard. That scalawag Taylor only gets you into more hot water. He always beats you at games of chance and drinks you and Longbeard under the table. You're better off if he stays away."

The Burgomaster gave a harrumph and wandered to his chamber. Iyaca Vassi hustled away and soon returned with a travel bag and his essentials. Rhiann, *p-Mayard*, Longbeard nineteen-names, Cecelia Darktop, and 12 armed Gnomes left Gnome-town with the heavily loaded wagon.

Rhiann rode beside *p-Mayard* on the wagon. Cecelia 21-names Darktop and Iyaca Vassi rode upon stout halvsies. Cecelia's steed Nuffin had carried her many times. The well-fed and rested brace of phi gamms effortlessly pulled the laden wagon along the well-maintained road that led out of Gnome-town westward into the foothills of the Copper Mountains. Halvsies also handled their burdens up the gentle grade easily. Four large workhorses carried the troupe's supplies. Longbeard 19-names rode his favorite halvsie Shadowdancer ahead of the column. Sergeant Rudy Nine-names and Corporal Roro Seven-names and two other Gnomes with seven names walked in front of the wagon. Two others walked on each side of the wagon where the width of the road allowed, and four others stayed behind the wagon. One of the rear guard, Lieutenant Donovan Ten-names rode a halvsie and another Corporal Alden Eight-names constantly watched the rear from a perch in a small halvsie-pulled cart. Longbeard's handpicked charges mostly carried axes and warhammers, but two in the front and one rear guard carried bows. The Gnomes sang and made no effort to hide their movement. Keeping two laboring phi gamms and a rolling wagon quiet was impossible. The Gnomes' detection skills paled in comparison to the Shapechanger. In his Mayard guise the doppelganger sniffed and glanced around. Twice he caught glimpses of Kobold scouts hidden in the brush above the road. The goblin-like Kobolds shied away from the heavily guarded wagon. *p-Mayard* also caught the more ominous glimpse of a large man hidden off the road and elbowed Rhiann to make him aware of the observer.

Rhiann asked, "Is he a highwayman? Is he going to rob us?"

p-Mayard chuckled, "In all likelihood he is a lookout or scout. Are you all right, Boss? They aren't going to rob us going to the mine. The miners value the goods we carry on the wagon, but they haven't paid up for them yet, so we don't have any gems or money."

Rhiann said, "It's unnerving to know we are watched."

p-Mayard answered, "Boss, you are as timid as a Thynna tower guard. We've traveled this road many times. These highwaymen know the power of your spells. I just look like you, so they see you sitting on this wagon seat. But you are you, though you are the spitting image of your great nephew Rhiann, and your Magick is still your Magick. I must again compliment on the effectiveness of your mimicking spell. You could even fool me. I'd swear you were Rhiann, but I know he's frolicking in the Hanging Gardens with that winsome Decima. Bottom line… if the highwaymen see you on the wagon, they are not going to attack."

Rhiann replied, "It's the mission. I'm anxious to get to the mines and retrieve the sword."

p-Mayard said, "Boss, you've never told me what is so special about that sword."

The one wagon party made good time and reached a small settlement called Dry Creek. A small brook had meandered through the area before the cataclysm, but its became a dry bed after the maelstrom. The settlement persevered and provided an austere social life for farmers and miners. The hamlet had a single tavern and inn. Only the very basics were available. Still it was a good stopping point on the route to the mines and provided an oasis of relative security from the wild beasts and lawlessness of the area.

CHAPTER 15

Highwaymen

The Man in Black leaned back in his rough wooden chair and stretched. The leader of the Fearsome Foursome acknowledged a knock at his door. A young brigand announced the arrival of one called the "Watcher in the Woods." The highwaymen's leader preferred not knowing the names of his henchmen and vice versa. Nameless faces are more easily forgotten. The Watcher entered.

The Man in Black said icily, "Why have you left your post? I specifically asked you to watch the road toward Dry Creek. What's so important that you couldn't wait for a courier?"

The Watcher answered timidly, "I thought you ought to know… he's back."

The Man in Black sat up straight and said, "What? Are you saying?"

The Watcher said, "Mayard Klarje. I saw him riding on a wagon pulled by phi gamms. He was escorted by a dozen armed Gnomes. The wagon was laden with goods. They have to be headed for the mines."

The Man in Black said, "You did well to let me know. I've long awaited my chance for a go with him."

The Watcher said, "There's more. Longbeard many-names is at the head of the column and the Burgomaster's mate rides with them."

The Man in Black now stood briskly. "What? That is good news! The only thing better would be for the scumbag Burgomaster himself to be along! Our friends will certainly want to hear about this good fortune."

The Watcher said, "I'm not sure it's good fortune. It is Mayard Klarje, the foremost sorcerer of his generation, and he is accompanied by a solid force of armed Gnomes. There are two youths with them. Must be pages of some sort. They were plainly dressed and unexceptional. One may be the waif you spared. Would be about the right age."

The Man in Black said, "I never thought the kid would survive. He wasn't worth wasting a sword stroke."

The Watcher said, "The other youth rode beside Mayard Klarje on the wagon. I'd swear he bore the same tell-tale birthmark on his face as old Klarje. Why do you hate Klarje and the Gnomes so much?"

The Man in Black sat back down and said, "A man needs no reason to hate Gnomes, but Longbeard and Storming Norman led the Gnomes that helped Mayard Klarje hunt down and capture my father Big Boy and Uncle Tiny. The same blokes broke up the renegade sorcerer Bailiwick's first alliance with the Kobolds. I'm sure the sorcerer and the Kobold chieftain Beeyo will want some of this action."

The Watcher said, "Mayard and the Gnomes were moving along at a pretty good clip. They will reach the safety of Dry Creek and its Gnomish garrison by nightfall. By the time messengers reach the sorcerer and the Kobolds it might be too late."

The Man in black answered, "This is why I'm leader and you spend most of your time shooing away flies in the woods. The goods they are carrying have little value. They have to be going to the mines. On the return trip they will be carrying the riches of the mines to take back to the greedy of Thynna. I've waited years for my vengeance. I can wait a few more days. In that time, we can plan our attack and assure we have enough strength to take them down. I want Klarje to suffer!"

The Watcher said, "Many share your feelings. What are your orders?"

The Man in Black answered, "Send runners to the Kobold encampments to the north and east. Beeyo oversees the northern warrens. Getting Kobolds to work together isn't easy. Beeyo has taken advantage of his ilk's enmity for Dwarves and Gnomes to gather a sizable force. His plan was to attack Gnome-town, but I convinced him that Dry Creek was a more realistic target. His encampment is about an hour's ride from here. Beeyo hates the Burgomaster of Gnome-town. One of Storming Norman's twenty-four names is 'Narg's bane.' Narg was Beeyo's father. Narg allied with the sorcerer Bailiwick. The renegade sorcerer Bailiwick was banished from Thynna. Storming Norman, Longbeard Nineteen-names, and Mayard Klarje led the raid that resulted in Narg's death and the scattering of his forces. Bailiwick barely escaped. Get word to Beeyo and Bailiwick that our elusive quarry is nigh within our grasp."

The Watcher said, "I'm less familiar with that area. How will I find them?"

The highwaymen's leader said matter-of-factly, "They'll find you. You'd best travel under my banner. They might kill you anyway."

The Watcher in the Woods said, "That's not very reassuring, boss."

The Man in Black said, "Seriously, make lots of noise. Don't hide your position. There will be no Gnomes to rob or sorcerers to evade in those woods. Now get going. Choose my fastest men."

The Watcher answered, "On my way."

The phi gamms lumbered into a large cleared area on the approach to Dry Creek. The field had been cleared and set with tobacco plants to produce the smokes enjoyed by the rustic miners and herdsmen in the area. The twin suns sank in the west and lent an orange haze to the cloudless sky. The guards breathed a sigh to have better vision. In the distance wisps of smoke rose into the sky from the homes and establishments in the settlement Dry Creek. On the far side of the two-hectare field a stout guard tower looked out onto the road. The tower stood twenty feet tall with a wall walk surrounding an enclosed area at the top. The merlons were gnome-height and width. Two guards faced the approaching wagons.

Longbeard nineteen-names muttered, "Guard duty at Dry Creek. About the only assignment more boring than guard duty at Gnome-town. There hasn't been an attack here since Burgomaster Storming Norman was Captain of the Guard and led an attack against the rogue sorcerer Bailiwick and the Kobold leader Narg. Remember, Mayard?"

On the wagon Mayard's doppelganger the Shapechanger uncomfortably shifted and said, "Uh…yeah."

He leaned over and whispered to Rhiann, "Boss, you never told me this story. You'll have to bail me out if he presses me."

Rhiann recalled Burgomaster Storming Norman's tale from his visit whilst p-Mayard was busy imbibing ale at the Gnome-town tavern and had figured the robust Gnomish leader had embellished the tale. He whispered back to p-Mayard, "Just play along."

Longbeard laughed and continued, "The Kobolds took such a beating that they aren't going to attempt further attacks. Still the Burgomaster insists on keeping a garrison here. Mostly blokes with four or fewer names draw the duty. They get experience in the local pub and get to meet the miners and hear their stories. So it's not boring all the time. The grub in the pub is pretty good, too. The guards will bunk in the barracks with the assigned garrison. The inn has enough beds for the rest of us. Madam Darktop, I'll assure you receive the best room."

Cecelia Darktop answered, "I'll take the same accommodation as the rest of you."

Longbeard laughed, "I'm glad you feel that way since all the rooms are the same."

Cecelia answered, "Longbeard, I've traveled to the mines many times. I've stayed in Dry Creek almost as often as you have. Your attempt at humor missed its mark."

Longbeard guffawed.

A standing log palisade surrounded Dry Creek. Wall stairs led to little watch points along the wall. *p-Mayard* urged the phi gamms into the town square. The small livery bustled with activity as the day ended and locals brought weary livestock in for keeping. The road guards reunited with acquaintances within the Dry Creek garrison. Longbeard, Madam Darktop, p-Mayard, Rhiann, and Iyaca Vassi headed for the town's only inn and tavern. The portly innkeeper Hojo welcomed them and made a fuss over Madam Darktop and *p-Mayard*. Rhiann and Iyaca relished the warm food and *p-Mayard* and Gnomes' stories, but soon the road weary party headed off to bed. Guards closed Dry Creek's gate to prevent the odd wandering nocturnal predator wandering into town. A typically quiet night ensued.

A Cabin in the Woods

Responders to the Man in Black's invitation trickled into the highwaymen's camp. The Kobold chieftain Beeyo and his entourage were first to arrive. Like all Kobolds, Beeyo hated Gnomes and Dwarves, but his hatred for Thynna and sorcerers exceeded his enmity for the smaller folk. Beeyo hated Mayard Klarje most of all.

His father Narg had been the Kobolds' most effective leader in a long while. Narg's efforts organized the chaotic Kobolds. He jumped at the opportunity to follow the renegade sorcerer Bailiwick. Narg died in the battle between the sorcerer's troupe and sentries from Gnome-town led by Storming Norman, Longbeard, and Mayard Klarje. Beeyo continued his father's efforts to organize Kobolds and gather a force strong enough to one-day challenge and destroy Dry Creek and Gnome-town and return stewardship of the Copper Mountain foothills to the Kobold ilk. The Man in Black's lieutenants Red-headed Stranger, Straight Arrow, and Waymore soon joined the meeting. The robed figure was the last to arrive. He entered the cabin with two Kobold escorts and took a seat at the roughly hewn table. The Man in Black sipped his beverage and barely acknowledged the new arrival. However, the Kobold chieftain Beeyo scarcely contained his excitement and said, "Lord Bailiwick, I'm so glad you could join us. My father spoke so highly of you."

Bailiwick grunted, "Your father… you are?"

Beeyo puffed out his thin chest and proudly said, "I am Beeyo, son of the great Narg. He served you steadfastly. I shall do the same."

Bailiwick accepted a mug of steaming beverage and replied, "Best I recall your father had his chance against the Gnomes and Mayard Klarje and failed miserably. I had Mayard Klarje and the others in dire straits, and then Narg got his a** kicked by a female Gnome. I barely escaped. Are you any better?"

Beeyo cleared his throat and answered, "My warriors and I are well trained. Our hatred makes us strong. I seek vengeance."

Bailiwick said, "That's all well and good. If the message I received is true, you may soon have your chance, Beeyo, son of Narg. I am waiting, Captain."

The Man in Black hazarded a glance toward the sorcerer and replied, "We all want the same thing, wizard. Klarje and the Gnomes kicked your ass too. Beeyo, you are not the only one of us to lose a father to Klarje and the Gnomes. The chance has come for all of us to gain a measure of vengeance. My watcher in the woods saw a heavily laden wagon headed for Dry Creek. Mayard Klarje, Longbeard Nineteen-names, and, yes, Madam Cecelia Darktop are in the party. Twelve armed gnomes and two youths accompanied them."

The Red-headed Stranger chided, "Why have we not attacked them. We could have used the supplies they carry."

Straight Arrow added, "They may pick up more support from the garrison at Dry Creek and the mines."

The Man in Black sat back in his chair and took a deep breath. He said deliberately, "We are talking about Mayard Klarje and two veteran Gnomish fighters backed up by a dozen more armed Gnomes. We'll need everyone here to overcome them. I want Klarje to suffer."

Bailiwick said, "As do I, but from my earlier experience, it is essential to silence the threat of the sorcerer first. Klarje is capable of powerful spells. Narg's charges had nigh won the battle after they incapacitated Klarje. I controlled the other leaders easily. Gnomes don't resist my Hold Spell. Eliminating Klarje early in the fight is essential. Knowing he's failed his group will be suffering enough for him."

The Man in Black asked, "If your spells don't affect him, how do you suppose we eliminate him. The Gnomes will protect him."

Bailiwick said, "I have a gift for him. It took great effort and the deaths of several assistants to prepare it. It's from the fruits of my thievery from Thynna's stores of spell components."

The Man in Black sharply replied, "I know tactics and hand-to-hand battle, not Magick. What are you talking about, sorcerer?"

Bailiwick hazarded a wry smile and carefully removed a cylindrical leather pouch from his pack. The sorcerer gingerly opened the pouch and allowed a sleek arrow to glide onto the table. The shaft was made of rare bluewood and the fletching was jet black.

Beeyo's lieutenant marveled at the arrow's construction and said, "It's well made" He reached out and touched the arrow.

Bailiwick shouted, "Don't touch the fletching!!"

His warning came too late. The stout Kobold's hand quivered and then he clutched his chest and dropped dead. The others shied away from the arrow.

Bailiwick said, "Idiot! It's a Tuscon feather! I took it from Thynna. Touching it means death! The tip of the arrow is made from the quill. Don't touch it there!"

The red-headed stranger said, "How can it be used?"

Bailiwick said, "With great care, you idiots! Nocking the arrow requires a deft hand and a thick glove. Three Kobold archers died trying to nock the arrow. My comrades are the best archers among the Kobolds of Doom Ridge. I can place one of them Invisible near the road to take out Klarje at the battle's onset. The rest will fall easily. We'll all have our revenge, as well as the treasures they will be carrying back from the mines."

The Man in Black protested, "He'll die instantly! I want him to suffer."

Waymore added, "Kobolds are not of much account in hand-to-hand combat. They are little better as archers. I guess a blind squirrel finds a nut once in a while. A Kobold might hit a target with the same regularity. He'll die if… I say, if this Kobold hits him with the arrow. If he misses, the Gnomes will turn the artifact on us."

The Kobolds as a group grumbled and then the archer said, "I won't miss."

Bailiwick added, "Impact will destroy the projectile. All stories I've read say the epistles only bring death once."

Straight arrow said, "Well, then it's already killed this bloke today."

Bailiwick argued, "It's already killed seven Kobolds. He touched the fletching."

Beeyo stood a safe distance away from the Death Arrow and said, "My father lost his life when reinforcements came to the Gnomes. We face the same scenario."

The Man in Black replied, "That's why the battle has to be carefully planned. Our Kobold allies give us strength in their numbers. Some of our Kobold allies will have to keep the garrison at Dry Creek occupied. Others will have to block the road to Gnome-town. We must have a perfect spot for an ambush."

The watcher in the woods said, "That's where I can help. I know this section of the forest like the back of my hand. I know a perfect place. A tall rock off the side of the road will be a perfect place for both your archer and a locale where you can cast spells uninterrupted, sorcerer. You wouldn't want a Gnome's axe digging into your hide while you were trying to cast a spell."

Bailiwick reflexively rubbed his upper left arm at the site of Cecelia's arrow's mark and said, "Or an arrow. Been there, done that, thank you. Again, eliminating the threat of Mayard Klarje's spells is foremost challenge. I've done battle with him. Don't let stories of his magnanimous deeds fool you. The man is vicious in a fight."

The Man in Black leaned forward, intertwined his strong fingers, snapped his knuckles loudly, and said, "My father Big Boy and Uncle Tiny could vouch for your words, were they still here. Klarje's generosity doesn't extend to highwaymen and Kobolds."

Bailiwick added, "And rogue sorcerers that fall from Thynna's grace."

The highwayman lieutenant Red-headed Stranger said, "Old Straight Arrow knows all about falling from grace. He used to be a sailor. Till he got a little too familiar with a dock master's daughter. Chased him all the way to these hills."

Muffled laughter filled the cabin.

Straight Arrow countered, "I notice you don't hang around Thynna and Low Gap, Red. You arrived in these woods with your tail tucked between your legs. I seem to remember something about the tavern barkeep's daughter at Low Gap. Old IRS said he was going to have your head on a stick!"

More laughter filled the room.

The Man in Black said sternly, "I'm glad you think this is funny. We are talking serious business here. We can't underestimate these Gnomes and Mayard Klarje. If we do, we'll suffer the same fate as our forebears. We have eyes on Dry Creek and the way station Jack's Refuge. Jack Taylor won't side with us, but he never refuses business. The bloke would sell his mother for a profit. Our allies assault of Dry Creek will serve as a diversion. We'll attack Klarje and the Gnomes on their return from the mines at the site between Dry Creek and Gnome-town chosen by the Watcher."

The watcher said, "They'll think they are home free."

Bailiwick nodded agreement. The highwaymen, sorcerer, and Kobolds settled into planning their attack.

CHAPTER 16

Copper Dragon

In the morning Rhiann awakened to boisterous activity in Dry Creek. The Gnomes were making ready. A second wagon laden with foodstuffs and tobacco joined them for the journey to the mines. Two merchants from Dry Creek rode on the new wagon, which was pulled by a team of four strong halvsies. Additional guards from the garrison brought the strength to twenty. The road widened and began a steady incline shortly outside Dry Creek. Halvsies and phi gamms pulled the wagons nigh effortlessly. The area on both sides of the road had been cleared to about thirty paces, leaving no cover for an ambush. The downside was the wide clearing made travelers vulnerable to attack from above, but large airborne predators were rarely encountered. About two hours into the trip a young Copper Dragon with a ten-foot wingspan approached the small caravan. Copper Dragons got their name from their habitat in the Copper Mountains and their love of copper. Great veins of the element stretched through the range. The beasts began life with tan coloration and developed their characteristic deep copper tone as they ingested the metal over time until they attained the reddish-orange color as very old adults. The little tan dragon flew around the wagons and unnerved the beasts of burden that pulled the carts. p-Mayard and the merchant driving the second wagon steadied the beasts.

p-Mayard whispered, "Boss, why don't you take care of this thing?"

Rhiann answered, "The Gnomes probably are wondering why *you* don't."

p-Mayard answered, "For the umpteenth time, I only look like you, Boss. You look like Rhiann, but both of you are sorcerers. Do something!"

The young copper dragon dove down toward the phi gamms. Mayard's doppelganger pulled the reins and steadied the big lowing beasts.

Rhiann said, "All right, but I don't like killing things."

p-Mayard muttered, "Say what?"

Rhiann quickly added, "Needlessly!" and began a spell.

The second merchant on the wagon from Dry Creek stood and threw a large piece of copper ore into the air. The dragon quickly circled away from the phi gamms and snatched the piece of ore in midair. The beast cooed happily and flew off toward the peaks. Rhiann interrupted his spell and stared at the retreating dragon.

The merchant said, "Happens all the time. It was just hungry."

The small caravan reorganized and headed toward the mines. Austere and oft abandoned cabins dotted the roadside. Near the midpoint of the journey they came upon the oft used way station called Jack's Refuge. The owner Jack Taylor had a longstanding relationship with the Burgomaster of Gnome-town and the Copper Mountain miners, but his neutrality allowed all sorts to utilize his facility. The beasts of burden were handling the trip well and only required a brief stop for water and a snack of hay. The travelers paid Jack Taylor's nonrefundable and always required entry fee and entered the palisade. The guards gobbled down a hot midday meal. Insalubrious types evaded the direct gaze of the Gnomes and particularly Longbeard Nineteen-names, who many referred to as the *short* arm of the law. Dwarves, Gnomes, Kobolds, mountain men, and a few miners wandered about the quadrangle of Jack's Refuge. Jack Taylor's guards quickly broke up an altercation between a Dwarf and Kobold and quickly escorted the pugilists to the gate. The fight ensued outside the gate. Taylor's guards on the allure actually cheered the fighters on. The dwarf's rounds of ale slowed him down and allowed the Kobold to keep the fight interesting for a while, but eventually the stout dwarf managed to get an arm bar hold on the wiry Kobold, who quickly tapped out. The dwarf accepted three JR tokens as payment to release his vanquished adversary. The three tokens would buy three rounds of ale at Jack's Refuge's tavern. Another couple of shouting matches broke out but did not lead to fisticuffs. Longbeard inquired of the barkeep as to the proprietor's whereabouts, but Jack Taylor was just said to be away. Longbeard told the barkeep that the party would stay over on their return journey. The barkeep made note of it and affirmed that rooms would be available in the rustic inn.

The two wagon caravan reorganized and started on for the mines. By late afternoon they arrived at the Copper Mountain mines. A stockade made of stout roughly hewn posts formed a semicircle around the company store, guardhouse, livery, armory, hostel, and buttery. The semicircle met the solid rock wall of the mountain that rose over the mine's entrance and served as protection from the west and north. A simple gate stood open between Guard towers that faced east and south. Miners' shacks occupied a cleared area in front of the palisade. Accommodations were available upstairs in the company store and very basic hostel. A barracks housed guards. The tight security rivaled Gnome-town, and there had not been a successful attack on the mines since the apprehension of the brazen highwaymen Big Boy and Tiny. The miners upgraded security after the highwaymen broke through the palisade and robbed the company store. Even then Big Boy and Tiny failed to penetrate the entrance to the mines proper.

Clerks with Iyaca Vassi's assistance busily unloaded the wagons. The miners' foreman Brady gathered Madam Darktop, *p-Mayard*, Rhiann, and Longbeard and lead them into the mine. Gnomes and Dwarves had some degree of infravision, but many miners were totally dependent on sources of light to find their way about the catacombs. Braziers were lit along the walls and Mayard's Continual Light Spells provided needed light. Rhiann added Continual Light Spells in two recent excavations to help the miners. The foreman led them to Roswell Kirkey's chamber and workroom.

Brady tapped on the door. A gruff voice from within bade them enter. Roswell Kirkey worked at his forge, did not interrupt his work, and kept his back turned to the entering group.

The dwarf muttered, "Why do you disturb me? I'm far behind. My brother Albie has sent an order for a hundred axes and swords. My work has piled up whilst I worked on the sorcerer's project."

Madam Darktop said, "Don't you have a better greeting for me, brother?"

Roswell dropped his hammer, turned, and said, "Hello, Sister, and hello, Sorcerer Mayard."

p-Mayard asked, "Have you finished the rapier, Roswell?"

Roswell answered, "I have kept my word, Mayard Klarje. The weapon is finished."

Longbeard Nineteen-names said, "A sword! A sword for a sorcerer! Why have you instructed the best metal smith on Sagain to create a warrior's weapon, Mayard?"

p-Mayard struggled for an answer. Rhiann spoke up, "Why are you questioning the motives of Sagain's greatest benefactor? Uncle Mayard always has the best interest of Sagain's people and Magick in mind."

p-Mayard said, "Now, easy, nephew. I have asked Roswell to fulfill a mission handed me long ago. We'll discuss this more."

Roswell Kirkey said, "Sister, Cecelia, why are you in the mines? I'm told there's increased activity on the roads. The highwaymen threaten our shipments and increased numbers of Kobolds are in the area. Some have been brazen enough to come to within the shadow of our doors. Our brother Albie must recognize the increased danger. Why else would he send such a big order? A messenger just preceded you."

Cecelia answered, "Yes, Albie's messenger traveled with us. Out brother. was just in Gnome-town. He is concerned. Is there any word of the renegade wizard?"

Roswell cast a glance at *p-Mayard* and Rhiann and said, "Only rumors, Sister. A sorcerer who consorts with Kobolds and Highwaymen needs reckoning with. You've had your chances with him, Mayard. But I see two with the mark of the Klarjes. I'd trust few sorcerers that didn't have the mark. So you have returned for your prize, Mayard Klarje. It won't disappoint. You will look upon my finest work. It shall be my legacy and gift to Sagain. Per your instruction and the will of Grayness I have kept it safe."

p-Mayard said, "I and most of Sagain will appreciate your gift, Roswell. I'd like to entrust the weapon to my nephew Rhiann."

Longbeard Nineteen-names protested, "Mayard, he is but a lad and another sorcerer at that. A weapon of that sort should fill the hand of a warrior."

Cecelia Darktop said, "Longbeard makes a valid point, Mayard. I'll carry the sword if you'd like."

p-Mayard shuffled a bit and insisted, "No, it should be in Rhiann's care for the moment. I'll explain later."

Cecelia Darktop said, "You've got a lot of explaining to do, Mayard. I've never seen you unnerved by a young Copper Dragon. Were it not for your escapades with my spouse the Burgomaster, I'd swear you were not yourself! But back to business… brother Roswell, I am only here for a little while. Would you come to the surface where I might see you in the light of our twin suns?"

Roswell said, "I have a lot of work to do, Sister, but I can't refuse you. Given our childhood closeness, that's nothing new. Allow me to fetch Mayard's prize and we'll go up for some food and fellowship."

The dwarf led the group to a sitting area in his chambers and left them.

Rhiann marveled at the energies and comradery of the Gnomes, Dwarves, and other miners. The sorcerers of Thynna reviled these people. While they were awaiting Roswell's return, the young Sorcerer went about the business of placing several more Continual Light Spells on areas of the walls and devices as well. The Continual Light Spells illuminated the far-reaching underworld passageways and made the miners work easier and safer. The hard working miners found the exceptional ore that Mayard had given the swordsmith to work with. He went into a back room and returned in a little while with a longsword.

CHAPTER 17

Exeter

Roswell returned with a longsword. The Dwarfish swordsmith said, "The odd piece of grayish red ore from which this weapon was forged was found deep in the earth by miners. The ore was discovered precisely at a point of impact of a visitor from deep space that produced the cataclysm that forever changed Sagain and heralded the Dawn of Magick. The miners and alchemists were unable to determine the nature of the ore and brought it under heavy guard to Gnome-town and the care of the burgomaster. Gnomish and Dwarfish gem masters extensively studied the irregular rock, which periodically gave off gray auras. Rarely thick red liquid oozed from the odd stone. By all accounts the ore was unique on Sagain. Burgomaster Altus Twenty-names Big Boy Stillwater Darktop presented the bizarre object to Mayard Klarje at dinner in appreciation for Mayard's help in subduing the highwaymen Big Boy and Tiny. Mayard, you carried the stone for many years before you brought it to me. The ore differed from when I last saw it. You said the stone found its heart and you brought her home. I'm not one for riddles and sorcerer talk, but I know my way around a forge. Here's Exeter."

Madam Darktop said, "Exeter?"

p-Mayard said, "Yes, her name is Exeter."

Exeter appeared as a well-made longsword, with a hilt formed of a reddish black material and a golden blade. The hilt of the weapon retained the reddish color. No runes appeared upon the weapon and no gems adorned the hilt. Exeter's beauty was in her simplicity.

Cecelia Darktop said, "She?"

Roswell Kirkey replied, "The bladed has a feminine nature. She's high-spirited. I could not scratch the blade with a red diamond."

Cecelia marveled, "There's nothing harder in the world."

Longbeard asked, "May I hold the blade?"

Roswell said, "It's Mayard's call, but you'll find it difficult to let her go once you've held her close."

Cecelia said, "Brother, you sound like you are writing folk music."

p-Mayard looked at Rhiann, who nodded a tad. Mayard's doppelganger had heard real-Mayard speak of the stone many times, used this knowledge to his advantage, and said, "I've no objections to any of my friends holding the weapon. I studied the reddish ore in Gnome-town. The alchemists and I tried to determine the nature of the ore. None understood it. We couldn't scratch the rock."

Longbeard Nineteen-names eagerly accepted the weapon and carefully moved it through the air. "It's fantastic! Wait! If a red diamond doesn't scratch it, how'd you melt it in the forge?"

Roswell smiled wryly and said, "I've some secrets. The ore wanted to be transformed. Mayard had altered it somewhat. Once in its finished form, the firmness returned. Has she spoken to you, Longbeard?"

Longbeard said, "Say what?"

Roswell said, "As I said, Mayard brought me an ore that had changed since I had last seen it. I believe you said, Sorcerer Mayard, that the rock was now whole and requested I forge it into the blade."

p-Mayard said, "I believe that's what I said. You've created a masterpiece."

Longbeard Nineteen-names held the sword up to his thick beard and said, "Tell me something, beautiful weapon."

Abruptly the stout Gnome lowered the sword and gasped, "I'll be a Kobold's uncle! It talks!"

Cecelia quizzically remarked, "What do you mean? We heard nothing!"

Roswell Kirkey asked, "What did she say?"

Longbeard twisted the sword's hilt in his strong left hand and replied, "She said, 'Thanks, noble warrior. I like having your hand gripping me. Flattery will get you everything. You are without enemies in this place, though things aren't always as they appear.' It was the most pleasing voice I've ever heard. Didn't you people hear it?"

A small symphony of "No's" rang out.

Roswell said, "She only talks to the one that holds her."

Cecelia asked, "What does she say to you, Roswell?"

Roswell smiled, "Her name is Exeter. She keeps thanking me and asks about Mayard's return. Maybe you should hold her Mayard."

p-Mayard hesitated and glanced toward Rhiann. Rhiann shrugged. Mayard's doppelganger reached out to Longbeard, reluctantly gripped the dark red hilt, and accepted the beautiful longsword. A pleasant voice appeared in the depth of his thoughts, "I sense no ill will toward the others in your shapeless heart, doppelganger. You have no enemies in this place, but your comrades think you are Mayard Klarje. Their attitudes will likely change when they learn the truth. Have you harmed Mayard Klarje?"

p-Mayard was at a loss as to how to communicate with the sword. Was spoken word required or was the entire affair telepathic? He concentrated and thought silently, "If you know your stuff, you'll realize the old sorcerer stands beside me in the guise of his great nephew Rhiann. Uh... you aren't going to sell us out, are you? I really don't want to cross these Gnomes! Gnomes aren't fond of deception!"

The sword's voice answered, "I'm committed to Mayard Klarje and never question his reasoning. But I'd really like to hear what he has to say about you! You are not a warrior. I serve a warrior best."

The doppelganger wryly thought, "I *can* be a warrior."

The sword said, "Perhaps Rhiann ... uh, Mayard should hold me, false Mayard."

p-Mayard said aloud, "Rhiann, the workmanship is second to none. Why don't you hold the weapon?"

The pseudo-sorcerer extended the longsword and Rhiann awkwardly accepted the heavy blade and gripped the hilt.

Exeter said telepathically, "Young Rhiann Klarje, nice to make your acquaintance. You have no enemies in this place. That includes your shapeless friend, the Shapechanger in Mayard Klarje-clothing. He very oddly is devoted to you, though he thinks you are your Uncle Mayard. One of Mayard's most unusual maneuvers, I must say. The Gnomes Longbeard and Cecelia and Dwarfish Sword master Roswell truly believe he is Mayard and you are Rhiann. So Mayard indeed remained at the Hanging Gardens in your guise. How was he feeling?"

Rhiann thought silently, "Mayard is well, at least, I think he is: he was fine when left him in his *Rhiann's* guise at the Hanging Gardens. The old codger might be having himself quite a time if lovely Decima thinks he's me."

The voice replied, "Does your shapeless companion really believe Mayard remains at the Hanging Gardens?"

Rhiann answered in his thoughts, "Yes, he does. I think. My great uncle wanted it this way."

Exeter asked, "Have you wondered why Mayard wanted you to come in his stead?"

Rhiann replied, "Well, yes, but he said he had tasks to perform in the Hanging Gardens. Also, he does many things that I don't understand."

Exeter said, "He clearly doesn't tell you everything. He can't keep things under his hat with me. Literally! As a heartstone I learned his thread of life was strained in his battle with the bewildebeest. He's aging rapidly. You'd best conclude this adventure and make haste to the Hanging Garden… if you desire his company again."

Rhiann said aloud, "No!"

He got quizzical looks from Cecelia Darktop, Roswell Kirkey, Longbeard Nineteen-names, and *p-Mayard.*

Exeter said, "Mayard asked me to guide and protect you as best I can. I have inherent ability to sense enemies, but only when you hold me. I'm always good for a kind word. I'll ask of you Rhiann Klarje, please keep my origins secret. In the wrong hands, I would do harm. One day perhaps you can bequeath me to a long line of warriors. That is my dream. The Gnomes are noble, but my destiny is not with them."

Rhiann this time remembered to only think his words and said, "Roswell and Mayard merely said you are derived from the odd ore the miners found deep within the mountain. What are your origins?"

Exeter softly replied, "I must have some secrets. Suffice it to say, I'm a sister of Grayness. The greatest mages will not understand the Magick that empowers me. My voice will appear in the mind of my wielder, but only when he grasps my hilt. I'm sympathetic and empathetic. I feel both the physical and mental wounds received by the person grasping my hilt. I'll do all I can to save my wielder from falling in battle. I sense enemies within thirty paces and determine the enemy that poses the greatest threat. I'll save my bearer and serve as a companion during dark, cold, lonely, and forsaken times. However, those within this room must swear to keep my existence secret."

Rhiann said, "Why?"

Exeter said, "Grayness wishes it. Mayard requests it."

Rhiann said, "So be it."

p-Mayard shuffled his feet nervously.

Rhiann returned the sword to the Shapechanger and said, "I have no experience with weaponry, but I have read every volume on the subject in Thynna's libraries. This artifact has every trait desirable in a blade. I agree with your assessment, Uncle Mayard."

p-Mayard said, "Uh...you do?"

Rhiann said, "Yes. The weapon told me your thoughts on the matter. The existence of Exeter is known only to those within this room, is that correct, Master Roswell?"

Roswell Kirkey answered, "Yes, Rhiann, just as your Uncle Mayard instructed. By the way, it's unnecessary to call me 'master.' Unlike nobles and most sorcerers, I work for a living. Sorry, no offense intended, Sister Cecelia. As Baroness of Flat Rock, you have always been an exception."

Cecelia Darktop said, "None taken, brother. When do I get to hold the sword?"

p-Mayard without speaking extended Exeter to Madam Darktop. Cecelia gripped the sword's hilt and indignantly said, "Well, I never!"

Cecelia indignantly returned the sword to Mayard Klarje's doppelganger.

Longbeard Nineteen-names asked excitedly, "What'd she say?"

Cecelia puffed, "She said that she usually preferred being held by a male, but in my case she'd make an exception. She likes my warrior spirit, but likes my bust line, hair, and beard most!"

Longbeard fought back a chuckle.

p-Mayard gripped the hilt. Exeter relayed to his mind, "*Rhiann* set things you up for you. Get on with it! Insure a bond of secrecy regarding my creation."

p-Mayard thought, "He held you so now you know that isn't Rhiann. If Mayard wants to keep you secret, here goes!"

The Shapechanger addressed the little group and said, "Exeter is a gift of Magick...of Grayness. We must keep her a secret. No one outside our small circle can learn of her existence."

Longbeard asked, "Why, Mayard? I should wield this sword! Many a Kobold and highwayman would fall before her!"

Rhiann said, "There'd be dire consequences if Exeter fell into the wrong hands."

p-Mayard energetically reinforced his companion's words, "Yes, yes. The weapon is Magick. I must study it. I ask you to accept my decision. Rhiann will carry the sword."

Longbeard said, "He's not a warrior! What value is the blade to a sorcerer, just a young one at that?"

p-Mayard stuttered, "I…I need you to trust me on this. It's Magick, what do the Kobolds say? Bad juju! After it's vetted, we can put it to use."

Longbeard conceded, "I prefer my axe and hammer anyway. I might be a bit short for a longsword. It's too big for a dwarf, too, Roswell and Madam Darktop. Mayard, you've always been a sorcerer of your word and as good a drinking buddy as a fellow could have! If you want the **** thing kept secret, I'll tell no one. Just you be careful young Rhiann. It's a might large for you, too."

Roswell Kirkey said, "I created the weapon at Mayard's behest.

It's a gift to Sagain. For my part, it's a secret till you want it known."

Madam Darktop said, "The things got a fresh attitude. I'll keep your secret. One question… should I tell the Burgomaster? He knew Roswell was doing a job for you. He also knew you carried the odd ore."

p-Mayard said, "True. However, he doesn't know the ore was modified before Roswell worked with it. Roswell has created many devices for me and others in Thynna. As much as I respect the Burgomaster, ale loosens Storming Norman's tongue. A night in the tavern would likely let our secret out. Maybe it's best we don't tell him. I'm not too sure about you holding your tongue, Longbeard."

Longbeard pulled on his dark red beard and said, "Guilty as charged. You can throw a Forget Spell on me if you want. Now I'm wanting some food. Is our business finished here?"

Roswell said, "How do you intend to carry the sword, Rhiann?"

Rhiann produced his small Bag of Holding. Exeter was much longer than the depth of the sack. Rhiann took the sword from Roswell. The young sorcerer easily slipped the sword into the sack.

Longbeard Nineteen-names grunted, "Magick!"

Roswell said quizzically, "What's in the little bag, Rhiann?"

Rhiann answered, "Odds and ends."

The others laughed.

p-Mayard thanked his comrades for their discretion. Roswell led them out of the mines. Rhiann quietly muttered the same arcane phrases and touched Longbeard's broad shoulder. Then he furtively repeated the phrases and touched Madam Darktop. He uttered the phrases a third time and touched Roswell Kirkey.

Rhiann, *p-Mayard*, Longbeard, Roswell, and Cecelia Darktop walked together to the dining area where they joined young Iyaca.

Longbeard Nineteen-names said, "Young Iyaca, you should see the beautiful red sword that old Roswell made for Sorcerer Klarje."

Cecelia Darktop bragged, "No one creates a better weapon than my brother. Though I can't understand what took so long brother. It's not like its Magick or anything?"

p-Mayard exchanged glances with Roswell Kirkey and gave a subtle wink.

p-Mayard managed to get a quiet word with Rhiann and asked, "What do they remember, Boss?"

Rhiann said, "They remember that Roswell made a pretty sword for you. Roswell fully remembers his deed. My spell didn't work on him. Will have to trust his discretion."

CHAPTER 18

Jack Taylor's Refuge

The company store's cooks prepared a hearty meal, and the group made do with rustic sleep arrangements. True to her word Madam Darktop insisted on regular accommodations. Roswell Kirkey preferred his austere quarters near his workshop in the mines. His sister joked the time underground was turning him into a Gnome. Rhiann shared a room with young Iyaca. The youth was curious about the activities within the mine. Rhiann told him that the swordsmith and Mayard had long discussions and actually showed the youth the longsword Exeter. Iyaca declined the opportunity to hold the weapon and in so doing saved Rhiann the work of another forget spell. The spirit of the blade had stressed the need to keep its essence secret.

Morning arrived quickly and the group enjoyed a breakfast of Johnny cakes, booderry syrup, and tomaters. Madam Darktop raved about the gemstones she had gathered for new projects. Roswell reappeared for a quick good-bye and headed back to his work, which had dramatically increased through his brother Albie Kirkey and the Burgomaster Storming Norman's orders of axes and hammers. Miners had loaded treasures from the mines onto the wagons. Large quantities of copper ore filled the smaller wagon, which was to return to Dry Creek. Gnomes busily readied for departure. The ores on the wagons slowed the return trip, and the precious gems increased the likelihood of misadventure. Longbeard Nineteen-names counseled and organized his charges and soon the group bade the miners farewell. Foreman Brady escorted them to the palisade and Longbeard Nineteen-names, *p-Mayard*, Cecelia Darktop, two merchants from Dry Creek, Rhiann

Klarje, Iyaca Vassi, and twenty other Gnomes headed up the road. Longbeard's guards included Lieutenant Donovan Ten-names, Sergeant Rudy Nine-names, Corporal Alden Eight-names, Corporal Roro Seven-names, and archer Dibbit Five-names.

Longbeard knew the route well and kept a wary eye toward the woods and ahead when the small caravan made it to the crests of small hills. Longbeard had a very good relationship with a number of the homesteaders along the route. On the way toward the mine camp, they had stopped at an establishment run by a rogue named Jack Taylor. Taylor was very good with livestock and meaner than most highwaymen, so roughnecks generally left him to mind his business. On the other hand, Jack Taylor was not opposed to dealing with anybody if there was a profit involved. Taylor called his place Jack's Refuge. He allowed folks of all ilk but forbade pugilism.

p-Mayard commented from the wagon perch, "The phi gamms are laboring with this load. Our speed is not even half what we averaged on the way to the mine camp."

Longbeard replied, "I've noticed. It's best we spend the night at Jack's Refuge. I made arrangements for us to have rooms. We'll be there in an hour."

Cecelia Darktop chagrinned, "You never know who'll be there. He lets in all types. We saw on our way to the mines."

Longbeard added, "Taylor runs a tight ship. His guards threw the fighting Dwarf and Kobold outside when we were stopped on the way to the mines. Sharing his space requires leaving conflicts at the door."

Rhiann asked, "What happens if another fight breaks out?"

Longbeard laughed and answered, "Then Taylor will knuckle some heads. He's a stout bloke and keeps some mercenaries on payroll. Don't look at them too closely, Mayard. Most have prices on their heads in Thynna."

Iyaca said nervously, "Will the Man in Black be there?"

Longbeard said, "If he is, I'll take exception to Taylor's 'no fighting' rules."

Cecelia Darktop said, "The last info we had placed the Fearsome Foursome east of Gnome-town. They frequent the roads where the greatest wealth travels. Makes sense. They are highwaymen. Their activity and reports of Kobolds again massing together have lead my mate the Burgomaster and my brother Albie to request the additional weaponry from my brother Roswell. The suns are dipping. We don't want to travel at night and camp in the woods. Jack's Refuge does have a palisade, though it keeps us inside with insalubrious blokes. You're awfully quiet, Mayard."

p-Mayard answered, "I'm just listening. Jack Taylor keeps some pretty good mead on hand. The wagons carry much heavier loads. The animals need rest."

The little caravan crossed tobacco fields and went up and down two hills and came upon the grassy area that surrounded Jack's Refuge. A stream traversed the large field. To the left of the road stood the way station's wooden palisade with a guard tower and open gate. Four men armed with longbows watched from the bartizan. *p-Mayard* guided the phi gamms to the gate. On both sides of the gate small gate towers were occupied by a single grizzled guard. The guards kept bows trained on the approaching wagons. Cecelia Darktop grudgingly parted with Jack Taylor's cover fee and the group entered. Diverse folks milled about the small quadrangle. Most shied away from the contingent of Gnomes. *p-Mayard* and Cecelia Darktop drew the most attention. Mayard Klarje frequently stopped at Jack's Refuge on his journeys and Madam Darktop commanded attention everywhere she went. *p-Mayard* guided the phi gamms to the small livery. The stable masters attended the beasts of burden… for a price. Madam Darktop again grudgingly obliged.

Longbeard Nineteen names barked commands, "Stay alert! This is not Gnome-town! I want six guards on the wagons at all times."

p-Mayard and Rhiann jumped down from the wagon. Longbeard, Cecelia Darktop, and Iyaca Vassi watered the halvsies. Two Kobolds wandered out the tavern door. Longbeard held back his guards and grudgingly suppressed his disdain from the gnarly goblin-like folk. The brace of Kobolds walked briskly across the enceinte and exited the trading post. The tavern staff busily scurried around and served patrons of many ilks. Madam Darktop and Longbeard bartered for the rooms Longbeard had reserved earlier when they stopped in route to the mine camp. Rhiann marveled at the diversity of the forest folks. Kobolds entered with fresh fish, game, nuts, and fruits. The barkeep paid the Kobolds, who nervously walked past the Gnomes.

The encounters only produced a few insults. Jack Taylor's guards closed the gates at sundown. Longbeard and Cecelia finished a hearty dinner and warmed by the fireplace. Longbeard's guards ate in shifts. When the first group finished their meals, they relieved their colleagues, who were guarding the wagons. p-Mayard, Cecelia Darktop, and Longbeard indulged in a mug of ale. Rhiann and Iyaca took in tales the threesome shared by the roaring fire. The proprietor Jack Taylor sauntered into the tavern, stared at the party for a time, and then came over to the table with refills. Longbeard Nineteen-names relayed Burgomaster Storming Norman's message. Jack Taylor barely acknowledged it and went into stories of increased lawlessness in the area and its threat to his livelihood. Longbeard allowed Jack's clientele brought with it risk. Madam Darktop quickly tired of the conversation and asked about their accommodations. Jack Taylor gave Madam Darktop a room he used at times... for a price, of course. Cecelia excused herself and went up the narrow stairs in the back of the room. Longbeard organized watch shifts. *p-Mayard* stretched. expressed his fatigue, and suggested everyone retire. They still had a day's journey to reach Dry Creek with the heavily laden wagons.

p-Mayard stood. Rhiann and Iyaca took it as their cue to made ready for bed.

Jack Taylor placed a strong hand on p-Mayard's shoulder and said, "Could we talk for a bit?"

p-Mayard reluctantly agreed and said, "Rhiann and Iyaca, go on to bed. I'll be up in a while."

Jack Taylor said, "You are not Mayard Klarje."

p-Mayard replied, "And you are not Jack Taylor."

p-Jack said, "Haven't been for a long time. What are you up to?"

p-Mayard answered, "I might ask you the same thing."

p-Jack said matter-of-factly, "I'm just making a living. You, on the other hand, are masquerading as the greatest sorcerer in the land and traveling with the leaders of Gnome-town, the strongest conurbation north of Thynna."

p-Mayard said, "Maybe these things ought to remain our little secrets. These law abiding Gnomes, particularly Captain Longbeard might start asking what really happened to the Burgomaster's friend Jack Taylor? How many of *us* are involved in your little masquerade?"

p-Jack said, "As if you didn't know. My six most trusted guards. The brace of Kobolds that left just as you were arriving. And some I'm not going to tell you about. The Kobolds who brought in the produce are really Kobolds. We wouldn't lower ourselves to till the soil. I could be a hero and tell your colleagues about your deception. They'd wonder about the real Mayard Klarje. The question has entered my own mind. Tell me one good reason why I shouldn't sell you out?"

p-Mayard said, "It'd be a bad idea. I am not alone."

p-Jack said confidently, "Don't try to con me! I know a Shapechanger's spirit. None of your companions share our essence!"

p-Mayard asked, "Did you see the young man who rides with me?"

p-Jack said, Yes. He's just a youth, and the younger whelp is only a boy."

p-Mayard said, "I'll call him down from his room. Look closely at his face."

p-Jack said, "I saw his face. He had the same cherry-red heart-shaped birthmark on his chin that you have created on your mug. Wait! Mayard does have the mark! The youth bears the mark of the Klarjes. Not to worry… he's too young to be much of a threat."

p-Mayard said, "It's the visage of Rhiann Klarje, the great nephew and apprentice of Mayard. You, I, and he are proof that things aren't always as they seem."

p-Jack said, "I'm not blind. He is not Shapechanger! He is, at most, an inexperienced sorcerer."

p-Mayard replied, "When you greeted Mayard Klarje as we entered, you did not misspeak. The youth is my boss, Mayard Klarje."

p-Jack said, "Not likely! Why does he travel as a youth and allow you to use his visage"?"

p-Mayard said, "I don't ask his reasons and he oft doesn't tell. Ask yourself… do you want to make him mad?"

p-Jack grumbled, "Sorcerers! Bah! I had one in here a few weeks ago. He was offering blokes payment to follow him on some quest. Tried to hire one or two of my boys. I sent one along just to keep an eye on him. Convinced him my guy was a Kobold archer. Even had him take some target practice. He never missed. Kobolds can't shoot for s***! But he fell for it! Sorcerers think they are so smart. We almost infiltrated Thynna, but the bastard got caught by Mayard Klarje. Don't know what happened to him. Don't care. I don't want to mess with Klarje. I'd question your decision to follow him."

p-Mayard said, "I'm the bastard that got caught by Mayard Klarje. You are showing good judgment in avoiding his ire."

p-Jack scoffed, "We can keep each other's secret. You'd best be a good boy and get off to bed or your nursemaid Madam Darktop will come to tuck you in."

Longbeard returned to the tavern after setting the order for the watches.

p-Mayard stood and said, "Thank you for your hospitality Jack. It's nice of you to forego the cost of the rooms. I'm sure the Burgomaster will be glad to hear of your generosity. He said you're overdue for a visit to Gnome-town."

p-Jack Taylor choked on his ale and sputtered, "Why... uh, OK. Give him my regards. Please tell me the business of running this joint is playing havoc with my social life. Wish him good health."

Longbeard smiled and added his thanks. The Gnome and doppelganger headed up the stairs to bed. p-Jack Taylor drowned his sorrows in another mug of bitter ale. p-Jack finished his ale and walked to the rear of the now deserted tavern. The doppelganger pushed on the third man's eye-level stone to the left of the third brazier from the end of the bar. A secret door opened with a slight grating sound and led to a stairwell. *p-Jack* descended the stairs. The door closed behind him. The stairs led to a dimly-lit passage that meandered underground. Two side passages ended in blind dead ends with traps. The long passage came to a dead end that really wasn't. *p-Jack* pushed on a rock in the wall. The wall opened and humid night air struck him in the face. A babbling brook flowed nearby. Two henchmen guarded the entry and kept a warhorse ready. *p-Jack Taylor* took the reins and rode away into the night. The guards resumed their game of chance.

Rhiann, Iyaca Vassi, Madam Darktop, Longbeard Nineteen-names, and Longbeard's Lieutenant Donovan retired to very rustic rooms.

Rhiann struggled with keeping the secret of Exeter from Rhiann and ultimately opted to have Iyaca grasp the hilt of the weapon.

Rhiann said, "Iyaca, you are my apprentice now. There's something I want you to know. If I should fall, do your all to protect my Bag of Holding and particularly one item within it." Rhiann opened the bag and continued, "Place your hand inside and grip the hilt of the longsword."

Iyaca said, "Longsword! Master Rhiann, the Bag is scarcely long enough to hold a dagger."

Rhiann said, "Remove the weapon."

Iyaca Vassi pulled Exeter from the Bag of Holding.

Exeter's voice placed the words in young Iyaca's mind, "Young Iyaca Vassi, I hope this is the beginning of a long relationship. You are now privy to my secret."

The night passed uneventfully. On the morrow the guards reported no trespasses against the wagons. After breakfast Longbeard organized the troupe.

Shouts rang from Jack's Refuge's guard tower.

Longbeard stopped his work and headed toward the still closed gate. He ascended the wall stairs and looked out. A Gnome riding on a straining halvsie rapidly approached on the road from Dry Creek. The rider shouted as he neared, "Kobolds! Dry Creek is under attack! We need help!"

At Longbeard's urging Jack Taylor's guards opened the door and allowed the rider to enter. Longbeard ran down the wall stairs and held the exhausted halvsie's reins while guards helped the distraught rider dismount. Farriers attended the brave little equine that carried the Gnomish messenger.

Longbeard said, "Talk!"

The Gnomish rider breathlessly said, "Last night the tower guards saw two Kobolds hanging around the woods' edge. Sergeant Rorke doubled the guard during the night. Before dawn it started. Two guards were picked off by arrows. They kept us pinned down on the wall walk. We fired back into the wood, but I don't think we hit anything."

Longbeard Nineteen names said, "Kobold archers picked off two tower guards! They normally couldn't hit the broad side of a livery stable. Kobolds usually prefer sneaky ambushes in the woods or else a direct attack when they have superior numbers, which isn't often, because of their chaotic nature. Only their greatest leaders like Narg have been able to gather sizeable forces. Narg had the Sorcerer Bailiwick's help. Old Bailiwick probably threatened to turn them into toads if they didn't fight."

The rider whose name was Nugget Six-names said, "These weren't typical Kobolds! They used duck and cover tactics effectively and were crack shots! Their attacks were organized and systematic. This morning they appeared out of nowhere near the palisade and lobbed flaming arrows into the quadrangle. We dropped a few before they could get back into the woods. But now putting out fires kept us busy. Then dozens of them charged the gate with a burning log. Our archers felled enough of them to make them drop the log. Flames from the log sent up smoke. Then the blighters charged with ladders and tried to climb the wall. We lost another guard to an archer's shot. He fell over the wall. They violated his body. Couldn't stand watching it! When we opened the gate and retrieved his body, six invisible Kobolds sneaked inside Dry Creek. Magick was afoot! They came into view when they attacked, but they killed two and injured three of us and also set fire to the livery. We retrieved the fallen guard's body and saw two highwaymen lurking in the woods. We finally whipped the once-invisible invaders and reestablished the perimeter. Everyone in town was involved in the fight and had to be wary of incoming arrows. Things were looking pretty grim. Sergeant Rorke sent me here to get reinforcements."

Longbeard asked, "Why didn't you send someone to Gnome-town?"

Nugget said, "We tried. Sergeant Rorke sent a rider through the gate to the east, but the Kobolds smote him before he got out of sight. I went west. The road to the west was guarded too, and highwaymen on large stallions pursued me, but my halvsie Lightnin Bug outran the enemies and I got away. There was a lot of smoke over Dry Creek last time I looked back."

A miner named Weijia said, "Invisible Kobolds! Highwaymen! Magick! A sorcerer is involved. A strange alliance!"

Madam Cecelia Darktop shouted, "What are we waiting for? Let's get going! They need help! We have Mayard Klarje! No other sorcerer can match him!"

p-Mayard said, "Well, yes, we do… I mean, I am ready to fight. Rhiann can help too."

Madam Kirkey sternly said, "Mayard, it's best the youths stay here or return to the mines where there's greater levels of security. But we should go! Can you teleport us to Dry Creek?"

p-Mayard remembered *real* Mayard's description of the spell and said, "Well, possibly, Madam Darktop, but it wouldn't help much. We'd arrive naked, I'm afraid. And only as many of us as I can carry. The distance is too great. What do you think, Rhiann?"

The others quizzically stared at *p-Mayard* and then toward young Rhiann. Rhiann said, "Of course you are correct, Uncle Mayard. But I should be by your side to help you with your spells."

p-Mayard gave an inward sigh of relief, "Yes, your help is invaluable."

Madam Darktop said, "Fine, he goes with us, but if your debate is over, we should get started."

Longbeard Nineteen-names said matter-of-factly, "Not we, Madam Darktop. You should not go to Dry Creek."

Cecelia Darktop argued, "I know you are concerned for my safety, Longbeard, but there's no way I'm going to miss this fight!"

Longbeard replied, "If you go along, it's the Kobolds and highwaymen who'd be in jeopardy, my lady. You fight better than any of us. But you can serve us and Dry Creek better."

Cecelia grimaced and said, "How? Dwarves serve best by fighting!'"

Longbeard Nineteen-names huffed, "I'm not a bad fighter, Cecelia."

p-Mayard quickly attested, "You are the best Gnome fighter among us, Longbeard."

Longbeard smirked.

Cecelia opined, "I'm growing impatient. I'm the best fighter! What could be more valuable?"

Longbeard looked at *p-Mayard* and said, "I'm surprised our distinguished sorcerer hasn't already suggested it. Madam Darktop, the answer lies on your feet."

Cecelia said, "My feet!"

Longbeard said, "Yes, the ruby slippers."

Cecelia said, "My shoes! They can only carry me back to Gnome-town. Not only that... I can't take anyone with me. How will that help you?"

Longbeard said, "The slippers will get you back to Gnome-town in an instant. We can give minimal assistance to Dry Creek. In fact, the guards who accompanied us would best serve by returning to protect the mines."

The messenger Nugget shouted, "Are you saying you are not going to send help?"

Longbeard answered, "No, to the contrary. Madam Darktop can reach Gnome-town through the Return Spell of her slippers. The Burgomaster can send a massive force to relieve the defenders of Dry Creek, and it can get there as quickly as we can. We will carry on to Dry Creek, but our movement is slow."

Cecelia Darktop said, "I don't want to leave you, particularly young Iyaca and Rhiann. I feel responsible for them."

Longbeard reassured her, "We have Mayard Klarje and me! If you go to the Burgomaster, Gnome-town can send a legion to help."

Cecelia asked *p-Mayard*, "I value your opinion, Mayard. What say you?"

p-Mayard said, "I say the more support we can get to Dry Creek, the merrier."

Rhiann said, "Merrier? It's not a party, Uncle Mayard."

Cecelia Darktop said, "Well, I can go to Gnome-town and still get to the fight as quickly. I suppose you're all correct."

The messenger Nugget impatiently said, "Let's do something!"

Cecelia Darktop said, "Rhiann, watch after Iyaca… and Mayard. I'm going to fetch Norman and the forces of Gnome-town."

Cecelia gathered her belongings. The Baroness of Flat Rock and life-mate of the Burgomaster lifted her raiment. Her ruby slippers glistened in the early morning suns' light. Cecelia said, "I'm ready."

The others stepped away from her and gave her three paces leeway.

Cecelia then clipped her heels together and said, "There's no place like home."

She clicked the heels again and said, "There's no place like home."

She then clicked the heels a third time and said, "There's no place like home."

Madam Darktop disappeared in a flash of blue light. In his bedchamber Storming Norman noted the flash of red light. His beloved Cecelia stood before him and began relaying the predicament of the defenders at Dry Creek.

CHAPTER 19

For Dry Creek

Longbeard said, "Someone must go the mine camp and warn Foreman Brady, Roswell, and the garrison of the Kobold activity."

Nugget quickly volunteered.

Longbeard said, "You have done more than your share in riding here alone. Your pony is exhausted."

Nugget said, "Sergeant Rorke chose me for my riding ability. Give me a fresh halvsie and I'll carry word to the miners."

Jack Taylor was away, but his top guard said, "You can't stay at Jack's Refuge. We must maintain neutrality. I will loan him a horse... for a price."

Longbeard said, "Understood. We will be underway. We are needed at Dry Creek. Thanks for the horse."

The top guard replied, "Nice doing business with you."

Nugget mounted up and rode toward the mine camp. Longbeard Nineteen-names organized the little caravan. The wagons had been loaded in anticipation of a return trip to Dry Creek and then ultimately Thynna. Now confusion ruled. Madam Darktop had reluctantly returned to Gnome-town via her Magick ruby slippers. The Gnomes debated their course. Some suggested they should return to the mines to shore up the defenses.

Longbeard's twenty guards strongly wanted to make haste to join the fray at Dry Creek. Eight had been assigned to the garrison and most had friends and relatives that served in the community's defense. Rhiann and young Iyaca Vassi stood in awe of the unfolding events and *p-Mayard* remained diplomatically silent.

Gnomish Lieutenant Donovan Ten-names, who was Captain Longbeard's highest ranking subordinate, insisted, "Our brothers in Dry Creek are overmatched. We must make haste to help them!"

Corporal Alden Eight-names said, "I agree. My skills are wasted guarding the mines. I'm a fighter! A mere squad can guard the entrance to the mines."

Sergeant Rudy Nine-names disagreed, "You heard the messenger. Magick is afoot! What can a few Gnomes and miners do against a sorcerer? When Dry Creek falls, the road to the mines is wide open. We must remain here."

Captain Longbeard said, "Mayard, what say you? You've been unusually quiet. No other sorcerer can match your skills. Come with me to Dry Creek. Should we leave the wagons and travel on fast horses? They might allow the young sorcerer and Iyaca to remain at Jack's. I could leave half my guards, too."

p-Mayard replied nervously, "The top guard says we can't stay at Jack's place anyway, and Jack is nowhere to be found. I can't leave Rhiann. He must accompany me. I'm reluctant to leave the wagons. The enemies might not come to Jack's place and the mines."

Longbeard whined, "Mayard! I've never known you to be tentative! They are Kobolds! Kobolds love shiny things! Of course they are going to attack the mines!"

The veteran Lieutenant Donovan ten-names said, "I agree with Longbeard. Eventually the enemies will seek the riches of the mines. But vengeance drives the sorcerer and highwaymen! They will first seek the destruction of the settlements and won't be happy until Gnome-town falls. The Burgomaster has pursued the highwaymen relentlessly and brought down their leaders. For them to show themselves, they must be confident in their strength. Mayard, we will need all our strength to defeat them. To inventory our steeds…we have Cecelia's halvsie Nuffin, my halvsie Shadowdancer, Donovan's halvsie, Iyaca's halvsie, the halvsie that pulled Alden's cart, two phi gamms, four workhorses that are no good for riding, and four halvsies that pulled the second wagon. That gives us nine steeds that we can ride. The four workhorses can pull the copper-carrying wagon."

Mayard looked to Rhiann. Rhiann weakly nodded affirmatively.

p-Mayard said, "Then let's make ready. What can we acquire from Jack's livery?"

The livery's blacksmiths quickly brought a large stallion for Mayard and three stout halvsies, including little Lightnin Bug that had borne Nugget to the mine camp. This gave them a total of twelve little steeds. Longbeard Nineteen names chose himself, Mayard *(p-Mayard),* Rhiann, Donovan Ten-names, Rudy Nine-names, Alden Eight-names, and seven other experienced guards. He ordered Roro Seven-names to take command of the wagons and follow the riders toward Dry Creek.

Iyaca said, "What about me?"

Rhiann said, "It's best you stay with Roro."

Iyaca said, "No, the Burgomaster told me to be with you. I want to go."

Roro said, "One place is as safe as another. I really can't guarantee his safety and certainly can't watch over him. So he's about as well off to go with you."

Little Lightnin Bug recovered quickly. Iyaca climbed onto the halvsie and replaced a loudly grumbling Gnome with six names. Thirteen riders left Jack's Refuge. Eleven Gnomes led by Roro Seven-names commanded the wagons. The two merchants from Dry Creek remained with the wagons.

Roro shouted, "Make safe Dry Creek!"

The Man in Black, Kobold Chieftain Beeyo, and Sorcerer Bailiwick sat upon equines on a hillock overlooking Dry Creek.

The Man in Black said, "The defenders are pressed. The battle goes well."

Beeyo said, "Yes, at the expense of my people's lives. When are your brigands going to enter the fray? What about some more spells, wizard?"

Bailiwick said, "Patience! I've fought battles with this lot before. We shan't reveal all our strengths. My surprise on the road between Dry Creek and the mines is set. The trap awaits its quarry. Mayard Klarje should be taking his last few breaths."

p-Mayard, Captain Longbeard Nineteen-names, Lieutenant Donovan Ten-names, Corporal Alden eight-names, Sergeant Rudy

Nine-names, Rhiann, Iyaca, and six veteran Gnomes rode hard across the open fields near the Copper Mountain mines. The woods were extraordinarily quiet. The trip was much quicker on steeds without the phi gamm-drawn wagons. The twelve halvsies kept up with *p-Mayard's* large horse. The topography of the rolling foothills of the Copper Mountains gave them glances into the distance, where they saw wisps of smoke. The riders approached a tobacco field before reaching the highest hill between them and Dry Creek. The field was about four hundred paces across.

Longbeard held up his right hand and said, "This is a risky place. We'll be riding in full view of the woods and the hill we are approaching."

The column moved forward and advanced halfway across the field. Then there was a disturbance from the woods to the left. A Kobold upon a large gray wolf charged out of the woods bearing a lance.

Longbeard shouted, "Mayard, take him out!"

p-Mayard steadied his horse and looked at Rhiann. The Kobold drew within a hundred paces. The snarling wolf oddly made no noise yet still alarmed the halvsies.

Longbeard reiterated, "Mayard, now. He's coming straight for you."

The Kobold quietly reached fifty paces.

Rhiann extended his left wrist and muttered a command. The Magick Missile struck the wolf. The beast fell forward and dumped its Kobold rider. The rider stood and continued to charge the cluster of Gnomes. The wolf's chest heaved and then it breathed no more.

Longbeard said, "Now that's suicide."

The Gnomish Captain dismounted, drew his hammer, and made ready to face the Kobold. The attacker abruptly stopped and hurled his spear.

Longbeard shouted, "Look out!"

The spear chunked harmlessly into the ground about five paces from the gathered riders. The projectile made no noise when it struck the ground. The Kobold turned and ran toward the woods. Alden broke ranks and started after him.

Longbeard ordered, "No! Hold your position! It's got to be a trick!"

p-Mayard whispered to Rhiann, "Thanks for bailing me out, Boss."

Another Kobold charged from the woods to the right. He also carried a spear and rode on a large wolf. Longbeard's charges turned to face him. The Gnome guard Dibbit Five-names readied his bow. The wolf-rider stopped about thirty paces from the group of Gnomes and hurled his lance. It also landed noiselessly a few feet from Dibbit. The Kobold turned the wolf away from the Gnomes and headed for the woods. Two more Kobolds rushed the group and repeated the maneuver. Captain Longbeard Nineteen-names ordered the group to move forward, but a group of Kobolds charged from the road leading to Dry Creek. At the same two other groups came out of the woods to the left and right. A fourth group came up behind the thirteen riders. Men on horseback blocked both the road to Dry Creek and the road back to the mine.

Longbeard said, "We can't outrun them, we can't ride through them, and I can't fight on this horse. Dismount! Form a tight circle. Mayard, Rhiann, and Iyaca in the center. We're going to need your help to get out of this jam, Mayard. I'd suggest you get started."

p-Mayard nudged Rhiann and said, "Let 'em have it, Boss1"

The thirteen riders dismounted, the Gnomes drew weapons, and the group moved together. The Kobolds to the east and north held their ground whilst the other groups menacingly edged toward the cluster of Gnomes. The group moved closer together and retreated to an area between the four Kobold lances. *p-Mayard*, Rhiann, and Iyaca stood about five feet from one of the lances.

Longbeard said, "About now would be a good time for a spell, Mayard!"

p-Mayard opened his mouth to speak but produced no sound. In fact, the entire area between the four spears was silent. Rhiann stood by Mayard. The young sorcerer held no weapon, but then reached for the sword in his bag of holding and grabbed Exeter's hilt.

"Imminent threat! Imminent threat! Imminent threat! Lethal danger! Enemy is at fifteen paces east of you and twelve paces south of the road." Exeter's warning ripped silently through Rhiann's mind.

Rhiann looked, opened his mouth, uttered, "Nobody's there!" but only the spirit of the sword heard.

"Danger! Danger! Danger!" Exeter warned.

Rhiann stared in the direction indicated by the warning and instinctively pointed the blade toward the spot. Movement! In less than a heartbeat a projectile appeared in midair and streaked toward *p-Mayard* and Rhiann. A Kobold brandishing a longbow appeared at the point of origin of the arrow. His offensive action cost him his invisibility. Rhiann reached out to shove *p-Mayard* but had no time. The arrow struck *p-Mayard* in the left shoulder. Mayard Klarje's doppelganger's mouth gaped open, and he fell silently to the ground. His body shimmered briefly and then returned to its amorphous shiny Shapechanger form. The dark red arrow with black fletching protruded from the amorphous mass. Rhiann reflexively reached for the arrow but Exeter warned, "No, no, no! Danger! Its fletching is a Tuscon feather. Touching it risks death!"

Iyaca Vassi and the Gnomes moved silently away from Rhiann and the fallen Shapechanger. The archer turned and ran toward the woods to the east.

Exeter informed Rhiann, "An area of silence extends thirty feet from the four lances thrown by the Kobolds. You must move thirty feet away."

Rhiann said, "So you can detect Magick?"

Exeter returned, "The area of silence poses a threat to you. I can detect threats to my bearer. Don't ask me how I know. It's Magick!"

Rhiann wildly waved his arms, pointed Exeter toward the clustered score of Kobolds to the north of the road, and ran toward them. He shouted, "Charge!" but only the sword heard the scream. Iyaca Vassi drew his little hunting knife and bravely charged behind Rhiann. Longbeard Nineteen-names recovered from the death and transformation of *p-Mayard's* body and ran with Rhiann toward the group of Kobolds. Donovan Ten-names, Rudy Nine-names, and Alden Eight-names followed Longbeard's lead, shrieked loudly, and charged toward the Kobolds. The screams became audible when they passed thirty feet from the northernmost lance. Dibbit Five-names still carried his bow. He regained his composure, pulled his drawstring taut, and silently released an arrow toward the fleeing Kobold archer, who had smitten *p-Mayard*. Though missing the twang of "string music,' the arrow followed a true course and ripped into the archer's chest. The archer fell forward with a thud, which Dibbit did not hear. The Kobold archer's body shimmered and changed into another amorphous featureless bipedal form indistinguishable from what had been *p-Mayard*.

The group of Kobolds to the east started toward their northern comrades. The archer's fall and transformation startled, spooked, and dissuaded them, and they hesitated. The group of Kobolds to the south charged forward and followed Rhiann, Iyaca, and the Gnomes toward the northern Kobold group. All in all, it looked like a fox chasing the hounds. As individuals separated thirty feet from the nearest lance their screams became audible. The Kobolds to the west held their ground and concentrated on keeping the road to the west and Jack's Refuge blocked.

Longbeard, Donovan, Alden, Rudy, and Rhiann reached the northern group of Kobolds. The powerful experienced Gnomes made short work of their first opponents. Donovan's great strength powered his axe through their shields. Most Kobolds managed to parry fewer than three rounds before they fell. Emotion and adrenaline fueled Rhiann's first foray into hand-to-hand combat. Rhiann had read every book on the subject in Thynna's libraries and also carried a Magick sword. Exeter felt nigh weightless in his hand, and the novice swordsman easily parried the unfortunate Kobolds' blows. Rhiann's every swing destroyed one of the goblin-like enemies. Donovan Ten-names clobbered Kobold after Kobold. By the time the southern cluster reached the battle, the Gnomes and Rhiann had already dispatched their northern foes and turned and met them head on. The number of the southern clutch was reduced by two unfortunates dumb enough to stop at *p-Mayard's* corpse and try to lull out the arrow with the Tuscon fletching from the dead Shapechanger. The fletching maintained its lethality and smote both. Dibbit five-names fired repeatedly and dropped four Kobolds in the eastern lot. All the while the Gnomes' disciplined halvsies remained in a cluster in the fringes of the field away from the battle. *p-Mayard's* stallion broke and ran through the Kobolds to the west and gravely injured two enemies. The Gnomes quickly overcame the southern group of Kobolds. A few survivors dropped their weapons, broke away, and ran for the woods to the south of the road. Two Gnomes suffered minor injuries. Thirty-one Kobolds' bodies littered the field. Reinforcements filtered into the group of Kobolds to the west. Longbeard Nineteen-names and Donovan Ten-names angrily pulled lances from the ground and hurled them toward the Kobolds. Two Kobolds fell. The silence spells centered on the lances silenced their screams. Both the east and west groups of Kobolds drifted backward toward the road's exits from the field.

CHAPTER 20

Regrouping

The Man in Black and Bailiwick sat upon horses on a nearby hillock and watched the conflict unfold. The Man in Black said snidely, "Nice plan, sorcerer. You managed to take out a Shapechanger at a cost of thirty-one lives. The Gnomes have effectively whipped Beeyo's warriors. Your ******* spells are little more than parlor tricks. You couldn't even tell Mayard Klarje wasn't in the fray."

Bailiwick snarled, "It should have worked! Your watcher said Mayard traveled with them! Why would a Shapechanger travel with Gnomes in the guise of Mayard Klarje?"

The Man in Black said, "While we're on the subject of Shapechangers! Why didn't you tell me your Kobold archer was a Shapechanger? I'm not exactly happy about your keeping such secrets from me. The Gnomes did not benefit from Magick, yet twelve of them and two boys have beaten fourscore of Beeyo's warriors."

Bailiwick defensively uttered, "I couldn't rely on the Kobolds to utilize the death arrow. Seven died trying! I couldn't tell the Kobolds a Shapechanger was among them. It would have offended Beeyo, and I… we need his numbers, unless you want to send your highwaymen against those Gnomish weapons. Furthermore, you assert the Gnomes were without Magick. One of the youths fought like a berserker! His sword emitted red auras! The Kobolds never scratched him. He's likely another Shapechanger."

The Man in Black retorted, "The watcher said the youth bore the mark of the Klarjes."

Bailiwick replied sharply, "Well, so did the Shapechanger in Mayard's guise. Can't say too much for your watcher in the woods. The youth is a Paladin of sorts, not a sorcerer, and he carries an exceptional blade. I hope the watcher is better at picking out ambush sites. Let's follow our plan and regroup at his favorite site. Mayard Klarje is not with this lot and somewhere still draws breath. Let them gather their wagons and treasure. They won't expect another attack."

The Man in Black shook his head negatively and commented, "I don't share your confidence. Longbeard did not gather nineteen names by being stupid and careless. It will be difficult to surprise him. His death, however, will be some consolation for not getting Mayard, and the men are hungry for treasure. I hope you can smooth that ****** Kobold's nerves over the loss of his so-called warriors. Personally, I've got my eye on that red sword!"

The remaining Kobolds abruptly left the field. The roads to both east and west were open. Longbeard Nineteen-names ordered defensive positions. Donovan Ten-names glared at Rhiann and cleaned his axe. The stout Gnome lieutenant said icily, "Rhiann, if you are Rhiann Klarje, you had to know the Shapechanger was not your Uncle Mayard Klarje, yet you led us to believe he was Sagain's great benefactor. You helped a Shapechanger into our homes, confidence, and inner ranks."

Longbeard added, "He certainly drank like your Uncle Mayard. Now I understand why the blighter never cast any spells. Donovan, lad, I've seen Rhiann produce Magick. He is at least a sorcerer, though I'd have sworn I was fighting beside a berserker from Valhalla or Paladin from San Francisco."

Rhiann answered, "I'm merely following my Uncle Mayard's plan. Until the moment of his death the Shapechanger thought *I* was my Uncle Mayard and the true Rhiann Klarje remained at the Hanging Gardens. The Shapechanger served my uncle loyally for many seasons. He was a true friend. I'm bereft and might add the Shapechanger served you well."

Longbeard also cleaned his weapon all the while keeping his eyes moving around the perimeter. The Gnomes skillfully gathered the halvsies and kept alert. Longbeard asked, "Does Mayard remain at the Hanging Gardens?"

Rhiann said, "My Uncle Mayard stayed at the Hanging Garden in my guise. I didn't understand my Uncle's plan. He merely said it was important that I complete his mission and business with Roswell Kirkey and insisted he was needed at the Hanging Gardens. I am truly sorry that you were deceived."

Longbeard nervously looked around at the carnage and said, "Just touching that vile arrow killed two Kobolds. The Shapechanger that mimicked Mayard only suffered a flesh wound yet it smote him instantly. It's too dangerous to try to remove and reuse it. Magick works against us, and no offense Rhiann, we do not have Mayard Klarje. The sorcerer opposing us has fomented invisible attackers, silence invoking spears, death arrows... what will that a****** think of next!"

Rhiann said timidly, "Yes, Captain Longbeard, I agree. The lethality of the arrow stems from its Tuscon fletching. I've read about such feathers. Few are the sorcerers capable of creating a Death Spell. Silence spells were placed on the Kobolds' lances. There's always a chance a spell won't work if placed against an individual. The Silence was tied to the lances' location. Invisibility always works if the recipient is willing, but a peculiarity of the Magick is that the invisibility is lost if the recipient attempts an offensive action."

Longbeard scanned the field and directed his charges to remain vigilant. He looked at the young sorcerer and said, "Rhiann, your Uncle Mayard has long been an ally of Gnome-town, and he's taught you well. However, his latest ploy is unsettling! Old Mayard isn't here to face the music, but you are. The Burgomaster must ultimately pass judgment on your part in the matter. Storming Norman Twenty-four names Darktop isn't fond of folks pulling the wool over his eyes. For my part, right now I need you. We all still face danger. The Kobolds oft leave their dead. It's in our best interest to burn their carcasses along with the Shapechangers. It's too dangerous to try to move the body of Mayard's doppelganger. Someone might touch the dark arrow's fletching. So he'll burn where he lies."

Gnomish Lieutenant Donovan Ten-names said, "Alden, please carefully inspect the Shapechanger archer and assure he carries no more death arrows. If not, drag his carcass to his likeness, the one that looked like Mayard Klarje. Everyone! Do not touch the arrow! Carefully carry the Kobold carcasses to the Shapechangers. Show them respect. Take nothing from their bodies! We'll create a pyre."

Sergeant Rudy Nine-names said, "Lieutenant Donovan, we have no oil. Igniting the bodies will be difficult. If we do start a fire, will it be safe to breath the smoke generated by that foul arrow?"

Rhiann said, "I'll ignite the bodies with a Fire Spell."

Lieutenant Donovan Ten-names said, "Young Klarje, you fight like a berserker from Valhalla. On this field, we have to trust you, but I am wary of Magick."

Captain Longbeard Nineteen-names said, "Well said, Donovan. Rhiann, we still have a sorcerer against us, so I agree with Donovan that we must trust you, and I do. The battle confirmed you can walk the walk as well as talk the talk. By the way, Dibbit, nice shooting! From this point forward, you are Dibbit Six-names I'm adding 'dead-eye' to your monikers. Now let's get on with it. We smote nigh two score Kobolds, and that's two less score to assail Dry Creek. Once we attend the pyre, we must gather the halvsies and back track toward Jack's Place and retrieve our wagons. Then we'll make a slow steady approach to Dry Creek. Reinforcements from Gnome-town should be well on the way by now. We must stay on high alert. Highwaymen, at least one sorcerer, and lots of Kobolds remain in the area."

Corporal Alden Eight-names carefully examined the doppelganger archer and found only a long bow and quiver of standard arrows. Alden and Newby Five-arms carried the archer's corpse to the body of *p-Mayard*. Other Gnomes collected the halvsies and brought the fallen Kobolds' bodies to the planned pyre site. Lastly the Kobolds' weapons and the four lances were thrown onto the pile. Rhiann directed the others to stand thirty feet away. The young sorcerer crushed a piece of sulfur, conjured, and uttered harsh words. A stream of blue fire flowed from his outstretched left hand to the bodies. Magick fire engulfed the bodies. The flames burned silently until the four lances were consumed, and then the flames began to crackle. The dark arrow gave off very dense black-gray smoke as it burned. The extremely hot Magick fire quickly consumed the bodies. The flames died down and left charred ground where the bodies had lain.

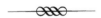

The Gnome Rider Nugget arrived at the Copper Mountain Mines. His new steed did not run as well as his beloved Lightnin Bug. Foreman Brady went about a well-established routine to shore up the mine's defenses whenever threats were manifest. Nugget paced impatiently and gazed toward Dry Creek. Roswell Kirkey armed miners, farriers, and innkeepers. Drills had prepared the tough mining community for such threats. Against Brady and Roswell's advice, after his steed rested a few hours the Gnome Nugget took to his halvsie and left the relative safety of the mine camp, and rode back toward Dry Creek.

Cecelia Darktop delivered Dry Creek's cry for help. Throughout Gnome-town the call to arms was answered. Soon a full legion of guards mustered in the town center. Burgomaster Storming Norman Twenty-four-names Darktop and his life-mate Cecelia sat upon halvsies at the head of the column as it left Gnome-town for a forced march to Dry Creek. Gnomish families living outside Gnome-town proper entered the walled conurbation. Able-bodied males and females took up arms as militia. Riders headed for Flat Rock to make Albie Kirkey and the dwarves aware of the hostilities.

The exhausted defenders of Dry Creek manned the allure and watched the woods and the smoking grass before the palisade. All fires inside the hamlet were put out. Dead and wounded were attended. Enemies were taken outside the gate and placed respectfully on a pyre. The field and woods around the walled hamlet remained quiet.

Lieutenant Donovan Ten-names, Sergeant Rudy Nine-names, and Corporal Alden Eight-names tended the fire that consumed the Shapechangers and Kobolds' bodies. Rhiann Klarje had read about Tuscon feathers in the tomes of Thynna's libraries and cautioned the Gnomes and Iyaca to avoid contact with the ash created by the fire. The grass beneath the bodies more than burned. It withered and all signs of life disappeared. When the fire went out only a circle of thirteen-foot diameter of bare black dirt sat where the bodies had been. Donovan caught a grasshopper as it flew by and tossed the insect onto the burned ground. The bug died and withered instantly. The circular patch of ground never again saw a sprig of life. In future years all manner of beasts that trod upon the cursed patch of ground lost their lives.

Longbeard organized the party into a column of twos and the riders rapidly rode westward toward Jack's Refuge. They found Roro, the two merchants, and ten other Gnomes with the wagons in defensive positions off the southern side of the road. Lieutenant Donovan took command of the wagon *p-Mayard* and Rhiann had brought from Thynna. The merchants nervously climbed aboard the second wagon. Longbeard added "Wagon driver" to his loyal lieutenant's list of monikers, and Donovan was henceforth known as Donovan Eleven-names.

Longbeard updated Roro Seven-names about the battle and the demise of pseudo Mayard Klarje. Roro's group had seen Kobolds in the woods and assumed defensive positions to assess the situation. In the best of circumstances, the wagons would not make Dry Creek by nightfall. The status of the walled community was unknown. Longbeard and Donovan debated whether to return to Jack's Refuge, hunker down for the night, or travel into the night. They chose to pull a bit further off the road and bed down in the woods for a fireless night. Rhiann offered to cast defensive spells and used his limited healing skills to help three Gnomes injured in the battle. Rhiann Klarje had cast more spells in the past day than any earlier time in his young life. He'd tasted hand-to-hand combat and taken lives... many lives. Lieutenant Donovan jokingly referred to Rhiann as "Kobold's bane." Donovan and Longbeard already numbered the name among their monikers. Longbeard Nineteen-names assigned watch shifts. Rhiann and Iyaca Vassi hunkered down in the center of the makeshift camp.

Fatigue overwhelmed Iyaca's apprehension of being in the woods surrounded by untold enemies, and the youth quickly slept. Rhiann battled exhaustion and reached into his bag of holding and grasped Exeter's hilt. The blade's enticing voice appeared in his thoughts, "Young Rhiann, you should be resting."

Rhiann thought, "I worry about Uncle Mayard. He relayed a story of fighting a bewildebeest during his travels with Nona, the eldest of the Three Sisters. He never said he'd been hurt. When did you learn of his injury?"

Exeter answered, "Some time ago, Rhiann. The injury involved the hair strand gifted him by Nona. His body has changed slowly, but the effects have been cumulative. He brought you into his life earlier than he'd hoped. Your Uncle thinks the future of Magick and continuation of Sagain's legacies rest in your hands. My last contact with him came when he gave the heartstone and remnant of the Gray Wanderer to the dwarf in the mines. I learned of his presence in the Hanging Gardens when I touched your mind. Your knowledge of the great sorcerer is more recent than mine. By the way... I regret the death of the Shapechanger. He was not typical of his lot."

Rhiann silently responded, "Thank you. Your voice is most reassuring. I am weary. Perhaps I should..."

Exeter said, "Sleep. Yes. Good night, Rhiann Klarje."

It didn't take long. Rhiann dreamed of his mother Caye, lovely Decima, and his cantankerous Uncle. Then the horrors of the battle crept into his dreams. Exeter's blazing redness, the flowing dark life's blood of the doomed Kobolds, the brief startled expression on *p-Mayard's* face after the death arrow struck him, the angry battle cries, and recalling the lust in his heart took their turns at tormenting the young sorcerer's sleep. As it had many times before, shapeless grayness mercifully entered his dreams.

Wisps...
Threads...
Threads of Magick...
Threads of fate...
Threads of time...
Threads connecting worlds ...
Dreams connecting worlds ...
Dreams of Magick...
The Magick of Dreams...
Magick connecting dreams...
Magick connecting worlds...
Grayness...

Grayness oft preceded the appearance of new spell incantations, but on this occasion the formless grayness simply covered the tormented young sorcerer's visions like a thick coat of paint. Rhiann dreamed of nothing! His vexed young mind found several hours' rest.

CHAPTER 21

Ambush

The Watcher in the Woods navigated the thick forest with ease and found the Man in Black and Bailiwick camped under the canopy of a Thyme Tree. Sage brush grew all around the massive tree and provided fragrant boughs for the highwayman and sorcerer's fire. Bailiwick drew on a briar pipe and the Man in Black rolled some locally grown tobacco. The Red-headed stranger, Waymore, and Straight Arrow sat at another fire and filled the air with folksy music with a cither, juice harp, and banjo. Highwaymen sat around and tapped their feet along with the songs. Beeyo the Kobold leader gathered with a group of ten of his underlings in the periphery of the noisy camp. A big man was tied to a tree near the group's horses. Three Kobolds taunted him. An exact visage of the man sat with Bailiwick and the Man in Black.

The Watcher approached the Man in Black and reported, "They have fallen back toward Jack's Refuge."

p-Jack interrupted, "They won't find old Jack there."

The Man in Black muttered, "I tolerate you because Bailiwick insists you are valuable to us. Yet you let a fake Mayard Klarje slip through your hands, and worse yet, our attack simply killed one of your ilk. I'd say you're not of much account and nigh worthless to us."

p-Jack replied, "Well, I did bring old Jack to you and filled his shoes."

The Man in Black said, "I never had a problem with Jack Taylor until now. He allowed my men to use his facilities. Having you available to spy on the goings on between the mines and Gnome-town hasn't borne much fruit."

p-Jack said, "I did let my colleague walk. He was fooling the Gnomes. I thought he might ultimately be an asset. I tried to get here and warn you of the deception. The attack came before I got here. ****** horse came up lame! Well, then here's a tidbit for you. Mayard Klarje does travel with them. It's the kid."

The Man in Black guffawed, "Balderdash! I spared that kid years ago! He's just a prestidigitator at best."

p-Jack said, "Not that one! The young sorcerer! He bears the mark of the Klarjes. For whatever reason, Mayard is traveling in the guise of his nephew. The Gnomes thought the Shapechanger was Mayard. I guest they know the truth now."

Bailiwick said, "It makes sense. The youth fought like a veteran warrior. All the while it was that ****** Mayard. Good thing we have an alternate plan."

The Watcher in the Woods waited patiently for the discussions to wane. He said, "The Gnomes did not go all the way to Jack's place. They reunited with their wagons and camped out in the woods. Per your instructions, we left them alone to relish their victory. My scouts tell me all the Kobolds have withdrawn from Dry Creek and now mass on both sides of the road between Jack's place and Dry Creek. Reinforcements from Gnome-town, a legion strong, are approaching Dry Creek."

The Man in Black said, "They are reinforcing for a battle that will not occur. Bailiwick's archer killed the wrong adversary. If the sorcerer still travels with the Gnomes, we could still be in for quite a tussle. However, we may never get another chance to have odds so much in our favor against Klarje."

p-Jack asked, "Might I go on ahead and whack old Jack Taylor? What good is he now?"

Bailiwick said, "I have no problem with your doing him in."

The Man in Black objected, "He is a pawn we might still employ."

The Kobold Beeyo stepped into the firelight and said, "My warriors are itching for a fight. Why did we stop the attack on Dry Creek? Why don't we attack the Gnomes in the woods while they are outnumbered?"

Bailiwick quipped, "You lost around forty blokes in the last skirmish, and the sorcerer only fought with a sword. How many of your people are you willing to lose?"

Beeyo growled, "I'll lose everybody if it means we get Klarje and Longbeard."

The Man in Black said, "Fair enough! That just might happen. Beeyo, the key to our success is surprise. Keep your Kobolds quiet and out of sight. The reinforcements from Gnome-town will be concerned about making Dry Creek safe. The sorcerer can cast only one spell at a time. There's a lot of treasure on those wagons. We still can get Klarje."

Beeyo slinked away to instruct his sergeants. *p-Jack* took another opportunity to menace Jack Taylor. The Fearsome Foursome and Bailiwick readied to break camp and go the watcher's ambush point.

Captain Longbeard Nineteen-names booming voice awakened Rhiann. Dawning light surrounded the camp in the woods. The twin suns twinkled in the east. The grateful merchants from Dry Creek provided victuals. Gnomes wolfed down their trail breakfast, busily broke camp, and made ready to head for Dry Creek. By now for better or worse reinforcements should be nearing Dry Creek from Gnome-town. Hopefully they arrived in time.

Longbeard's charges broke camp at dawn. Captain Longbeard and Rhiann rode beside Donovan and Iyaca's wagon. Rudy Nine-names rode at the head of the column. Alden Eight-names rode at the rear. Four pair of Gnomes rode halvsies and positioned behind Rudy, between the first and second wagon, behind the second wagon, and with Alden in the rear. Eight Gnomes walked as foot soldiers by the wagons. The octets of walkers and riders swapped places every hour or so. The archer Dibbit kept his bow ready and rode with Donovan and Iyaca. Lieutenant Donovan Eleven-names relished his new "wagon driver" moniker and continued to drive the phi gamms. Iyaca Vassi yielded his halvsie to Roro and rode beside Donovan. The veteran lieutenant had traveled much more than most Gnomes and entertained the youth with his stories. Donovan Eleven-names was quite fond of dragon tales and spun tales as well as he fought. The veteran lieutenant remained wary of the environs.

Iyaca asked, "Have you fought dragons, Lieutenant Donovan?"

Donovan proudly answered, "There's a green dragon with a big lump on his head after his misfortune of going up against me. I've had a go with quite a few Copper Dragons, too. You can usually buy them off with a bit of copper, but the old ones get cranky and might enjoy a taste of Gnome. Not all dragons are bad. I met a Prismatic Dragon once. It passed through Gnome-town. Yes, sir, I've had some pretty good friends with wings."

Iyaca asked, "Old Ones, Lieutenant Donovan? Have you known Old Ones?"

Donovan said, "Yes, a few. Keep your eyes and ears open, young Iyaca. I feel like we are being watched."

Longbeard drew alongside the wagon just then and said, "Me, too. It's unnerving. I'll be glad to get to Dry Creek."

Rhiann caught up to Longbeard and said, "We are. Kobolds are on both sides of the road. Not many, and they scamper off into the woods after we pass."

Donovan urged the big phi gamms and said, "How'd you know Rhiann? Kobolds are stealthy, quiet, and blend in. Is it a Magick thing? Are you using a spell?"

Rhiann replied, "No, it's the sword. She tells me if an enemy is within thirty feet. I could get used to it."

Longbeard said gruffly, "I still think it'd be best for me to carry the weapon. Good thing halvsies are so good natured. You can have a free hand to grip the weapon's hilt. Come to think of it, Mayard Klarje really was not in the mines. Does our agreement to keep the weapon secret still hold?"

Rhiann said, "The sword relayed Mayard's wishes, so I'd say 'yes'."

Donovan Eleven-names cleared his throat and tipped his head toward Iyaca, who sat next to him on the wagon and well within earshot. Rhiann saw the less than subtle effort and said, "Iyaca knows Exeter is more than a simple long blade. He is now my apprentice and must learn to stand in my stead when needed."

Longbeard Nineteen-names muttered, "Strange days! Shapechangers on our side! Shapechangers against us! We depend on children to fight for us. Bedlam! Fits dealing with Mayard Klarje, though. The Shapechanger handled his ale well and told Mayard's stories as though he had lived them. Truth be known… I rather miss the blighter."

Rhiann said, "p-Mayard had shared many adventures with Uncle Mayard. I also miss his company."

Donovan asked, "Does Magick tell you anything about your Uncle, Rhiann?"

Rhiann honestly answered, "No."

The phi gamms trudged along and set the pace moving steadily toward Dry Creek. Around midday the two-wagon caravan neared the hillock that p-Mayard had considered a perfect spot for an ambush. The road cut between two rocky outcroppings that sat like small buttes placed in the woods.

The Gnomish Captain Longbeard halted the column and asked, "What does your Magick sword tell you, Rhiann?"

Rhiann said, "We are too far away, Captain Longbeard. I sense nothing nearby."

Donovan urged, "We might as well get on with it. There is no way around. Necessity forced the road through this little gap and now forces us through it."

Longbeard replied, "Proceed. Stay alert! Weapons at ready! Dibbit, keep an arrow ready."

The column moved forward into a small open area the gap. About sixty feet separated the tree lines with grassy areas about twenty feet wide on both sides of the road. The first riders entered the thirty-foot-wide gap between the stone buttes. The rock on the south or right was twenty feet height whilst the left was about fifteen feet high. Donovan's wagon neared the opening of the stone gap. The merchant from Dry Creek followed on the second wagon.

Exeter sent a message to Rhiann, "I feared this would happen! Too many to count! Defend!"

Rhiann shouted, "Enemies surround us."

Shouts erupted. Kobolds charged from the woods onto the road behind and in front of the caravan and ran onto the stone buttes. Five men stood on the larger and less elevated rise. The Gnomes dismounted and gathered around the wagons. The well-trained halvsies clustered between the two wagons.

Longbeard said, "Odds are against us, but we'll let them know they were in a fight!"

Bailiwick, the Man in Black, Waymore, the Red-headed Stranger, and Straight Arrow glared menacingly at the cluster of Rhiann, Iyaca, the merchants, and twenty-one Gnomes. The Fearsome Foursome remained strategically behind Kobolds and avoided the direct gaze of the Gnomes. The Man in Black typically warned his colleagues to try to remain from view.

Bailiwick shouted, "Mayard Klarje, long have I awaited this day! Know you are going to die, but know also that you fail your comrades."

Rhiann shouted, "Mayard Klarje does not travel with us."

The Man in Black said, "Nice try, Klarje. Even in disguise you can't hide your red mark. We know you travel in the visage of your nephew."

Another tall figure came to the front and stood at the edge of the rise. *p-Jack Taylor* walked forward and said, "I've learned your nefarious comrade that looked like Mayard Klarje was in fact of Shapechanger ilk, but he told me your true identity Klarje. I know it's really you looking like a youth."

Longbeard shouted, "Jack Taylor, you are a scumbag! After all Gnome-town and Dry Creek have done for you!"

Bailiwick uttered a phrase and pointed toward Longbeard. The stout Captain shivered briefly and then was unable to speak. The Hold Spell took full effect.

The Man in Black said derisively, "You are truly a coward, Mayard Klarje. You try to save yourself by forcing a Shapechanger to take your appearance and then travel as a youth. But you'll receive no mercy. This day you'll pay for many transgressions, not the least of which is the fall of my father Big Boy and Uncle Tiny."

Then a Kobold wearing a ragtag collection of small furs stepped forward and added, "You'll pay for my father Narg!"

Donovan Eleven-names muttered, "Your Uncle Mayard isn't a very popular guy in these parts, Rhiann. I'm afraid we've had it. Looks like they've brought their entire force from Dry Creek just to wipe us out."

Bailiwick pointed toward Donovan and muttered harsh phrases. A mauve ray headed toward the Gnomish lieutenant, but Rhiann touched Donovan's shoulder and uttered a Protection dweomer. The Hold Spell failed. The wily Donovan stopped moving and gave the appearance he was disabled.

Bailiwick screamed, "You can't stop my spells now, Mayard!"

Rhiann answered, "I'm not Mayard Klarje."

The Kobolds shouted louder and worked themselves into a frenzy.

Dibbit 'Dead-Eye" Six-names took aim. The sorcerer was shielded but the Gnomish archer had a clear shot at Jack Taylor. Dibbit fired. The arrow struck the visage of Jack Taylor in the chest. *p-Jack* clutched his chest and fell off the little escarpment and landed with a thud. He drew his last breath and changed into the increasingly familiar amorphous bipedal form.

Rudy Nine-names said, "Center shot!"

The Kobolds howled in unison.

Beeyo shouted, "Quite honestly I don't know how much longer I can hold them back."

Bailiwick said, "Not yet! I want to taunt Klarje!"

Dibbit fired again. Beeyo quickly pulled an unfortunate Kobold sergeant in front of him and into the arrow's path. Dibbit's shot struck down the Kobold sergeant.

Straight Arrow took two steps back and uttered, "That old boy's a pretty good shot!"

Bailiwick concentrated on Dibbit and sent a successful Hold Spell his way. The brave little archer dropped his bow.

Exeter sent Rhiann a message, "He's more than thirty feet away, but I don't have to tell you the sorcerer is your greatest enemy. Mayard's fear that I'd fall into an enemy's hands may quickly come to pass."

Rhiann returned the thought, "I can't block all his spells. We can't run."

When Dibbit dropped his bow, the Kobolds and highwaymen grew more brazen and stepped to the edge of the rise. Bailiwick and Beeyo strategically kept at least one Kobold between them and the Gnomes. Scores of Kobolds menacingly edged forward from front and rear of the trapped caravan.

The Man in Black taunted, "Klarje, you'll enjoy knowing that a thousand Gnomes now defend Dry Creek against an attack that is not coming. The Burgomaster will find your worthless hides in this gulley."

Bailiwick rubbed his left shoulder and added, "I'm just sorry Madam Darktop is not with you. I still owe her. Save Klarje for me. Send in your warriors!"

Beeyo screeched, "Attack!"

The Kobolds gave a yell.

Wings fluttered overhead. Two Copper Dragons swooped down over the caravan and then flew over the masses of Kobolds. The larger copper dragon grabbed an unfortunate Kobold in its claws and then dropped him unceremoniously on several of his fellows, knocking them down and disrupting their advance. A reddish creature as large as a warhorse with the body of a lion, the head of a man, three rows of sharp teeth, a trumpet like voice, two small horns, a long tail resembling that of a dragon, large spines protruding from the tip of the tail, and large wings extending from its back landed between the Kobolds to the west and the Gnomes.

On the rise Bailiwick shouted, "That's a Manticore! What the…"

Two griffons landed between the eastern Kobolds and the Gnomes. Six Copper Dragons circled the caravan. The Manticore menacingly checked the Kobolds to the west. Then wonderfully soft lyrics of a lullaby filled the air. Rhiann's eyes felt heavy.

CHAPTER 22

Cragmore

Young Iyaca Vassi awakened and found himself in a rocky grotto. He was resting on a bed with a soft mattress and pillow. Rhiann Klarje slept beside him. Rhiann's Bag of Holding was neatly packed under his left shoulder. Iyaca sat up. Other than a few scrapes and scratches, the youth was no worse for the wear. Braziers lit the room and very pleasant incenses burned. Iyaca stood and started toward Rhiann's bed.

A very pleasant feminine voice said quietly, "Please don't awaken him." Iyaca recalled the voice from the road between Dry Creek and Jack Taylor's place and stopped in his tracks. The female sat on an overstuffed chair in the corner of the chamber. She was beyond beautiful. The lovely longhaired creature was so stunning that he had to catch his breath. Long reddish-orange locks flowed down her neck and crossed over to the front of her chest, falling far below her curvaceous perfect breasts. She had…soft feathered wings that sprouted naturally from the small of her back. Her wings extended almost involuntarily, and a soft plush tail swished gently behind her as she talked. There was radiance to each beautiful hair, as though every strand had its own life. Her melodic voice was beyond description. Determining whether she was more pleasing to the eye or ear was impossible.

His mother's words had always soothed the pangs of scrapes and abrasions, which he had suffered during his play. Madam Darktop kindly assumed the role after the youth arrived in Gnome-town. But what he heard now was beyond the comfort of their most tender words. The youth would amble off a cliff should she request it.

Iyaca asked, "Where am I? Who are you?"

The soothing voice continued, "I take it you've never looked upon a siren. I'm glad you've awakened, little one. How do you feel?"

Iyaca said timidly, "I'm not sure. Am I dead?"

The siren said, "No. You survived. I've never sung to one so young and wasn't sure how it'd affect you. But it was the only way I knew to save you and Rhiann. The odds were overwhelming."

Iyaca then asked, "So your song put everybody to sleep."

Maranna said, "Yes, it was a lullaby."

Iyaca said, "Before I lost consciousness, I saw other winged beasts. Did your song put them to sleep, too?"

Maranna said, "No. Before I sang, I gave them ear plugs. The fuzzy little critters fill the ear canal, harmlessly remove ear wax, and block out all sound. Earlier I sang to a group of copper dragons and convinced them to help carry the Gnomes. The dragons feasted on the copper in the wagon when they were finished."

The siren's pheromones overwhelmed Iyaca. The youth breathed heavily, extended his left hand and touched her soft chest, allowed his hand to linger, sighed, and barely managed, "You are so… wonderful… soft… I can't stop…"

Maranna smiled, removed his hand, and said, "Yes, you can."

Iyaca most horribly wanted to touch her again. The siren held his hand away from her and said, "maybe in a few years, little one."

Iyaca sighed again and said, "Where are we, and *who* are you?"

She replied, "I am Maranna. I've travelled with Rhiann and Mayard Klarje. We are in Cragmore. It's my home and a work in progress. We are far to the east from Thynna."

Iyaca asked, "Is Rhiann OK?"

She said, "I… think he is only asleep. He's older than you, and you survived. So I think he has a pretty good chance. The lullaby affects males differently."

Iyaca's mind filled with questions but he had difficulty formulating them. He managed, "Are the others here?"

Maranna answered, "No. Only you and Rhiann."

Iyaca asked, "What happened to the others?"

Maranna replied, "You are awake now, and quite inquisitive, my little friend. You should be happy that I saved you. We'll talk more of the others when Rhiann wakes up."

Iyaca asked, "Why shouldn't I wake Rhiann up?"

Maranna answered, "I only have experience with allowing those under the lullaby influence to awaken on their own. Have some nectar."

Iyaca saw the dark amber liquid in an ornate glass decanter. The thirsty youth gulped down the fluid and said, "It's delicious."

Maranna said, "Why don't you go explore outside. My sister Serena will show you around."

Iyaca said, "Another Siren?"

Maranna answered, "Yes, she's helping me with Cragmore. You'll find more of my friends outside. Be careful. Don't go near the ledges."

A lovely green-haired siren entered the chamber and said whimsically, "He's cute. May I have him?"

Iyaca gulped.

Maranna laughed and answered, "No, Sister. Just show him around."

Serena said, "Come on, kid. I've already carried you halfway across Sagain. I won't bite you… very hard."

Iyaca gulped again.

Maranna answered, "Iyaca, you will be fine. She's only teasing."

Serena extended her hand and took Iyaca's left hand. The duo left the sleeping chamber. Rhiann continued to sleep. Serena and Iyaca walked into warm morning light sent from the distant twin suns and looked about the area. Maranna's beautiful home Cragmore was nestled upon a rocky ledge above a river that had cut a deep gorge in the mountains far to the east of Thynna. The site sat upon a roughly circular mini-plateau surrounded by sheer cliffs a least a thousand paces in height. The circular gorge appeared to have no beginning, end, or exit. The circumventing river and sheer cliffs isolated the lair. A tall rim of rocky peaks surrounded the grassy plateau. Three shadowy gunmetal gray six-legged steeds meandered about the grassy area and munched on the plush green stalks. The stalks grew back as fast as the equines ate them. The mares were larger than typical workhorses and ghostly in appearance. When he stared at them, Iyaca saw the outline of the rocky cliffs behind them. A voice appeared within his head and simply warned, "Don't stand too near the edge. An updraft might carry you over."

Iyaca jumped back and said, "She spoke to me! Inside my head!"

Serena said, "Cloudmares communicate telepathically, without spoken word. They have a powerful intrinsic Forget Spell. You won't remember seeing them… unless they want you to do so."

Iyaca said, "Rhiann used such a spell at the mines."

Serena said, "The Cloudmares' spell is more powerful and pretty much always works."

Iyaca curiously asked, "How do you remember them?"

Serena smiled and said, "The Cloudmares can choose to allow you to remember them. Urra, Syrrth, and Shyrra are great friends of Mayard Klarje. They allowed me to resist the Forget Spell effect."

Iyaca moved nearer the beautiful siren. Serena flipped her long green hair and said, "You may touch me."

Iyaca sighed. The massive Manticore stood on the fringes of the plateau and stared intently at the youth.

Rhiann Klarje moaned and turned. The light of the twin suns broke through the small window where the young sorcerer rested. Rhiann wasn't sure how long he had slept. The softness of the bed and the warmth of the Phoenix down blanket were difficult to abandon. Dreams had infiltrated his sleep. Maranna's face and her soothing voice had repeatedly appeared in his slumber, and when she spoke he felt strangely secure and warm. Rhiann stretched and sat on the side of his bed.

Maranna said with relief, "Rhiann. I'm so glad you've awakened."

Maranna sat in a large chair near his bed. Her tail swished nervously behind her and she pulled up and twirled her long reddish hair, the act exposing her right breast.

The young sorcerer blushed and asked, "Where am I?"

Maranna said, "Welcome to Cragmore, my home. I've still got a lot of work to do on it."

Rhiann said sleepily, "Maranna? How'd…where…?"

Maranna said, "Are you rested? We have much to discuss after you have fully recovered. I'll get you some nourishment."

Rhiann asked, "I think I am rested physically. In other ways I still feel like I'm having a bad nightmare. But I am really here. My hunger tells me it's not a dream. Where is Iyaca?"

Maranna sighed and said, "I can fix the hunger. Iyaca has already eaten. My sister Serena arrived for a visit and is showing him around

Cragmore. She promised to behave. It's unlikely she will, but he's too young to… never mind. Let me fetch you some nectar and waybread."

The siren left the sleeping room and returned shortly with a carafe of fluid and scrumptious looking biscuits. She placed the food on a table by Rhiann's bed. Rhiann munched on the nutritious bread and drank the delicious fruity beverage.

Rhiann finished his food and said, "Maranna, you are beautiful and I am enjoying your hospitality, but I really must I must get to the Hanging Gardens and give Uncle Mayard the sword Exeter. I've tarried too long."

Maranna said hesitantly, "Rhiann, we have much to discuss. I… I have something I must tell you, and there's no easy way. I can't sing everything away."

She stepped away again and returned with a bundle of items and an old tattered leather bag.

Rhiann frowned and muttered, "Wait… that's Uncle Mayard's hat… and holding bag… and cloak. He'd never be without them. Is he here, Maranna?"

Maranna shook her head negatively, extended her soft fingers, and softly stroked his face. The siren whispered, "Rhiann, your Uncle Mayard only lives in our memories. He passed peacefully at the Hanging Gardens. His greatest and oldest friends were with him at the end. Nona honored him with a pyre. A hundred centaurs and six Manticores trumpeted his farewell lament."

Rhiann said, "No… he said he was going to help shore up the defenses of the Gardens! That's why he wanted me to fetch the sword in his stead!"

Maranna sighed and continued, "He wanted it this way. Rhiann. He did not want you to remember him by his final weak moments. Nona stood by and comforted him. Mayard was too weak to make another journey and he knew it. His strength faded fast after you returned to the Gardens."

Rhiann sobbed, "But I should have been with him!"

Maranna said, "No, Rhiann. Again, that's the way he wanted it."

Rhiann sobbed a bit and asked, "What are Cloudmares?"

Maranna said, "Read his journal about the Cloudmares. You'll remember them the next time you see them. They carried you to the

Gardens The cloudmare's intrinsic Forget Spell is more effective than sorcerer's."

The young sorcerer did not remember traveling to the Hanging Gardens on the Cloudmares. Maranna briefly described the beasts and relayed were friends of Mayard Klarje.

Rhiann scratched his head and said, "Déjà vu… all over again. I feel like I should have known that already. But the sword, Exeter, told me to get back to The Hanging Gardens to see him again. She said he was sick."

Maranna answered, "The spirit of the blade gave you the best and most honest answer she could. She knew only of his infirmity, not the extent of it."

Rhiann said, "He told me about the battle with the bewildebeest but never talked about a serious wound. I know he was wounded by an amazon's arrow. He told me to give it to the Burgomaster of Gnome-town."

Maranna said, "The Amazon's arrow hurt only his backside and pride. The bewildebeest was about to kill or maim Nona. Mayard saved her, but the animal hit him across the scalp and partially tore his life strand, the gift from the Spinner. Once that happened, Mayard's days were numbered. He has left his possessions and legacy to you. He told me to give these to you."

Maranna opened the old tattered bag and removed rune covered journals and spell books. The bag contained untold quantity of spell components and artifacts from around Sagain. Maranna said, "Your Uncle Mayard has entrusted Magick's safekeeping to you, Rhiann Klarje. This is difficult… this epistle… Nona gave it to me. It bears his seal. I am to give it to you."

The Siren tucked her wings behind her, tried to control her bushy tail, and placed her soft hand on Rhiann's shoulder. She rethought kissing him for she feared her kiss's effect, given his youth. She gave Rhiann a rolled parchment, which was sealed with hardened wax. Mayard's seal was imprinted in the wax. Maranna stepped back. Iyaca Vassi returned to the chamber and stood by Maranna. The Siren wrapped her right wing around the youth. Iyaca's knees buckled, but he caught himself before falling. Rhiann broke the seal. Three runes formed in the air between Rhiann and Maranna.

$$Ø \infty Ø$$

The glowing runes persisted for thirteen heartbeats and faded. Rhiann wiped away a tear and began to read…

Rhiann,

It's important to preserve rarities, Rhiann. Once we lose plants or animals to extinction, we cannot get them back. After the Dawn of Magick, little dragon-like beasts called shypokes flourished. Unfortunately, they were rather defenseless and easy to catch. Compound this by the facts that they tasted good and their bones and eggshells were valued as spell material components, the little blighters were driven to extinction. Sagain lost many species as a result of the cataclysm that awakened Magick. However, we gained others. Greedy and short-sighted folks have led to our losing many again. Plants, trees, animals, and the defenseless need our protection.

Our world is changing. Nona, Mors, and Decima's influence fades. The sorcerers and leaders of Thynna evermore abandon reason. Voices in the Council praise even the scoundrel Bailiwick and call for his return. This would be a baneful thing for Magick. I'm sure your travels with my Shapechanger friend *p-Elliott* acquainted you with the conflicts and intolerances of the north. I regretted sending you, but I trusted no one else. If you are reading this letter, then Maranna found and brought you to safety and I'm certain has presented you my heirlooms. I leave our world with many worries. Sorcerers are tapping into unexplored realms of Magick. I've cautioned, but my words fell on deaf ears. Arcane forces take advantage of foolhardy spell casting, enter, and threaten our world from without, while Thynna's arrogance threatens Sagain from within. The Three Sisters and their folk in the Hanging Gardens refuse to capitulate to Thynna's demands. After you and Elliott left the Hanging Gardens, calls went out to all the wonders of the Veldt and other Old Ones sanctuaries. General Chiron now commands a great army. His centaur brethren organize the defenses of the Gardens. I had many sessions with Chiron and the Three Sisters, but I grew weaker. I use my last energies to compose this epistle. My nephew, Sagain has many great reassures and traditions, many of which predated the Dawn of Magick. Our Seven Wonders must be preserved, and if they cannot be preserved, they must not be forgotten. I'd have liked to share them with other worlds, other civilizations. I've dreamed of many. I challenge you to finish my work, to accomplish hat I could not. I have dreamed of a Source of Magick. Within this source there is a means to travel between worlds and times. I never found the source.

My nephew, seek the source of Magick.

Hold true to the spirit of Grayness at all times.

Guard well and preserve Sagain's treasures. If you cannot save them, find a means to carry them away.

Try to be a voice of reason in Thynna, but don't exhaust your energies in the city of Magick. Therein may have been my greatest mistake. Your mother Caye and father Kurth are good people, but they are too embroiled in the affairs of Thynna. Expect no help from them; in fact, they'll resist your efforts. Likewise, the Three Sisters and most Old Ones mistrust Magick and resent everything that is Thynna. Like the two toughest kids on the playground, eventually Thynna and the Hanging Gardens are going to fight. The warring peoples of the north… I don't know what direction they'll follow. But you have a reliable resource in Maranna. She professes neutrality in most affairs of the world. Try not to get involved in the affairs of the north. Gnomes and Kobolds will always hate each other, and Dwarves will always do anything for a profit. I thank you for retrieving the treasure from the mines. The spirit of the sword is a true sister of Grayness. She has a role… I… don't understand it. Burgomaster Storming Norman gifted me the odd ore. It had a connection to the Source of Magick. I started dreaming of the source when the ore came into my possession. In fact, the heartstone came to me after a dream. The sword will be a companion to you. I have left journals detailing my travels in the Veldt. I've looked in all the Seven Wonders for the Source of Magick. Time is near… I'm sorry to burden you with my unfulfilled task. My body is dying, but my love for you lives on, and my love of Magick and Sagain lives on in you.

Most fondly,
Your Uncle Mayard
MK

Ǿ ∞ Ǿ

Rhiann held the thick vellum loosely in his hand. A tear trickled down his cheek and crossed the heart-shaped, cherry-red birthmark. Maranna and Iyaca stood quietly. A second siren with long green tresses entered and stood by Maranna. Serena shared many of her sister's traits.

Rhiann said, "I hardly know where to start."

Maranna replied, "You may stay at Cragmore as long as you want. I still have lots of work to do. Serena has agreed to help me."

The green-haired siren said, "You spoke truthfully sister. He bears Mayard's mark. He's quite pretty, too. May I kiss him just once?"

Rhiann blushed.

Maranna said, "Not a wise move, sister."

Iyaca Vassi edged toward the shapely Serena and said, "I wouldn't mind if you kissed me."

Serena quipped, "Watch it, Kid, you don't know what you're asking for."

Iyaca now blushed.

Rhiann asked, "The last thing I remember is the arrival of the Manticore. He was fearsome. Next thing I know I'm nodding off and we're here. What happened after we left the road to Dry Creek?"

Maranna said, "My friends and the copper dragons carried the sleeping Gnomes to Dry Creek. Venla said the place was teeming with Gnomes. The Gnomes in your party will sleep for a couple of days and then wake up. The dragons carried the men to their cabin in the woods. Venla found a bloke tied to a tree and released him. Said his name was Jack Taylor."

Rhiann rolled Mayard's parchment, applied a lump of the old sealing wax, muttered a Heat Spell, sealed the letter, and stored it in his ever-filling Bag of Holding. He straightened his back, wiped a solitary tear from his face, and asked of the Siren, "Are you sure my friends are safe?"

Maranna brushed back her long red hair and fluttered her plush multicolored wings. Both were mannerisms she oft employed when asked an uncomfortable question. She replied, "Well, Rhiann, normally I don't concern myself with the affairs of men, Gnomes, and Kobolds. My concern was saving you. Gnomes live in the wild north and deal with danger on a daily basis, so I can't assure their safety. On the other hand, Venla Faxxine assured me that his entourage carried the Gnomes and merchants to the relative safety of Dry Creek. If you'd care to ask him yourself, he's outside. He oft visits the Cloudmares and enjoys the grasses of Cragmore."

Iyaca timidly confirmed, "The Manticore is outside."

Maranna said, "Yes, he is my true friend."

Rhiann asked, "If the Manticore and the others carried the Gnomes and merchants, who brought Iyaca and me to Cragmore?"

Maranna sighed and said, "Serena and I carried you."

Rhiann scratched his head and said, "I'm remembering everything about the journey to the Hanging Gardens now. The Cloudmares! And you! When we traveled to the Hanging Gardens with Uncle Mayard and *p-Elliott*, you said you weren't a beast of burden and refused to carry folk, particularly males."

Maranna grumbled, "First time in over a thousand years, but I promised my old friend Mayard that I'd look after you. Don't make too much of it."

Rhiann queried, "How'd you know where we were?"

Maranna answered, "I've shadowed your movements. We didn't intervene in the first Kobold attack because it was just a diversionary attack."

Iyaca asked, "Why doesn't the Manticore enter?"

Maranna said, "Venla is very considerate. He knew you'd be sleeping. It's always safest to awakened from the effects of a Siren's lullaby gradually and at your own paced. I just sing people to sleep. I am an expert on waking them up. Now that you're awake, I'll ask him to come in."

CHAPTER 23

Manticore's Version

The Manticore Venla Faxxine squeezed through the entry and entered the spacious living area of Cragmore.

Maranna said, "Venla, Rhiann and Iyaca have questions about the affair in the woods near Dry Creek. Will you fill them in."

The Manticore Venla's deep voice contrasted with the Siren's melodic tone. The massive Old One always sounded impatient. Venla Faxxine said, "Well, after you and Serena left with Rhiann and Iyaca for Cragmore. I took charge in the woods near Dry Creek. Everything went smoothly for the most part. The six Copper Dragons remained under your Charming Song. I grabbed the Gnomish Captain Longbeard, who remained under the effect of the wizard's Hold Spell and awake."

Young Iyaca interrupted, "He wasn't asleep! Why?"

Rhiann explained, "It's Magick. The Hold Spell kept Longbeard from doing anything else, including fall asleep. The spell's duration depends on the level, the power, of the sorcerer who cast it. So Longbeard saw and heard everything."

Venla Faxxine gruffly cleared his throat and said, "If I might continue. Yes, he was truly 'held.' I grabbed this Longbeard bloke and ordered Copper Dragons to carry Gnomes to Dry Creek. One grabbed the archer Dibbit. An unlucky dragon grabbed the wagon driver."

Iyaca blurted, "Donovan Eleven-names! The wizard placed a Hold Spell on him, too."

The Manticore grunted, "The blighter faked being held. Suppose he wanted to surprise the attackers. But he wasn't 'held' so he did fall asleep. The young copper dragon pinched him a bit too hard and woke him up. He played 'possum' and pretended to be asleep whilst the dragon carried him. When the dragon landed and dropped him on the ground, the sneaky Gnome popped up and shouted, 'No beast is going to get away with carrying Donovan Eleven-names like a sack of feed.' The Dragon initially just tried to get away, but the Gnome fought him on the field in front of the Dry Creek stockade, beaned the dragon with his hammer, and broke the effect of your Charming Song. Then they really had a go. The other five dragons didn't know whether to **** or go blind. Your charm commanded them to carry the combatants to their respective lairs, but they saw a colleague embroiled in conflict with a tenacious Gnome. Bottom line was the power of your charm overpowered the dragons' instincts and they stayed out of it and just watched. It was the meanest Gnome any of us had seen. To be honest I got caught up in watching the fight. Gnomes were charging out of the gate to help their comrade. After receiving three or four knocks to the head, the copper dragon beat a hasty retreat. The wagon-driver Gnome directed his friends to gather their sleepy colleagues and started dragging them inside the walls. The five remaining dragons and I returned to the sleepers and picked up another load of Gnomes. The griffons carried the highwaymen to their not-so-secret cabin in the woods. The copper dragons had always known about it. On the first trip they released some bloke who was tied to a. tree. He muttered something about 'pay back' and an imposter, but we already knew the Gnomish archer had smitten his doppelganger. The Griffons sent him on his way and returned for the other highwaymen. After two loads, the griffons helped us carry Gnomes and merchants to Dry Creek. Chaos ruled, but we dropped off our cargo uneventfully. Hauling Gnomes is not duty I'd recommend. I wouldn't do it for many folks."

Rhiann asked, "What of the sorcerer?"

Venla Faxxine replied, "Let sleeping sorcerers lie. I didn't want to wake him up."

Rhiann said, "You likely saved the lot of us. I was hard pressed to counteract Bailiwick's spells, and we were so outnumbered."

Venla sighed, "Yes, and in so doing, we violated unwritten rules of neutrality. I… we have new enemies."

Iyaca asked, "What happened to the Kobolds?"

Maranna curiously asked, "What does that concern you? They were going to kill you."

Iyaca shrugged.

The Manticore continued, "They were too many. We left them sleeping in the woods and on the field. The dragons may have eaten a few once Maranna's charming song wore off. Gnomes... I carried. Kobolds... not so much. They'll wake up with only each other to fight."

Maranna answered, "We saved Rhiann... and you, Iyaca. I didn't want either the Kobolds or Gnomes to gain advantage because of my interference. So Venla and the others moved the Gnomes. After hearing Venla's tale of the wagon-driver Donovan, I'm thinking we may have saved the thousand Kobolds. It's hard to tell who'll wake up first after hearing a siren's lullaby."

Serena twirled a strand of her green hair and smugly said, "Some never wake up."

Maranna snipped, "Sister, that's not usually our intent. Iyaca, eventually the Kobolds and Gnomes we separated on the field today are going to fight. No action on our part will change their enmity toward one another. If a predator stumbled upon the disabled sorcerer that stood with the Kobolds and highwaymen, so be it."

Burgomaster Storming Norman Twenty-four names Darktop stamped the ground in Dry Creek's quadrangle. His large force was strategically deployed and ready for an attack. His legion used their digging abilities and constructed redoubts composed of semicircles of raised dirt thirty paces in front of the east and western gates of Dry Creek. Reinforcements swarmed over wall walk and guard towers. Scouting parties had risked entering the woods to look for Kobolds and found little sign that their adversaries had been here. Nonetheless ambush parties were set up in the woods. The folk of Dry Creek busily repaired the damages fraught by the Kobolds' earlier attack. The Burgomaster and Madam Darktop finished preparations as afternoon headed into night. Several hours passed uneventfully. Then at dusk a watcher in the tower shouted, "Winged creatures approach! Dragons!"

Storming Norman Twenty-four names charged up the wall stairs and shouted, "Not to worry! Hold your fire! It's only a gaggle of Copper Dragons! Get some copper ore ready!"

The guard in the tower shouted, "One is much bigger! They bear burdens!"

Storming Norman shouted, "Wait! That's not a dragon! It's a Manticore! It carries...my stars! Longbeard Nineteen-names!"

The sentry yelled, "They are getting closer! They all carry Gnomes, and the Gnomes are not moving! Shall I fire?"

Norman hesitated. Then five dragons and the Manticore landed about fifty paces from the palisade, unloaded their motionless cargo, and flew upward. A sixth dragon landed, and the Gnome it carried stood up, began shouting, and whacked the dragon up the side of its head with his hammer. The dragon staggered backward, shook its head in bewilderment, and then swung its tail mightily and knocked the Gnome down. The Gnome jumped up and grabbed the dragon's tail.

Storming Norman shouted, "That's Donovan Eleven-names! I'm adding dragon-buster to his titles! Those in the eastern redoubt! Go help him!"

The young copper dragon shook free. The Manticore and five other dragons circled overhead. Gnomes in the hastily constructed fortification rushed toward the dragon and Donovan. The Manticore growled a command to the young dragon on the ground that was engaging the Gnome, but the beast ignored him. The Gnome Donovan was holding his own and easily dodged the young inexperienced dragon's attempts to bite. Donovan Eleven...twelve-names now with dragon-buster... expertly delivered three blows in succession with his hammer. The dragon recoiled and puffed out its chest. Norman's troops neared the fray. From the allure Norman shouted, "It's going to breathe!" Before the copper dragon exhaled, Donovan walloped it up the side of the head and redirected its gooey spittle to the ground near him. The acidic breath weapon merely befouled some grass and dissolved the tip of Donovan's boot. The dragon thought better of further action and flew away toward the Copper Mountains to the west. The Manticore and other five copper dragons flew northwest and away from Dry Creek and toward Jack's Refuge.

Donovan Eleven-names shouted, "You've ruined my boot! Come back and fight, you shameless wyrm!"

Norman's troops arrived. Donovan and others carried Longbeard, who was awake but unable to move or speak, Sergeant Rudy Nine-names, Corporal Alden Eight-names, archer Dibbit Six-names, who also was awake but unable to move or speak, a guard with six names, and Corporal Roro Seven-names into Dry Creek. Donovan relayed details of the battle to Storming Norman, Madam Darktop, and their entourage. In a little while the Manticore and dragons returned with more sleeping Gnomes. The winged beasts deposited their sleeping cargo a safe distance from the palisade and were soon away again. Griffons joined the Manticore and Dragons in the next load. Soon all of Longbeard's party including two snoozing merchants were inside the walls of Dry Creek. Storming Norman's technique for awakening the sleepers was a quick slap to the face. Some of the younger Gnomes, those with fewer than six names, required several smacks to awaken. Many awakened with headaches, dizziness, and disorientation. No manner of smacking roused Longbeard and the archer Dibbit. The sorcerer Bailiwick's Hold Spells remained in effect. Longbeard saw everything but was unable to tell Norman about the events. His naked ears were tortured by the siren's sweetly singing, but he was unable to fall asleep. However, Donovan detailed everything that happened up to the point he fell asleep. Storming Norman Darktop was particularly incensed by the deception and whole situation with *p-Mayard*. Mayard Klarje had enabled the Shapechanger to gain Gnome-town's trust and access to the conurbation's innermost ranks. The Gnomish leaders felt betrayed by their sorcerer friend. Most Gnomes had little regard for Magick and sorcerers to begin with. Mayard Klarje had slowly gained their trust over long periods of time and had assisted Longbeard, Norman, and their predecessors in many sticky matters, including the capture and defeat of numerous highwaymen. But on this day Old Ones had filled the skies and consorted with dragons. The renegade sorcerer Bailiwick had wreaked havoc and was still at large. The highwaymen the Fearsome Foursome had not been captured or killed, and huge numbers of Kobolds remained in the area. Norman was now in need of a sorcerer to remove the spells on Longbeard and Dibbit. Cecelia Darktop's slippers only worked to return her to Gnome-town. They were a one-way ticket. The Gnomes could do little more than hunker down. A few hours passed and no attacks came. Captain Longbeard and archer Dibbit remained immobilized but their bodily functions worked. Madam Darktop teased it was akin to caring for babes. A while after the Manticore's lot delivered the last of the sleeping Gnomes, Longbeard's steeds galloped into the field before Dry Creek, led by the halvsie Lightnin Bug.

Burgomaster Storming Norman Twenty-four names Darktop judged, "The Klarjes are either gone or were never here. Whatever the case we are fresh out of sorcerers. We will have to get Longbeard and Dibbit to Thynna to have the spells removed from them. Promotions are in order. Donovan, you are now Donovan twelve-names, with wagon-driver and dragon-wrestler now added. Longbeard is Longbeard twenty-names with 'stone-face' as his new moniker."

Dry Creek, reinforced by a thousand Gnome soldiers, remained on high alert.

CHAPTER 24

Aftermath

The Man in Black felt a pinch to his left leg and jumped up in alarm. He was lying in the dirt in the woods in front of the porch of his hidden cabin in the woods. A young Copper Dragon had a firm grip on his left leg. The highwayman took a deep breath and readied for the worst, when the small dragon released his leg and abruptly flew away. Two griffons and another dragon were depositing the still sleeping Red-headed Stranger, Waymore, and Straight Arrow on the ground nearby. These beasts also simply snorted and flew away. The last thing the highwaymen's leader remembered was melodious sound filling the air. The Man in Black went to his colleagues and awakened them with difficulty. He used Storming Norman's technique of repeated face slaps. The Fearsome Foursome suffered headaches and disorientation, but the quartet managed to make their way into the cabin. The Man in Black collapsed in his chair and rubbed his sore leg. Straight Arrow peered out the window. None of their underling rogues had returned. and notably Jack Taylor was no longer tied to the tree. Straight Arrow gripped his rapier and watched intently. However, the winged beasts did not return. The Kobolds and Bailiwick were nowhere to be seen.

The Man in Black unleashed a chain of expletives and growled, "Cursed Old Ones! Cost me my chance to even things with that ****** Mayard Klarje! And to think! I turned down an offer to serve with Thynna's mercenaries against them. The offer came with full pardon and better pay than we are scrounging out of these woods. Mayard Klarje has gotten the better of me again! He's probably relaxing at the

Hanging Gardens and enjoying himself! **** every Old One! I pledge my blade to their downfall!"

Straight Arrow rubbed his throbbing temples and timidly noted, "But you hate Thynna, Boss! By joining their mercenaries you'll be helping the sorcerers."

The Man in Black muttered, "I hate Mayard Klarje and his progeny most of all! We'll accept Thynna's pardon and take her money. We'll serve as it behooves us, and right now it behooves me to take vengeance against Klarje and the Old Ones! Keep your eyes open! The winged vermin may return!"

The Red Headed Stranger asked, "What about Jack Taylor?"

The Man in Black answered, "He'll seek vengeance. That's just another reason to make ourselves scarce around these parts!"

Bailiwick eased his left eye open. The fading light of the twin suns made him wince. His temples throbbed mercilessly and the hard rock beneath him stiffened his back. Kobolds were laying all around him. The sorcerer painfully raised his head and scanned the area. The Gnomes, merchants, young Klarje, the steeds, and beasts of burden were gone. Both wagons remained. The wagon bound for Thynna still carried all its treasures, but the second wagon had been stripped of all its copper ore. The Man in Black and his fellow Fearsome Foursome comrades were missing. The Kobold Chieftain Beeyo snored loudly.

Bailiwick stood and scanned the skies and saw only a solitary Copper Dragon slowly circling in the distance. Smoke was no longer rising from Dry Creek. The hour of the day told him he had slept several hours. Last things he remembered were the appearance of the winged beasts and melodic voice on the air. He resisted the urge to sleep and mumbled Dispel Magick to no avail. The sorcerer muttered to no one, "****** Old Ones! Mayard Klarje remains my greatest enemy, but now my anger for the Old Ones and Hanging Gardens surpasses my ire with the Council of Thynna."

Bailiwick let the sleeping Kobolds lie and scampered off the rock. He awakened his horse and whistled for his familiar Windy. The ferret had served him well. It detected the scents of Klarje's entourage long before Beeyo's Kobold scouts had seen them. Now Windy's senses told the sorcerer the way was clear to his hidden abode. Bailiwick cursed his dependence on the Highwaymen and Kobolds. He took some choice gems from the wagon. They'd come in handy for his future plans.

Sagain's skies blessed the forest with a rain shower sometime after the sorcerer's departure. The rain awakened a few Kobolds, who in turn awakened their many comrades. Beeyo yowled from the pain of his headache. The early awakeners had first choice at the bounty from the mines on the wagon. Many fights ensued. Eventually Beeyo took charge and most of the best stones.

The griffon dropped Jack Taylor off a short distance from Jack's Refuge and flew away. Jack didn't resist the big beast's efforts to pick him up and carry him. It'd have been futile in the first place, and secondly, the beast had released him from his bondage. Jack preferred to stick around and have a go at his doppelganger and the highwayman, but that option was not placed before him. Now he was at least in familiar surroundings. The proprietor made his way through the woods to the exit point of the secret passage into his establishment. His henchmen were not at their posts. Given recent events Taylor was going to be hard pressed to know who was really himself. The doppelganger gained power by replacing Jack's trusted helpers. Jack went to the rocky outcropping behind two thyme trees and manipulated a section of the rock. The entry to the secret passage opened. Jack entered and went down the first false passage and avoided the trap. He retrieved his long blade and made his way to the tavern. Behind the closed door he listened and heard his top guard's voice. Jack triggered the opening mechanism and the secret door opened.

Top guard said, "Jack, where have you been? We've had all kinds of trouble, but business has been good. Thanks to Madam Darktop and Gnome-town."

Jack nodded to his number one and said, "I want to hear all about it. First I've got to take care of something."

Jack Taylor walked over to the bar and asked the barkeep for a mug of ale. The barkeep started to fill a mug from the tap. Jack Taylor abruptly thrust his long sword into the barkeep's chest. The barkeep moaned, shimmered briefly, and collapsed onto the floor in a bipedal amorphous mass. Two Kobolds seated in the corner stood and made for the door. Taylor shouted, "Stop those two!"

Top guard threw his knife into the first Kobold. Again the Kobold fell and changed into its Shapechanger form. Two miners caught the second Kobold short of the door. The p-Kobold delivered a wicked bite to the miner's arm, but Taylor made its way over and ran the Shapechanger-Kobold through. Another featureless bipedal form fell on the floor.

Taylor growled. "Get this trash out of my establishment and send word to Thynna, Gnome-town, and Low Gap that I am in need of a barkeep. We have three guards to attend on the outside, Turbo, Hatchet, and Diamond."

Top guard said, "Might explain a couple of defections, Boss. How'd you know?"

Taylor said, "Bastard laughed at me while I was tied to a tree. My former Barkeep, Turbo, Hatchet, and Diamond aren't as lucky as I am. Not sure why they kept me alive. One thing's for sure. They going to wish they had killed me."

Top Guard took some friends and dispatched of the three doppelgangers on the wall walk. Jack Taylor downed several mugs of ale and sharpened his blade.

CHAPTER 25

Return to Thynna

Maranna's home provided safety and comfort for Rhiann and Iyaca. The siren and her sister Serena, the Cloudmares Urra, Syrrth, and Shyrra, and the Manticore Venla Faxxine constantly monitored the skies above Cragmore. Rhiann and Iyaca slept for the better part of two days and replenished their bodies with waybread and nectar. A young man with multicolored hair appeared and brought numerous fruits of the forest and news of the realms. His comings and goings were quite subtle and oft accompanied by small gusts of wind. Maranna called him Eyerthrin. Rhiann asked to meet him.

On the fourth morning since his arrival Rhiann awakened and went into the living area. Iyaca, Maranna, Serena, and the young man Eyerthrin sat in the room and conversed.

Maranna said, "Rhiann, I want you to meet Eyerthrin. He is from the far north. He brings us fresh fruit today."

Rhiann was taken back by the man's glistening hair and deep blue eyes. The youth extended his hand and accepted Eyerthrin's in return. He noted the man's strong grip and said, "Are you a sorcerer, Eyerthrin?"

Eyerthrin said, "Pleased to meet you, Rhiann. I see you indeed bear the mark of the Klarjes. Sagain owes a great debt to your forebears, particularly your Uncle Mayard. Though I never made his acquaintance, I am well aware of his deeds. I am touched by Magick, though it's stretching it to call me a sorcerer."

Rhiann said, "I thought you might travel with the Fly Spell. I hear you leave and arrive. The Cloudmares and sirens fly noiselessly and I've grown to recognize Venla."

Eyerthrin smiled and said, "I fly, but I don't use a spell."

Rhiann said, "You lack wings."

Eyerthrin laughed, "In this bipedal form, yes. It's a bit hard to navigate in my natural form. I am a Prismatic Dragon, Rhiann."

Rhiann said, "I've read of your ilk in Thynna's libraries. But I've never seen one… at least not until today. Your transformation spell is remarkably effective., I'd say as effective as a Shapechanger. You look like a man. How small can you become?"

Eyerthrin laughed, "This is about as small as I can get. But I can become invisible. My ilk has scouted Thynna for a long time, but we haven't gotten involved. Yet. I recently spent some time in the market square. Not a lot of good vibes coming from the city of Magick these days."

Rhiann fought back a tear and asked, "Eyerthrin, has word of my Uncle Mayard's death reached Thynna?"

Eyerthrin glanced at Maranna as though he sought her permission and then spoke, "No, Rhiann. But there is growing unrest. Many sorcerers want him to return to address goings on in the council of Thynna. Your father Kurth's voice is seldom heard. The general ill will toward Old Ones persists. Resentment of the Three Sisters' influence grows. The Council of Thynna moves precariously close to war with the Three Sisters and the Old Ones. More mercenaries arrive daily. The mercenaries are confined to barracks constructed outside the city proper. The Council of Thynna offers pardons and payment for service. Some rather insalubrious blokes have turned up. I actually heard your Uncle's name besmirched."

Rhiann said, "I must go to Thynna."

Maranna asked, "What can you do? Rhiann, you are young. Your Uncle Mayard grew stronger as he grew older. His dreams bettered his Magick. He entrusted his journals to you. They detail his studies and travels. Study them. Get stronger before you challenge the Council of Thynna and debate the Three Sisters. Most of our Old One colleagues adhere to neutrality and avoid getting involved in the affairs of men and sorcerers. This Magick thing is relatively new to all of us. Recent events in the northern lands muddy your course. You won't be welcomed in Gnome-town and Flat Rock. The Burgomaster is an unforgiving little bloke. Mayard's relationship with Nona formed the basis of his influence in the Hanging Gardens. Now the Three Sisters will stubbornly oppose Thynna. Mayard balanced the Council of Thynna. Without him... let's just say I worry about your facing their ruthlessness. Stay in Cragmore."

Rhiann replied, "My uncle entrusted the Klarje legacy to me! His legacy! My legacy! It's a lot more than a red birthmark! Burgomaster Storming Norman and Baron Albie Kirkey provide strong leadership for their communities and I respect them and understand why they'd be angry with Uncle Mayard and me. Uncle Mayard could have smoothed things out with them. He could at least temper the aggressiveness of the Council of Thynna and act as a go between for Thynna and the Hanging Gardens. I need Uncle Mayard! I share the mark of the Klarjes, but I'm not capable of the Mimicking Spell that he used to look like me. Had *p-Mayard* not fallen in the battle! His copy of Uncle Mayard was perfect. Eyerthrin, your man-visage is convincing. Might you become Uncle Mayard?"

Eyerthrin smiled and answered, "No, Rhiann, I can only be Eyerthrin. This is my appearance in bipedal form. It is what it is. I'm not a Shapechanger. I also lack your Uncle's command of Magick, though I dabble in it a bit. My ilk has intrinsic capabilities, such as the invisibility I mentioned. Long ago our leaders opted to observe and not attempt to alter Thynna's course. I'm scarcely a thousand years old and lack the age and knowledge of my elders, but Maranna says you are a person of character, so I'll support you howsoever I can. I've many duties that I've neglected and must return to them. I'll check in, Maranna. Good luck, Rhiann Klarje."

The tall rainbow-haired man respectfully bowed to Maranna and Serena and bade them farewell. He shook Rhiann's hand and gave Rhiann a wondrous scintillating dragon scale and said, "I don't freely part with these, but occasionally I shed one. It'll come in handy as a spell component. Now I'll say good-bye." Eyerthrin exited the room.

Serena said, "Come Iyaca, let's see Eyerthrin off."

Eyerthrin extended his arms as far as he could reach in both directions. He inhaled, bowed his head, and touched his chin to his chest. He then lifted up his head, bent his neck into full extension, and exhaled. Scintillating lights surrounded him. His tall muscular frame shimmered in the lights, paled to a man-sized white light, and changed to a repeating pattern of brilliant lights. The man-sized form slowly expanded to a great-multicolored sphere. The expanding sphere gradually acquired a form with a massive head, four powerful legs, two great wings, an immense body, and a long serpentine tail. The large roughly reptilian shape briefly flashed many colors and solidified to the form of the young prismatic dragon.

The prismatic dragon was a wondrous sight. His scales glowed with all the colors of the rainbow. The beast was the height of several men and the mass of many horses. The dragon's sparkling eyes made available a window to his great wisdom.

Transformation for the prismatic dragon was an innate ability, not a spell. Eyerthrin and his ilk had the ability to change their size and shape. Their weight decreased proportionately when they assumed their smaller size. If they got smaller, they weighed less, too. Density, weight, and mass were measures of Nature, not Magick. Dragons were creatures of Magick. But even Magick had limitations. The dragon could not become much smaller than his favorite man-sized form that enabled him to walk the halls of buildings, stroll the streets of towns, and ascend stairs. In his glorious dragon state, he attained a length of eighty feet and stood twenty feet tall at the shoulders with his great neck extending another fifteen feet. Innumerable scales of many sizes and shapes covered his body. The largest were about a cubit (20.6 inches) in length and width, while the smallest were the size of the tip of Nona's sewing needle. Everyone was every color, one color, and no color; each and every one of the scales changed repeatedly to a colorless shimmering reflective surface, any one color of the prism or rainbow after a summer storm, or a multitude of colors.

Serena's eyes mirrored the Dragon's scales. The siren stroked his powerful foreleg and marveled at the softness and warmth of the scales, a feature unique to the prismatic dragon ilk. Eyerthrin inhaled and took flight.

Iyaca said, "He makes quite an exit, doesn't he?"

Serena laughed and then took Iyaca for another walk around Cragmore. Inside Maranna and Rhiann heard the ghostly neigh of the Cloudmares outside followed by the sound of the beating of great wings. The glimmer of brilliant light of all colors of the rainbow streamed through the open door and mimicked Dancing Lights and Fairie Fire dweomers.

Maranna closed the door and then left Rhiann alone in his bedchamber. The young sorcerer gripped the again sealed epistle from his Uncle Mayard. Mayard Klarje's tattered hat, cloak, and worn bag of Holding sat by Rhiann's bag on the floor. Mayard's bag contained many rarities including rare spell components such as a goodly number of irreplaceable fossilized shypoke eggshells, phoenix feathers, red diamonds, unicorn tears, which Mayard had accumulated over time. Rhiann placed the prismatic dragon scale gifted by Eyerthrin in the bag of holding. The silence in the chamber brought back the silence created by the Kobolds' lances in the fight that cost the Shapechanger p-Mayard his life. The subsequent encounter with the sorcerer Bailiwick, Kobolds, and outlaws brought to light the enemies' hatred of Mayard and all he stood for. Along with his collection of rarities Mayard had passed the torch to Rhiann. How might Rhiann with his youth and inexperience succeed where the learned Mayard had failed? Thynna, the Old Ones, the peoples of the North were more conflicted than ever. Sorcerers grew more powerful and stretched the boundaries of Magick without considering consequences. Had word of Mayard's death reached Thynna? What impact would his death have? His words had fallen on deaf ears of late, but his presence tempered the course of the Council of Thynna. Common folk of Thynna still had great respect for Mayard, as indicated by the monument in the courtyard before the council building. Now Mayard's letter warned of little support from Thynna's leaders. Still, Rhiann felt the need to return to the city of Magick and plead Mayard's case for peace with the Hanging Gardens and the Old Ones.

Although the Hanging Gardens likely represented his only source of allies, Rhiann missed his family most horribly. The context of his Uncle's death deepened his being alone. Maranna and Serena's beauty and sensuality did not equal his mother Caye's loving touch. Rhiann finally found sleep. Grayness left him undisturbed. When he awakened, the young sorcerer made the difficult decision to leave Cragmore and hazard a trip to Thynna. First came the problem of arranging transportation. Shouldn't be a problem with so many Old Ones capable of flight hanging around Maranna's home. He left his cozy bed and went to the common area. Maranna sat with Iyaca and gently brushed his long sandy locks.

Maranna shared Caye's ability to look into Rhiann's eyes and see into his mind, it seemed. The siren said, "You've decided to go to Thynna."

Rhiann answered simply, "I must."

Maranna said, "I worry for your safety. The mark of the Klarjes no longer assures respect in the city of Magick. Eyerthrin reported your Uncle Mayard's enemies have grown more powerful and vocal in his prolonged absence. Mayard's well-known fondness for the Three Sisters and the Hanging Gardens has alienated many sorcerers. It's been quite a while since his last address to the Council of Thynna, and you and I know that was his last address."

Rhiann said, "I must go in his stead."

Maranna said, "I expected you to come to this conclusion. Before you make your final decision, there's one more voice I want you to hear."

Soft footsteps shuffled into the room. Rhiann looked up and saw lovely Decima in a white robe standing near the entryway.

Rhiann said, "Decima, why have you left the Hanging Gardens in these uncertain times?"

Decima walked over to Rhiann and softly rubbed the heart-shaped, cherry-red birthmark on his left chin. She purred, "I wanted to see you. I arrived on a flying centaur named Margaret. How'd you think your Uncle's things got to Cragmore?"

Rhiann said, "I just assumed Maranna retrieved them."

Decima said, "No, twas I. I brought his things and then had to return to the Gardens. That was before you arrived. Then I heard through Eyerthrin that you were here."

Iyaca said, "Eyerthrin certainly gets around."

Decima replied, "Eyerthrin's ilk is always welcomed in the Hanging Gardens. He is a reliable source of news. To be honest he helps keep us apprised of goings on in Thynna. Rhiann, don't go to Thynna! The Council of Thynna had grown to pay little heed to your Uncle Mayard's words. Nona. Mors, and I fear they will totally ignore your pleas."

Rhiann said, "I must go and carry on his work. Perhaps the Council of Thynna has not learned my Uncle's fate. I'll say my words are his words."

Decima cautioned, "The Council of Thynna has many eyes and ears, and I'm not just talking about familiars. Flight and subterfuge are not restricted to Old One ilks. Just as we spy on them, the Council also has knowledge of the goings on in the Hanging Gardens. Commander Chiron's defenses guard against frontal and broad scale attacks. The skies over the Gardens are easily penetrated. Maranna proved that when she interrupted us when you and I were walking in the Gardens."

Maranna interrupted, "Good thing I came along."

Decima retorted, "That's a matter for debate. Bottom line is that Thynna may well know about your Uncle Mayard's passing. Eyerthrin's forays into Thynna only scratches the surface of the city's cleverness."

Rhiann said, "I am well aware that all portals to the chambers of the Council Tower building in the inner ward are guarded by Magick Mouth and other protective spells that will detect invisible beings and non-sorcerers. As good as p-Mayard was at being Elliot and mimicking others, he never gained access to the innermost chambers."

Decima added, "Nor has Eyerthrin been able to penetrate the security."

Rhiann continued, "Decima, it means a lot to me that you returned to Cragmore, but I must carry on my Uncle Mayard's work, and I can't do it here. Every passing day sees the Council of Thynna grow more powerful and defiant."

Decima said, "Know, Rhiann, that I care for you deeply, as deeply as my sister Nona cared for your uncle. She shared the spinning of her distaff with Mayard, but this did not protect Mayard in his encounter with the bewildebeest. Likewise, I have given my 'lock of life' to you. It does not shelter you from danger and physical harm."

Rhiann said resolutely, "What I am seeing today… your friendship and caring, Decima, the sirens Maranna and Serena's beauty and grace, the Manticore Venla's power, the Cloudmares, the winged Centaur, the beautiful prismatic dragon… everyone's loyalty! Old Ones have much to give our world and deserve respect and tolerance. I understand my Uncle Mayard's liking you. He respected Magick and used it judiciously. As much as he loved Magick, he loved Sagain more. His eyes sparkled whenever he talked of the wonders of the world. I have spent the last several days reading his journals. When I read his words, I see the sparkle in his eyes in my mind. I must treat with the Council of Thynna, Old Ones within and outside the Hanging Gardens, and the peoples of the north,"

Serena quipped, "Listen to the young philosopher! You'd best temper your enthusiasm. There are just as many Old Ones that'd eat you if they got a chance! Gnomes and Dwarves are crude little folk. They always poke fun at our tails and are forever looking to see if I have a hollowed out back." The green-haired siren proceeded to spin around, spread her feathery wings and flipped her tail to the side to reveal her smooth firm backside. She continued, "How's that for a butt?"

Young Iyaca gulped and said, "It certainly doesn't look like a hollow tree!"

Maranna scolded, "Sister, youths are present! Behave! I was rather enjoying Rhiann's discourse. Continue, Rhiann."

Rhiann pulled his gaze away from Serena's curvaceous posterior and said, "I must continue Uncle Mayard's search for the Source of Magick. His journals confirm his resolve that it exists and finding the source of Magick is the key to Sagain's survival, or at least her continuation. If I'm given the chance, I must explore the seven wonders of the Veldt. I hope that my dreams will guide me. I beseech Grayness for knowledge! The first steps of my journeys must carry me to Thynna. I lack the ability to leave Cragmore on my own power."

Decima said, "Nona was right when she said there is a lot of your uncle in you, Rhiann. A lot more than I realized. My sisters Nona and Mors and I will always welcome you in the Hanging Gardens. Go to Thynna. Stay safe. Once you are inside the walls of the city of Magick there's little we can do to help you. Once you have attended to your business and met your goals, come to me. I'll comfort you."

Maranna cleared her throat and said, "I'm not sure he needs the kind of comfort you're thinking about, Decima. But I thank you for coming to Thynna and your words."

Decima managed a smile for the siren, stood and walked to Rhiann, and planted a soft lingering kiss on his lips. Rhiann wrapped his arms around her and relished her warmth and softness. Decima's hair and the single strand in Rhiann's locks emitted warm yellow light. She pulled away from Rhiann, placed her left index finger gently against his lips, and said, "Farewell, Rhiann Klarje. Walk in Grayness."

The young flying Centaur Margaret stood at the foyer door. Decima walked briskly to the equine and deftly climbed onto her back. The centaur silently flew away. Rhiann watched the winged equine fly over the rocky cliffs to the south.

Maranna placed her hand on his left shoulder and asked, "When will you leave?"

Rhiann answered, "I must arrange Uncle Mayard's things in my bag of holding. Will you please look after Iyaca?"

Iyaca defiantly said, "Rhiann Klarje, I am bound to you! Where you go I go. I'll not leave your side in these difficult times."

Rhiann objected, "Iyaca, you'll likely be killed."

Iyaca bravely replied, "Then so be it."

Rhiann said, "Oh, well, it'll probably be the end of both of us anyway. Prepare your things. Maranna, we'll need transportation."

Maranna said, "I promised Mayard Klarje that I'd look after you. I'm coming, too. The Cloudmares Urra and Syrrth have agreed to carry you to Thynna's gates. As I said before, we won't be able to help you much once you are inside."

CHAPTER 26

Defying the Council

Caye Klarje Marsh aimlessly went about her tasks. She'd already gotten her younger son Arthur Seigh Klarje off to his middle school classes and her husband Kurth Marsh to another likely unproductive day of debating the actions of the Council of Thynna. Kurth's dissenting voice had been pushed further and further into the corner and minority. Mayard Klarje had been gone for a long time and had dragged Kurth's son Rhiann along on this extended walkabout. Word had come from the north of a skirmish between Gnomes and the renegade sorcerer Bailiwick. Envoys from Gnome-town led by newly promoted Captain Donovan Twelve-names had arrived at Thynna's gates with two unfortunate colleagues who had fallen victim to the sorcerer's nefarious Hold Spell. The Council of Thynna initially denied the Gnomes entry to the city. Council members were furious that the wagon of riches from the Copper Mountain mines had been hijacked by Kobolds. The persistent, strong-willed Captain Donovan blurted that 'Mayard wasn't Mayard, Rhiann wasn't Rhiann, Rhiann might have been Mayard." Shapechangers had fomented mischief on both sides, and Old Ones had nefariously attacked. Rhiann or Mayard or whoever he was had disappeared. Mayard certainly had the ability to make himself look like Rhiann, but the reverse was not true. Rhiann had never mastered the Polymorph Self Spell. At least he had not the last time his mother had laid eyes on him. The memory of Rhiann's last departure brought tears to Caye's eyes.

The Council of Thynna had denied the Gnomes entry. Captain Donovan Twelve-names created quite a ruckus at the gate. The unfortunate victims of the Hold Spells slowly deteriorated, and the Gnome Captain refused to stay silent while his friends suffered. Caye Klarje Marsh defied the Council of Thynna's order and exited the city to assist the Gnomes. She used multiple Dispel Magick Spells and freed Longbeard Nineteen-names and Dibbit Six-names from the Hold Spells. Kurth Marsh stood firmly against the Council and supported his life-mate Caye. The council relented and allowed the Gnomes entry to Thynna but restricted their movements to the outer ward. Caye Klarje brought the party from Gnome-town to her home and fed them. Afterward she had to replenish her entire pantry. But Caye gained a standing invitation to Gnome-town and received vigorous hugs of gratitude from Donovan, Longbeard, and Dibbit.

Longbeard and Dibbit suffered consequences from their prolonged inability to move. Both required Heal Spells and aqua therapy in Thynna's warm springs. Their progress was slow. Donovan Twelve-names remained in Thynna, kept up with his friends' progress, and spent his days waiting for his friends' recovery studying Thynna's outer curtain and the armaments of the guards. Donovan made many constructive comments, and the veteran officers of Thynna's guard welcomed his comments and looked forward to his visits. Though the Council of Thynna had delayed the Gnomes entry, many mercenaries straggled into the city in answer to the council's call for arms. Donovan Twelve-names watched from the allure. Four riders approached the city.

Donovan commented to the sergeant of the guard, "Those are rather rough types. Fact is… the red-headed bloke looks remarkably like a highwayman we encountered when Longbeard got caught in the wizard's Hold Spell. I'd question the wisdom of allowing them entry."

The sergeant on duty Redbrick replied, "The Council has sent out envoys offering pardons and pay for rogues like these. Nobody's vetting these guys! The sorcerers want men that are able to fight. They won't be trusted to be tower guards and inner ward militia. Most will be relegated to serving in expeditionary forces intended to have a go against the Hanging Gardens. They won't see the inside of the city. Look! The outer guards are directing them to the commandant's gatehouse."

Donovan said, "I'm well familiar with the gatehouse. When I was younger and only had five names, I served as courier for the

Burgomaster. It's the first position of responsibility for Gnomes rising in rank and considered an honor. I made many trips to Thynna, and my journeys from Gnome-town always ended at the gatehouse. I'd never been in the city until Sorceress Caye's invitation with my current trek with Longbeard and Dibbit."

Redbrick replied, "I served in the gatehouse. Most all of us do. Messengers from Gnome-town arrive every fortnight. Got to admit. I don't remember you."

Donovan replied, "I'm not surprised. Messengers and envoys doing business for the Burgomasters don't tarry and make small talk. We carried communications to and from the Council of Thynna. Duty wasn't particularly hazardous. We didn't carry treasures… usually. Also, Gnomish trained halvsies can outrun and outmaneuver most every other horse on the planet, so we didn't have trouble with highwaymen and beasts of the forest."

Redbrick chuckled and said, "I don't imagine highwaymen would value letters from the Council of Thynna to outlanders. The letters always say, 'no' to their requests and 'send payments now.' I can remember taking leather pouches from the Gnomish riders and giving them another in return. Didn't ever talk much. getting to know you makes me wish we had. You Gnomes aren't bad blokes."

Donovan asked, "I'd say the same about you, Redbrick. We as soldiers tread common ground. Do you think the Council of Thynna intends to go to war against the Three Sisters?"

Redbrick said, "Everything points to it. The council covets the resources of the Veldt. I'm just a soldier. I do what I'm told. Right now I'm told to guard these walls. The sorcerers secure the gate. It works well unless one goes rogue like the woman who disobeyed orders and went outside the gate and saved your friends. I heard some say the older guy with the really long beard was almost a goner."

Donovan smirked, "He's my senior Captain and didn't have far to go. Not of much account."

Redbrick and his underling Corporal Tybert laughed.

A gravelly voice behind them protested, "I heard that Donovan! I'll drink your *** under the table any day of the week!"

Donovan said, "Why Captain Longbeard, I'm surprised to see you up. Do you need help emptying your **** pot?"

The guards laughed again. Longbeard Nineteen-names grumbled, "If you hadn't just helped save my ***, I'd kick yours. It's good to be up old friend. Sorceress Caye says I still can't drink ale and need a few more days. The Hold Spell really sat me back. I'd like another go at that sorcerer one day."

Donovan replied, "So would we all, Captain Longbeard."

Longbeard squinted in the morning light, stood on tiptoe at the merlon, and watched goings on outside the city. He commented, "Lots of men coming from the north. Times are tough. It's hard to get ores from the mine past the Kobolds and Highwaymen."

Donovan said, "I just saw a quartet of unsavory types checking in. On had long red hair. Did you get a look at the blokes that bushwhacked us near Dry Creek?"

Longbeard replied, "Not really. There were too many Kobolds around, and I got hit by the Hold Spell early on. Made it hard to focus. I got a pretty good look at the sorcerer and the Siren that sang to us. By dang, Donovan, she was pretty! Might near pretty enough to make it worthwhile to get paralyzed."

Several soldiers gathered around and more laughed. The Gnomes entertained with stories. Some were quite embellished. Donovan bettered Longbeard at storytelling! Men, a few Dwarves, three Gnomes, and a Kobold wandered into the gatehouse.

Longbeard muttered, "They are taking anybody."

Donovan added, "Look! Halvsies! It's the envoys from Gnome-town!"

Three Gnomes on halvsies rode into the cleared area between Thynna's outer curtain and the woods and approached the gatehouse. Guards met them and accepted their satchels. The perimeter guard removed parchments and carried them to the gate, where Redbrick's subordinate accepted them and brought them to the veteran sergeant. One of Redbrick's responsibilities was screening communiques. The sergeant only bothered the Council of Thynna with such matters if the messages were urgent. Redbrick studied the epistle and said, "Most of this concerns you boys. The Burgomaster inquires as to your condition, Longbeard, and warns Donovan to avoid spending too much time in the taverns. Security remains high at Dry Creek and Gnome-town, but the Sorcerer Bailiwick and the Fearsome Foursome's entourage have disappeared. Storming Norman's troops engaged and routed a Kobold army commanded by a Chieftain named Beeyo. The roads between Gnome-town and Flat Rock and the Copper Mountain mines are safer, at least for the time being. The Burgomaster wants you to return as soon as possible. Donovan… he says the horse stalls need cleaning and he's saving that duty for you."

Now Longbeard had the chance to laugh with the Thynna guards.

Redbrick added, "Don't get your beard in a knot, Captain Donovan. He really says you are now Donovan Fourteen-names and your new rank of Captain is permanent. Based on reports from the recent campaign, the younger soldiers spoke highly of your campfire tales. Your added names are 'story-teller' and 'strong-heart.' Captain Longbeard is now Commandant Longbeard Twenty-one names, and his given his twenty-first name, 'spell breaker.'"

Donovan Fourteen-names humbly said, "I'm honored. I shall continue serving Gnome-town with all my strength."

Donovan watched the mustering of the four new arrivals with interest. The veteran Gnome shouldn't shake the feeling he'd seen them all before. Longbeard Twenty-one names carefully and awkwardly descended the wall stairs and headed for the solarium for more physical therapy. Dibbit six-names' youth helped him recover more quickly, and he insisted on helping Caye Klarje with her chores and ran errands for the sorceress. Thynna's guards denied Dibbit entry to the inner ward, and sorcerers gawked at the Gnome as he went around the outer ward performing tasks for Caye. Longbeard slowly improved.

Caye Klarje stared at her plate of mostly uneaten food. Kurth had prepared what was her favorite meal, roasted blooter with cibbage, caramelized onyum, pinanas, and blue beets. The couple took turns preparing meals and preferred to use old natural cooking methods instead of using Magick. Caye's Uncle Mayard had encouraged sorcerers to use Magick wisely, but more and more sorcerers employed spells to accomplish mundane tasks. Caye had merely picked over her food, and after several failed attempts to converse, Kurth had retired for the evening. Caye's troubled mind returned to her son Rhiann. Rhiann had left on walkabout with Mayard and the last word of him came from the Gnome visitors. Caye's son was last seen in the company of Old Ones. Mayard was allegedly still at the Hanging Gardens. Kurth had learned nothing of his activity from the meetings of the Council of Thynna. The Council's eyes and ears in the Hanging Gardens had gone blind and deaf. Centaurs vetted those entering the city closely and prismatic dragons patrolled the skies, making it harder to gather intelligence. Mayard's plans were oft hard to understand. Why had he sent her son off to the north in the company of a Shapechanger, purportedly the same Shapechanger that had tried to kill Mayard years ago? Caye cleaned her plate and made her way upstairs. She veered her path from the bedroom she shared with her life mate and entered Rhiann's room. Her son spent little time at home and even less in his bed since he'd become Mayard's apprentice.

Rhiann's room had been his refuge from outside stressors. His little brother Arthur Seigh Klarje lived in the former nursery down the hall. Rhiann enjoyed childhood heirlooms that had belonged to Caye, Kurth, and their ancestors. His favorite toys were a set of building blocks that stuck together until he wanted them to fall apart, a jack-in-the-box that produced a different visage each time it opened, and a horse-of-a-different-color that was a different color each morning when he awakened. His bed was stuffed with moongoose down and he slept on a pillow filled with rare lullaby bird feathers. When he lay down on the pillow, the soft pillow emitted gently melodies that aided his falling to sleep. His chest of drawers was made of durable semper fi tree wood that grew on Wombat Mountain to the south of Thynna. A bluewood desk sat against the wall. His chair was made of flexible fibers from a living morphing bush that grew as Rhiann did. He had to water the chair once a week with nutrient rich water. The mirror that hang on his wall was named ICU. A painting of a rambling bramble bush decorated his wall. The painting was in a different location every morning.

Caye sat on the edge of the bed.

The mirror ICU soothingly said, "I see you, Madam Klarje. I miss Rhiann, too."

Caye said, "ICU, I see you, too."

The mirror said, "I see less of you, Madam Klarje. You are not eating well. You must take care of yourself, as well as you look after everyone else, including the noisy Gnomes. You should talk with me more often."

Caye said, "I'm glad the Gnomes have needed my help. It's given me purpose. Too bad you only converse and aren't clairvoyant. Or able

187

to see beyond these walls and across the world, particularly into the Hanging Gardens."

ICU answered, "My Heartstone was bound to this mirror long ago, Madam Klarje. I have sympathy and empathy with those in this room. Hello, Rhiann."

Caye looked up and saw Rhiann's reflection in ICU. Rhiann was wearing Mayard's old hat and cloak and carried his Uncle's tattered catch-all bag. A wondrous siren and a youth not much older than Arthur Seigh stood by Rhiann.

Rhiann said, "Hello, Mother."

Caye jumped from the bed, ran to her son, and hugged him.

ICU said, "Beautiful. Will you sing for me?"

Maranna said, "Not a good idea. There are impressionable young males among us."

Caye Klarje interrupted her hugs and joy to say, "And an impressionable older man just down the hall. My life mate need not hear a siren sing. Rhiann, I'd ask how you got here, but I believe I know. Where is Mayard? Who are these folks? Why are Old Ones in Thynna?"

Rhiann kissed her face gently and replied, "One question at a time, Mother. I have... news. It's not good. Uncle Mayard... has gone to our ancestors. Maranna was his... and is my friend. She saved me from Bailiwick's revenge. Iyaca Vassi is my... apprentice."

Caye said, "Mayard is... dead? How? The Gnomes said he did not travel with you. They said a Shapechanger traveled in his guise and was killed by Bailiwick's treachery."

Rhiann answered, "That's true, Mother. The Shapechanger traveled as Uncle Mayard and thought that I was Mayard till the moment of his death. Uncle Mayard remained at the Hanging Gardens in my visage. He told me he had business to attend to in the gardens and asked me to attend to business for him in the north. That's how I came to be with the Gnomes."

Caye sobbed, and said, "Shapechangers? The very vile being that tried to assassinate Mayard in the guise of the merchant Elliott!"

Rhiann said, "Yes, Mother. Uncle Mayard and Elliott, as you called him, became true friends. *p-Elliott* served most loyally. Word came to me of Uncle Mayard's death while I was staying at Maranna's home."

Caye raised her eyebrows, scanned Maranna's curvaceous body, and asked, "Are you saying you have been living with this siren?"

Rhiann said, "Yes, Mother, along with other people, including my apprentice. This is Iyaca Vassi. He is bound to me as I was to Uncle Mayard."

Caye said, "Apprentice? You are barely old enough to..."

Maranna interrupted, "You have a fine son, who is mature far beyond his years, Yes, I find him attractive, but his eye is on another. Decima of the Three Sisters."

Caye said, "What? The Three Sisters? You are involved with the Fates?"

Rhiann removed Mayard's tattered hat and allowed the long hair to fall. Decima's strands and those woven from Nona's distaff illuminated the room. Caye gasped and said, "Now you share more than the mark of the Klarjes with your Uncle Mayard."

Iyaca Vassi broke through an awkward moment of silence, "Hello, Sorceress Caye. Pleased to meet you."

Caye Klarje took a deep breath and exhaled loudly. She said, "Hello, Iyaca, are you a sorcerer?"

Young Iyaca answered, "I'm afraid I'm not of much account."

Caye replied, "That's not what I've been told by the Gnomes. Donovan the story teller is seldom quiet and always relaying stories of his adventures. He spoke highly of you. You have performed well in difficult situations. Welcome to my home. All of you."

Caye cast another glance toward Maranna. Maranna turned and looked into the mirror and asked, "Madam Klarje, have you any suggestions regarding my tail? It's always getting in the way."

Caye Klarje said, "No. I don't know much about tails."

Iyaca said, "You should ask Donovan twelve-names, Maranna, he says he knows a lot about everything."

Rhiann said, "Iyaca, Donovan was speaking in generalities. Besides, he's in Gnome-town."

Caye said, "Well, actually, Donovan is in Thynna. Though I don't think you should be asking him about tail."

Rhiann said, "Donovan is in Thynna?"

Caye said, "Yes, he brought two colleagues who were in duress. Bailiwick's Hold Spell was slowly drawing the life out of them, because they were unable to effectively eat and drink. The council forbade them entry, but I helped them. Longbeard and Dibbit are getting better, but they aren't well enough to return to duty yet. Donovan has been helping Sergeant Redbrick out at the outer curtain. The Gnomes are staying in the infirmary. Donovan insists staying near them and camps out in the foyer."

Rhiann said, "I'm not sure they'll be happy to see me. The Shapechanger and I did not tell them about our ruse. They found out when he died. Maranna's friends removed the Gnomes from the battlefield. I still have to face the Burgomaster over the deception."

Caye asked, "How'd you get past the guards?"

Rhiann said, "I bear the mark of the Klarjes. I entered through the gate. Maranna carried Iyaca to the house. She flew silently and invisibly. I met them on the street. Maranna brought me to the window ledge and I climbed in through the window."

Caye said, "You've always enjoyed sitting on the ledge and looking out at the skies. You must be tired. And hungry. Let me fix you some food and prepare some bedding. I've never had a siren... as a house guest. How do you sleep?"

Kurth Marsh entered the room rubbing his eyes. The baffled sorcerer looked about the room and muttered, "Rhiann? And a siren?"

Maranna looked into Caye's eyes and said, "Sleep is Nature's gentle nurse. I close my eyes and relax. Old Ones don't differ all that much from sorcerers. Mayard Klarje understood us. Don't worry. I have no plans to seduce your life-mate."

Caye stared back and muttered, "What about my son?"

Maranna coyly whispered, "That might be another matter. We'll have to wait and see."

Caye whispered back, "That's not funny."

Maranna answered, "It wasn't meant to be. Mayard Klarje was my friend. I promised him I'd look after Rhiann. I appreciate your hospitality. I know my kind is not welcomed in Thynna."

Kurth Marsh picked up on Maranna's last comment and said, "Did you say 'was'? Is Mayard...?"

Caye blurted, "My Uncle Mayard has passed away. I just learned myself. The siren brought Rhiann and his friend to Thynna. We're barely beyond introductions."

Kurth worriedly replied, "Caye, what are you thinking? We're already in hot water with the Council over your actions with the Gnomes. If

Mayard is indeed dead, we've lost our greatest buffer against further censorship. The Council will develop more backbone if he is gone. Their policy regarding Old Ones in the city is quite explicit. We can't harbor a siren in our home."

Maranna flushed.

Rhiann said, "Maranna and others of her ilk saved us from the sorcerer Bailiwick and highwaymen. But for her intervention, Iyaca and I'd be dead, too. She is my friend."

Kurth said, "The Council of Thynna would seriously question your choice of friends, son. Mayard got away with things because... he was Mayard. We lack his influence."

Rhiann said resolutely, "I'm here to speak in his stead. If the council does not know of his death, I'll relay my words are his. I know what he wanted. Uncle Mayard wanted peace between Thynna and the Hanging Gardens! We wanted Old Ones welcomed in Thynna."

Kurth Marsh tore his eyes away from the siren and looked at his son. He said, "Son, I admired your uncle and loved him like a blood relative. I do not share the mark of the Klarjes as you do, but I share his philosophies. But the Council is ever more set in its ways. The Castellan Yerko succeeded Stewart Leftbridge and grows more powerful and influences his colleagues. The High Chancellor and Lord President invariably agree with Yerko's decisions. I fear the council's path is set. I fear for your friend the siren's safety. The Castellan calls for the Gnomes' expulsion daily."

Caye interjected, "All the while the Council welcomes vermin from all of Sagain into the war machine."

Kurth said, "I agree, Caye, but my opinion matters little. Siren... uh, I didn't catch your name... please remain hidden. I'd suggest you leave as soon as possible. Also, Rhiann, your young friend Iyaca must be vetted. The Castellan's troops will be very unhappy that he entered Thynna covertly."

Caye said, "Kurth, he's a boy!"

Kurth said, "On some things I agree with the Castellan. All who enter the city must be vetted. The Shapechanger that got near Mayard illustrates this fact. It's best you take him to the gatehouse and allow the sergeant of the day to give him papers to properly enter the city."

Caye puffed, "I'll ask Donovan to escort Iyaca. The Gnomish Captain goes daily to check on communication from Gnome-town.

He's proven very helpful. Sergeant Redbrick has requested Donovan be given security clearance to join the guard force as a liaison. The hour is late. Nourishment and rest are needed now."

Maranna looked at her reflection in ICU. The mirror commented, "Such beauty."

Maranna smiled.

Caye and Kurth took their unexpected guests to the dining area for an impromptu meal. Rhiann and Iyaca bedded down in Rhiann's old room. Maranna accepted a pallet on the living area floor, and most spent a night of minimal sleep.

CHAPTER 27

Mercenaries

On the morrow Donovan Fourteen-names and Dibbit arrived to assist Caye in her tasks. The Gnomes headed to the front gate area with Iyaca. Donovan greeted Sergeant Redbrick.

Donovan said, "Good morning, old chap. Hope all is going well. I need some papers for my young friend Iyaca Vassi. He's Rhiann Klarje's apprentice."

Sergeant Redbrick uttered, "How the bleep did he get into the city?"

Donovan replied, "Don't ask me about sorcerer stuff. All I know is Rhiann Klarje returned to Thynna last night. This young fellow lived with the Burgomaster and Madam Darktop for a time after his parents fell victim to highwaymen. The Burgomaster more or less gave him to Rhiann and Mayard Klarje, except it wasn't Mayard Klarje."

Redbrick answered, "Sometimes you talk sideways, my Gnomish friend. So Rhiann's back. Is Mayard with him? The Council has been doing a lot of things the old sorcerer wouldn't care for. We saw Mayard Klarje leave Thynna with Rhiann on a wagon bound for the mines and haven't seen hide nor hair of either since. Of course we learned it wasn't really Mayard when you blokes got here and relayed the story about Bailiwick's attack. Still can't believe the old bloke allowed a Shapechanger into the city in his visage. The Council was up in arms about the whole affair. There's even been some support for Bailiwick. You know, Castellan Yerko and Bailiwick were good childhood friends. Their antics put most kids to shame. Mayard needs to come back and explain his actions."

Iyaca remained quiet. Donovan said, "Well, I thought the Shapechanger was old Mayard. The rascal was a straight up guy the entire time. He served well, but then again Master Rhiann said he thought Rhiann was actually Mayard. It gets confusing when you look back at it."

Redbrick said, "I suppose Old Mayard's lot doesn't affect this young fellow. He can't wander around the city without papers or sponsorship. I suppose Caye Klarje will cover the sponsorship, but Sorceress Caye is still in a bit of hot water over you guys. Your performance since you've been in the city has bailed her out some. I still haven't heard from my request to have you as a liaison from Gnome-town. If it falls through, you probably could muster in the army. I saw them take in six Kobolds today. By the way, the four blokes you saw coming in the other day were top notch recruits. They had glowing resumes. Their leader was given a commission and now supervises the gatehouse screening. The other blokes were assigned cavalry duty and patrol the road to the south."

Donovan said, "I didn't like the looks of those guys. The red-haired fellow looked familiar. Déjà vu, I suppose."

Redbrick said, "The criteria for acceptance into Thynna's mercenary corps is to be living, breathing, ornery, and not opposed to fighting Old Ones."

Donovan said, "I have nothing against Old Ones. My ilk has always had a live and let live association with the Three Sisters and the Hanging Gardens. Fact is… Old Ones likely saved us from Bailiwick's lot. I was mad about being hauled around by a dragon at the time, but not so much now. Maybe war won't come. Rhiann and Mayard oppose it."

Redbrick said, "Let's take him over to the gatehouse. They're not busy at the moment. Should be routine!"

Redbrick, Donovan, and Iyaca passed through the gate and made the short walk to the gatehouse outside Thynna. Soldiers walked around the cleared area. Iyaca walked behind the Gnome and Tower Guard. They entered and found the gatehouse bustling with activity. Soldiers directed them to a desk in the back of the large entry room. A tall man sat and the table and scribbled on a parchment.

Redbrick said, "Are you the document clerk?"

The man said, "If you are asking am I the only ******* they've recruited that can read and write in a while, the answer is 'yes.' So you need paperwork. We don't see many Gnomes on the rosters."

Redbrick said, "No, it's not for the Gnome. He's an emissary from Gnome-town. It's for the kid. He needs papers."

The tall man said, "I saw you walk in. From the distance he looked a little young to muster in. What's his name?"

Redbrick said, "I'll let him give you the information. Iyaca, come up here. Let's get this done. I've got duties to get to."

Redbrick turned, but Iyaca was missing.

Redbrick said, "Where'd he go?"

Donovan said, "I don't know. He was just here. I was looking around to see if I knew any of these blokes. Iyaca? Iyaca!"

The clerk frowned and said, "I got tons of muster papers to fill out. Where is he?"

Red brick said, "Aw, get back to your work. If Rhiann Klarje wants his assistant to have domicile in the city, he can bring him here himself!"

The tall man said, "Did you say Rhiann Klarje? Is he in the city? I didn't see him enter?"

Redbrick said, "Are you kidding? Klarjes don't have to check in. I haven't seen him but Donovan says he's back."

Donovan looked at the tall dark-featured man and said, "Do I know you? What's your name? Yes, Rhiann Klarje is back in Thynna. I saw him this morning at his mother's house."

The tall man looked at Donovan and said, "I don't think we've met. I don't spend a lot of time with Gnomes. My name's... Money. John Money. Some call me the cash man. Was...uh, Mayard Klarje back, too?"

Donovan said, "No, I didn't see him, Mr. Money. Your voice sure is familiar."

John Money replied, "You may have heard me singing in a tavern. I dabble in music. If you blokes don't mind, I've got a ton of paperwork to do."

Sergeant Redbrick said, "Sorry we bothered you, Money. The kid must have wandered off. We'll leave you to your business."

Donovan and Redbrick left the gatehouse and headed back toward town. The short walk led them past the many merchant shops set up on the plaza outside Thynna. Redbrick said, "That little blighter wasted all our time. I'm going to whip his butt!"

Just then a voice whispered from a nook between two shops. Donovan turned and saw Iyaca cowering among baskets and barrels. The Gnome asked, "Iyaca, what gives? Why'd you run away? We only needed a few minutes."

Iyaca quietly said, "It was the clerk."

Redbrick said, "Do you mean Money, John Money?"

Iyaca said, "He can call himself whatever he wants. He's the Man in Black. He's the one whose men killed my parents."

Redbrick said, "The highwayman? Are you sure?"

Iyaca answered, "Donovan, I'll never forget his face. He probably remembers me, too."

Donovan said, "You were little more than a tyke when they brought you to Gnome-town. Redbrick, I wouldn't know. I never saw his face in the road to Dry Creek. His voice was familiar."

Iyaca said, "Go arrest him, Redbrick!"

Redbrick scratched his chin and muttered, "I can't rightly arrest him, Iyaca. Technically, he is my superior. Part of his mustering package included full pardon for all previous acts. On top of all that, he can read and write, which makes him quite a commodity to the Council of Thynna. He mustered in with three other guys."

Donovan said, "Undoubtedly the Fearsome Foursome are now in the employee of the Council of Thynna and there is naught we can do about it."

Redbrick said, "That's about the size of it. Copies of the muster logs are kept in the Guard Tower. We'll check."

The three returned to the gate. Redbrick's presence enabled them to pass inspection easily. It was a pretty safe bet that Thynna guard patrols wouldn't stop and check companions of a senior officer. Redbrick led them to the records room. They quickly found the week's rosters. John Money, Chris Tofferson, Billy Nelson, and Jennings Waymore mustered in on the same day. John Money was assigned duty in the gatehouse and the other three were dispatched as cavalry recruits to patrol roads south of Thynna.

CHAPTER 28

Treating with the Council

After Donovan and Iyaca headed off toward the city's gates, Rhiann, Kurth, and Caye sat down to breakfast. Rhiann insisted on going to the council meeting with his father Kurth Marsh and addressing the body of sorcerers.

Caye said, "I'm going to visit Longbeard this morning. I don't know what to do with the siren. I've too many tasks to keep up with her."

Rhiann said, "Don't worry about Maranna. She'll fend for herself. She is like a cat in the dark, and then she is the darkness. She moves like a bird in flight. If she doesn't want to be seen, she won't be seen."

Kurth finished his coffee, stood, and said, "Then you can tell me all about it tonight. Caye, I may be late. Rhiann will see lots of action today. The Elders have called another meeting of the Council of Thynna. More restrictions to entry to Thynna and strengthening of the walls are on the agenda."

Caye sighed and said, "How much more power does the council desire? How many more restrictions can they add? Their restrictions almost prevented my helping the Gnomes. Longbeard wouldn't have lasted much longer. It was not the intention of our ancestors to restrict knowledge and citizenship. They intended all touched by Magick to feel welcome. The elders are little better than the barbarians to the north. Their attitudes drove my Uncle Mayard from the city."

Kurth answered, "They are concerned about the safety of the Gem Bush among other things. The guards intercepted mercenaries from the Veldt. They disguised themselves as merchants and almost made it to the inner curtain."

Caye said, "The inner curtain! They'd have been near the school. How'd they get so close?"

Kurth replied, "Some think they had inside help."

Caye continued, "I'd rather Uncle Mayard and the emissaries to the Hanging Gardens had left the Gem Bush where it was. The Three Sisters really just got rid of a headache and dumped it on Thynna. Baubles and trinkets! Who cares about them?"

Kurth answered, "Many people both within and outside Thynna's walls treasure gems. Every insalubrious bloke on Sagain would love to steal the Gem Bush. Successfully stealing the gem bush would give them a replenishing supply. Besides, how could the elders refuse a gift from the Spinner, Allotter, and Unturning?"

Caye answered, "Most thieves are poor orchardists and horticulturalists. Keeping plants healthy is a lot of work. Caring for the Gem Bush is one of many tasks entrusted to my gardening group. One must know the nutrients and spell components needed to keep the Gem Bush healthy. The bush is the pride of the Council of Thynna! Protecting and nurturing it has become their top priority. Harvested gems adorn the garb of the council members. New gems replace those harvested by the council. Greed is greed, whether from a thief from the Veldt or a Council member from the inner ward of Thynna."

Kurth replied, "I share your opinion, Caye, but bear in mind your legacy entitles us to live in the inner ward. You… uh, we chose to live in the outer ward."

Caye quickly entered, "Yes, away from the snobs!"

Kurth suppressed a chuckle and said, "Now you sound like your Uncle Mayard."

Rhiann quipped, "I'm glad we live in the outer ward."

Caye, Kurth, and Rhiann made ready. Maranna was conspicuously absent from the morning gathering.

Rhiann and Kurth made their way into the inner ward. Kurth exchanged pleasantries with many sorcerers along the way. He spoke to merchants, city workers, and guards as was his fashion. Most residents of the inner ward held themselves above talking with the helpers and workers. Kurth Marsh was very popular with everyone other than the elite members of the council. Kurth stopped off at the merchant Elliott's place.

Rhiann cordially addressed his old childhood nemesis. Elliott treated them to pastries and refreshing cream. Refreshing cream was a reliable food source. It was always fresh. The security had tightened since Rhiann had left the city of Magick. The homes in the inner ward had grown more opulent. The courtyard of the Great Hall of Thynna remained the center of activity. The statue of Mayard Klarje remained in place. Another fence had been erected around the Gem Bush. The brilliant gems on the tree glistened in the morning light from the suns. The wondrous tree flourished under Caye Klarje's horticulture care. Caye and other prominent members of the community and spent many hours nurturing the Gem Bush and other plants in the courtyard. Young sorcerers meandered about the courtyard and many ascended steps leading into the well-constructed School of Magick. The school's construction was financed through the efforts of Mayard Klarje, who oft returned to Thynna with priceless jewels and spell components. His most valuable addition was the Gem Bush, which was planted in the courtyard near the Great Hall of Thynna, the assembly place of the Council of Thynna and the city of Magick's center of government. The Gem Bush was a gift from the Old Ones of the Hanging Gardens, specifically the Three Sisters, the Spinner, Allotter, and the Unturning. The Gem Bush was thought unique; it was certainly the only one known in all of Sagain. It grew after the impact that created the cataclysm and never increased beyond its current size. The bush was thirteen feet tall. Its diameter was thirteen inchworm lengths. The tree had thirteen limbs, thirteen leaves on each limb, thirteen veins on each leaf, and drew nourishment through thirteen roots. Each limb bore one gem of thirteen different colors, including one ultra-rare red diamond. Only one gem of a given color could be removed every thirteen years. A second gem could not be removed, even with the power of a Limited Wish or Alter Reality Spell. As they passed the little tree, Rhiann recalled the history of the Gem Bush. The Three Sisters entrusted the plant to Mayard Klarje and hoped it would improve relations between Thynna and the Old Ones community. Suspicion and greed overrode the gesture and the Council of Thynna accepted the gift, but more restrictions were placed on entry and approach to the city by the preternatural Old Ones. Mayard protested to no avail. Nevertheless, he painstakingly planted the Gem Bush in the Great Hall's courtyard and entrusted its care to his niece Caye and her colleagues.

Rhiann and Kurth ascended the steps leading to the Council of Thynna's meeting chamber in the very secure inner ward. Guards were posted at the double doors. Initially the guards held Rhiann at the chamber entrance. Castellan Yerko had forbade entry to all but bona fide members of the Council of Thynna. Rhiann insisted he was speaking in Mayard's stead, but it held little import to the guards. Kurth Marsh berated them to no avail. Members of the council filtered into the chamber, with most casting contemptuous glances at young Rhiann and Kurth. One particularly haughty inner ward resident referred to Rhiann as "another ****** Klarje. His companion said something to the effect "their facial mark buys them nothing" and "their time is past." Others mumbled derogatory comments about Mayard, mostly centered on his relationship with the Three Sisters and the Hanging Gardens. Finally, Castellan Yerko made his way to the chamber door, and Kurth appealed to him to allow Rhiann to speak.

Yerko said, "He's a boy, Kurth. The Council has pressing business, including discussions about your wife's insubordination. Why should I allow him before the Council?"

Rhiann implored, "I carry my Uncle Mayard's message."

Yerko answered derisively, "Then let him speak for himself! I grow weary of his messages!"

Kurth said, "Rhiann brings word from the Hanging Gardens."

Yerko gruffly replied, "So he's kowtowing in the Gardens with his harlot Nona. The only word I want from the Three Sisters is their total submission and dissolution of their power. When Nona shatters her distaff and leaves the Veldt, I will treat with her. Mayard's ways are old ways, Marsh. Your young relative must learn he can't follow Mayard's path. Thynna moves away from the old ways."

Rhiann said, "Please allow me to speak, Castellan."

Kurth added, "Let him be heard, Castellan. If you are so comfortable with the Council and Thynna's course, what harm can he do?"

Yerko looked up at the twin suns sparkling in the east and said, "The day is wasting while we tarry here. You want to speak, whelp? Well, if you want to make a fool of yourself, proceed. You'll be as big a laughing stock as your senile Uncle Mayard."

Rhiann said excitedly, "I'll be brief, but thorough."

Yerko clapped his hands together and the guards separated and granted access to the doors. Rhiann and Kurth followed the Castellan into the large amphitheater. Murmurs passed through the captive audience.

The Castellan headed for the podium and addressed the Council of Thynna members, "Fellow Council Members, you are honored to be addressed by an adolescent sorcerer, Master Rhiann Klarje. He intends to enlighten us about the Hanging Gardens. His Uncle Mayard has sent him to face us in his stead. I'm sure his Uncle's lack of courage makes young Rhiann proud of the mark he wears on his face."

Mocking laughter coursed through the auditorium. Childhood memories reentered Rhiann's mind. Kurth Marsh took his seat. Rhiann approached the podium and looked out into the crowd. Almost all council members lived in the inner ward and were unfamiliar to him. Rhiann began by reciting part of Mayard's letter. The audience and Castellan frequently interrupted him. Laughter drowned his words. Kurth stood twice to speak up for Rhiann. On the first occasion the Castellan harshly ordered him to remain seated. On the second occasion the Castellan threatened to expel Kurth from the building and censure him. Calls to "Go back to your ****** Old Ones, you traitor", "You are a disgrace to Magick" and "Let old Mayard speak for himself." Rhiann relayed Mayard's worries and Nona's warnings, but everything fell on deaf ears. Eventually the Castellan Yerko moved Rhiann away from the podium and declared the council; had "heard enough." Yerko ordered Rhiann from the chamber and Kurth to stay and hear the council's judgment on Caye's activities. Cat calls, various insults, and hoots and howls followed Rhiann as he exited. The young sorcerer fought back tears as he exited the chamber to raucous laughter. Kurth stood to follow his son, but Yerko demanded Kurth remain seated. Rhiann's father watched his son walk dejectedly from the chamber.

Rhiann walked down the steps and into the courtyard. Young sorcerers busily pelted Mayard's statue with blooter eggs and rotten tomatoes. Two arms guards simply stood by and laughed. The merchant Elliott ran from his store and brandished a broom. The shopkeeper shouted, "Ruffians! How dare you deface the statue of Thynna's greatest benefactor! Young Sorcerer Klarje, you're here at an opportune time. Turn them into something disgusting!"

Rhiann said, "Merchant Elliott, thank you for speaking up in my uncle's behalf. May I borrow your broom?"

Elliott extended the broom and said, "The hooligans would never attempt such behavior if Mayard Klarje were here. He's been away too long. I hope he returns soon."

Rhiann went over to the statue, used the merchant's broom, and cleaned the statue. He returned the broom to the merchant.

Elliott said, "Young Klarje, the Shapechanger would have certainly done me in, had you and your uncle not discovered his treachery. The disrespect for the statue occurs daily. I hear stories of Bailiwick's return and other rumors that Mayard Klarje will not come back to Thynna. If you have any influence on your uncle, please implore him to return to this wayward city."

Rhiann said, "I wish Uncle Mayard were here, too, Elliott. Thank you again for your concern."

Elliott said, "Allow me to fix you a cup of tea. Come into my shop for a moment."

Rhiann said, "I must be going…"

Elliott said, "I mistreated you when you were young. You and Mayard saved me. You've nowhere to be in the next little bit. Please come along."

Rhiann shrugged and followed the wiry merchant into his shop. Elliott's visage brought back memories of Rhiann's first encounter with p-Mayard. The young sorcerer rested his laurels on one of Elliott's beer barrels and took in the thriving shop. Soon the merchant returned with a nice cup of herbal tea and some biscuits. Rhiann rather enjoyed the respite.

Elliott relayed stories of interactions with Mayard Klarje. He said, "Your Uncle Mayard is very fond of my tea and biscuits. I look forward to his next visit for many reasons, not the least of which is restoring order among these hooligans."

Rhiann simply smiled and sipped his tea. The young disheartened sorcerer spent the better part of the morning mainly listening to Elliott's rambling. Finally, after three cups of tea, Rhiann excused himself and bade the merchant farewell.

While Rhiann was sipping tea, his father Kurth was being raked over the coals by the Council of Thynna. Castellan presented forms; papers of censure against Caye Klarje and the full council voted overwhelmingly to approve the censure. Kurth objected and avowed such action would never occur if Mayard were present.

Yerko icily replied, "Mayard is not here. His interest in Thynna's affairs has taken second seat to hobnobbing with his Old One friends. If he wants to dispute my actions, let him return and challenge me. Kurth Marsh. Your spouse Caye Klarje Marsh has yet to stand before the council to answer for her actions involving the Gnomes, when she disobeyed the guards. I suspect she'll be called during the next general session in a few days. It'd be in her, and your, best interests to summon Mayard Klarje to Thynna."

The entire chamber remained quiet. Kurth gathered his papers and left the chamber room.

CHAPTER 29

Ferret and Dragon

Rhiann made his way through the crowded inner ward, passed through the gate in the inner curtain, and headed for his mother's house. He passed the infirmary and rehabilitation center on the way. Donovan Fourteen-names and Dibbit sat outside the rehab center.

Donovan said, "Young Rhiann, why so down in the mouth? You look like you lost your best friend."

Rhiann replied, "I have, Donovan. My address to the council accomplished nothing. How goes Longbeard's treatment?"

Dibbit said, "The old geezer didn't bounce back as quickly as I did, but we received good news. The healer and sorceress Caye say he's well enough to travel. Looks like we'll be able to return to Gnome-town very soon."

Rhiann noted concerned looks on the Gnomes' faces and said, "That is good news. You should be happy. Why are you looking out of sorts? And where's Iyaca? Did he get his papers?"

Donovan said, "Well, not exactly. He's back at your mother's house. We thought it best he stays there till we sort things out."

Rhiann said, "I know you have enjoyed your time in Thynna, Donovan. You have given great advice to the sergeant of the guard. I realize you might not be ready to leave."

Donovan said, "It's not… Rhiann, the Man in Black has mustered into Thynna's mercenaries and received rank. He works in the gatehouse. Iyaca ducked out just before the bloke saw him. The blighter has received a full pardon from the Council of Thynna so there's naught we can do. We really need Mayard Klarje."

Rhiann placed his hand on Donovan's broad shoulder and said, "Donovan, he is not coming."

Donovan said, "It'd take him a while to get here from the Hanging Gardens, but your siren friend could get a message to him quickly."

Rhiann said, "Donovan, he is never coming."

Dibbit said, "Mayard Klarje would never abandon Thynna. He's really added to this city."

Rhiann fought back a tear and said, "My friends, there are few in Thynna that know that my Uncle Mayard has gone to our ancestors. I'm now the bearer of Magick's standard, and I'm clearly not wanted in Thynna."

Donovan objected, "Sure you are! You have the mark of the Klarjes!"

Dibbit added, "Then come to Gnome-town! We'd be glad to have you."

Rhiann said, "I'm not so sure. The Burgomaster is probably rather upset with Uncle Mayard... well, now it'd just be me."

Donovan asked, "Can't you find another Shapechanger to mimic Mayard."

Rhiann said, "I'm afraid *p-Mayard* was rather unique among his chaotic ilk. It's inevitable that word of Mayard's death will reach Thynna."

Donovan asked, "What are you going to do now?"

Rhiann said, "I'm going to my mother's house to consult with her. And Maranna, if she remains in Thynna."

Donovan said, "We'll head that way. We must begin preparations to return to Gnome-town. The Burgomaster will want to hear of the Fearsome Foursome. He's not going to be very happy."

Rhiann said, "Maybe he'll be less angry with me."

Donovan asked, "Should I inform him of Mayard's passing?"

Rhiann replied, "Yes, take him into confidence. I've learned a lesson. I won't deceive him again."

Donovan Fourteen-names placed a strong hand on Rhiann's shoulder. Then the brace of Gnomes and dejected young sorcerer made their way along the crowded streets toward Caye and Kurth's home.

Nona's tears fell onto the fertile soil in the garden outside her living quarters. She twisted her long hair and broke off a single hair. It fell to the ground. A small shrub grew instantly where it fell. She looked upward at the sky and glanced toward the lovely distant body some called Andromeda. The oldest of the Three Sisters sang a lament for Mayard Klarje. She then sat on a stone bench and sobbed. Soft footsteps approached. Decima said, "Sister, you must rest. Please come inside."

Nona looked up and said, "I can't believe he is gone, sister. Mayard was such a part of my life. We shared so many adventures. I hoped for another five hundred years."

Decima said, "But for a bewildebeest's fangs you may well have shared that much time or longer. You must turn your thoughts to your health and our tasks. Come with me."

Decima extended her hand and took her sister's. Nona stood and followed her sister toward the sitting area she had shared so many times with Mayard Klarje. Nona said, "I hope you'll have long years with Rhiann, sister."

Decima said, "I'm not sure, sister. He shares his Uncle's dedication to Magick… and Sagain. I'm low on his priorities."

Nona managed a smile and said, "A few of your kisses will change all that."

Skittering sounds from the garden caught their attention. Both sisters turned. Nona said, "Who's there?"

Decima said, "No one can get past Chiron's defenses, sister. We're safe here."

A ferret scurried across the garden into the trees.

Nona said, "Oh, it's only a woodland creature. A friend of the forest."

The sisters entered the sitting room.

Mighty Chiron interrupted a futile attempt to sleep and went to the edge of the invisible bridge across the river that surrounded the Hanging Gardens. The death of his old friend Mayard had disturbed the centaur. His sentries always welcomed his companionship. Just a day earlier the guards had to repel a giant from Hinderburgh. Chiron turned quickly. A small ferret raced between his legs and started across the bridge. Chiron's companion nocked an arrow and started to fire.

Chiron said, "No. Let it go. It's just a ferret."

The ferret cleared the bridge and scooted across the cleared area, running between the hooves of the many centaurs on guard duty and entering the woods to the north. The ferret ran through the underbrush. It stopped at a pair of well-worn boots. A dark robe fell to just above the top of the boots.

The sorcerer said, "Oh, Windy, my eyes and ears, you have returned. The value of a familiar! So he's passed on. The great Mayard Klarje is dead. I'm saddened only by the fact his death did not come by my hand. There's no need for my current plan and naught to do here at this time. I'll release the giants." The sorcerer uttered some guttural phrases. Four Hinderburgh giants interrupted their phi gamm feast and answered his summons. The sorcerer spoke to them in the same gruff tone. The giants grumbled their disappointment, but the sorcerer assured them the fight they hoped for with the centaurs was merely delayed. The sorcerer gave a shrill whistle. Beating wings appeared. He mounted the large old copper dragon, gave the beast a large chunk of copper ore, and muttered, "To the woods near Thynna. Stay out of sight."

The dragon flew straightaway to the propinquity of the city of Magick. The sorcerer stayed in the fringes of the woods until the next day's shift began their tasks in the morning. He made his way to the gatehouse. An old acquaintance provided him a change of clothes and papers to enter the city as a merchant from Low Gap.

CHAPTER 30

Returning to Gnome-town

Kurth Marsh made his way home. He, his life-mate Caye, and their son Rhiann talked long into the night. The siren Maranna respectfully remained away from the family. The Gnomes rejoined Longbeard Twenty-names, who was released from his rehabilitation. Young Iyaca Vassi spent time alone in Rhiann's room conversing with the mirror on the wall. ICU relayed stories of Rhiann's youth, including the tale of his first encounter with the Shapechanger later known as *p-Mayard*. Rhiann joined Iyaca after a time and the youths commiserated. Kurth and Caye retired to their bedroom, but the light remained on through the night. Rhiann finally napped. Too soon his mother's voice awakened him.

Caye said, "Rhiann, the Gnomes are at the door. They ask to speak with you before they leave for Gnome-town. Also, your father and I have been summoned before the Council of Thynna."

Rhiann rubbed the sleep from his eyes and said, "The Council was set to adjourn this session yesterday. They were not to meet again for a fortnight. I'll go with you."

Caye solemnly answered, "They have called an emergency session today. Our instruction specifically ordered us to come without you. The Castellan's Sheriff Janet Rhino is waiting to escort us, and she has ten inner ward sentries with her. Please awaken your friend."

Rhiann awakened Iyaca, they quickly dressed, and the duo went downstairs. Donovan Fourteen-names, Longbeard Twenty-names, and Dibbit Six-names waited in the foyer. They were dressed in travel clothes and carried their bags. Their weapons remained in the armory at the outer curtain's gate. Sergeant Redbrick had managed to garner papers for the Gnomes to roam the outer ward, but he had to store their arms. Longbeard still looked a bit thin and peaked, but the Gnomish Commandant walked now without the cane he had employed only a few days earlier. High Sheriff Rhino patted her foot impatiently, and her ten heavily armed deputies with disdain reproached the Gnomes for tarrying in Thynna. High Sheriff Rhino and her twin brother Pinochynose had been childhood friends of Castellan Yerko. High Inquisitor Pinochynose mastered the spell Detect Lie and its reverse Lie. He could half tell some whoppers... and usually got away with it. It was very hard to mislead him. The Gnomes nervously avoided Pinochynose's gaze and questions.

Newly-promoted Captain Donovan said, "Rhiann Klarje, we came to say goodbye for now. Our duty calls. Fact is... I'm really missing my axe and hammer, and I get the feeling we are wearing out our welcome. Madam Darktop's cooking will fatten up old Longbeard in no time at all. He's Commandant Longbeard now. That means he gets to hobnob with the Burgomaster's guests."

Longbeard quickly said, "I'm not kissing anybody's a**, Donovan! I'll summon you for that duty!"

Dibbit chimed in, "Don't you mean doody, Longbeard?"

The Gnomes shared a laugh. Donovan said, "Rhiann, being in Thynna has helped me learn a lot about sorcerers. Trouble is... there's a lot more to know about them than I thought. I'll never pretend to understand your Uncle's motives, but I'll put in a good word for you with the Burgomaster. I surely hope your path brings you to Gnome-town soon. We'll be in touch. Now than the most notorious outlaws in the north have mustered into Thynna's army, we may not have much to do. Suppose old Bailiwick is still at large. We are returning with the courier today."

Rhiann looked at High Sheriff Rhino and her ever more impatient deputies and said, "I hope you have safe travels, my friends. My course is less certain. Today... well, I'm going to... walk you to the gate." The young sorcerer turned to his parents and said, "Mother, Father, fare well."

Caye answered, "Rhiann, we'll see you later in the day. I want to plan some tasks for you in the middle school."

Rhiann and Iyaca joined the three Gnomes and headed toward the gate. Six of High Sheriff Rhino's deputies accompanied them. Rhino and the other four deputies muttered directives to Caye and Kurth. Caye said, "If my Uncle Mayard were here, you'd be singing a different tune."

Rhino quipped, "OOOH, I'm scared now. Guess I'm lucky the old codger isn't here."

Rhino's confidence shook Caye's. Did the High Sheriff know of Mayard's passing?

Rhiann, Iyaca, Captain Donovan, Commandant Longbeard, and Archer Dibbit walked among the Castellan's deputies. Rhiann felt a subtle tug on his cape. Unmistakable pleasant pheromones besieged his senses. Maranna was near. Touching him did not betray her invisibility. Innate abilities differed from spells. Had she been made invisible by a sorcerer, her action may well have exposed her. Suddenly one of the deputies went sprawling. His armor and weapons clanked loudly. His curses filled the air. His comrades laughed and one commented something along the line of "two left feet." The Gnomes fought back laughter. Then another deputy stopped laughing and stared off idly into space. His colleagues started shaking him, but the hulking centurion did not respond.

In the confusion Maranna whispered in Rhiann's ear, "I only gave him a little kiss. He'll probably come around in a couple of days."

Rhiann, Iyaca, and the three Gnomes made their way on to the massive outer curtain. Donovan received many greetings along the way. The Gnomish Captain had made many friends and helped many outer warders with tasks during his short tenure in Thynna. Two deputies caught up with the small party. Sergeant Redbrick met them at the gate and returned their weapons. One of the deputies started to object. Suddenly he stopped talking, smiled, and stared off idly into space. His comrade began shaking him. Sergeant Redbrick gave Donovan a vigorous handshake and slap on the back. Redbrick then opened the gate. Rhiann and Iyaca stood by Redbrick as the Gnomes exited.

The new gatehouse clerk who called himself John Money stood just outside the gate and said facetiously, "Sorry to see you leave, boys. Be sure to turn in your temporary papers. Remember you'll have to see me to get papers to enter the city in the future. I'm scrutinizing all visitors. Oh my. Young Rhiann Klarje. Are you harboring an undocumented visitor? That's a punishable offense! You'll have to go before the Council. He must…"

Suddenly the tall man stopped talking, smiled a silly smile, and smiled off idly into face. Dibbit turned, walked to Iyaca, and slipped his temporary papers into Iyaca's pocket.

Dibbit whispered, "In case you get stopped on the way back to the house, kid."

Dibbit rejoined Donovan and Longbeard. Outside guards took the entranced John Money to the infirmary. Other guards closed the gate. Iyaca, Rhiann, and Sergeant Redbrick climbed the wall stairs to the wall walk and gazed across the massive cleared area in front of Thynna's outer curtain. Donovan, Longbeard, and Dibbit joined the courier who was returning to Gnome-town. Rhiann and Iyaca watched their friends ride off to the north and fade into the forest at the base of the foothills. Healers rushed to the infirmary to attend John Money and Rhino's seconds-in-command who remained somewhat catatonic, though they bore expressions of delight on their faces.

Maranna whispered to Rhiann, "Would you mind going home. I going to develop a case of chapped lips, and its not particularly pleasing to kiss these blokes."

Rhiann and Iyaca thanked Sergeant Redbrick for his help, descended the wall stairs, and made their way home. It was mid-morning.

Caye and Kurth's day of misery was only beginning. The deputies walked on all sides and followed Pinochynose and High Sheriff Rhino into the inner ward.

Caye muttered, "I feel like I'm under arrest."

High Sheriff Rhino said sharply, "You aren't far from it. Keep in line."

Kurth whispered, "Caye, we must see this through. We have no choice."

Loud clanking sounds greeted their arrival into the courtyard near the Council Tower. Workers hammered at the statue of Mayard Klarje that sat near the Gem Bush. One of the statue's arms crashed to the ground. The merchant Elliott stood in the entry to his shop and shook his head negatively. A crowd of inner warders stood around the statue and cheered. The same lot jeered the couple as they passed.

Caye muttered, "What is the meaning of this disrespect?"

High Sheriff Janet Rhino muttered, "What does it look like? It's the changing of the guard, and it's long overdue."

Kurth added, "Why aren't you…"

The High Sheriff said, "Shut up. Let' get on inside. They will be waiting."

The deputies prodded the couple, and Caye and Kurth stumbled up the stairs. The guards at the chamber door separated and allowed the party to enter. Two straight chairs were set up near the podium. High Sheriff Rhino directed Caye and Kurth to the chairs. Every seat in the amphitheater was filled with wealthy prominent sorcerers of the inner ward. Castellan Yerko stood at the podium. The elected Lord President Homer and High Chancellor Odell wore normal garb and sat quietly in the first row of seats in the amphitheater. A sorcerer named Lubick wore the Lord President's robe and sat in a plush chair behind the castellan Yerko. Another sorcerer named Bogni wore the High Chancellor's robe and sat beside Lubick. Lubick and Bogni were lifelong friends of Castellan Yerko. Both sat quietly.

Caye and Kurth walked over to the austere chairs and sat down.

Castellan Yerko sarcastically said, "Nice of you to join us."

Caye Klarje Marsh angrily blurted, "What is the meaning of this farce, Yerko? Why have you replaced the rightfully elected Lord President and High Chancellor? Uncle Mayard will never stand for this! Defacing his statue! After all he's done for Thynna! None of you would face him and do these things!"

Yerko said, "If you are quite through, Klarje, you will address me as Castellan Yerko. Mayard Klarje is not here. Reliable sources tell me he's not returning. Just when were you going to inform this governing body of his death? Was it your intention to keep his demise secret so you could continue to bask in his ill-gotten privileges in Thynna? Long have the Klarjes led this city for their own gain! For your information, members of the Council spent the better part of the night using spells to weaken the stone in that cursed statue!"

Caye quickly stood and blurted, "Well I never!"

Kurth grabbed her hand and pulled her back into her seat and said, "Castellan Yerko, that's unfair. We live modestly in the outer ward. Mayard never asked for the statues and monuments. We gave to the city willingly. As to his death, we only learned of it yesterday. We haven't come to grips with it ourselves. Please forgive us for our weakness in our grief."

Yerko angrily replied, "You knew yesterday. Yet the young whelp presented his words as Mayard's. Mayard Klarje is dead and can no longer defend Thynna from threats outside her walls. However, I know of one powerful enough to do so. My emissaries sought the great Bailiwick. I've offered him sanctuary and a seat of the Council of Thynna. He has graciously accepted. Enter, Lord Bailiwick."

The door in the back of the chamber opened and Bailiwick audaciously entered the chamber. A handsome ferret was wrapped around his shoulders, and the sorcerer lovingly stroked the beast's soft fur.

Kurth wailed, "That's treason!"

Yerko countered, "On the contrary, Marsh, it's treason to speak against me. You are henceforth deprived of your seat on the Council of Thynna. You are your spouse are denied entry to the inner ward until further notice. Because she disobeyed the Council's orders and treated with the Gnomes outside the city and brought them into the city proper without proper vetting, Caye Klarje Marsh is excluded from the inner ward for five years. The length of your exclusion depends on your compliance to this council's orders, Kurth Marsh. Any further acts of defiance will result in your expulsion from the city. Your son Rhiann is forbade entry to the inner ward. Any further association with Old Ones and other enemies of the city of Thynna and this council will result in his permanent expulsion from the city. Lord Bailiwick is now in charge of all regulation of Magick. My deputies will harvest gems from the Gem Bush to cover the costs of mercenaries needed to protect the city. Is anyone in this chamber opposed to my decisions?"

Caye's sobs were the only sound.

Yerko said harshly, "Then it is done. Kurth and Caye Marsh are forbidden entry to the inner ward. Anyone who abets them shares their punishment. Is that clear? Now, former Council member Kurth Marsh, take your sorry a** back to the outer ward."

Kurth helped Caye to her feet and led her from the room.

As they left the guard said, "Good riddance, Marsh."

As the couple descended the steps, the statue of Mayard Klarje crashed to the ground. Throughout the inner ward, monuments to the benefactor of Magick were torn down or defaced. Pranksters placed a fake Gnome beard on a small statue near the inner curtain. Caye and Kurth received taunts and an occasional splat from an overripe fruit during their trek through the inner ward. Once they reached the outer ward, they found more gentile treatment, though most sorcerers thought better of greeting them. The beleaguered sorcerers finally reached their home. Rhiann, Iyaca Vassi, and the wondrous siren sat in the family room. Kurth relayed the Council's decision.

Kurth said, "The Council has learned of Mayard's death. His statues are being torn down. Yerko has brought the sorcerer Bailiwick to Thynna and bestowed stewardship of Magick to him. Pinochynose's deputies are planning to strip the gems from the Gem Bush to cover the cost of hiring mercenaries."

Caye dejectedly said, "Stripping the gems will kill the tree. They must be removed one at a time in order for the tree to replenish its fruit."

Rhiann said, "Mother! Father! We must dispute Yerko's actions."

Kurth said, "The Castellan has seized total power. Now he has Bailiwick to back him up. Say what you will about him, but Bailiwick is an accomplished sorcerer. Few resist his Hold Spells. Yerko has replaced the Lord President and High Chancellor with his minions. Many in the inner ward resented Mayard's association with the Old Ones. Mayard stayed away too often and too long. While the cat was away, the mice played, and all that… Your mother, you, and I are under banishment, Rhiann. We are denied entry to the inner ward. Failure to comply with Yerko's orders will result in our permanent expulsion from the city. Any association with old Ones will lead to our expulsion. I'm afraid your beautiful friend must leave. Iyaca's presence puts us at risk, too. The Castellan and High Sheriff's deputies roam the city. If they find him without proper papers, again we'll bear the brunt of punishment. The mark of the Klarjes no longer gives us prestige. Now it marks us as adversaries of the Council of Thynna."

Rhiann asked, "How did the council learn of Mayard's death. I only told you and the Gnomes?"

Kurth said, "Bailiwick is a powerful ally for Yerko and Pinochynose. Who knows what resources he may have employed!"

Caye said, "Yes, he looked so confident when he entered with his ferret. Mayard's greatest adversary is now the steward of Magick! Alas!"

Maranna quizzically asked, "Did you say 'ferret'?"

Caye said, "Yes, it's a lovely creature, but it's Bailiwick's familiar."

Maranna said, "A ferret. I flew to the Hanging Gardens. Chiron and Nona commented on seeing a ferret about the gardens. It's not unusual. Forest creatures are welcomed in the Gardens."

Rhiann huffed, "Not that it matters now, but that likely explains how the council learned about Uncle Mayard's demise. The Gem Bush is the lone remaining vestige of Uncle Mayard's legacy."

Kurth said, "Rhiann, you are my son, and as such, you may stay and work with me in the outer ward. However, Iyaca must return to Gnome-town, and Maranna must leave Thynna. I can't risk expulsion. I don't have the strength to extract a living off the land. Your mother must continue her teaching, but she must stay within the guidelines given her by the council. As I look out the window, I see one of High Sheriff Rhino's deputies posted on the corner of our street. Castellan Yerko has eyes and ears all about Thynna, and his mercenaries are loyal only to the wages he pays them. We cannot speak of Uncle Mayard outside these walls. I'm sorry. It can't be any other way."

Rhiann looked to Caye, but his mother merely hung her head dejectedly.

Maranna said, "I'll carry Iyaca outside the wall and make sure he gets safely back to Gnome-town. Donovan and Madam Darktop will look after him."

Rhiann touched her shoulder and said, "Come to my room. We'll gather Iyaca's things." Kurth said, "I'm glad you understand, son."

Rhiann said, "Yes, father, I know exactly what I need to do."

Rhiann, Iyaca, and Maranna ascended the stairs. Iyaca sobbed loudly.

In Rhiann's room, Iyaca said, "The Gnomes were very good to me. I'll assist the couriers."

Rhiann said, "You'll do no such thing. You will stay with me."

Maranna said, "Rhiann, he can't. The Council of Thynna forbids his staying here. He must leave."

Rhiann said, "Thynna is no longer my home. My parents abandon our family's heritage and forget all Uncle Mayard has done. Inwardly, I shall always treasure my name and heritage. Outwardly I must become nameless. I shall ever strengthen my Magick and pursue the goals of Mayard Klarje. I am born of Thynna but I reject everything the council is doing."

Iyaca said, "So you're… nameless…enchanter… from Thynna. NET…"

Rhiann said, "Put simply, yes. My Uncle Mayard took me to many locations. One of his favorite was by a stream near Wombat Mountain. It'd be a good place for a home… and a good place to hide a treasure."

Maranna said, "Rhiann, I'm not sure I like what you are implying. Is leaving Thynna best for you? And what are you talking about hiding?"

Rhiann said, "Uncle Mayard tasked me with preserving the best of Sagain and Magick. Lord Bailiwick may have a title, but I am the true steward of Magick. I can't allow the rape and murder of the Gem Bush. Maranna, go now to Wombat Mountain. Take Iyaca and my rucksack. There is a tent inside it. Set up a camp. Maranna, I'll need some help. The only chance we have to save the Gem Bush is to steal it tonight."

Iyaca asked, "How are you going to steal a tree?"

Rhiann said, "The Nameless Enchanter of Thynna can do many things. It'll leave Thynna the same way it got here. My Uncle Mayard used Dig and the reverse of Plant Growth and Enlarge Spells to move the Gem Bush. It reduced its size to a twig. He carried it in his pocket."

Maranna said, "The security in the inner ward is higher than ever. More light spells, guards, familiars, Magick Mouth Spells… you name it."

Rhiann said, "I have a plan. We must leave my parents out of it. Meet me near the gatehouse outside Thynna after dark."

Maranna said, "I told Mayard I'd help look after you. I'm not sure that includes helping you with half-witted schemes. I'll go along as long as you are not in jeopardy. I know the place you speak of. I went there with him, too."

Rhiann said, "Maranna, the mark on my face places me in jeopardy. I'm in jeopardy where I now stand."

Maranna shrugged. The siren and young Iyaca exited through the opened window. Rhiann went downstairs and informed his parents of his friends' departure. Caye stared blankly. Kurth looked out the window at the deputy on the corner.

Rhiann said, "Maranna and Iyaca are gone."

Kurth said, "Good. The deputy did not react. You must comply with the council's order, Rhiann. Your mother and I are depending on it."

Rhiann said, "Father, I'm going to tell the guard that I'm leaving Thynna and have him escort me to the gate."

Rhiann kissed his mother's face, gathered his old bag, hat, and cloak, and went outside. He asked the guard to escort him to the outer curtain. The young sorcerer felt numb as he placed houses where he had built childhood memories. At the gate he nodded to Sergeant Redbrick. When the gate opened he stepped outside and trekked toward the woods' edge. At dusk activities in the shops, barracks, and gatehouse were winding down. The tall new clerk remained in the infirmary recovering from the siren's kiss he received a day before. Paperwork was piling up and new recruits camped out waiting to muster into Thynna's mercenary corps. Rhiann used the waiting time to study Mayard's notes. The spells were rather straightforward. Maranna arrived and he revealed his plan. Maranna objected briefly. She disliked carrying males and had already taken Iyaca for a journey earlier. She faded from view and whisked Rhiann over the wall. The siren easily evaded Thynna's airborne defenses and carried him to an alley in the inner ward. Several guards stood around the Gem Bush. Souvenir hunters had taken away most of the chunks from Mayard's destroyed statue. Maranna wrapped her wings around Rhiann. Walking was a bit awkward but they made their way to the fence around the bush. Maranna sang a gentle lullaby. The guards nodded off. Rhiann removed ear plugs from his ears, used a Rock to Mud Spell to get through the fence. He approached the Gem Bush and muttered a series of spells. A sorcerer rounded the corner on an evening constitutional. Maranna approached him and gave him a kiss. His life-mate would search for him for three days before she found him smiling in the alley behind Elliott's store. Rhiann completed his spells. Now only a hole in the ground occupied the spot where Mayard Klarje had planted the Gem Bush. Maranna spirited Rhiann away from Thynna to Wombat Mountain. Iyaca had prepared a site for the tree. Rhiann reversed the spells and planted the Gem Bush near the creek at the base of the mountain. An illusory Terrain Spell create the illusion of purplanana bushes, complete with the nefarious phase spider webs. The deadly spiders were the most feared arachnids in all Sagain. Mayard and Rhiann's bags of holding contained ample items to make their campsite comfortable. The hidden Gem Bush took root. It was no worse for the wear. Rhiann expressed his satisfaction with the transplanting of the rarity and his mastering of his Uncle's regimen.

On the morrow Castellan Yerko, High Sheriff Rhino, Pinochynose, Sorcerer Bailiwick, puppet Lord President Homer, and likewise puppet High Chancellor Odell gathered and launched a full investigation into the loss of the tree. The first suspects were the Klarjes, but the deputy assigned to watch them reported Caye and Kurth remained in their home all night, and Rhiann Klarje had voluntarily left the city. Numerous mercenaries saw the young sorcerer enter the woods north of Thynna alone. Bailiwick and Yerko still pondered his involvement, but there was no evidence to implicate Caye and Kurth Klarje in any wrongdoing. Castellan Yerko ordered all remaining monuments to Mayard Klarje be removed. Bailiwick suspected Old Ones. The bewildered guards were punished severely and reassigned latrine duty for a year. Though they staunchly denied malfeasance, the guards were thought to have imbibed intoxicants. Yerko, Rhino, and Pinochynose had no experience with sirens. Bailiwick's lone encounter was on the road to Dry Creek.

CHAPTER 31

The Source of Magick

Rhiann, Iyaca, and Maranna sat around a fire in the wood's edge at the base of Wombat Mountain. Thick growths of Semper fi trees gave the mountain its fuzzy appearance. The Gem Bush sat in its new home surrounded by semper fi trees. The fire reflected in the Gem Bush's sparkling fruits. The three talked long into the night.

Rhiann said, "This place held a special place in Uncle Mayard's heart. It shall be our home, Iyaca. Maranna, it will provide you a roof whenever you desire."

Iyaca said, "Boss…do you mind if I call you, 'boss'? Begging your pardon, but we are sitting in a tent."

Rhiann chuckled and said, "We'll build a home. A home where all Old Ones will be welcome and any sorcerers who are tolerant. We'll call the place Harmony House."

Iyaca said, "You are handy with spells. Construction should be easy enough."

Rhiann said, "Iyaca. I want to honor Uncle Mayard's feelings that Magick should be used appropriately. We'll use standard construction methods whenever possible. We'll use Magick to hide the Gem Bush. The leaders of Thynna cannot learn of its location."

Iyaca said, "We'll be in hot water if they catch us with it."

Rhiann said, "More importantly the Castellan and his cronies will abuse the wonderful tree. Its priceless gems will buy them many mercenaries. This fertile ground will serve my plans well."

The walls of Thynna did not bar entry to Maranna. The siren flew over the wall unnoticed like a great cat in the dark, and then she was the darkness. Under Maranna's tutelage Iyaca Vassi had developed unequaled stealth, which enabled him to wander the streets, alleys, and recesses of the City of Magick. Young Iyaca's undocumented presence had angered Thynna's privileged. Not being a spell caster also made him an outcast. Nonetheless, Maranna and Iyaca became valuable eyes and ears for Rhiann Klarje in Thynna. Guards like Redbrick and Rhiann's old childhood nemesis Jethro were sympathetic to the young sorcerer. Rhiann pushed his Nameless Enchanter of Thynna moniker. Most began to refer to him as simply NET. Rhiann reentered Thynna sometimes alone and on rare occasions with Iyaca and Maranna. His friends had to avoid contact with his parents. His parents strictly adhered to the orders of the Council of Thynna. The Castellan's minions searched for the Gem Bush and never found clues. Thynna's armies grew and tensions with the Old Ones increased. Rhiann relayed to his parents Mayard's suggestions that Rhiann explore the Veldt and the Seven Wonders. His parents were opposed. Arguments always followed Rhiann's visits. By the spring of Iyaca's sixteenth year the homestead Harmony House provided basic housing. Progress was very slow. Maranna left development of Cragmore in Serena's hands and visited often. On one of her visits Rhiann expressed the desire to retrieve his personal possessions from his room in Thynna, including the mirror ICU and his bed, which had always grown with him. Maranna agreed to stay with Iyaca and mind Harmony House.

After his travels with his Uncle Mayard, Rhiann Klarje asked questions, like why, where, how, and when? Libraries, tomes, teachers, and his parents answered few of his questions. The inquisitive sorcerer had exhausted all sources of knowledge within the city. The youthful sorcerer felt the elders' policies were unfair, iniquitous, and unwarranted. He again found attitudes in Thynna had not changed. His parents grew ever more in line with the Council's thinking. Lord Bailiwick and Castellan Yerko further solidified their hold of the city of Magick. Deputies monitored Rhiann's movements in the outer ward, and he, Caye, and Kurth were still forbidden to enter the inner ward. The inflexibility and intolerability of leaders of Thynna chagrined the aspiring son of Kurth Marsh and Caye Klarje. Rhiann extended his visit to try to help his parents deal with their plight.

Dreams troubled Rhiann Klarje. Sometimes he awakened with knowledge of a new spell. More often odd facts appeared in his thoughts. Invariably what he saw in his dreams came to be true.

Rhiann suffered through a particularly difficult argument with his parents about the elders of Thynna. The young sorcerer retreated to his room and brooded for several days. The Siren Maranna worried about his absence from Harmony House and silently flew over the walls of Thynna and stealthily entered his bedchamber. Rhiann scarcely acknowledged her and simply stared into the mirror.

Maranna queried, "Hello, Rhiann. What have you been doing? I… uh, we've missed you."

The siren folded her wings behind her and stood by Rhiann's open window.

Rhiann Klarje said, "I am weary but can't find sleep."

Maranna answered, "I can help you. Close your eyes."

Rhiann said, "You are beautiful in the starlight. If you sing, I shan't be able to resist you.""

Maranna cooed, "Would that be so bad?"

Rhiann answered, "I value our friendship more than a night of passion!"

Maranna replied, "I won't seduce you. I've had many chances and have not. Reason has left the leaders of Thynna. We need you at Harmony House. The Old Ones need you at the Hanging Gardens. I'm told Decima opines over your absence. Eyerthrin seldom visits. I've little news to report."

Rhiann said, "Why did you risk coming to Thynna?"

Maranna blushed and said, "Iyaca and I worry about you. Our concerns are justified. Your mind is troubled. You need rest. Close your eyes."

NET sighed and lay back onto his comfortable cot and stared at the beautiful winged siren. Maranna sang. Rhiann wanted to hold her more than take his next breath. Her soothing voice instead lured him to sleep.

Maranna sighed and said, "Perhaps one day, my love, I'll share your bed."

The siren left the sleeping sorcerer.

Pleasant memories filled Rhiann's dreams. The siren's song sent him into the deepest sleep he'd ever attained. He dreamed of the depth of the siren's eyes. Then shapeless grayness entered his dreams.

Wisps…
Threads…
Threads of Magick…
Threads of fate…
Threads of time…
Threads connecting worlds …
Dreams connecting worlds …
Dreams of Magick…
The Magick of Dreams…
Magick connecting dreams…
Magick connecting worlds…
Grayness…

Grayness oft preceded the appearance of new spell incantations. For the first time in Rhiann's dreams the formless grayness spoke. Words formed in the young sorcerer's mind. "Seek the source of Magick. Go to the point of impact in the Lonely Cliffs."

Rhiann said, "How will I find it?"

The voice answered, "Head southeast from Wombat Mountain. Approach the tallest butte. Follow the red sand. Greatness awaits you."

Rhiann managed, "Who are you?"

The voice answered, "I am the grayness of Andreas. You may call me Xenn."

Grayness faded. Rhiann slept soundly for the better part of a day and awakened refreshed and with great resolve. When he awakened, new dweomers appeared in his mind. His dreams fired them in his memory like a kiln.

When the young sorcerer discussed his intention to explore the uncharted region with his parents, a bitter fight ensued. Both Kurth and Caye expressed their disdain, but this did not dissuade the youthful spell caster. Rhiann planned an excursion with his two most loyal and steadfast friends, the ageless Siren Maranna and Iyaca Vassi.

Rhiann Klarje left Thynna and reached Wombat Mountain by dawn. The twin suns slowly rose in the east. Maranna flew over the expanse of desert to the south. The womanly creature returned and reported searing heat, great expanses of sand, and a table rock formation ten leagues into the desert beyond the fringe of the grassy prairie. Fine smoke rose above the stone ridge. Both Maranna and Iyaca hoped to accompany NET.

Rhiann said, "Thank you, but I must go on alone. It's time to erect a permanent home outside Thynna. Erect a cottage at this site. Use the wood of the semper fi trees. Semper fi trees cover Wombat Mountain and create its fuzzy appearance. Their wood molds like butter and hardens with time."

NET entered the desert alone, followed the directions from his dream, and grew stronger with every southeasterly step. He traveled across burning sands for several days. Then he noted red rivulets in the hot sand. Small vermin eagerly lapped up the red moisture and parted from it unwillingly. The sorcerer bent down to the ground and closely inspected the moist red sand. The redness was not the blood of an unfortunate beast. Rhiann scooped up some of the red soaked sand. He sniffed the odorless sand and rubbed granules of sand between his fingers. The sand sifted between his fingers and left behind droplets of deep ruby red fluid, which pooled in his right palm.

Ingestion of the strange ichors did not harm the denizens of the desert. His tankard was near empty. He gently touched the tip of his left index finger to the growing pool of liquid and found the consistency of red grape juice. Rhiann gingerly tasted the liquid with the tip of his tongue. The slightly bitter fluid left a pleasant after taste. The sorcerer waited a moment and licked the moisture from his right palm.

NET felt warm, flushed, and suffered a slight headache. The symptoms soon passed. He scooped up more reddened sand, filtered it thorough his fingers, and drank the small quantity of liquid. His thirst and hunger disappeared. Rhiann worked diligently, collected four ounces of the fluid, and stored it in a small spare canteen.

Carefully the wandering wizard followed the crimson path in the sand to the Lonely Cliffs. Even small vermin deserted the arid purlieu of the odd butte. The fine scarlet lines ended at the base of the cliffs. Careful inspection revealed a secret, cleverly concealed mechanism that opened a door in the seemingly solid rock wall that led to a crudely hewn stairway leading into the interior of the cliffs. Rhiann cast Detect Magick and Find the Trap Spells. The spell caster found no traps or evidence of Magick. Rhiann laboriously negotiated the stairs and eventually found his way to a dimly lit grotto. A column of light fell from the ceiling of the massive cavern, illuminated a small area of the cave's floor, and hit squarely on an irregular dark gray rock, which was imbedded in the softer rock of the cavern floor. NET peered upward. An irregular opening similar in size to the gray rock on the cavern's floor allowed a bit of outside light to enter the cavern. Gray light emanated from the ugly rock and masked the rays from the distant twin suns. Detect Magick revealed blinding auras throughout the odd grotto. The young sorcerer tentatively extended his left leg and tapped the solid floor of the cavern with his well-made boot. No traps... only the desert and concealed opening secured the grotto.

Rhiann Klarje stood in an opening about five feet high and three feet wide. The smooth stone walls of the cavern extended twenty feet to the left and thirty feet to the right. The ceiling was probably thirty feet high at the point where the sky was visible. Dim gray light made it difficult to estimate the depth of the cavern. At some time, the cavern had witnessed extreme heat like dragon fire or Fire Magick. Stale air belied the open ceiling. A stone table sat to his left. From his vantage point he couldn't tell whether the waist high table was contiguous with the floor of the cavern. Something sat upon the two-foot long by three-foot wide table. Carefully the young sorcerer inched into the cavern and moved along the wall.

Rhiann felt very mature, very powerful, and strangely comfortable in the cavern. Had no one discovered this place? The sorcerer heard only his labored breathing. Rhiann held his breath, listened, reached into one of the pockets of his vest, and removed a small rounded device. He gently squeezed the device, and light flowed from his hands. The Continual Light Spell illuminated the ancient cavern. The grayness dimmed the effect of the usually brilliant light. Nothing moved in the shadows. Rhiann was alone. He cautiously approached the stone table.

A small closed chest and narrow cylindrical tube rested upon the table, which was an extension of the stone floor. The sorcerer inspected the chest. It was the length of twenty inchworms, height of twelve, and depth of fifteen. The scroll tube was made of an amalgam of silver and other metals; its diameter was the length of two inchworms and its length twenty. (The inchworm had a consistent length, which had served as a standard of short measure since antiquity. A grown man's foot was typically the length of twelve of the little critters stretched end to end. Twelve inches was termed a "foot.") Intuition told him not to touch the chest and scroll tube.

The sorcerer was drawn to the odd gray stone. Grayness emanated from the stone and diminished the Continual Light Spell. Odd gray light covered him and felt strangely good. Red fluid emerged and flowed from points on both the right and left side of the large gray stone. Two gray stone fragments lay on the cavern floor below the points where red fluid trickled from the stone. The two fragments emitted the same grayness. The larger fragment rested to the left. It was one by one-half cubit. The smaller on the right was one-half by one-half cubit. Ominous red auras flashed unpredictably, briefly overpowered the grayness, and filled the room with redness.

Rhiann gingerly touched the stone and felt the coldness of a rock undisturbed for thousands of centuries. The gray stone reacted to his touch, shimmered, warmed, and mimicked soft flesh. He felt a powerful wave of Magick. Lights, visions, and every spell he had ever read or cast briefly rushed through him. Placing both hands on the gray stone refreshed Rhiann Klarje. The sorcerer lifted the stone fragments and held the larger stone in his left hand and smaller in his right. The stones had little weight.

Searing pain flowed into his hands and coursed through his body. Rhiann dropped the stones and muttered aloud, "Fool!"

The larger stone hit the stone floor and shattered into one large and seven smaller fragments. The fragments changed from gray to yellow color. The seven smaller stones were indistinguishable in shape, size, and color. Yellow light flashed from the eight fragments.

The smaller stone shattered into one large and four smaller fragments. The fragments changed from gray to purple. The four little fragments were impossible to tell apart in shape, size, and color. Mauve, purple light flashed from the five stones.

Images of numbers appeared in his mind.

Thirteen and two…

Then an unseen force knocked Rhiann to the floor and scraped his knees. An unfamiliar incantation flowed from his mouth. The Create Wood Spell produced thirteen unremarkable identical lengths of common hardwood akin to an old man's walking stick.

The thought of touching the yellow and purple fragments of rock to the ends of the staffs entered his mind. Initially he avoided the seven small yellow fragments. Folklore of Sagain held seven heralded bad luck.

Rhiann touched one of the four smaller purple stones to a length of wood. Nothing happened. Then he cautiously picked up and touched the large purple stone to a length of wood.

Great auras of Magick filled the cavern!

Gray, then purple light…

The large purple stone adhered to the end of the length of wood. Symbols appeared on the shaft of the staff.

Ǿ ∞ Ǿ

The name **"Atlas"** appeared in his mind and he spoke it aloud.

The staff emitted eerie purple light that filled the cavern. Instantly the four smaller purple fragments moved to four lengths of wood nearest the staff he called Atlas. The four stones simultaneously meld with the wood; then the four aligned facing north, south, east, and west. The four emitted less intense purple auras. Four sets of the same runes **Ǿ ∞ Ǿ** appeared around the circumference of each staff at its midpoint. A single rune appeared on the handhold of each staff. Runes of N, S, W, and E differentiated the four otherwise identical staves. The runes were from an old language that NET had learned from his mother by the hearth fire.

The name **"The Staves of the Four Winds"** appeared in his mind and he spoke the words aloud.

The large yellow fragment hummed and the yellow glow intensified.

The enchanter touched the larger yellow stone to one of the lengths of wood. Again there were great auras of Magick and the stone merged with the staff.

The name **"Pleione"** appeared in his mind and he spoke it aloud.

The staff Atlas sent a mauve ray of light to the glowing yellow stone.

Then simultaneously the staves Atlas and Pleione sent respectively rays of purple and yellow light to the seven remaining yellow fragments. The colored rays hit the yellow stones, merged, and created a red glow. The seven stones merged with the seven remaining lengths of wood and the archaic symbols **Ǿ ∞ Ǿ** again appeared and repeated seven times on the circumference of the staves at their midpoint.

Monikers appeared in his mind and he spoke aloud, "I deem you the Pleiades, **the Seven Sisters,** the seed of the union of Atlas and Pleione. Your names are **Alcyone, Merope, Celaeno, Electra, Maia, Taygeta, and Asterope.**"

His voice echoed from the walls of the cavern.

Then blackness...

He fell unconscious.

Shapeless grayness again entered his mind.

Wisps...

Threads...

Threads of Magick...

Threads of fate...

Threads of time...

Threads connecting worlds ...

Dreams connecting worlds ...

Dreams of Magick...

The Magick of Dreams...

Magick connecting dreams...

Magick connecting worlds...

Grayness...

Rhiann shivered in his deep sleep.

The voice said, "You have done well. Sagain's legacies have reached other worlds. Knowledge must be passed forward."

Rhiann dreamed of fabulous places. His mind's eye traveled to the Seven Wonders of Ancient Sagain in the Veldt and found them exactly as his Uncle Mayard described. He dreamed of faraway worlds, including an odd world with three suns, a beautiful blue world, and a primitive world. He dreamed of supervising the creation of analogs to Sagain's Seven Wonders in the "blue world." He dreamed of standing at the edge of a Green Vale in the World of Three Suns, whilst standing amongst reds, oranges, and yellows. He dreamed of a primitive world barely touched by Magick. He dreamed of laboriously writing detailed descriptions of these places in tomes. Images of ancient Sagain and the grotto of the bleeding gray stone filled his mind. His hands recorded the deeds of others. Fabulous spells… rare material components… Old Ones… arcane forces… grayness.

Rhiann awakened, stiff, tired, and cold. The working of a great spell appeared in his mind. The incantation was more complex than any he had ever read; yet he knew it well. The incantation was also etched in a strange tome with violet parchment pages beside him on the floor of the cavern. The text was written in the old language in shimmering silver runes.

The writing was without question by his hand!

In some fugue state he had written the incantation upon the magnificent pages, but such an intricate effort would have taken years for the greatest scribe to record. Flawless, flowing runes filled the volume, recorded the Spell, and detailed the thirteen staffs. The cover of the tome read in the old language the **Tome of Translocation**. The same symbols

$$\emptyset \infty \emptyset$$

were etched upon the cover of the Tome. Alien material composed the pages, ink, and cover of the tome. The Great Spell required exceedingly rare shypoke eggshells as a material component.

Rhiann was alone. He scanned the walls of the cavern, which were bare before his lapse of awareness. His handwriting now covered the walls. The thirteen staves rested on the floor of the cavern. The small chest and elongated silver tube sat upon the table. His handwriting also appeared on the far wall. He studied the etchings further and muttered a Comprehend Languages Spell and read the runes. The Old Language apparently written by his hand. He read the archaic writing aloud, "Bloodstone: The Fountain of Magick."

The old runes told of "fire" falling from the sky and striking the land. After a time of cooling ancients braved the desert, came to the Lonely Cliffs, created the stairs with their primitive tools, and discovered the gray rock, the two shards fractured from the rock, and the flow of red liquid from the rock. None touched the Bloodstone and its fragments. Rhiann had been the first to do so. His hand had written the story on the cavern's walls. Additional runes detailed the creation of thirteen and two staves. Only thirteen cudgels lay in the cavern.

The sorcerer turned his attention to the table.

The uninspiring chest and the elaborate scroll tube now bore the same symbols.

Ǿ ∞ Ǿ

The sorcerer gingerly picked up the surprisingly heavy chest and found no opening mechanism. Eerie lights flickered from the chest, the large gray stone in the center of the room, and the thirteen staves. Rhiann returned the chest to the table, walked over to gray stone, and studied the purple staff. The sorcerer reached down and picked up the staff. Instantly the cudgel meld with his hand and he heard a single word of the Old Language in his mind. He muttered the word aloud: "Open!"

Rhiann Klarje heard a clicking sound. Chest on the table opened.

The numbers "thirteen and one" appeared in his mind. The light surrounding the gray stone again dimmed. Another length of wood lay by the gray rock. The purple staff glowed, passed a ray of mauve light to the fourteenth length of wood, and transformed the simple cudgel to an elaborate staff. The staff bore only one set of the now familiar symbols.

Ǿ ∞ Ǿ

Atlas communicated to the young sorcerer, "This is a gift from the grayness of Andreas. Xenn. The Staff of Entry is a means to enter places that are closed to you."

Perplexed, Rhiann muttered aloud, "How?"

Rhiann Klarje felt safe, warm, and cozy.

The fourteenth staff rested by the gray stone in the center of the cavern.

The sorcerer turned his attention to the silver cylinder, carefully picked up the tube, noted its minimal weight, curiously removed the stopper from the tube, found, and removed ancient rolled vellum. The same material composed the pages of the blank parchment and Tome of Translocation.

Rhiann held the staff Atlas, peered into the opened chest, and saw another book. He studied the cover of the tome and then carefully opened the book. The volume, titled, **"The Traveler's Tome,"** contained blank and handwritten pages. The material was identical to the Tome of Translocation and blank vellum from the silver cylinder. The handwritten pages told fantastic stories of travel to faraway worlds.

His handwriting created the extraordinary script!

Had he visited the Seven Wonders of the Ancient World of Sagain in the Veldt? He had seen them in his dreams and had detailed knowledge of the Hanging Gardens from his travels with Mayard. Rhiann only knew of the other wonders from Mayard's descriptions, yet *his* handwriting described them in detail.

The Seven Wonders of the Veldt enjoyed a prominent place in the literature of Sagain. Though many wrote of the seven extraordinary places, the locations of most were long lost. Death had been the reward of most who sought the Seven Wonders, and this resulted in the number seven becoming synonymous with bad luck.

The Travelers Tome detailed the histories, mysteries, and hidden locations of the storied Wonders. Ancients of Sagain constructed the Hanging Gardens of Redcreek, the Statue of Jove at Sparta, the Temple of the Amazon Huntress Artemis, the Equine Shrine of Halicarnassus (A lost city), the Colossus of Bourmorck, the Continual Light House of Alexandria (another lost city), and finally the Great Pyramid of Deception. The site of each wonder filled a hexagonal area 13 leagues on a side. Thirteen such hexagonal areas separated each wonder from the Great Pyramid and one another.

Rhiann Klarje opened the rare vellum and read,

"Of the Seven Ancient Wonders of Sagain:

"Of the First Wonder: "In the south and west of the Veldt, the waters of Red Creek became enriched with minerals and nutrients. There Magick, Nature, and the ancients created the Hanging Gardens of Sagain. The foliage and opulence of plant growth was unequaled anywhere in the world, even at the Laurels, the citadel of the Light Sorcerers.

"Of the Second Wonder:

"The Temple of Jove at Sparta in Sagain honored the Old One who created the legendary nectar which bore his name. Jove's nectar had legendary properties, but no recipe survived. The statue of Jove was created in the Veldt at the little village Sparta.

"Of the Third Wonder:

"The Temple of the Amazon Huntress Artemis sat at the gap that led to the lands of the Amazons in the great mountains at the far western fringes of the Veldt. The highly intelligent Amazons disdained contact with other peoples, particularly their ancient enemies the giants. Magick touched the Amazons. There had been a queen named Artemis whose deeds filled many campfire songs and legends, but no written records existed of her activities on Sagain. The specifics of the Temple of Artemis and the queen to whom it was dedicated had always been a cause for debate among Sagain's scholars. Hunters paid homage to the queen of the Amazons. Archers sought the expertise of the Amazons, for the great warriors' bow making was unparalleled. Although the Amazons bartered with hunters and archers, the huge warriors kept secret the location of Artemis's temple.

"Of the Fourth Wonder: "The Equine Shrine of Halicarnassus recognized the importance of the steeds, which bore and labored for the ancients of Sagain. Many varieties of these animals were indigenous to Sagain, including simple warhorses and equines that flew, sang, danced, talked, and performed all manner of fantastic tasks. Massive figures of such equines filled the huge temple.

"Of the Fifth Wonder:

"The Colossus of Bourmorck was created by one of the earliest sorcerers to call himself a Dark Sorcerer. Bourmorck built a massive golem at the Crossroads of Infinity, near the small oasis hamlet Rhoades. The golem stood at the intersection of great lines that formed a symbol of infinity on the soils deep in the Veldt, near the eastern sea. Given the proper command, the great golem created by Bourmorck uprooted and walked about.

"Of the Sixth Wonder:

"The Continual Light House of Alexandria served as a prototype on Sagain. The Spell of Continual Light was cast upon the summit of the building, and the Magick served as a beacon much more effectively and predictably than a flame. The spell was cast upon half of a spherical stone that was set in motion by a Rotation Spell. A Permanence Spell completed the project, which resulted in an alternating light that could be seen from afar.

"Of the Seventh Wonder:

"The Great Pyramid of Deception of Sagain sat at a central point equidistant from the other six wonders. Legends held it contained great treasures. The expanse of the Veldt helped keep the secrets of the great pyramid."

The Travelers Tome told of other civilizations, including civilizations of other worlds. The hauntingly familiar handwriting described them in detail. The detailed descriptions were written in first person. Were his dreams real? Had he actually been to other worlds? He had written on the walls of the grotto and the chronicle, but he remembered the immaculate details of the story only after reading the narrative.

The plot thickened further.

Numbers appeared in his head and he spoke them aloud, "Thirteen and two."

Yet another length of wood lay by the gray stone. Atlas's mauve glow intensified and the staff sent a ray of dark violet light to the fifteenth staff. Was this staff identical to the Staff of Entry? This cudgel had a different single set of symbols at its midpoint.

∞ **Ø** ∞

The fifteenth staff aligned end to end with its antithesis the Staff of Entry.

Atlas communicated, "This is the Staff of Closure. Use its power to bar entry. The Staves of Polarity are gifts of Andreas. Grayness. Xenn. Thank the Bloodstone."

Rhiann rested Atlas against the gray stone, reached with his right hand to retrieve the staff of Entry, received a powerful shock, and collapsed to the floor. Grayness filled his dreams. More travels… more places… more writing.

Rhiann awakened and pondered the length of his sleep. The young sorcerer shook off the stiffness and looked around the cavern. Nothing had changed. The Staves of Polarity had realigned end to end. There was a well-healed scar on his right hand where he had touched the Staff of Entry. The purple staff Atlas emitted mauve auras.

"That was stupid! But, what should I do," he mused and took the purple staff in his left hand.

Atlas glowed intensely and sent the message, ""Use the other hand."

Rhiann placed Atlas in his right hand, bent down, extended his left hand, picked up the Staff of Entry, and braced for another shock. None came. He comfortably held Atlas in his right hand and the Staff of Entry in his left. He rested the Staff of Entry against the gray stone, extended his left hand, and started to take the Staff of Closure.

Atlas again communicated, "Use the other hand."

Rhiann transferred Atlas to his left hand, bent down, took the Staff of Closure in his right hand, and felt comfortable.

"What now?" he mused.

"Use both hands," the voice, which was growing familiar and also sounding a bit impatient, implored.

Rhiann rested Atlas against the gray stone, and picked up the Staff of Entry with his left hand. He now held the Staves of Polarity, the Staff of Entry in his left hand and the Staff of Closure in his right hand. He experienced no discomfort, but a great force tried to push the staves apart.

A logical thought appeared in his mind. "Opposites repel."

NET turned the handhold of the Staff of Entry toward the ground and attempted to touch the tip of the Staff of Closure. The handhold of the staff neared its opposite's tip but violently turned away at the last moment and avoided contact. The sorcerer was unable to touch the staves end to end.

"You risk Thunderstruck!" appeared in his mind.

A loud clap of thunder echoed though the cavern and rattled the twelve staves lying on the floor. Atlas rested against the Bloodstone and sent the message, "Touching opposites destroys. Touching the Staves of Polarity to one another creates a powerful destructive spell, which does not spare the bearer of the staves."

Rhiann Klarje attempted to approximate the handholds of the staves. As the handholds approximated an arc of energy passed between them.

The sorcerer yelped, "Ouch!"

Another shock drove consciousness from him, and again he slept. He dreamed of not only wondrous places and times but also horrific and disturbing images.

Fire...evil...the stuff of nightmares...

Names...

DECKSTEQ.

Dreamraiders...

Redness replaced grayness.

Wisps...

Threads...

Threads of Magick...

Threads of fate...

Threads of time...

Threads connecting worlds ...

Dreams connecting worlds ...

Dreams of Magick...

The Magick of Dreams...

Magick connecting dreams...

Magick connecting worlds...

Dream raiders...

Elf pressure...

Albtraum...

Albträume, elf dreams, nightmares...

Others probed his dreams.

Nameless...

A gravelly voice muttered, "I see you and thank you for showing me the path."

Redness faded to blue. Grayness returned.

NET awakened, glanced quickly around the cavern, and detected subtle changes. The Staves of Polarity again lay end to end but did not touch. The purple staff Atlas leaned against the gray rock and kept mauve lights on both the Staff of Entry and Staff of Closure. The chest was again closed, the scroll tube remained open, and the vellum stretched across the stone table. NET walked over to the table. Writing written by his hand in the Old Language covered the previously blank vellum from the silver scroll tube. Rhiann could not translate the writing.

Atlas telepathically suggested, "You'd feel stronger if you held me!" Rhiann walked over to Atlas, took the purple staff in his left hand, and returned to the table. Holding Atlas enabled Rhiann to read the limerick written on the ancient vellum.

"I thank grayness. I thank Atlas and Pleione. I thank the Seven Sisters. I thank the Staves of the Four Winds, the Windward Staves, children of the Bloodstone, the Source of Magick."

Ǿ ∞ Ǿ

Reading the words aloud opened the chest.

Opening the chest by reciting the limerick and holding the purple staff and uttering "open" disarmed multiple Glyphs of Warding, which protected the chest. Attempting to open the chest without reciting the limerick written on the parchment or holding the purple staff Atlas triggered and exploded the Glyphs. Disarming Glyphs was beyond most sorcerers.

Rhiann Klarje's nap refreshed him, and the sorcerer returned to the gray stone and again touched the lump of rock. Now he felt a cold and lifeless boulder. Red liquid steadily oozed like ichors from wounds from the two previously noted sites. The red fluid flowed from the stone, ran across the hard floor of the cavern, extended to the wall, seeped through, exited to the soil of the desert, and created red lines in the sand. He touched the flowing red liquid. The crimson ichors thickened… like… blood.

Rhiann Klarje heard a low-pitched rhythmic rumble akin to the sound of distant thunder or slow heartbeat of a sleeping giant. The sound emanated from the Bloodstone and reverberated against the walls of the small cavern. Dark maroon fluid gushed from the stone with each thump. Rhiann rubbed his fingers against his dirty vest. The sorcerer took a deep breath, left the strange rock, returned to the opened chest, and peered into the little trunk. The chest contained the Tome of Translocation, the Travelers Tome, and fragments of fossilized eggshells from the long-extinct Shypoke. Shypoke eggshell was the essential material component for the spell detailed in the Translocation Tome. The Translocation Spell became one of Sagain's greatest treasures.

Low-level Teleportation Spells worked over short distances and allowed no encumbrance. The spell caster arrived at his destination nude and defenseless. Word of Return Spells instantly brought the sorcerer back to his sanctuary and allowed some burden. Teleportation and Word of Return enabled little more than escape and produced tiny ripples on the sea of Magick. The boundless dweomer Translocation created great waves. The complex incantation of the Ninth Level Translocation Spell was far beyond the power of most sorcerers. Traveling beyond one's world was dangerous. Assuring a habitable destination required refinement and amplification of the spell.

Rhiann accepted the gift of the scarlet liquid and drank deeply from the Bloodstone's flowing crimson ichors and stored some of the red fluid in his tankard. The Bloodstone's life's blood granted Rhiann new energies and etched the incantation of the great Translocation Spell in his mind. The mysterious gray boulder of unknown origin had fomented the dawn of Magick on Sagain. NET placed the Tome of Translocation and precious supply of the rare shypoke eggshells in the little chest, and returned the vellum to the silver cylinder. He placed the Staff of Closure in his right hand and touched the scroll tube with the staff. The chest and scroll tube sealed and all writing disappeared from the chest. Without Atlas, opening the artifacts required Spells of Detect Magick, Comprehend Languages, and finally Dispel Magick.

NET held Atlas and said, "I thank grayness. I thank Atlas and Pleione. I thank the Seven Sisters. I thank the Staves of the Four Winds, the Windward Staves, children of the Bloodstone, the Source of Magick."

Another aura of Magick filled the cavern and a small rucksack appeared on his belt. Rhiann placed the Traveler's Tome in the Bag of Holding. One by one and by their own volition, the other fourteen staves entered the little sack. The last to enter were the Staves of Polarity. When the Staff of Closure followed its antithesis into the storage device, the little Magick sack rumbled a bit. The staves and tome did not increase the weight of the wondrous sack.

Rhiann said, "I thank grayness. I thank Atlas and Pleione. I thank the Seven Sisters. I thank the Staves of the Four Winds, the Windward Staves, children of the Bloodstone, the Source of Magick."

The Nameless Enchanter of Thynna then held a snow white Phoenix feather and uttered a simple incantation. He raised the purple staff Atlas in his left hand, levitated, and flew through the opening in the roof of the cavern. Rhiann explored the Veldt. The writings of the Traveler's Tome accurately depicted the locations of the Seven Wonders. Rhiann planned to keep the cavern and its treasures secret and safe from the squabbling factions of Sagain.

CHAPTER 32

600 Years

Rhiann then returned to Wombat Mountain to rejoin Maranna and Iyaca Vassi. The cottage was completed. Extensive gardens grew around the homestead. Rhiann felt disappointment. His friends must have commandeered Magick to produce such growth, and he'd asked they adhere to Mayard's wishes and limit its use. Rhiann found Iyaca working in the cottage. His apprentice looked older.

Iyaca said uncertainly, "It's you, isn't it?"

Net marveled, "Of course it's me. I realize *p-Mayard* and real-Mayard mimicked me, but they are gone. Why'd you doubt me?"

Iyaca said, "You look the same. It's like you've not even been away."

Rhiann answered, "Iyaca, are you well? In this dim light, I'd swear you look older. Nice work on the cottage! I'm amazed you finished it so quickly! I'd rather you had avoided using Magick, but the end result is impressive."

Iyaca replied, "What do you mean quickly? I am older, and we didn't use Magick. Rhiann, we'd nigh given up on you. Only stories of powerful Magick to the south and east and reports from Old Ones saying they'd spotted you in the Veldt gave us the hope that you would yet someday return. You've been gone six centuries, six hundred changes of the seasons!"

Rhiann said, "You jest! I see my reflection in ICU! I look the same. How?"

Iyaca replied, "I see you still need convincing. You have been away six centuries." Iyaca called, "Maranna, the wayfarer has returned." The mature apprentice stared at Rhiann.

Rhiann said, "I feel like I'm on display in Thynna's museum."

The siren Maranna entered the room.

Rhiann said, "Maranna, you are as lovely as ever. Is Iyaca teasing me?"

Maranna said, "It's true. You are not of the Old Ones, yet time has not touched you. How? Where? I flew over every inch of the Veldt, including those cursed buttes."

Rhiann said, "I was oblivious to the passage of time."

Iyaca noted, "You were unaffected by the passage of time."

Maranna touched the heart-shaped, cherry-red birthmark on Rhiann's face, bent over and gently kissed him, and said, "I wasn't the only one who searched. Decima implored Chiron to send out search parties. She rode centaurs throughout the Veldt for years. Your parents Kurth and Caye used their limited resources and searched for you. The Council of Thynna looked for you also, but only because they considered you a suspect in the disappearance of the Gem Bush. Search parties came around here, but Venla Faxxine and others scared them off. Your illusory Magick has served us and the little tree well. It's thrived, by the way."

Rhiann said, "Decima... searched for me? Has she changed?"

Maranna said, "Doesn't look a day older. Constantly opines over your absence. The Three Sisters are as stubborn as ever. Many occasions have brought Thynna and the forces of the Hanging Gardens close to war. Thynna's allies now include the Giants from Hinderburgh and the Kobold legions of the north. Bailiwick and Yerko have solidified their hold of Thynna. Aging has not softened their dispositions. Shortly after you disappeared, the truly elected Lord President Homer and High Chancellor Odell both died mysteriously. Yerko's puppets President Bogni and High Chancellor Lubick are very old now. They have never been more than figureheads."

Rhiann blurted, "My parents? And brother Arthur Seigh?"

Iyaca said, "Your parents are still in fairly good health. Many sorcerers now see their thousandth year. They sent your brother Arthur Seigh Klarje away to attend school at the Laurels, a small village to the north near Hunter's Peak. Kurth and Caye hoped to remove your younger brother from the discord that gripped Thynna and lessen the likelihood he'd follow in your footsteps. The Laurels has become a gathering point for thinkers and philosophers. As you suggested, we call the cottage Harmony House."

Rhiann said, "You've done well. Finishing the house and protecting the Gem Bush at the same time. My time away enlightened me. I found the Source of Magick. In so doing, I may have discovered a means to fulfill my Uncle Mayard's dreams of preserving what is good of Sagain and her Magick. In fact, ... I may have already done some things."

Iyaca said, "You *may* have? How can you not know?"

Rhiann Klarje shook his head, "Grayness? Magick? Even I don't understand, my friends. I have artifacts that cannot fall into the hands of the Council of Thynna. Maranna, is this center of knowledge where my brother resides being true to Uncle Mayard's ideas?"

Maranna answered, "I'm not versed in Magick. The world is for the most part just as you left it. The Laurels is the exception. Unlike Thynna, outcasts and learners are welcomed there. Your brother Arthur Seigh is a highly-regarded educator. Those who flock to the Laurels deem themselves Light Sorcerers and concentrate on academia and study. There is another center of growth near Mt. Airie. I know little of the small hamlet called Koorlost other than its occupants call themselves Dark Sorcerers and are a bit secretive. Loggers have denuded large tracts of timber on Mt. Airie's slopes to provide building materials for Koorlost's construction."

Rhiann said, "When I went into the desert, I had no idea I'd be away so long. It saddens me to know my Gnomish friends have long passed on. When I saw them leaving Thynna, I had no idea it'd be the last time I'd see them."

Maranna said, "Not all of them have passed on."

Rhiann said, "That's impossible. Gnomes are not sorcerers. Even if they enjoy good health and accumulate thirty names, Gnomes are lucky to live a hundred seasons."

Maranna said, "True. However, the spirit of adventure filled one of your friends. Right after you left, Burgomaster Storming Norman Twenty-four names sought to open relationships and trade with the Hanging Gardens and the Three Sisters. He sent his most reliable officers, including Captain Donovan. The envoys met with the Three Sisters. Mors became enamored with Donovan and shared a strand of her hair. Nona tied Mors' lock to Donovan's hair and bound the strands with fibers from her distaff, just as she did you and Decima and herself and Mayard. Donovan Eighty-four names still journeys to the Hanging

Gardens. He has served as Burgomaster now for over four hundred years. Gnome-town has flourished under his rule. Copper dragons are domesticated. Thynna reacts very little now with the Gnomes. Bailiwick and Yerko even accused Donovan of hiding you and the Gem Bush. But it's all water under the bridge now. Gnome-town allies with the Hanging Gardens. Donovan always asks about you. Thynna's pardon did not extend to Gnome-town. Of course, everyone else you knew in Gnome-town has gone to their ancestors. You'll be glad to know that Donovan's troops captured three of the Fearsome Foursome on the road and made them pay for their crimes. Castellan Yerko objected, but Longbeard, rest his soul, and Donovan held fast. The Man in Black, or John Money, was reassigned duty inside Thynna, and to my knowledge never left the city again. He choked to death on a blooter bone at Elliott's shop. Yerko accused Elliott of fomenting the deed. There were suspicious marks on the body, but Elliott eventually evaded prosecution."

Rhiann said, "So my parents have never gotten back into the Council's good graces."

Iyaca said, "Actually, Kurth Marsh regained his status as a Council member in a few months. He, uh, denounced you and your Uncle Mayard publicly. Your mother remains distant to the council."

Rhiann said, "I understand. He had no choice. He had to think of my mother. I want to go to Thynna and the Hanging Gardens."

Maranna asked, "Should I summon the Cloudmares to carry you?"

Rhiann said, "Who?"

Maranna said, "Oh, I'm sorry, I suppose you are still affected by their Forget Spell. Urra..."

Rhiann chuckled, "That's OK. I remember Urra Shyrra, and Syrrth. My time at the source of Magick changed me. Couldn't resist teasing you."

Maranna quipped, "Not funny."

Rhiann said, "I'd like to send some items to my brother. Maranna, will you carry them to the Laurels. I'm trust you with a big part of Sagain's destiny."

Maranna nodded affirmatively and said, "I'll still carry your items. You didn't answer my question."

Rhiann took the Staff of the West Wind from his ruck sack and said, "No, as long as I have a supply of phoenix feathers, I can get there with this staff. Flying is old hat for me now."

Iyaca said, "Old Hat? What has your hat got to do with flying?"

Rhiann answered, "It's just a figure of speech, Iyaca. It means I've done it enough that I am very comfortable with doing it. I long to see Decima, but I must see my mother first. I'm going to Thynna."

Iyaca said, "If you insist on going to Thynna, you need to know the defenses have been shored up. Your Uncle Mayard's defenses are still employed. By orders of the Council of Thynna the outer gate is Wizard Locked at nightfall. None came pass through without disabling the spell. The guards are carefully chosen and given Gems of Seeing to detect Magick and Invisible Creatures. Rings of Protection make the guards unsusceptible to spells such as Sleep, Death, and Stun. Every night a sorcerer places Protection from Magick Spells on the oncoming shift. The outer curtain is made of Stone of Ooranth, dark black stone impervious to most forces and nigh as hard as red diamonds. The wall stands thirty feet high. Guards on the allure have an unobstructed view of the ground in front of the wall. The bartizans rise another thirty feet and are positioned so that guards see several hundred yards. Continual Light Spells placed on Semper Fi Wood poles long ago illuminate the area on the outside of the wall. Outside the outer curtain, armed guards monitor the activities. During the day the guards control all who enter. Bailiwick installed three combination locks on the door. Failure to open them properly activates a Glyph of Warding. Every day, the combinations change. The sergeant of the guard only opens the door for those thoroughly vetted. Getting into the city is difficult, even for me. I sneak in every now and then just to keep my skills up. I've gotten pretty good at it after 600 years. Be careful. Bailiwick and Yerko's minions are ruthless and thorough. If you get inside, don't expect any help. Bailiwick and Yerko have firmly consolidated their control of the city of Magick. Your parents Kurth and Caye remain compliant to the council's orders. Kurth sits quietly in meetings of the Council of Thynna, and Caye becomes more and more withdrawn. Both fear you are dead. Bailiwick, Yerko, and most leaders relish the idea. Thynna has not seen the mark of the Klarjes since you left. Don't expect it to afford you any advantage."

Rhiann said, "When I left, I was the master and you the apprentice. Now in many ways our roles are reversed. You have great knowledge of Thynna and the world, whilst I have spent my time in a lost grotto.

Thank you for your information. I don't doubt your word, but I must see for myself."

Maranna's reliable wings carried Pleione and the Seven Sister Staves, the Pleiades, to Arthur Seigh Klarje at the Laurels. The eight staves nurtured Magick and became the cornerstone of Light Sorcery. Arthur Seigh accepted the treasures and proclaimed great Pleione "The Staff of the Order of Light Sorcery."

The little chest containing the Tome of Translocation, a supply of shypoke eggshells, and silver scroll tube containing the opening instructions of the chest remained with the hallowed Bloodstone.

CHAPTER 33

Return to Thynna

Rhiann Klarje retained the purple Staff Atlas, Staves of Polarity, ("Left Hand: Entry" and "Right Hand: Closer"), Staves of the Four Winds, Travelers Tome, and the Bag of Holding with its plethora of contents. He had memorized the incantation of the great Translocation Spell. He dispatched Maranna to the Laurels with her precious cargo of the Staff Pleione and the Seven Sister Staves. Rhiann organized his bag of holding and combined some of the items he received from Mayard. He bade Iyaca farewell and used the Staff of the West Wind to fly to the woods near Thynna.

Construction had transformed the area in his absence. Outsiders had created a city outside the great outer curtain. The gatehouse and mercenary barracks had grown into great edifices. Rhiann made his way through visitors, merchants, and soldiers and approached the gate. An officer on duty stood in front of the closed gate. The intimidating officer had turned away several persons who had petitioned for entry. He referred some to the gate house for papers and flatly told others to stay away from the gate. His booming voice unsettled others to the point they retreated to regain their courage. The soldiers wore uniforms emblazoned with the crests of Yerko and Bailiwick. Three complex opening mechanisms had been added to the door. Three large dials dominated the odd black door. Rhiann pulled his cowl over his face and approached the gate keeper.

The sergeant at arms said, "State your business or be away!"

Rhiann answered, "My name is Rhiann Klarje. I petition for entry to the city."

The soldier said, "Your garb implies you are a sorcerer. I'll attribute your choosing to claim to be the infamous lost sorcerer Rhiann Klarje as a mistake of your youth. You even have his mark on your chin. I'm in a particularly generous mood, kid. Here's some free advice. Drop the Klarje act. Lord Bailiwick and Castellan Yerko detest the Klarjes, particularly the one you are mimicking. You don't want to cross the Castellan and High Sorcerer of Thynna. The Klarjes are relics of the past. Now they are relegated to outer ward residents. You'd better wipe that red mark off your face. Here! I'll do you a favor."

The burly sergeant extended a thick index finger and rubbed the heart-shaped, cherry-red birthmark on Rhiann's chin. A small spark left Rhiann's face and burned the sergeant's finger. The big man yelped, "Ouch!"

Obviously the birthmark remained after his gesture. Rhiann bit his tongue and tersely replied, "I am Rhiann Klarje. Please grant me entry."

The soldier said gruffly, "Don't play sorcerers' tricks on me! You could be charged with assaulting an officer. Now you're trying my patience. You have to get papers to enter the city. Go over to the John Money Building and apply. If you get papers, I might let you in."

Rhiann said, "The John Money building? Where…"

The soldier huffed, "Where have you been? The John Money Gate House. It's named in honor of the greatest non-sorcerer to ever serve Thynna. Money became a member of the Council of Thynna before the end of his days. There are statues honoring him all over the inner ward. He's in all the school books. He led the parties searching for the legendary Gem Bush. Rhiann Klarje, the very one you mimic, disappeared about the same time the tree vanished, gosh, over six hundred years ago. Castellan Yerko, High Sorcerer Lord Bailiwick, and Money suspected Rhiann Klarje had a hand in the bush's disappearance, but they never found the rogue or the Gem Bush and were never were able to prove anything. Klarje probably wandered off into the desert and got eaten by one of his Old One friends. Bottom line is he'd be over 600 years old if he were alive and you don't appear to have seen more than 25 seasons. Now… one last time. All newcomers have to be processed. Get in line at the Money building."

Several guards gathered around. Rhiann Klarje was inclined to acquiesce to the sergeant's request. The sorcerer turned away from the massive gate and started toward the building named for Gnome-town's old nemesis. He blended into the crowd near the gate house and observed the activities at the outer curtain.

The sergeant turned and shouted to colleagues on the allure, "Send word to the Castellan. There's a young bloke at the gate calling himself Rhiann Klarje."

The Captain of the Guard challenged, "Are you crazy? I'm not going to message the Council of Thynna that a sorcerer that disappeared 600 years ago wants to enter the city. I saw the man! He's barely twenty!"

The sergeant said, "Did you see he bears the mark of the Klarjes?"

The Captain answered, "Like all the rest of you, I've only read about the birthmark shared by many descendants of the founder of Thynna. Lord Bailiwick has long forbidden mention of the founder's name publicly. I'll send word to High Sheriff Clank's office. If he approaches the gate again, detain him. If he's a Klarje, he's not welcome. If he's not a Klarje, he's taunting the Castellan and High Sorcerer, and that's a pretty dumb move."

More guards gathered near the gate. Rhiann chose to await nightfall. One by one the guards left their posts and returned to the barracks. Per usual the nighttime ritual of closing the gate ensued. When darkness arrived, Rhiann removed the Staff of Entry from his bag of holding, placed an Invisibility Spell on his person, and approached the gate. He touched the staff to the intricate gate. Auras flashed about and the gate opened. Rhiann slipped inside. All manner of confusion ensued. Guards hustled about to try to close the gate. The Captain of the Guard called for battle stations. Rhiann made his way toward his parents' home. The outer ward had changed little in his long absence. Taller spires filled the inner ward and more opulent high rising structures were readily evident inside the inner curtain. Sorcerers were exiting their homes to investigate the ruckus caused by the opening of the gate. Squads of heavily armed inner ward guards rushed toward the gate. The chaos facilitated his trek to Caye and Kurth's modest home. The neighborhood remained familiar. Few things had changed. Curious folk stirred about and moved toward the outer curtain. Rhiann stood outside the door for a while. He sighed and approached the door and knocked.

Rhiann said, "May I enter?"

From within an elderly man's voice cracked, "The hour is late. Return on the morrow."

Rhiann's spirits dropped. Another voice said, "The city is abuzz, Kurth. It might be important."

The door opened. An elderly, unkempt Caye Klarje looked at the young man on her door stoop.

Rhiann said, "Hello, Mother."

Caye Klarje coldly said, "This is a cruel hoax. You are a minion of Bailiwick, and you mock my son all the way down to his birthmark! Have not my mate and I adhered to every request of Lord Bailiwick, Castellan Yerko, and the Council of Thynna?"

Rhiann said, "Mother, it's me. May I enter?"

Caye answered monotonically, "We cannot refuse entry to agents of the Council of Thynna. It's part of our clemency deal. So enter, finish your tormenting, and be gone."

Sorcerers and more guards rushed past. Caye and Kurth's neighbor said as he ran by, "Someone opened the gate."

Rhiann crossed the threshold. Clutter and decline marred the once immaculately maintained home. Rhiann stepped over old clothing and entered the sitting room. Kurth Marsh sat in his overstuffed chair and stared blankly at the wall. The elderly sorcerer scarcely acknowledged Rhiann's entering the room.

Rhiann said, "Father, are you well?"

Kurth looked up at the new arrival and said, "Rhiann left long ago. It strains my memory to recall his appearance, but you look remarkably like him. The birthmark is particularly accurate. Now you've effectively brought back painful memories to my mate... and to me. Tell Lord Bailiwick he has succeeded."

Caye entered and curtly said, "I suppose we'll be accused of opening the gate. Tell High Sorcerer Bailiwick that I haven't uttered a spell in centuries. Magick is as dead to me as my son. Kurth and I have been here all night."

Rhiann pulled the Staff of Entry from the bag of holding and said, "I opened the gate. With this staff. Look! I have... Uncle Mayard's hat... and robe... and spell books. Here's the scarf you made me. And the token you gave me when I lost my first tooth." Rhiann pulled other items from the old bag.

Caye quizzically asked, "Only Rhiann know the significance of these things. You must be… him. You look so young. Are you using a Transformation Spell?"

Rhiann replied, "No, Mother, I was away. Time moved at a different pace for me. I discovered what Uncle Mayard sought. My purpose in life is follow his path and preserve what's good of Magick and Sagain."

Caye said, "Kurth, this *is* our son."

Kurth said, "Then he must leave immediately. There's nothing for him in Thynna. The Castellan, High Sheriff, and Lord Bailiwick can't know he's been here. It's trouble for us."

Caye said, "Your father is correct. When something goes awry in Thynna, we are always the first to blame and be investigated. Deputies will be here soon. You must go."

Rhiann tearfully said, "I… I just wanted to see you… to let you know I'm alive…I…"

Caye said, "Then you have done so. Now, you must leave Thynna. You'll find no help and no sympathetic ears. All traces of your Uncle Mayard are gone. Lord Bailiwick always blamed you for the theft of the Gem Bush. We have suffered in your stead. It's best we live out our days in anonymity."

Kurth stood and demanded, "You have been away over 600 years. Now you return to complicate our lives. We sent your brother as far away from Thynna as was practical. Mayard was an old fool. You are a fool to follow him. Please leave, and don't involve any Old Ones."

Rhiann fought back tears. He bent down and kissed his mother's cheek and said, "I love you, mother. I'm sorry…"

Caye interrupted him, "Son, in my mind you died long ago. I've spent 600 years grieving you. Your father and I remain under constant scrutiny. Bailiwick is powerful. No one in Thynna will stand against him. He has alienated many peoples of the world. Thrice Thynna's forces have repelled attacks from the nomadic Moonglows. Several times the Old Ones from the Hanging Gardens halted forays of Bailiwick's armies into the Veldt. But he's never been stronger. His alliance with the Hinderburgh Giants may swing the balance of power against the Three Sisters. Leave Thynna, my son. I cannot grieve you again. Perhaps you can find purpose with your brother Arthur Seigh at the Laurels. If Magick has a worthwhile future, it's with the thinkers there. I'll always remember your time before your journeys with Uncle Mayard. I wish you'd never taken the first step on his path."

Shouts erupted outside and a loud knock on the door interrupted Caye. Rhiann uttered phrases and disappeared. The door flew open, and High Sheriff Clank burst into the foyer.

Clank screamed, "Where is he? Where is this bloke who claims to be your lost son?"

Caye gulped and said, "We are alone. We have been alone for six centuries."

Clank's deputies tore through the house and searched every nook and cranny. The Chief Deputy Klodno reported the house was occupied only by the elderly sorcerers.

Clank snarled, "I'll get to the bottom of this matter, Caye Klarje. Lord Bailiwick does not tolerate tomfoolery. Someone presented to the outer curtain gate yesterday and claimed to be Rhiann Klarje. Then the impassible gate gets violated! Lord Bailiwick and Castellan Yerko do not believe in coincidence. If I find out you are hiding knowledge of this person, I'll have you scrubbing the floors of the mercenaries' latrine."

Rhiann moved stealthily through the streets and approached the inner curtain. Many Magick defenses had been added to the guards. He used the Staff of the West Wind and flew over the wall. He avoided going more than three or four feel above the wall walk to evade the airborne defenses of the inner ward. The opulent homes and edifices were well lit. Many monuments honoring Bailiwick, Yerko, and their associates dotted the area. The most painful for Rhiann was the large statue of John Money, the nefarious Man in Black, which stood precisely on the site of the old statue of Mayard Klarje in the central courtyard near the school. The largest houses now belonged to Bailiwick, Yerko, and High Sheriff Clank. Rhiann avoided contact and silently flew over the inner and then the outer curtain and made his way back to Harmony House.

Iyaca greeted him and said, "You are back so soon."

Rhiann said, "Anonymity. Nameless. To all but my closest friends it's what I'll become. Please refer to me as NET… the Nameless Enchanter of Thynna. I'll send communiques to the Council of Thynna to warn them about their risky activities. Bailiwick practices dangerous spells.

Some of Bailiwick's efforts creep into my mind. Powerful spells affect all touched by Magick. I fear Bailiwick has summoned arcane forces to Sagain. During the time I was in the grotto with the Bloodstone, the situation in Sagain has only gotten worse. My Uncle Mayard's fears look evermore as though they're coming to pass."

CHAPTER 34

Translocation
The First Three Spells

Rhiann travelled to the Hanging Gardens and shared a tearful reunion with Decima. The Three Sisters remained set in their positions regarding Thynna. Thynna's burgeoning armies bivouacked on the fringes of the Veldt. Hinderburgh giants bolstered their ranks. Donovan's responsibilities kept him busy in bustling Norman, formerly known as Gnome-town. Rhiann returned to Harmony House. When Maranna returned from the Laurels, NET gave her his tankard filled with red liquid. The tankard refilled after someone drank the ichors of the Bloodstone. When imbibed outside the Bloodstone's grotto, the thick scarlet liquid merely refreshed and nourished. Maranna called the juice Jove's nectar and treasured the bottomless tankard.

Rhiann commissioned Iyaca the task of recording events. He enjoyed fellowship with Maranna, Iyaca, and the Manticore Venla Faxxine at the cottage on Wombat Mountain. Maranna poured Jove's nectar and Iyaca piled fire logs from the sloburn tree on the grate in the fireplace at Harmony House. NET easily fostered a roaring blaze with a simple Fire Spell, but just as did his Uncle Mayard, the wandering sorcerer preferred the heat and light of a natural fire. Lost in thought NET pensively stared into the flickering flames. Maranna and Iyaca encouraged their worried friend. Rhiann submitted to fatigue and slept.

Shapeless grayness again entered his mind.

Wisps...
Threads...
Threads of Magick...
Threads of fate...
Threads of time...
Threads connecting worlds ...
Dreams connecting worlds ...
Dreams of Magick...
The Magick of Dreams...
Magick connecting dreams...
Magick connecting worlds...
Grayness...

Shapeless grayness took form, specifically the visage of his Uncle Mayard Klarje. The visage spoke, "I thought you'd enjoy this visage."

Rhiann answered his dream, "I'd have preferred to have had the opportunity to say goodbye to my Uncle."

The voiced replied, "You should proceed with carrying out his wishes. It's time to use the great spell. The very fabric of Sagain's existence is tearing."

Rhiann said, "I don't have a destination... I don't want to waste the shypoke eggshells."

The visage changed to formless mist and said, "The eggshells will define your focal point, the point to which you will return. The eggshells fix the passage of time. Once you travel to a place the eggshells will fix a focal point as well. It's not necessary to use the eggshells to return to a place you've previously visited, but you fix time only by using the eggshells. Maybe. You'll learn. It's Magick. Magick defies definitions and rules."

Grayness faded. Rhiann slept fitfully for a bit.

Then...

Redness entered Rhiann's dream.

He dreamed again of horrific and disturbing images, including a great lake of flaming water.

Fire...evil...the stuff of nightmares...

Names...

DECKSTEQ.

Bailiwick…
Summoning spells…
Dreamraiders…

Wisps…
Threads…
Threads of Magick…
Threads of fate…
Threads of time…
Threads connecting worlds …
Dreams connecting worlds …
Dreams of Magick…
The Magick of Dreams…
Magick connecting dreams…
Magick connecting worlds…
Dream raiders…
Elf pressure…
Albtraum…
Albträume, elf dreams, nightmares…

Others probed his dreams.
Unnamed…
A gravelly voice muttered, "I shall follow you."
Redness faded to blue. Rhiann dreamed of his travels with Donovan Eighty-four names. He awakened with mixed feelings.

Maranna had returned to Cragmore, and Iyaca returned to Thynna to assess the Council's activity and deliver communiques from the *Nameless Enchanter of Thynna* to the counsel. The letters warned of the dangers of summoning spells and tapping unknown forces of Magick.

Rhiann sat alone in Harmony House and mulled the phrases of the great Translocation Spell in his mind. The sorcerer held a fragment of fossilized shypoke eggshell in his hand.

There was nothing for it.

It was time to try the spell… outside the grotto with the Bloodstone.

Rhiann uttered the phrases perfectly and pinched the fossilized shypoke eggshell. The hard shell dissipated into powder as the sorcerer conjured. As an extra bit of precaution, Rhiann applied amber to his left palm and grasped the Staff of the West Wind. He tied his bag of holding to the Staff of the West Wind.

Rhiann cast the spell.

To the north, the prismatic dragon Eyerthrin felt a great foreboding wave on the sea of Magick. Lord Bailiwick stood abruptly and spilled the potion he was creating. Caye Klarje Marsh felt foreboding feelings. Throughout Thynna uncertainty gripped sorcerers in the inner and outer ward. Ninth level Magick created great waves on the surface of Magick's sea.

Rhiann knew he had performed the complex incantation correctly. The spell should have worked.

But...

Ruin...?

The young Sorcerer felt his body and mind ripped through the fabric of space and time.

Absolute darkness...

Cold...

Void...

Then colors, and energies...

His thoughts were spinning violently out of control. He passed through vortex after vortex of color and energy. Pain coursed through very nerve ending. He felt the air sucked from his lungs.

Then, grayness...

Alas!

Had he died and entered the abyss?

Was there nothing more?

His feeling of hopelessness ended when he unceremoniously hit marshy ground. His lungs hungrily engulfed the fetid air of a swamp. Scents and sounds overwhelmed his senses. Quickly he sloshed across the shallow water on his hands and knees to get out of the open area of the bog and gain cover behind some trees. But where was he?

A single sun brightened the sky. The area was flat, so he could see little, and as he looked over the bog he saw only similar plants on the opposite side. A large bug crawled across his hand and he slung it away. Rhiann clutched the Staff of the West in his left hand. Just as the Tome described and the incantation promised, the staff remained with him.

Perhaps the small amount of amber had helped the staff stay in his hand. Rhiann explored the land and learned its inhabitants called it Donothor. Nature and preternatural beasts dominated the world. Diverse bands of inhabitants lived in small hamlets or lead nomadic lives. Great swamps occupied the southern reaches of the land. Mountain ranges divided the northern areas. Most of the world was wild. A tiny hamlet named Lyndyn provided a rare organized community in the north. Occasionally a dragon flew overhead. Donothor was a wild, primitive, and mundane world, which was untouched by Magick. It was not a suitable place for his plans. Rhiann concentrated on his focal point... the cabin Harmony House at Wombat Mountain, where the powdered shypoke eggshells had fallen to the floor. His return was instantaneous and much less traumatic.

The door opened and Iyaca entered.

Rhiann felt exhausted. He asked, "What year is it? How long was I away?"

Iyaca said, "I left you here this morning and you are still here. Have you sampled Maranna's nectar?"

Rhiann slept. Grayness crept into his somnolence.

Wisps...
Threads...
Threads of Magick...
Threads of fate...
Threads of time...
Threads connecting worlds ...
Dreams connecting worlds ...
Dreams of Magick...
The Magick of Dreams...
Magick connecting dreams...
Magick connecting worlds...
Grayness...

Shapeless grayness took form in the visage of lovely Decima.

The voice said, "I thought you'd enjoy this visage."

Rhiann answered his dream, "Seeing Decima makes me want to go to the Hanging Gardens instead of another world. Translocation was painful. I felt my soul was being ripped from my body."

He ersatz Decima said, "It will get better. I'm leaving you a gift."

Grayness faded. Rhiann awakened and found a goodly supply of fossilized shypoke eggshells tucked neatly in a ruck sack. Maranna returned from Cragmore, and Rhiann talked with her and Iyaca.

Rhiann prepared for another journey and carefully ground the shypoke eggshells and began the complex gestures. Every movement required precision. The movements of his hands could not vary by one-thousandth of an inchworm's length! Rhiann cast the Translocation Spell. His level of discomfort diminished each time he crushed the shypoke eggshells.

To the north, Eyerthrin felt another great wave in the sea of Magick. Rhiann adjusted to the travel. Bailiwick shuddered in the warm midday sun. Caye Klarje felt apprehensive. Everyone touched by Magick felt the spell. Rhiann took deep smooth breaths as he traversed the vortices. He gripped the Staff of the West Wind firmly.

Clouds and seas covered the small world. Rhiann warily peered through squinted eyes as he traversed the darkness of space and neared the beautiful world with a single moon. As near as he could tell, it was the third world of a system of worlds revolving around a very plain single sun. He descended, as though suspected from a great string, to an island. He landed with a thud within a stone circle. He stood among sarsen stones. A heel stone lay north east of the sarsen circle. The heel stone was a rough stone about 16 feet above ground and leaning inward toward the stone circle. As Rhiann looked northeast he saw the single little sun rising above the heel stone. The sorcerer used the power of the Staff of the West Wind to explore the quaint little world.

This was a world heavily dominated by Nature.

The world of the single bright sun presented little opposition. The simple people of the blue world noted unusual occurrences wherever the sorcerer traveled. This was another world worth defending. Rhiann's mind was clear. This world was an appropriate place to share Sagain's legacies. It would be a good home for replications of Sagain's Seven Wonders. He traveled to a places called Virginia, Babylon, Rhodes, Alexandria, Roanoke Island, the Bermuda Triangle, and Egypt. He planned to share bits of this world with his home Sagain.

Rhiann returned to his focal point at Harmony House. He had found some of what he wanted. A simple world to share Sagain's Seven Wonders.

Soon Rhiann tried the spell again. Maranna and Iyaca sat with him as he prepared to cast the spell. Rhiann crushed shypoke eggshells and uttered the complex incantation. He moved through grayness. The sorcerer felt as he did when, as a boy, he took an ill-advised draw on an oldster's pipe and filled his lungs with smoke of strong pipe weed. Thoughts of impending doom streamed through his mind. Rhiann felt progressively weaker, stumbled, and fell to the ground. It hurt more than before. Reluctantly he took a shallow breath, tentatively tested the air, and quickly followed with a deep inspiration. Thankfully, the air was clear. Alien plants surrounded him. His eyes detected reds, yellows, oranges, but nothing green. He lay on red moss and stared upward.

An eerie gray moon almost filled the sky. Perhaps he was lying on a moon spinning around a bizarre world! No, the massive body that filled the sky above him emitted gray light. It was a sun. The grayness was strangely familiar. Rhiann pinched his thigh to assure he wasn't dreaming. There was another sun …small and yellow like the twins that warmed Sagain and a third, very dark, large, and distant. A cone of gray light flowed from the hovering celestial body, focused, and concentrated on the sorcerer. The sky above was largely hues of yellow-orange with bits of blueness, but the massive gray celestial body hovered near and almost filled the sky. Deep gray rays filtered from the gray body and creative a twilight effect. The gray rays struck and refreshed him. The Staff of the West Wind in his hand emitted purplish auras and sent fine mauve rivulets of light toward the giant in the sky. The grayness was familiar and comfortable. He had sensed it in the grotto with the Bloodstone. Red, orange, and yellow foliage surrounded him. In a few paces the red and orange foliage changed to deep green. Taller trees and bushes rimmed the entire roughly circular area of green ness around a valley filled with short shrubby plants. A knoll in the center of the valley obscured the far side of the circular vale. Bright green plush grass covered a rim that extended several paces. At the edge of the green moss, the terrain inclined gently at about fifteen degrees for thirty paces and reached the floor. The floor of the green vale extended several hundred paces and rose gently in several areas. The flattened area circled the central knoll. A grassy upslope began where the floor ended and extended fifty or so paces to the top of the central hill. Many small rivulets coursed through the landscape. A gentle breeze crisscrossed the warm valley.

Shrubby enhancing plants filled the hillsides and the floor of the Vale. The enhancing plants did not grow in rows. Instead the plants were arbitrarily set in the gently rolling terrain. None grew on the central hill. Very few other plants intermingled with the enhancing plants.

Rhiann said, "Perfect."

Rhiann reached into his ever-present rucksack and removed three windward staves. He placed the Staff of the West Wind at his feet and the artifact aligned with its handhold facing west. He placed the other three staves on the ground and they positioned facing north, south, and east. The runes on the four staves emitted glowing purple auras. Gray auras surrounded the staves and moved outward until they encircled the vale. The grayness amplified around the four artifacts that were created in the grotto with the Bloodstone. The windward staves created a circle of protective Magick. Also the spring in the center of the hillock began to effervesce. Next Rhiann climbed to the hillock's top and inserted the four staves into the water of the pool. Its waters changed to prismatic spray. Rhiann Klarje walked the circumference of the hillock and touched the four staves to the ground in thirteen places. Depressions formed in the periphery of the hillock at each place he touched the staves to the ground. Rhiann touched the four windward staves to the bottom of each hole in the ground. Deep mauve auras formed in the holes and produced purplish gray smoke that remained in the depressions. When Rhiann touched the soil in the last hole in the ground, a small geyser erupted in the effervescing pool and bathed the hillock with sprays of prismatic fluids. Gray light from the hovering massive gray sun focused in beams onto the four staves and the thirteen holes in the ground. Rhiann felt strong. Thirteen had always felt lucky. Uncle Mayard had made several requests regarding Sagain's rare flora, but he had not suggested thirteen. Rhiann had ideas to fill the gaps. Emanations from the massive gray sun filled the air with grayness. Rhiann grew tired, stretched out in the plush grasses, and slept.

Rhiann awakened warm and cozy. Someone had covered him with a deep purple silk blanket. He sat up. No one was around. Dark yellow light bathed him. The huge gray sun had retreated from the land and now appeared as a large gray circle in the sky. A small bipedal creature peaked *out of* a large oak. The figure stood about three-quarters the height of an average man and had orange-yellow skin and long brown hair. He slowly exited the tree and cautiously approached Rhiann.

The smallish bloke verbalized. Rhiann gripped the Staff of the West Wind and thought "Languages." This activated the staff's languages spell.

The denizen of the World of the Three Suns asked, "Are you a friend of the forest?"

Rhiann rubbed his aching backside and answered, "Most definitely."

The creature rifled questions, "Why are digging the earth on top of the hill where nothing grows? Why have the waters of the spring turned into a rainbow? We are blessed by the Approximation of Andreas, so all things can happen. You certainly are not Drelvish, Kiennish, or Droll. Are you a Spellweaver?"

Rhiann said, "My name is Rhiann. I am touched by Magick and feel comfortable and charged by the grayness. I follow my dreams and grayness' direction. Why does nothing grow on the hill?"

The little bloke replied, "I am a simple keeper of the enhancing plants. My ilk, the Drelves, grow strong from the shrubs, the enhancing plants that grow in this island of green ness. The tubers give us health. My home is in the village Meadowsweet, a short walk from Green Vale."

Rhiann said, "Most everything in this lush valley is green. What's special about the green ness? In my home most plants are green."

The Drelve laughed, "You are funny, traveler. Uh, Rhiann… my name is Ulysses. I've only seen seventeen seasons, but I can tell you the rest of the world is red, orange, and yellow. Are you from the Emerald Isle? It's supposed to be green, though some say it's just a legend."

Rhiann said, "Ulysses, I'm from… another place. I'd like to learn more about your world."

Ulysses quizzically asked, "Don't you mean our world?"

Rhiann smiled, "Will you show me your home?"

Ulysses answered, "The elders tell us to remain hidden and guard closely our homes. Our friend the forest provides us protection from our ancestral enemies, the Drolls and Kiennites. But the Gray Wanderer Andreas has given protection to Green Vale. Those with ill will toward the forest have never been able to enter. Yet you are here. I'll take you to Meadowsweet, Rhiann. Meadowsweet is our ancestral home. The Drelves have long lived at Meadowsweet. Our forebears expanded into the forests. It is every Drelve's heritage. The plants flourish under the great red elms and in the soil of the meadows. The waters of the brooks in the meadows are sweet. Thus, the name."

"What is the origin of the enhancing root?" Rhiann asked.

"That's like asking where the Drelves came from," the Drelve answered. "You may stay in my tree if you want."

Rhiann pondered, "In your tree?"

Ulysses said, "Sure. It's a small tree, but it's comfortable. Of course, you may use the guest tree unless someone is visiting from Alms' Glen. But the time to harvest the enhancing root tubers is still a dark period away. We can make in time for enhancing root tea."

Ulysses led Rhiann through a nigh imperceptive narrow opening in the trees that surrounded the Green Vale. The duo moved silently along the cushioned ground. Plush, dense moss covered the ground. The moss was a myriad of colors but mostly deep orange intertwined with bright red and blue hues. Stepping on the moss gave the sensation of walking on air. Breathtakingly beautiful great red oak trees towered above the surrounding forest. Except for their coloration, the red oaks were similar to the great green oaks located in the forests of Sagain.

Occasionally a face peered out through the bark of a red elm or red oak. Not all Drelves lived in communities. Occasionally a lone Drelve or a small family inhabited a large tree in an isolated area of the forest.

Abruptly Ulysses held up his hand, motioned for Rhiann to stop, paused on the pathway, and gave a pleasant whistle that mimicked the purring of a meow-meow skat. New mothers treasured the meow-meow skat's company. The rare feline's gentle purring sounds soothed a restless babe and helped bring sleep, the forest's gentle nurse.

After a few moments Ulysses motioned for them to continue. They came to a clearing. An edifice crudely constructed with large rocks filled the center of the area. The rocky building blended into the natural landscape and minimally disturbed the environment. The ever-present multihued moss covered the building. When Ulysses led the group into the clearing, a hundred Drelves came out of the forest and surrounded him. Some older, some smaller, some fetching females, the Drelves were an extension of the forest.

An older Drelve emerged from the largest tree in the central area. Carrying an oaken cudgel and wearing a crown of woven vines, the elder Bruce said, "Welcome to Meadowsweet. The Approximation blesses us. I hope a Spellweaver comes to us. The time of the harvest is nigh."

Addressing members of the community, young Ulysses said, "Elder, I have found a friend of the forest in Green Vale. He is not of our ilk, but says Magick touches him."

The elder curiously asked, "Are you a gift of the Wandering Sun Andreas? Are you to be our Spellweaver?"

Rhiann said, "No, I'm only a visitor, but I will assist you in protecting your Green Vale. First, tell me of your world... uh, land."

Drelves brought nutritious fruits of the forest. Green Vale was the only place of greenness in the great forest. The elder gave a description of the land of the Drelves.

Three very different suns gave light to Parallan, the world of the Drelves. Total darkness never covered the land. The little yellow sun Meries traversed the sky in sixteen hours. When Meries drew high in the sky, the little star bathed the World of the Three Suns with amber light, warmed the world, and gave imparted beautiful yellow and orange hues to the skies of Parallan. Rather than a round bright spot, the dark sun Orpheus was akin to a large dark unmoving spiraling defect in the sky. Giant Orpheus gave little light and controlled the movement of Meries. Andreas, the Gray Wanderer, appeared in the sky irregularly. Oft times Andreas came into view as a gray speck on the horizon. From time to time the wanderer left the skies altogether. Every now and then the gray sun wobbled a bit closer to the World of the Three Suns.

Eight-hour periods of waxing and waning amber light made up one cycle of Meries. The little yellow sun never left the horizon, but every sixty cycles Meries slunk down in the amber sky and lingered at its zenith for a time of fifteen cycles, or 240 hours. These nadirs of Meries's light were called dark periods. During the dark period the scant light that reached the World of the Three Suns derived mostly from great Orpheus with variable contribution from the Gray Wanderer. Thus the times of greatest light were called light periods, the lesser light were amber periods, and the cyclic extended periods of least illumination were called dark periods.

Some peoples used the arbitrary term "day" to describe one eight-hour cycle of bright light and the term "night" to describe the eight-hour amber periods. The terms day and night had little meaning during the 240 hour-long time of decreased illumination of the dark period. Most folk simply used the term dark period. But the time from the beginning of one dark period to the beginning of the next was consistently the equivalent of 75 cycles of Meries, or 1200 hours.

On the odd occasion the Gray Wanderer drew near Parallan. The Approximations of Andreas gave wondrous gifts to the fauna, flora, and folk of Parallan. During these totally unpredictable Approximations, the Gray Wanderer filled the sky, bathed the land with its deep gray light, and augmented the forces of Magick in the world.

Many peoples of Parallan celebrated the significant rituals of their given ilk during dark periods. For instance, the Drelves harvested the tubers of the enhancing plant only during the dark period. Vital to the Drelves, the enhancing plant's tubers matured in eight dark periods. Thus, a season of the harvest encompassed eight dark periods, and equaled the time of 600 cycles of Meries; 480 cycles of light and amber periods and the equivalent of 120 cycles of relative darkness. Drelves called the time between harvests a "season of the harvest," a change of season," or a "year."

Drelves usually matured in fifteen to thirty *years* and chose life-mates when they found love. If blessed by good health and bountiful harvests of the disease fighting enhancing root, the forest folk lived to see hundreds of harvests. Teachers oft lived longer, and the ultra-rare Spellweavers had uncommonly long lives.

Elders relayed stories of the Approximations of the Gray Wanderer and its Magick giving rays. The gentle forest folk welcomed Rhiann and made him welcome. After the repast Ulysses led Rhiann to a babbling brook to freshen. Rhiann encountered a yellow-leafed Tree Herder who was resting his roots in the brook's waters. Ulysses led Rhiann to a large red oak and muttered, "Home, sweet home." The Drelve gently rubbed the tree's bark and sang melodic phrases. The Drelve then stepped through the tree's bark. Rhiann shrugged and followed. Inside he found a soft comfortable mossy bed. Rhiann spent a very comfortable night inside Ulysses' tree home. Rhiann removed the four Windward Staves and muttered the incantation of his Forget Spell. The Drelves remembered nothing of his visit. Rhiann had found a world touched by Magick to receive Sagain's Magick and rarities. He immediately returned to Sagain to begin fulfilling his Uncle Mayard's requests.

CHAPTER 35

Mayard's Legacy

Lord Bailiwick and the Council of Thynna ignored warnings of someone calling himself the Nameless Enchanter of Thynna. Epistles arrived at the doors of the meeting chamber and in message centers. These letters warned of the dangers of such Magick. Casting such a spell opened doors that should have never been opened and bore incomprehensible consequences. and inquired of his travels. Bailiwick persisted in his efforts. Bailiwick dreamed of spells like all other sorcerers. On one occasion redness permeated his dreams and left him with an incantation for a spell he called "coax a demon." The dweomer enabled the summoning of arcane forces to Sagain.

Rhiann, Iyaca, and Maranna enjoyed some quiet moments at Harmony House. Rhiann relayed stories of his travels. NET stared at the multicolored flickering flames and pondered the dangerous situation in Thynna.

Rhiann somberly said, "Perfecting the spell Translocation will be my legacy to our world. I've recorded my efforts and travels in this Travelers Tome."

Iyaca respectfully asked, "Although you are gone a long time, you leave and return safely. Doesn't that mean the spell works?"

Maranna nodded agreement.

NET managed a weak smile. "My friends, your ignorance of Magick is bliss. At this point, I've mastered *where* but not *when* I come and go. Time allies with neither Magick nor Nature. It resists everyone's efforts. You record the passage of time on Sagain. My inner clock tells me that I age the same whether I'm on Sagain or in another place, a heartbeat is a heartbeat. Time passes constantly. When I travel to the world of the little yellow sun, I arrive at different times. Sometimes I arrive much earlier than when I last departed. Reestablishing relationships is frustrating. Someone I knew for years may have never met me. When I arrive earlier than my last departure, I create something I call a time wrinkle. Not a comfortable thing! And it…it could be devastating in their world. I am working on the wording of the incantation. It's going to take at least the power of an Alter Reality, or Limited Wish, Spell. Once I visit a world, my focal point to return is the point and time of my previous departure. I require the irreplaceable precious shypoke eggshells only when traveling to another world for the first time. However, if I use the precious shells, no time passes in a given world whilst I have been away. Variable time passes in Sagain during my journeys. Time passage relates to the Windward Staves, too. I'm learning."

Maranna queried nervously, "What of our world?"

NET answered, "Not to worry. I always arrive forward of when I left."

Iyaca curiously inquired, "What is your name in the other worlds?"

NET answered, "My intention is to observe and learn. I've various monikers. Merlin, Croatan, Anastasia, Maya, Aristotle, Socrates, Leonardo, Nostradamus, and Confucius are among them. Merlin is my favorite."

Maranna asked, "Do you want us to call you Merlin?"

Rhiann replied, "NET is good enough. On the positive side, I've contrived a way to carry others with me, though it's risky."

Both friends enthusiastically volunteered.

NET said, "I've not finished my work. Harmony House is my focal point and anchor in space and time. Stupidity runs rampant in Thynna. I fear evermore for our world Sagain. One of you should remain here to monitor goings on."

The Cloudmare Urra carried Rhiann on journeys into the Veldt and easily avoided dragons and other airborne predators. Rhiann found flying with the Cloudmare was safer than using the Fly Spell power of his staff. It also enabled him to conserve his supply of Phoenix feathers. NET used Invisibility dweomers and blended into the Cloudmare's misty form. Palindromes' excellent sense enabled them to see through the invisibility. Vicious palindromes looked the same whether one looked at them from the left or right. Should a palindrome lose a fang, another appeared to maintain the creature's symmetry.

Thynna's armies grew larger and ever threatened the Hanging Gardens. The disturbing redness that entered Rhiann's dreams in the Bloodstone's grotto on occasion found its way into his dreams. Arcane forces touched Sagain. Bailiwick and his cronies had opened gates to other realms. Rhiann felt a sense of urgency. He used Translocation to travel to the blue world and the Green Vale in the World of the Three Suns. His protective Magick had held. The power of the four staves and the Grayness bathing the land from the hovering gray sun potentiated one another and made safe the area. Only the forest dwelling Drelves knew of the Green Vale. Rhiann shared the secret of his protective Magick with them, and then used his Forget Spell to selectively erase their memories of him. The Drelves remembered Green Vale was protected by powerful Magick, but the forest dwellers had no memory of how the protective Magick came to be. The Forget Spell gave them something that would come to be known as plausible deniability.

GATHERING THE
THIRTTENE FRIENDS

CHAPTER 36

A New Home for the Gem Bush

Rhiann said, "Time is not on my side. I'm going to carry the Gem Bush to a new home. If it's all I accomplish, I'll at least fulfill some of Uncle Mayard's wants. I have found a suitable place to take the tree."

Iyaca said, "It's been safe here for six centuries, Rhiann. Do you think it's necessary to move it?"

Rhiann said, "I'd prefer you called me NET. Now, there are forces afoot from within and outside our world. Uncle Mayard specifically mentioned certain tasks. He wanted our Seven Wonders duplicated on another world. I've done it, though it seems a dream to me. My visits to the blue world confirms duplicates of the wonders are there. In that world they are called the Hanging Gardens of Babylon, the Statue of Zeus at Olympia, the temple of Artemis, the Mausoleum of Halicarnassus, the Colossus of Rhodes, the Lighthouse of Alexandria, and the Great Pyramid of Giza."

Iyaca said, "Strange names, strange places, NET. How are you planning on moving the Gem Bush? Its roots have had six centuries to dig into the soil. Are you taking the Gem Bush to the same place?"

NET replied, "No, the first world is largely a world of Nature. The second world is touched by Magick, though at times more than others. Grayness appears whenever the third sun draws near the world. I was fortunate to be there during one of these so-called Approximations. The Grayness enhanced my Magick. The location I've prepared for the Gem Bush should be safe, though I'm in need of a caretaker."

Iyaca said, "I'll do anything you ask of me, though I don't have what your mother calls a green thumb. I'm not good at growing things."

Rhiann said, "I need you here, Iyaca. I still haven't mastered carrying others with me. It'll likely require shypoke eggshells to take others. Since I've already traveled to the hillock in the Green Vale, I won't need them to go back alone. It looks like rain. Let me get at it."

Rhiann and Iyaca exited the cabin and walked a short distance into the semper fi trees. Rhiann's illusions posed no real barriers. The Gem Bush had flourished. Thirteen colors of rare gems covered the bush, including rare red diamonds.

Rhiann scurried around the base of the Gem Bush with a little shovel, scooped up morsels of dirt, placed the soil in a tiny bucket, and uttered what sounded like a child's limerick. Rhiann then reached into his rucksack, got a pinch of powdered iron, recited the incantation for the Enlarge Spell *backwards,* and completed a Shrink Spell. The Gem Bush decreased in size until it was small enough to fit in the palm of his hand. The Gem Bush retained its weight. Rhiann then used a small leather loop, muttered another group of phrases, and touched the tiny Gem Bush. The gem-laden bush rose into the air. Rhiann wrapped his arms around the tiny bush. She scattered a bit of soil he brought from Green Vale onto his shoes. Next he crushed the Shypoke eggshells and painstakingly cast the Translocation dweomer. The young sorcerer and the gem Bush disappeared.

Rhiann reached Green Vale in an instant. He arrived in the brightly lit light period. The vale was devoid of activity. Rhiann guided the Gem Bush over one of the thirteen holes he had dug in the hillock. He eased the bush into the hole. NET then recited the Enlarge Spell and touched the Gem Bush. The wondrous bush expanded to its natural height and size. The Circle of Green Vale had its first inhabitant. Gray auras surrounded the tree. The geyser erupted from the effervescing pool and bathed Rhiann and the Gem Bush.

The gem bush…

$$\acute{Ø} \infty \acute{Ø}$$
$$\mathbf{X}$$
$$\infty \acute{Ø} \infty$$

Rhiann Klarje concentrated on Harmony House and muttered a simple command. In an instant he stood before Iyaca and Maranna in Harmony House.

Iyaca finished the sentence he was saying as Rhiann left. Essentially no time had passed.

CHAPTER 37

The Snowberry Bush

The Cloudmare Urra removed the effects of her Forget Spell and carried Net to the beautiful Hanging Gardens. To the best of everyone's knowledge, the Snowberry Bush in the gardens was unique. The remarkable bush produced blooter-egg sized perfectly round white fruits. When picked, the fruits became cold. The fruits were quite useful to chill beverages on a hot day. The snowberry bush allowed the harvesting of thirteen fruits at a picking and replaced the fruits once the thirteenth was removed. Picking a fourteenth fruits resulted in all the picked fruits turning to dust. The bush still replaced its stolen fruit, but additional harvesting was delayed by the number od days equal to the number of fruits over thirteen that were picked. Trial and error over time had established the idiosyncrasies of the Snowberry Bush. The Three Sisters treasured the bush. Taking it jeopardized Rhiann's favorability in the Hanging Gardens, but Mayard Klarje had listed the Snowberry Bush among the treasures of Sagain that he wanted preserved. Rhiann smiled when he remembered this Uncle's reason… "nothing beats a good cold ale, Rhiann, and fruit of the Snowberry Bush chills better than anything else in Sagain."

The noble centaur Chiron greeted Rhiann and said, "Welcome, young-looking Klarje. My step lacks the spring it had when last we talked. I'm pleased you continue your Uncle's legacy. Those many years there was no word of you. Decima kept hope you'd return, and now you have. Our world teeters on the edge of war. Thynna's armies mass in the deserts in the north of the Veldt. On several occasions they have all but invaded. Only strong presence of myriads of Old Ones deterred Bailiwick and Yerko from all out attacks. Bottom line is they are cowards and remain within the ever tightening walls of Thynna veiled by their dark Magick. The Sisters hold firm in their resistance. No other voice has risen to replace Mayard. Eyerthrin has sensed powerful spells in the propinquity of your sanctuary. Quite honestly, it concerns him, me, well, all of us. There's more. Thynna's leaders jeopardize our world in many ways. Forces probe Sagain from without. Eyerthrin and others sense their presence. At first Eyerthrin thought it came through you, but he senses their presence when he cannot feel you. Oddly that you at times are not detectable to those touched by Magick. Even great Mayard never accomplished this ability. Pardon my thinking out loud, but the security of the Hanging Gardens has been my responsibility now for three millennia. I must ask, do you fully share your Uncle's commitments?"

Rhiann tried to take in all that Chiron said as they walked. Sometimes he forgot that six centuries passed while he lingered in the Bloodstone's grotto. Powerful Chiron looked as strong as ever and the defenses around the beautiful gardens had been ever strengthened. He responded, "Chiron, it's my intent to fulfill every request my Uncle Mayard gave me, even though some may jeopardize... friendships. I lost many friends while I was pursuing the source of Magick. Time is everyone's enemy."

Chiron said, "You are the only ally Old Ones can number among those touched by Magick. That you are here says many things. But time has not taken all your friends, Rhiann Klarje, and one of them is here now. His beard is longer and he is no better looking than the first time I saw him, but the Burgomaster of Gnome-town, Donovan eighty-something names is here for a visit. He comes periodically to give us updates on the north... and to spend a little time with Mors. You'll notice the strand of her hair in his beard right off. He wears it like a crown."

Rhiann said, "It will be good to see him. I haven't been able to work a trek to Gnome-town into my schedule."

Chiron led him across the invisible bridge into the city. The young sorcerer relished a brief reunion with beautiful Decima. A comely Dryad led him to the same room he shared with Mayard those many years before. Rhiann removed his ever-present hat and chuckled when he saw how it now rivaled Mayard's in its wear. The sorcerer walked into the garden and looked upon the beautiful Snowberry Bush. He felt guilt over his plan to make off with the exceptional plant. His discussion with Chiron left him feeling Sagain was closer to all-out war than ever and a battle in the Hanging Gardens in all likelihood meant the death of the Snowberry Bush. A hand on his shoulder brought Rhiann back.

Decima said, "You are lost in thought. Were you thinking about me?"

Rhiann honestly answered, "No."

Decima said, "Were you thinking about that red-haired siren Maranna?"

Rhiann laughed and said, "No. I do marvel that you look exactly like you did 600 years ago."

Decima coyly replied, "So do you."

Rhiann shrugged and said, "It wasn't 600 years to me. It felt like I was in the grotto for only a few days." He remembered she knew nothing of the grotto. He added, "Relations between Thynna and the Old Ones have deteriorated."

Decima said, "They couldn't get much worse. We are grateful for our friends. Let's go to dinner. One thing that hasn't changed in 600 years is Burgomaster Donovan's appetite and impatience at meal time. He's excited about seeing you."

Decima led Rhiann to the dining area. Nona, Mors, and the robust Donovan sat in plush chairs and snacked on grapples and pinanas. Donovan's beard now extended the length of his chest and maintained its reddish color. A polychromatic strand of Mors' hair intertwined with the Gnome's beard. His worn axe was strapped across his back and he wore robes designated for the Burgomaster. Mors' gift had given the Gnome extraordinarily long life and allowed him to accumulate the unheard total of eighty-four names., which far exceeded the thirty-six Storming Norman attained. Donovan stood and met Rhiann in the center of the room.

Donovan said, "Rhiann Klarje, Decima's description holds true. You look little older than the day the siren's song subdued us and when I last saw you on the allure of Thynna. You are a sight for sore eyes."

Rhiann replied, "As are you, Donovan. I always regretted that I had been unable to return to Gnome-town."

Donovan laughed, "It's a good thing you didn't my friend. Old Storming Norman was fit to be tied when he learned about the deception. He wanted to scrub your head. Eventually he got over it. He had many adventures with your Uncle Mayard. Sagain has not been the same without him."

Rhiann asked, "Tell me about Gnome-town, Donovan. What happened to..."

Donovan interrupted, "Time eventually took our old friends, Rhiann. When the Fearsome Foursome mustered into Thynna's army and old Bailiwick made his triumphant return to Thynna, matters improved in the north. It's well documented in the history books. Storming Norman, Longbeard, Albie Kirkey, Madam Darktop, and Roswell Kirkey consolidated the governments of Gnome-town and Flat Rock. The wealth coming from the mines fueled growth. It's thought of as a golden period in our history. Dwarves and Gnomes worked together better than ever. The leaders diminished relations with Thynna and developed trade with Greensborough, the Laurels, and the Hanging Gardens. Storming Norman named me emissary to the Hanging Gardens. I got to spend a lot of time here and developed my relationship with the lovely Mors. She graced me with her gift and gave me all these wonderful years to look upon her face. Storming Norman attained thirty-six names, by far the greatest number ever for a Gnome. Longbeard reached twenty-nine. They ruled justly for many years. Norman had statues of Mayard Klarje erected in the courtyard of Gnome-town. Our people demanded similar tributes be made to the five leaders, and statues of Norman, Longbeard, Madam Darktop, and the Kirkey brothers were erected."

Mors cleared her throat and interrupted, "And a statue of Donovan was erected, too. Donovan did more to advance Gnomes and Dwarves than anyone!"

Donovan smiled and said, "Thank you, my ...uh, love. Yes, Rhiann, they erected a statue of me. Our strength deterred enemies and we lived in peace. Thynna's armies drew many insalubrious lots and in so doing made things better for us. The criminals went south and became mercenaries. Norman was fond of saying "The foxes are guarding the chicken coop." Eventually Storming Norman Darktop, Longbeard, Ablie Kirkey, Madam Darktop, and Roswell Kirkey grew old. I accumulated names and became Burgomaster when Storming Norman joined his forefathers. The first thing I did was change the name of Gnome-town to Norman. The Dwarves followed suit and changed the name of Flat Rock to Albiekirkey. The road to Dry Creek and the mines is secure and developed. There hasn't been a robbery in centuries. I can't say the same for the roads to Thynna. We do not secure them. Travel to Thynna is risky. We travel to the Hanging Gardens through Albiekirkey. I spend as much time here as I can. I've made friends with the Cloudmare Syrrth. She removed her Forget Spell for me. The Three Sisters have treated us fairly. I believe most folk of Sagain trust the fates more than the sorcerers of Thynna. But I've rambled long, our food is here, these beautiful women are with us, and I am with a long, lost, dear friend. Let's enjoy this evening."

Dryads brought food and drink. The lovely servers dropped Snowballs into the beverages to chill them. Donovan, Rhiann, Mors, Nona, and Decima made small talk whilst enjoying their meal. Rhiann talked about peace with Thynna, but everything indicated the die was cast.

Donovan continued, "During the time you've been away, the Three Sisters sent many overtures and emissaries. Shortly after Mayard's death and your disappearance one of the emissaries was murdered by the inner ward guards. A recruit from the north named John Money quickly rose to the leadership of Thynna's special constabularies. High Sheriff Rhino and her twin brother Pinochynose died under mysterious circumstances. Rumors circulated in the outer ward that John Money was responsible for their demise. John Money disdained the robes of his predecessors and dressed entirely in black. He brought colleagues that mustered with him into positions of leadership. The constabularies abused their privileges and the citizenry, but protests from prominent sorcerers, namely your parents and their friends fell on even deafer ears than you and Mayard found in the Council of Thynna. John Money and his crew grew very popular in the inner ward. I was serving as courier during those days. Everyone kept hoping for your return. Sergeant Redbrick held onto his principles, but he could do little to prevent the atrocities fomented by John Money and his lot. You and I know John Money was none other than the Man in Black. Your apprentice Iyaca bravely kept a presence in the outer ward. He was almost caught several times. Money's lot eventually grew too old to carry on their meanness, but Bailiwick and Yerko had little trouble finding rascals to replace them.

When Redbrick passed on, I lost any source of information on Thynna. I encouraged our leaders to take our trade and business elsewhere. Bailiwick and Yerko have cast lots with the Giants of Hinderburgh and barons further west of the Copper Mountains. Thynna's armies mass in the deserts to the north of the Hanging Gardens. The rhetoric of Castellan Yerko's speeches grows more inflammatory. The lieges of Thynna support, feed, and water the host with Magick. I came to update the sisters, but their flying friends have a handle of the armies' movements. Our scouts have seen large numbers of Hinderburgh giants and wild men moving toward the desert. Thynna's forces have angered and on several occasions fought nomadic warriors called Moonglows. To be honest, we have traded with the Moonglows. Some carry swords and axes forged in Norman and Albiekirkey."

Rhiann asked, "Nona, Mors, and Decima, have you considered Thynna's demands?"

Nona replied, "Rhiann, you have been gone a long time. Statues of Bailiwick, Yerko, and the Man in Black now stand where once stood your Uncle Mayard's statue and the Gem Bush. Yerko continues to accuse us of stealing the Gem Bush. Thynna offers no terms, only total capitulation and surrounding all resources of the Hanging Gardens to them. They have detailed knowledge of the Gardens. We don't fully know how they attained it. Mayard gave us significant protection from Magick before we... lost him."

Rhiann pleaded, "Sisters, give them this site. Give them dominion over people of the west that insist on remaining their allies. I'll help you move your most treasured flora to another site. We can create another Hanging Gardens."

Nona said, "No, we can't, Rhiann. This is our home. We will remain here."

Rhiann made a few more suggestions. The Three Sisters' minds were set. After dinner Donovan Eighty-four names walked into the gardens with Mors and Rhiann spent some time with Decima and exchanged a few gentle kisses. He feigned fatigue and excused himself. When he was sure everyone was in bed, he made his way to the main garden. He chased a ferret away from the Snowberry Bush.

Rhiann scurried around the base of the Snowberry Bush with a little shovel, scooped up morsels of dirt, placed the soil in a tiny bucket, and uttered what sounded like a child's limerick. He sprinkled a bit of the soil on his boots and into his rucksack. Rhiann then reached into his rucksack, got a pinch of powdered iron, recited the incantation for the Enlarge Spell *backwards,* and completed a Shrink Spell. The Snowberry Bush decreased in size until it was small enough to fit in the palm of his hand. The Snowberry Bush retained its weight. Rhiann then used a small leather loop, muttered another group of phrases, and touched the tiny Snowberry Bush. The white berry-laden bush rose into the air. Rhiann wrapped his arms around the tiny bush. He scattered a bit of soil he brought from Green Vale onto his shoes. Next he crushed the Shypoke eggshells and painstakingly cast the Translocation dweomer. The young sorcerer and the Snowberry Bush disappeared. The activity created a defect thirteen feet wide in the garden. The ferret scurried into the defect and sniffed. In Thynna, Bailiwick sensed a great wave on the sea of Magick. Eyerthrin sensed the disturbance as well.

Rhiann arrived in Green Vale in an instant. He arrived in the dark period. The vale was devoid of activity. Rhiann guided the Snowberry Bush over one of the thirteen holes he had dug in the hillock. He eased the bush into the hole. NET then recited the Enlarge Spell and touched the Snowberry Bush. The wondrous bush expanded to its natural height and size. The Circle of Green Vale had its second inhabitant. Gray auras surrounded the tree. The geyser erupted from the effervescing pool and bathed Rhiann, the Snowberry Bush, and the Gem Bush.

The snowberry bush…

Ǿ ∞ **Ǿ**

III

∞ **Ǿ** ∞

Rhiann Klarje concentrated on the Hanging Gardens, scattered a bit of the soil he had taken from the Snowberry Bush's former home, and muttered a simple command. In an instant he stood in the main garden just a few feet away from Decima's cottage. The startled ferret fled from the hole in the ground. Rhiann muttered a phrase and gestured as the ferret ran away. All the Detect Magick Spell told him was that the furry beast was indeed a *familiar.* A furry little spy! Rhiann followed the beast a bit. He reached into his ever-present rucksack and grasped Exeter's hilt.

The soothing feminine voice entered his thoughts and said, "It's a woodland creature, Rhiann. It's not an enemy, but an extension of an enemy."

Rhiann thought, "It's a familiar! Whose familiar?"

The voice replied, "He's more than thirty paces away, Rhiann, and I'm not privy to the nature of familiars."

Rhiann thought, "Familiars are Magick, not Nature."

The sorcerer watched it run toward the invisible bridge. The ferret scampered across Red Creek and headed off toward the woods to the west.

CHAPTER 38

The Green Oak Dryad's Home

Rhiann returned to his opulent room and removed Mayard's diary from his rucksack. He reviewed his Uncle's comments about an unusual Great Green Oak near Greensborough. Large green oaks were common, but the tree that interested Mayard served as a home to a dryad. The exceptional tree stood alone on a hilltop near Greensborough. Approaching the tree would be difficult. In addition to housing the dryad, the tree's upper branches were the favorite roosting place of a large green dragon named Limenose. Everyone who lived in Greensborough was green. Rhiann would stand out. The odor of freshly squeezed lime juice filled the air. Rhiann had encountered copper dragons in his adventures around Gnome-town, now called Norman. Copper dragons could be bought off with a bit of copper ore. He'd met the prismatic dragon Eyerthrin at the Hanging Gardens. However, Rhiann had no dealings with green dragons, but serendipitously Donovan's fate placed the elderly Gnome at the Hanging Gardens. After all, the Three Sisters were the Fates. He'd tap Donovan's knowledge of the green wyrms. Carrying the Snowberry Bush to the Green Vale in the World of the Three Suns had left him a bit tired, but the pain associated with his early travels had abated. Two of Mayard's chosen now rested in Green Vale.

Rhiann awakened to shouts and wails. His handiwork had been discovered. He dressed and climbed the stairs. Chiron paced the main garden. The noble centaur approached Rhiann and said, "Someone has stolen the Snowberry Bush. The guards assure me the only traffic across the invisible bridge was a scared ferret. I've seen the darn thing mucking about myself."

Rhiann asked, "Do you think the ferret was involved?"

Chiron growled, "Don't insult my intelligence, sorcerer! He was seen leaving the crime scene, but he wasn't carrying a tree! What were you up to last night?" Decima walked up, and Chiron continued, "I think I know."

Decima said, "Lord Chiron, my relationship with Rhiann is no secret, but his intentions have remained honorable. But he *was* with me."

Rhiann blushed but was grateful for the alibi. Decima flashed him an odd glance. Did she suspect?

Nona and Mors arrived at the crime scene. Nona said, "This is the work of Thynna! Mayard loved this tree! It makes me feel I've lost him again!"

Burgomaster Donovan Eighty-four names hustled up to the uproar. The Gnome comforted Mors. Rhiann stood with Decima. Nona railed against Thynna and sorcery in general. The eldest of the Three Sisters fumed, "Thynna will rue this day. I'd prefer Magick had never come to Sagain. But for Mayard and others of the Klarje family, sorcerers have abused and used Magick for ill-gotten gain. Chiron, send our people into the woods and find that ****** ferret!"

Rhiann felt horribly guilty. Inside he knew he'd done his Uncle Mayard's will, but like deceiving the folk of Gnome-town and Dry Creek those years ago, his Uncle's schemes oft bent the rules. For the moment the Snowberry Bush was safe. It would not fall to a Hinderburgh giant's axe! The reports of Thynna's enlarging armies and the boldness of sending familiars into the Hanging Gardens spurred Rhiann to hasten his agenda. He drew Donovan aside and led the Gnome to his room.

Donovan said, "What's on your mind?"

Rhiann said, "I need some of your expertise. My Uncle Mayard left me several tasks. There is a tree near Greensborough that he had great interest in. Its...uh, the favorite resting place of a green dragon, and the home of a Dryad. I'd like some advice on dealing with green dragons."

Donovan tugged his long beard and puffed out his chest and said, "Woah! The dryad is a greater threat, young Rhiann! I know you are over 600 years old by my reckoning but you still look young. If you want to know about green dragons, you've come to the right Gnome. I...uh, made the acquaintance of a green witch, a green barrette from Greensborough. The green witches are Old Ones. They are an ancient folk who long predate the dawn of Magick. Greensborough is sometimes called the Emerald City. Lime trees and huge jade deposits give character to the region. Long have the green barrettes lived with green dragons. They have mastered resisting the green wyrms' infamous poison gas breath weapon. My acquaintance gave me this."

The Gnome separated his thick beard and carefully moved Mors' life strand aside. An ornate jade hair bow sat deep within his beard. Donovan said, "I've long treasured this green barrette. Doubt you'll ever see one outside of Greensborough. It gives me a fighting chance against green dragons. But you're talking about old Limenose now. As they get older, and particularly since Magick came to Sagain, the blighters pick up spell abilities. If all else fails, they can fall back on the old claw, claw, bite routine. Old Limenose isn't going to like your wanting to take away his tree."

Rhiann said, "Donovan, you sure know a lot about this dragon and the Greensborough area."

Donovan answered, "Well. I did a lot of traveling in my youth. As I said, I had an acquaintance in Greensborough. When Limenose was young, he accosted me and some…uh, friends. I smacked him around a bit. He remembers me well. Nowadays most folk in Greensborough stay away from his hill and tree. The tree is enchanted, anyway. Dryads are quite unpredictable. Are you sure you want to tangle with Limenose?"

Rhiann nodded affirmatively and said, "My Uncle specifically requested I save this tree. He avows there's no other like it in all of Sagain."

Donovan continued, "Yes. Your Uncle had a thing for unique things. Things like a Snowberry Bush. Is it in your best interest to get out of here and on with your next task? Old Chiron is quite an investigator."

Rhiann said, "Just say I know the Snowberry Bush is safe. I do feel pressed for time. I need to make my way to Greensborough. I'm counting on Urra knowing the way."

Donovan said, "Ah, you are allowed to remember the Cloudmares. Urra knows. So do I."

Rhiann said, "I can't ask you to go with me, Donovan. It's too dangerous."

Donovan said, "Now how can I miss another go with Old Limenose. Trouble is, I can resist his spittle, but his Magick is another matter, and there's the matter of the Dryad. It won't be easy."

Rhiann and Donovan told Mors and Decima of their need to run an errand. The sisters gave "see you later" hugs and kisses. The sorcerer and Gnome found Urra and Syrrth waiting outside the Gardens. The Cloudmares agreed to carry them to the Greensborough area. Donovan resisted the urge to enter the Emerald City. Rhiann and Donovan found the old haughty green dragon sitting upon the lone tree standing on top of Lime Mountain. The sweet smell in the air belied the risk one took in climbing the mountain to try to sample the fruits of the little trees that abounded on the lower slopes. The Lime Trees produced the scent along with rounded fruit, which was green when green and greener when ripe. The juice was treasured in many recipes and poultices. Limes were not Magick. They were the work of Nature. The scent of the mountain, ever-present regardless of season, was a bit of Magick.

The stately green oak stood alone on the top on the peak surrounded by deep green tall grass. A huge green dragon sat on the upper limbs and peered out over the landscape. The air hung heavy with the scent of ripening limes.

Donovan said, "Limenose has attacked merchant convoys from Athenia and Vallidale, the lands to the east, and interrupted our trade. Maybe we can teach the old boy a lesson and stop the attacks. It'd be like killing two ogles with one rock."

Ogles were big-eyed birds that raided crops in the plains. Hunters often slew the dimwitted Ogles with slings. Of course only a stone affected by Magick could kill two at once, but the old adage of killing two Ogles with one stone had come to mean getting two things done at the same time.

Donovan continued, "Green dragons are arrogant and overconfident. Sometimes, if we play it smart, they whip themselves."

Rhiann spent a bit of time conjuring and touched Donovan several times. The Gnome sharpened his axe and straightened his beard and mithril armor. Donovan said, "My armor was a gift from Roswell Kirkey. There was never a better armorer. Are you finished?"

Rhiann said, "I've done about all I can do."

Donovan said, "Then, there's nothing for it! Time to go!"

The Gnome brazenly left the cover of the lime trees and walked into the tall green grass. Donovan shouted, "Look at me, you ugly *******! I've come back to kick you're a** again!"

The big green dragon flew into the air and sped toward Donovan. Limenose growled, "What a sight for sore eyes. Your little a** is mine this time!"

Donovan answered, "Don't take me lightly. I have beaten your ilk many times. I'm going to teach you a lesson for interfering with my trade."

Limenose confidently shouted, "Do you think I mean to be satisfied with consuming marsh rats and scraps, when the caravans carry fat luscious Enigmas and Nus. Do you think me a fool? I'm a lot stronger than I was the first time we tangled! I've power of Magick."

Donovan replied, "You must refrain from attacking the caravans."

The Gnome gulped. Limenose was now the largest green dragon the Gnome had seen. His scales were emerald and pea green. A sea green cornea and lighter green sclera surrounded his dark slit-like feline pupils. Green dragons had no "whites of their eyes"- only greenness! Limenose's long tail curled above and behind him and his innumerable scales rattled menacingly.

A wry smile crossed the green dragon's face. He beat his heavy wings and hovered over the Gnome, and shouted, "Let's get to it! Repel this!" Limenose spewed a cloud of thick gas, green of course, toward Donovan. The thick liquid splashed over the Gnome and coated his fine armor. Donovan's green barrette protected him and his goods from the green dragon breath.

Donovan shook vigorously and sent green dragon spittle in all directions. The powerful acid within the thick gooey substance destroyed everything it touched. Plants sizzled!

"Confound it, you dirtied my armor!" Donovan protested.

Undaunted, Limenose inhaled deeply, exhaled, and sent a gust of rapidly spinning green smoke toward Donovan. A green tornado left the green dragon and covered the Gnome. The swirling wind turned faster and faster as Limenose exhaled. The force of the windstorm turned Donovan violently. Limenose stopped exhaling and pounced toward her opponent, but Donovan stopped spinning and jumped to the side. Limenose thumped hard against the ground, but injured only his pride. Rhiann muttered a Push Spell and struck the off-balance green dragon. Limenose crashed backward to the ground, rolled over three times, and quickly righted himself. Limenose angrily uttered a three-phrase incantation. A Magick Missile streaked from the green dragon's left forepaw and struck Donovan, but Rhiann's shield spell protected the Gnome.

Shield Spells gave immunity to Magick Missiles.

Limenose said something in the green dragon tongue.

"That wasn't very nice," Donovan chided.

Limenose conjured the Confusion Spell. The accuracy of the green dragon's incantation surprised Rhiann, but the spell didn't work.

Rhiann's Protection Spell protected Donovan. Limenose roared and uttered a Power Word Stun. Rhiann's protection Spell did just enough to temper the powerful Stun. Donovan feigned falling under the spell and stumbled haphazardly and fell. Limenose laughed and approached to finish the job. The dragon opened his maw to snack on Gnome, but Donovan delivered a powerful blow to his sensitive nose. Limenose recoiled. Rhiann sent an Entangle Spell to the beat's legs, and Limenose fell hard and rolled over on the ground. Donovan closed on the dragon and popped him on the head with his axe. Limenose shook his head and then snapped his maw at Donovan. Donovan jumped back with blinding speed. Rhiann's Haste Spell assisted the Gnome's movement. Donovan smacked the dragon three times and fell back. Limenose roared, flew high into the air, dove toward the Gnome. Donovan jumped aside at the last moment, and hit the dragon's right wing. This disrupted the beast's balance and Limenose hit the ground hard again. Donovan sped over to the dragon and clubbed him several times. Limenose saw stars.

Donovan asked, "Have you had enough? Will you say 'calf rope'?"

The big dragon dejectedly muttered, "Yes, I'll say 'calf rope' or anything else you want me to say. You whipped my a** good!"

Donovan said, "References to your posterior are unnecessary. Get out of here while you can."

Limenose limped away and finally managed to take off and fly toward the distant mountains.

Donovan said, "Well, there's your tree, Rhiann."

Rhiann said, "There's still the matter of the Dryad."

Donovan said, "I can't help you there. How do you talk her into taking her tree?"

Rhiann answered, "I don't. She goes with it. The tree and the sprite it contains are an inseparable symbiosis. From my reading… we should play her lots of compliments, but be wary of her charms. I've read they are quite persuasive and hard to resist."

Donovan replied, "You've resisted sirens and Decima…haven't you?"

Rhiann didn't answer. He motioned toward the great green oak. Donovan and Rhiann approached the great green oak. The sorcerer rubbed the great oak tentatively but jumped back when a small blue-haired nymph walked quickly through the bark.

After sleepily rubbing her dark purple eyes, the diminutive forest creature gently stroked Donovan's long red beard, winked at him, and asked, "Why are you rubbing my tree? Who are you, pretty thing?"

Rhiann asked, "Are you the Lady of the Tree? A dryad?"

The diminutive tree sprite warbled, "Of what do you speak? I'm not a matron! Dryads are huge, nigh as big as Gnomes, four feet tall! I'm a simple sprite! I've been sleeping in my tree having the best dream. I was drinking the juice of byneberries. I've never seen you, young…ooh! Sorcerer! You are a Sorcerer! You are cute. Would you like to come into my tree and share a few moments? I have some passion fruit."

Donovan chuckled and said, "He'd best stay with me, Lady of the Tree."

The tree sprite answered coyly "I won't keep him long."

Donovan said, "Oh, I suspect your beauty would forever detain him, my Lady."

The tree sprite blushed, but her bright green skin turned purple instead of red. Rhiann studied the cute little creature. The tree sprite's blue hair and purple eyes contrasted with her bright green skin. The greenness returned after her blushing ended. The little creature appeared perfectly at home in the green ness of Greensborough. As tall as thirty-six inchworms stacked end-to-end, the three-foot-tall sprite was about two-thirds the height of Donovan, who was a bit above average height for a Gnome.

Knowing the sprite's vanity might be used to their advantage Donovan said politely and redundantly, "Thank you for allowing our eyes to behold your beauty, Lady of the Tree. We don't often look upon such beauty. Please bear with us, and we thank you for allowing our glances."

The tree sprite accepted the compliments and offered, "You may come inside and try some of *my* wondrous fruits."

Rhiann said, "Please reenter your tree. There's naught I can offer to improve on perfection, but with your permission, I'll prepare spells to enhance your home's beauty and make it safer for you."

The tree sprite winked at Donovan and said, "I'm thinking how good it'd feel to have your strong arms around me, great warrior. I watched you stand down the dragon. I have no fondness for the vile beast. Its foul spittle burned my plush grasses." She then gave the Gnome a gentle kiss.

Donovan said, "I could go inside with her for just a little while, Rhiann."

Rhiann said, "No, strong warrior. I need your help."

Rhiann gave Donovan a gentle pinch and interrupted the sprite's charm spell. The tree sprite turned and entered the tree. Without hesitation, Rhiann scurried around the base of the great green oak with a little shovel, scooped up morsels of dirt, placed the soil in a tiny bucket, and uttered what sounded like a child's limerick. He sprinkled a bit of the soil on his boots and into his rucksack. Rhiann then reached into his rucksack, got a pinch of powdered iron, recited the incantation for the Enlarge Spell *backwards,* and completed a Shrink Spell. The huge green oak decreased in size until it was small enough to fit in the palm of his hand. The green oak retained its weight. Rhiann then used a small leather loop, muttered another group of phrases, and touched the tiny oak tree. The tree rose into the air. Rhiann wrapped his arms around the tiny bush. He scattered a bit of soil he brought from Green Vale onto his shoes. Next he crushed Shypoke eggshells and painstakingly cast the Translocation dweomer. The young sorcerer and the great green oak disappeared. The activity created a defect thirteen feet wide in the soil of Lime Mountain. Bailiwick sensed a great wave on the sea of Magick. Eyerthrin sensed the disturbance as well.

Rhiann arrived in Green Vale in an instant. He arrived in the amber period. The vale was devoid of activity. Rhiann guided the great green oak over one of the thirteen holes he had dug in the hillock. He eased the tree into the hole. NET then recited the Enlarge Spell and touched the green oak. The massive tree expanded to its natural height and size. The Circle of Green Vale had its third inhabitant. Gray auras surrounded the tree. The geyser erupted from the effervescing pool and bathed Rhiann, the Green Oak, the Snowberry Bush, and the Gem Bush.

The green oak…

$$Ǿ \infty Ǿ$$
$$V$$
$$\infty Ǿ \infty$$

Rhiann Klarje concentrated on Lime Mountain, scattered a bit of the soil he had taken from the oak tree's former home, and muttered a simple command. In an instant he stood beside Donovan on Lime Mountain. The Gnome was saying, "How long will you be gone?" Then Donovan added, "Oh, you're already back."

The Cloudmare Urra carried Rhiann back to the Hanging Gardens. Her colleague Syrrth carried Donovan *Eighty-five* names to the Hanging Garden, where he visited briefly. She then carried him back to his Burgomaster duties in Norman.

Rhiann received updates from Chiron and Decima. A skirmish north of the Gardens cost the lives of seven centaurs and over a hundred of Thynna's mercenaries. No clues were found in the disappearance of the Snowberry Bush. Rhiann visited with Decima and then bade Urra carry him to Cragmore.

CHAPTER 39

The Sick Amore from Andalusia

Rhiann's next target was a Sick Amore tree in Andalusia. Mayard Klarje described the rarity in his journals. It was the prized possession of a sorceress named Madam Ruth who used the tree's heart-shaped fruits to create Love Potions. Her ninth potion was said to be as potent as a Charm Spell or Dryad's kiss. Rhiann joined the sirens Maranna and Serena and young Iyaca Vassi for dinner and talked about the task.

Serena fumed, "Ruth plays with fire. Her potions don't hold a candle to one of our songs. Would you like me to sing to you, Iyaca?"

Iyaca said, "Oh, yes, please."

Maranna and Rhiann simultaneously uttered, "No!"

Iyaca asked many questions about goings on in the Hanging Gardens. Rhiann updated his friends about his progress.

NET said, "I don't know why my Uncle listed items in the order he gave in his journal, but I'm following his order. He only said the Sick Amore Tree grew in Andalusia. According to legend, the Sick Amore bears thirteen heart-shaped fruits, and ingestion of its fruit was the equivalent of imbibing a love potion. One who consumes the bittersweet fruit becomes intoxicated, loses reason, and longs for more."

Maranna said, "I know where the tree grows. Rhiann, your Uncle Mayard may simply have written things as they came to him. His travels took him to Andalusia several times. Once he fell under the influence of one of Madam Ruth's potions. Urra and I had to retrieve him. He was quite mad at us. If you insist on going on with your plans, Andalusia lies far to the east and borders the great eastern sea. Many wild areas are lowly populated. The wood from Andalusia trees is highly sought after. Andalusia breeds of horses are popular, too. The vintners produce decent wine. Few sorcerers live in this largely agricultural area. If memory serve me right, Madam Ruth is an exceptional potion maker, but only a mediocre sorceress. Guard dawgs protect her home… and the tree."

Rhiann said, "Uncle Mayard wanted to save the tree. It seems it's already in a rather safe place. Will you show me the way?"

Maranna said, "Urra will carry you."

Rhiann said, "Thanks. I'll use soil from Cragmore as a return point."

Urra carried Rhiann to the east. Maranna led them to Madam Ruth's complex. The silent flyers found the special tree easily. There were no dragons to fight, only a tall fence augmented by Wall of Thorns, Entangle, Plant Growth, Ensnare, and Magick Mouth Spells and six rather vicious guard dawgs. Rhiann used a cricket, uttered an incantation, and cast a Sleep Spell on the guard dawgs. An area Silence Spell, quieted the Magick Mouths, which warned the sorceress of trespassers. The Silence Spell halted verbal communication among Rhiann, Maranna, and Urra, but the sorcerer and Cloudmare communicated telepathically. Rhiann used the Staff of Entry to separate the branches of the entangled vines and gain access to the Sick Amore Tree. Rhiann repeated his ritual. He moved around the base of the Sick Amore Tree with a little shovel, scooped up morsels of dirt, placed the soil in a tiny bucket, and uttered what sounded like a child's limerick. He sprinkled a bit of the soil on his boots and into his rucksack. Rhiann then reached into his rucksack, got a pinch of powdered iron, recited the incantation for the Enlarge Spell *backwards,* and completed a Shrink Spell. The Sick Amore Tree decreased in size until it was small enough to fit in the palm of his hand. The Sick Amore retained its weight. Rhiann then used a small leather loop, muttered another group of phrases, and touched the tiny Sick Amore. The tree rose into the air. Rhiann wrapped his arms around the tiny tree. He scattered a bit of soil he brought from Green Vale onto his shoes. Next he crushed Shypoke eggshells and painstakingly cast the Translocation dweomer. The young sorcerer and the Sick Amore disappeared. The activity created a defect thirteen feet wide in the soil of Madam Ruth's Andalusia garden. Bailiwick sensed a great wave on the sea of Magick. Eyerthrin sensed the disturbance as well. Sorcerers throughout Sagain felt the waves created by the dweomer. The Dream Master felt the spell, looked up from his scrying stone, and smiled wryly.

Rhiann arrived in Green Vale in an instant. He suffered no discomfort. He arrived in the light period. The lovely tree sprite came of her tree, greeted him, and thanked Rhiann for bringing her to such a beautiful place. Rhiann guided the Sick Amore Tree over one of the thirteen holes he had dug in the hillock and eased the tree into the hole. NET then recited the Enlarge Spell and touched the Sick Amore. The tree expanded to its natural height and size. The Circle of Green Vale had its fourth inhabitant. Gray auras surrounded the tree. The geyser erupted from the effervescing pool and bathed Rhiann, the Sick Amore, Green Oak, Snowberry Bush, and Gem Bush.

The sick amore…

Ǿ ∞ Ǿ
XII
∞ **Ǿ** ∞

Rhiann Klarje concentrated on Cragmore, scattered a bit of the soil he had taken from the oak tree's former home, and muttered a simple command. In an instant he stood beside Syrrth. Urra and Maranna had not yet returned from Andalusia.

CHAPTER 40

Jellybean Bush

Rhiann and Maranna returned to Harmony House and joined Iyaca. NET told them his plans to sneak into the Temple of Artemis and steal the Jelllybean Bush. Mayard Klarje tried to steal the whimsical Jellybean Bush from the Temple of Artemis in the Veldt. The Amazons discovered his plot. The old sorcerer escaped with his life and an Amazon's arrow in his butt. At Mayard's request his great nephew Rhiann had presented the arrow to the Burgomaster Storming Norman Darktop of Gnome-town long ago. The old wandering sorcerer had written about his fascination with the thought-to-be unique plant often. The bush always bore 169 speckled berries. The berries developed specks as they ripened. Thirteen specks meant a berry could be picked, but the Amazons prohibited taking berries from the bush and only consumed the fruits when they voluntarily fell from the bush. Eating the fruit was considered a great honor by the powerful feminine warriors. Less than thirteen berries left the bush at any given time. Harvesting more than thirteen resulted in the immediate spoilage of all that had been picked. Mayard recorded great detail about the bush in his journals. Rhiann discussed his Uncle's writings with his friends.

Maranna said, "Rhiann, I've gone along with your decisions. But Mayard was unable to take the bush, and he was much more experienced."

Rhiann said, "My Uncle had not drunk from the source of Magick and did not have Translocation at his disposal. Preserving the Jellybean Bush was on his agenda, so I must proceed."

Iyaca cautioned, "She's right, NET. I read about the bush in your Uncle Mayard's journals. Its fruit is simply a sweet treat. Is that worth risking your life?"

Rhiann said, "I am committed to fulfilling my Uncle Mayard's requests. I have read his journals about the Temple of Artemis in the Veldt. He writes…

"The Temple of the Amazon Huntress Artemis sat at the gap that led to the lands of the Amazons in the great mountains at the far western fringes of the Veldt. The highly intelligent Amazons disdained contact with other peoples, particularly their ancient enemies the giants. Magick touched the Amazons. There had been a queen named Artemis whose deeds filled many campfire songs and legends, but no written records existed of her activities on Sagain. The specifics of the Temple of Artemis and the queen to whom it was dedicated had always been a cause for debate among Sagain's scholars. Hunters paid homage to the queen of the Amazons. Archers sought the expertise of the Amazons, for the great warriors were unparalleled bowyers and fletchers. Although the Amazons bartered with hunters and archers, the huge warriors kept secret the location of Artemis's temple. For the Amazons, it was not just a temple…it was the most beautiful structure in all Sagain. The foundation of the temple was rectangular in form, similar to most temples at the time. Unlike other sanctuaries, however, the building was made of marble, with a decorated façade overlooking a spacious courtyard. Marble steps surrounding the building platform led to the high terrace, which was approximately 80 meters by 130 meters in plan. The columns were twenty meters high with ionic capitals and carved circular sides. There were 127 columns in total, aligned orthogonally over the whole platform area, except for the central cella or house of the goddess. The temple housed many works of art, including four ancient bronze statues of Amazons sculpted by the finest artists of the time.

Iyaca said, "I've read and reread the descriptions of the wonder in the Veldt. Nowhere are there clues to safely enter and evade the Amazon guards. NET, on this task, I think you should ignore your Uncle Mayard's wants."

Rhiann said, "I must follow his instructions."

Maranna said, "You assume there is a method to his madness. Sometimes he just did things for the adventure. His tryst with the Amazons may have been just that. Mayard had barely escaped sentries of the closely guarded Amazon Temple of Artemis and got away by the skin of his teeth with an Amazon's arrow impaled in his butt. I carried the wounded sorcerer to the Hanging Gardens. Healers removed the arrow and Nona used thread spun from her distaff to sew up the wound of Mayard's butt."

Just then another voice. Nona's said, "That's right. The old blighter tried the amorous approach. He was pretty good at it. At least he thought he was."

Rhiann said, "Nona. How'd you find us?"

Another voice, Decima's said, "It was your fate."

Rhiann said, "Decima. Nice to see you… I think."

Decima said, "The Cloudmares brought us to Harmony House. I've sensed its location in your thoughts."

Mors entered and said, "We want to help you. To honor Mayard and spite Bailiwick and the Council of Thynna."

Nona looked into Rhiann's eyes and said, "A ferret came to the gardens with an epistle tied around its neck. The letter from High President Bailiwick of Thynna said that Rhiann Klarje was a thief and an enemy to all Sagain. He alleged you stole the Gem Bush from Thynna centuries ago and now pilfer rarities of Sagain, including our treasured Snowberry Bush. Mayard spoke to me often of his concerns for our world and his desire to preserve the best of Sagain in any way possible. I see much of Mayard in you, Rhiann. You continue his work. He talked often of the Jellybean Bush and wanted to treat me to samples of its fruit. He was injured trying. I never believed he was seriously enamored with the Amazon queen."

Rhiann said, "Guilty as charged. I'm sorry, Decima… and Nona… and Lady Mors. You have been more than kind to me. Uncle Mayard feared for the plant's safety… as well as yours."

Nona said, "We understand. He, as well as you, warned us of Thynna's imminent threat. We feel committed to our roles in the world. I hope you have given the Snowberry Bush a good home."

Nona said, "We have another deed. Fact is… Mayard is gone. My gift to him gave him longevity and he used the time well. He saved me from the bewildebeest's talons. We have a gift to bequeath. Young Iyaca step forward."

Nona took a spinning wheel and drew forth a length of multicolored thread. Mors snipped the thread with her shears and gave it to Nona, who kept her face about three inches from Iyaca and enticed him ever more with her sweet breath and soft touch. Nona's inestimable charisma overwhelmed Iyaca. His fingers and toes tingled with excitement. Nona took a strand of her long platinum hair and twisted it around the thread of Iyaca's dark hair wrapped around her finger and bound the pair of threads with the fiber that Mors snipped from Nona's distaff. Scintillating lights surrounded Iyaca and the beautiful matronly Fate. Nona gently stretched and braided the interwoven strand. The interwoven hair and fiber grew ever longer and surrounded Nona and Iyaca. She smiled, gave Iyaca a kiss, and stepped away from him. Mors deftly snipped the strand of hair where it left Nona's head. Iyaca's locks shimmered briefly and then resumed their dark color. The long strand he received from Nona meld with his hair and the fiber from Nona's distaff.

Nona purred, "My gift to you, Iyaca Vassi. May Rhiann long follow his Uncle Mayard's steps and may you long assist Rhiann Klarje."

Maranna said, "You'll never take the Jellybean Bush with a show of force. The Amazons are too powerful. A mere squad of Amazons defeated an entire company of Hinderburgh Giants, and they were only fighting over hunting rights in the Dawgskill Mountains. They'll fight more fiercely defending their home and treasured temple."

Rhiann suggested, "Invisibility?"

Maranna said, "Mayard tried it. The Amazons other senses are too keen."

Rhiann said, "Well, we know the location of the Temple and the Jellybean Bush within the Temple of Artemis. I could shrink you, Maranna, and you could fly me in."

Maranna said, "You are not going to be able to shrink me, Rhiann. Even if I am willing, Magick oft doesn't affect me.'

Iyaca said, "You could sing to them."

Maranna said, "I tried it. Amazons are attractive, but they are fighters not lovers. Their warrior spirit wins out every time. I did distract them with a battle cry. Might have bought Mayard a little time."

Rhiann said, "I can use Silence until it's time to cast the spells."

Maranna said, "We won't be able to hear you."

Rhiann said, "I'll have to have a bit of luck. I don't want to jeopardize anyone other than myself."

Maranna said, "That's not going to happen."

Decima added, "I'm pretty good with a bow. I can create a diversion."

The Cloudmares Urra, Syrrth, and Shyrra carried Rhiann, Decima, and Iyaca to the proximity of the Temple of Artemis. Maranna and Serena flew with them. Rhiann busily cast several spells and Urra bore him over the Temple. Large red arrows flew toward the Cloudmare, but Urra evaded them. She dipped low. Rhiann used the effect of The Feather Fall Spell to leave the Cloudmare and fall near the Jellybean Bush. He was Invisible, Silent, and Shrunk to the size of a mouse when he jumped off Urra's back. He telepathically relayed his plans to Urra so the Cloudmare anticipated his actions. An Amazon's arrow came precariously close to the small, silent, invisible, gently free-falling little sorcerer. Fortunately for Rhiann he got his bit of luck and the arrow missed. Several arrows hit Urra but only passed through the big wingless flying equine. If the arrows affected her, Urra did not show it. Outside the Temple of Artemis, Decima shouted and fired an arrow toward the wall. Twenty-five Amazons answered her shot, but the Shield Spell that Rhiann had uttered just before he left on Urra's back deflected them. Iyaca pretended to send spells toward the wall. More arrows flew toward him, but he was likewise protected by a Magick Shield. Maranna flew over the temple. Arrows flew about, but the siren's maneuverability helped her evade them. The Amazon archers were quite accurate with their volleys, so the siren had to stay well out of range. The siren sang battle cries. A hundred Amazon warriors ran from the temple toward Iyaca and Decima's position.

Iyaca said, "No shield is going to protect us from those blades. This is our signal to run!"

Decima gave him a quick kiss and said, "That's for luck, and I can't agree with you more."

Decima and Iyaca climbed aboard Syrrth and Shyrra. Urra flew around the bartizans and guard towers twice and drew fire. The Cloudmare then flew off toward her comrades.

Tiny, invisible, silent Rhiann broke his silence and invisibility, shouted a Magick Missile command, and shattered a mirror in the courtyard a distance away from the Jellybean Bush. Amazons rushed to investigate. Rhiann reversed the order of his spells. He muttered the reverse of Enlarge and touched the Jellybean Bush with his tiny hand. The bush shrank to the size of a booderry bush. He then hurriedly dug around the base of the shrunk Jellybean Bush with a little shovel, scooped up morsels of dirt, placed the soil in a tiny bucket, and uttered lyrical phrases. He sprinkled a bit of the soil on his boots and into his rucksack. Per usual the Jellybean Bush retained its weight. Rhiann then used a small leather loop, muttered another group of phrases, and touched the tiny Jellybean Bush. The speckled berry bush rose into the air. Rhiann wrapped his arms around the tiny bush and scattered a bit of soil he brought from Green Vale onto his shoes. Next he crushed Shypoke eggshells and carefully cast the Translocation dweomer. The young sorcerer and the Jellybean Bush disappeared. The activity created a defect thirteen feet wide in the garden. In Thynna, Bailiwick sensed a great wave on the sea of Magick. Eyerthrin sensed the disturbance as well.

Rhiann arrived in Green Vale in an instant. He arrived in the dark period. The tree sprite was playing in the pool in the center of the hilltop. Rhiann guided the Jellybean Bush over one of the thirteen holes he had dug in the hillock. He eased the bush into the hole. NET then recited the Enlarge Spell and touched the Jellybean Bush. The wondrous bush expanded to its natural height and size. The Circle of Green Vale had its fifth inhabitant. Gray auras surrounded the tree. The geyser erupted from the effervescing pool and bathed Rhiann, the Jellybean Bush, Sick Amore Tree, Green Oak, Snowberry Bush, and the Gem Bush. A speckled fruit fell off the jellybean bush. Rhiann counted 13 specks. Another fruit replaced the one that fell off. Rhiann ate the fruit. Apple flavored… brought back fond memories of visits to an apple orchard in Virginia in the blue world … Mayard left one slot open. Rhiann now knew what to put in the open spot.

The jellybean bush…

Ǿ ∞ Ǿ

VIII

∞ Ǿ ∞

Rhiann Klarje concentrated on Harmony House, scattered a bit of the soil he had taken from Iyaca's garden, and muttered a simple command. In an instant he stood alone in the cottage. In a little while Iyaca, Nona, Decima, Mors, and Maranna returned, and the group shared Jove's nectar.

Iyaca said, "That's a relief."

Maranna agreed and said, "Some angry Amazons are wanting your hide."

Rhiann mused, "Now, five trees stand in the growing circle. The tree sprite is unsupervised. I need a shepherd. Uncle Mayard told me where to find one."

Maranna urged, "Please rest tonight."

The Cloudmares carried the Three Sisters back to the Hanging Gardens.

CHAPTER 41

The Tree Shepherd's Origins
The Silver Maple

The ageless Tree Shepherd gazed toward the ominous dark citadel Koorlost that dominated the valley below Mount Airie. The immense tree herder had wandered among and lovingly cared for the diverse flora of the dense forests that covered greatest peak of Sagain. While caring for the plants the green giant had witnessed the growth of the black walled citadel from a hamlet to an imposing fortress. The citadel now filled the valley that led toward the deserts to the west. The Tree Shepherd sprouted at the time of the great cataclysm that heralded the dawn of Magick and grew as a sapling on the slopes of Mount Airie. Time had not dulled his vision and awareness.

Conflict gripped the peoples of the world. The Tree Shepherd didn't understand the waste of life and Magick. Folks calling themselves Dark and Light Sorcerers fomented the disputes. Their demands on his forests made them indistinguishable to the towering tree herder.

The shepherd stretched his huge upper boughs and enjoyed the warming rays from the distal twin suns that sent light to the world of Magick. Such a simple pleasure…simply looking upon the beauty that Nature and Magick had created. Many of the trees and plants he tended possessed only simple Magick, such as the ability to change the color of their leaves or produce a delicious fruit. The nameless Tree Shepherd appreciated even these simplest of abilities and painfully felt the felling of every tree needed to fulfill the needs of construction. Uprooting and moving about exhausted him, and maintaining his illusory appearance as a great green oak became increasingly difficult as the sorcerers became more adept at Magick. To this point, he had remained successful.

No threats at the moment. The Green Giant concentrated, instantly moved a league to the west, and arrived at a small clearing deep in the wood. Again the distant binary suns warmed and energized him. He surveyed the area. Alas…

The woodsmen continued their assault on the silver maple growth. Silver was in great demand. Tiaras, chalices, spears, knives, trinkets, bling… Three more trees had been stripped of their silver leaves. Only lush green leaves remained on the thirteen-foot tall trees.

"Why must they take every silver leaf?" the grumpy green giant mused painfully and silently, and of course to no one.

Stripped of their silver leaves, the trees were no longer fertile and would now live only another thirty, or forty, or perhaps fifty seasons.

"Unless an interloper requires their heartwood for a fire!" the Tree Shepherd muttered silently with angst.

Had the harvesters left only a single silver leaf the magnificent denizens of Sagain's forests would beget more saplings.

As far as the green giant knew, the silver maples and four nearby ultra-rare trees with fluted fruits were the only source of the metal in all of Sagain.

Sagain…

Before the Great Fire in the Sky and subsequent Time of Darkness only a flicker of Magick existed. The Fire in the Sky gradually changed everything. The flicker grew to a roaring flame. For the most part the new powers concentrated around the small community Thynna. Sorcerers grew more powerful, lived longer, and developed discord, greed, jealousy, covetousness, and maliciousness. Thynna became the center of power and culture. Rivalries ensued and sorcerers differentiated into rival groups called Light and Dark Sorcerers. Dark Sorcerers gathered in Koorlost and Light Sorcerers clustered in the hamlet the Laurels, but the most powerful still lived in Thynna's inner ward and followed the aging High President Bailiwick and Castellan Yerko.

Despondently the great tree herder laboriously tended the remaining trees. Abruptly he froze and drove his trailing roots into the ground.

A robed character stood nearby! Had to be a Light or Dark Sorcerer!

How did the robed character appear so swiftly and without warning? Ah…simple teleportation…more of them were learning the spell. Still he should have detected the cumbersome Magick. The fellow was not nude and defenseless. The green giant peered at the face beneath the cowl. This was no woodsman or simple harvester. The Tree Shepherd had seen this sorcerer many times. The tall sorcerer approached one of the three denuded silver maples. A single tear rolled down the sorcerer's cheek.

The sorcerer lamented, "Foolishness! Wanton waste! Why? They are going to strip the entire forest! More trinkets for the greedy of Thynna and Koorlost! Will nothing natural remain of our world? Uncle Mayard was right. At least one silver maple must be saved."

The sorcerer looked toward the distant suns. The green giant read his unwelcomed companion's thoughts. The man's name was Rhiann. Rhiann's mind struggled with the fate of the distant suns. Many doomsayers claimed the suns grew larger and spoke of Sagain's doom. Others avowed the suns that bathed the world of Magick were merely going through one of many cycles that had occurred since the dawn of Magick. Thynna's conflict with the Three Sisters, Old Ones, and the Hanging Gardens troubled the sorcerer standing before him. The sorcerer lowered his gaze from the sky and stared directly at the green giant.

"I know you are reading me, tree shepherd," the sorcerer said aloud.

The green giant remained silent.

"Don't fear me, tree shepherd. I don't come to destroy your forest. I see they've taken more of them. The silver maple stands in the Samm Hills are no more. This stand was one of the last. It's too bad the silver maples can't move about as you do," the sorcerer continued.

The green giant did not answer.

"I've known of you for a long time. My Uncle Mayard Klarje wrote about you in his diaries. He said you love and care of the forest is unsurpassed."

The tree shepherd recalled visits from the old haggard sorcerer who called himself Mayard. Still the great tree herder remained silent.

The sorcerer continued, "Know that I seek the continuation and preservation of what is good of Sagain. I know a place. A time…I can make this possible. Already I have gathered a great green oak from the forests around Greensborough. I had to best a green dragon to secure the tree and the winsome dryad that lives within the tree. I've taken a snowberry bush from the Hanging Gardens. It grew nowhere else in the world. I had to deceive the Three Sisters to take the bush. The Spinner, Allotter, and Unturning enjoyed using its fruit to chill their beverages on a hot day. Under cover of darkness I sneaked a Gem Bush from the clutches of the greedy sorcerers of Thynna. I've taken a Sick Amore tree from a sorceress who lives in Andalusia. She used the heart shaped fruits to make love potions. The effect surpasses most Charm Spells. I took a whimsical jellybean bush from the temple of Artemis in the Veldt. The Amazons nigh caught me. The hard speckled fruits look identical, but taste differently and never the same. Will you hear me?" the sorcerer asked.

Slowly he moved a few steps closer to the silent towering green oak.

The Tree Shepherd sighed silently.

"At least that's a response. The beauty of Sagain need not end, Tree Shepherd. I have seen the source of Magick. I've also seen other worlds where you might practice your stewardship. Are you interested?" the sorcerer queried silently.

The Tree Shepherd only emitted another sigh.

The sorcerer continued, "The inner ward of Thynna grows more exclusive. The Council of Thynna sends a juggernaut into the deserts to challenge the Three Sisters and Old Ones. Conflict is inevitable. I don't know if the doomsayers that talk about the distant suns have any basis for their fears. However, the greed of Thynna and the pillaging of our world's beauty are readily evident. Arcane forces from without probe Sagain. I've seen them in my dreams. The bastion at the base of the great mountain and the city to the north grow stronger. The orders of sorcerers further divide the world. Magick has splintered the world. Conflict between Light and Dark Sorcerers is inevitable. Look at the young silver maple to your left. It's perfect! 13 feet tall…it's diameter equals the length of thirteen inchworms. Its leaves have thirteen veins. It stands by three denuded brothers. I suppose it's the harvesters' next target. I know a place…a place of refuge where this little tree will survive. It could grow under the light of three suns and be touched by Magick. Someone should watch over it. Ponder my words. I'll return."

The loquacious sorcerer strolled over to the silver maple. He raised an ornate staff, uttered an incantation, lowered the staff to the ground, walked in a circle around the lovely little tree, and traced a circle in the ground around the silver maple. He used a tiny shovel and removed a bit of topsoil. He sprinkled it on his boots and place a bit in a rucksack he carried on his hip. An aura surrounded the silver maple. The sorcerer looked back at the tree Shepherd, smiled, touched the shiny bark of the maple, and sang another lyrical incantation. The lovely tree shrank to the size of a tiny sapling and then floated into the air. The aura surrounding the silver maple intensified. Those touched by Magick sense little ripples on the great sea of Magick when spells are cast. The Translocation Spells created great waves on that complex sea. Intense green light briefly filled the area. When the green light faded, the silver maple and the sorcerer were gone. The Tree Shepherd recognized the Magick of the Translocation Spell. He had sensed its unique tidal wave many times. Many sorcerers knew teleportation spells. Teleportation was a simple spell and served one's purpose so long as the caster didn't mind reaching his destination naked and defenseless. Translocation was ninth level Magick...Magick of the highest level.

Rhiann arrived in Green Vale during a light period. The tree sprite sat on the lower limb of her tree home. Rhiann directed the silver maple over a prepared spot and performed the usual planting ritual. The geyser erupted and bathed the silver maple, jellybean bush, sick amore tree, green oak, snowberry bush, and gem gush with its sparkling waters.

The circle had its sixth occupant.

The silver maple...

$$\acute{Ø} \infty \acute{Ø}$$
$$\mathbf{X}$$
$$\infty \, \acute{Ø} \, \infty...$$

Rhiann scattered some soil from the silver maple's former home on Mt. Airie. He concentrated, muttered phrases, and returned to the Tree Shepherd.

CHAPTER 42

The "Toot and see scroll" Tree

After the sorcerer and silver maple disappeared, the Tree Shepherd went about his work on the slopes of Mt. Airie and next attended the small stand of "toot and see scroll" trees. He hoped the ultra-rare trees would remain undiscovered. The Tree Shepherd's limited teleportation spells restricted his movement to the area around Mount Airie. He arrived at the small grove of trees with flute shaped fruits and chased away a three-eyed roc eater. Rocs favored the fruits of the purplanana trees that grew in this area. Three-eyed roc eaters favored rocs. The third eye in the back of the roc eater's head improved the predator's hunting. The Tree Shepherd gave a sigh of relief. The "toot and see scroll" trees were unharmed. The trees had had sprouted like the Tree Shepherd at the time of the great light and stood at this place as long as he had walked and rooted in Sagain's soil. The four thirteen-foot tall trees had thirteen branches, thirteen-inch diameter trunks, leaves divided by thirteen veins, and bore thirteen fruits. The fruits were shaped like small fluted silver scroll tubes.

In all of Sagain only these four "toot and see scroll" trees remained. The old tree herder had cast illusory Magick on the quartet. Observers saw only a stand of common purplanana bushes. A sorcerer's Dispel Magick dweomer would remove the illusion, but why would a sorcerer waste Magick in a stand of purplananas and risk picking a purplanana's fruit? Webs of deadly phase spiders intertwined with the purplanana's leaves and thirteen fruits. The spider's venom acted quickly. There was no antidote. Only a seventh level Cure Spell afforded any chance for the victim. Phase spiders always appeared three inchworm lengths to the right, left, front, or rear of their actual location. Also the dastardly spiders were proficient jumpers. As a quirk of Nature, Magick, or both, the big burly rocs were resistant to the spider's venom. The green giant had scarcely finished tending the fourth tree when the sojourning sorcerer reappeared.

"Nice work, Shepherd," the sorcerer commented.

The green giant only silently grunted. The response was not lost on the traveler.

"That's a bit more of a response. Have you considered my offer?" the man called Rhiann asked.

The green giant silently, "You are no better than the woodsmen and harvesters. In fact, your destruction exceeds the silver mongers. At least the greenness of the tree remains after the silver leaves are taken. At least, that is, until the tree feels the woodsman's axe. Those woodsmen will meet with accidents! So shall you, if you touch one of these trees! You made off with the silver maple before I could stop you! My great limbs and roots have been known to fall upon unsuspecting usurpers of the forest!"

The sorcerer asked politely. "If you deter the first, others will follow. You can't stand guard constantly. Nor can you stop me. I'd rather have your permission. May I sample the odd fruits? Are the fruits scrolls of Magick?"

The Tree Shepherd said, "Each tree bears but thirteen fruits. There's always been thirteen. Never more, never less."

"Does the fruit mature every season?" the sorcerer asked.

"There have always been thirteen fruits on the tree. They appeared as nubbins when the trees were saplings and matured in thirteen seasons," the shepherd replied illusorily. "I've never felt the need to pick one. If you pick one, will you go away?"

"Thank you for your permission. I've seen nothing like these fruits in all of Sagain. The tubes have an aura of Magick beyond that of the tree and the background. You contribute greatly to the strength of Magick in the area, Tree Shepherd! I'll take the lowest fruit," Rhiann suggested.

The green giant stood quietly and communicated nothing telepathically.

The sorcerer gently twisted and removed the nearest of the shimmering silver fruits. A green aura briefly covered the area and the nubbin of another fruit appeared where the "toot and see scroll" fruit had been.

"Magick replenished the fruit," Rhiann marveled.

"It would seem so," the Tree Shepherd grumpily conceded.

The silver tube was precisely the length of thirteen inchworms laid end to end. (Many worlds used the invariable length of the universally ubiquitous insects as a standard of measure.)

The sorcerer inspected the silver tube closely. The fruit was clearly inedible. The little scroll had clear lenses at both ends and holes spaced along the slender tube. Was it a simple flute? The sorcerer peered through the end of the flute-like structures. Lenses! The lenses magnified objects viewed in the distance.

The fluted tube was a looking glass!

Rhiann Klarje flipped the lenses to the side, blew air through the end of the device, covered the other holes along the length of the devices, and played melodiously haunting notes.

"A novel fruit. You said the fruit grew in thirteen seasons. This tree should be preserved. May I remove another fruit for my brother Arthur Seigh Klarje?" the sorcerer respectfully asked.

"I should doubt any protestation would stop you," the Tree Shepherd disconsolately muttered silently.

Rhiann carefully removed a second "toot and see scroll" fruit. At the instant the fruit separated from the tree, the remaining eleven mature fruits and recently developed nubbin fell from the tree, landed on the green grass, shimmered briefly, and crumbled into gray dust. Patches of gray earth remained where the scrolls fell onto the grass. The dirt had the consistency of soot from an old fire and no aura of Magick. The tree was now simply an attractive green bush thirteen feet tall. Rhiann removed the first fruit from his pocket. It remained intact.

Rhiann cried out, "****!"

The Tree Shepherd commented aloud, "A painful lesson. Magick seldom rewards greed. One must remove only one fruit and allow the harvested fruit's bud to mature."

"Gauging Magick is difficult. Magick pervades all of Sagain. I propose a place where one of the remaining trees might be safe. Magick touches that world, though not at all times. Still the little tree might flourish," Rhiann proposed.

"Now only three trees remain. I can't allow you…" the green giant argued.

Rhiann interrupted, "Do you really feel the woodsmen will resist removing the silver scroll tubes?"

"I doubt they'll possess the powers I see in you, sorcerer," the Tree Shepherd answered.

"Your illusion may deter them with the help of the spider webs. But they'll only fire the forest. They've burned large areas to gain access to the bluewood trees. Phase spiders have but one power of Magick. They lack fire resistance. Once the webs are burned, they'll harvest the scrolls and roasted purplanana fruits. Do you agree it's be best that I harvest one of the remaining scroll-bearing trees?" the sorcerer retorted.

"Your powers exceed mine. Cover them with Invisibility!" the Tree Shepherd pleaded.

"Flames indiscriminately consume invisible objects and dispel illusion. Also, the ability of many commoners is detecting illusion. Magick is ubiquitous! Detect Magick has little utility in our world!" the sorcerer answered.

The Tree Shepherd argued, "Many years ago another requested one of the trees but lacked the power to move it. Mayard was his name. Use your ability of Translocation! Every sorcerer on Sagain feels the inimitability of the spell! Transfer the scroll-bearing trees to a bluewood stand! Leave them to Sagain!"

Rhiann answered, "The woodsmen felled the bluewoods. There's no place on Sagain I can hide them. Let me preserve this piece of our world."

The Tree Shepherd despondently replied, "I can't really stop you."

The sorcerer calmly replied, "You cannot."

The sorcerer again traced a circle around the nearest toot and see scroll tree, raised his staff, and uttered lyrical phrases. He meticulously repeated the incantations he'd employed in transplanting its predecessors. An intense aura followed. The tree and sorcerer vanished.

Rhiann arrived in Green Vale and set the toot and see scroll tree in one of the remaining spots. The geyser erupted and bathed the trees with its nourishing waters. The circle contained seven occupants.

The toot and see scroll tree…

Ǿ ∞ Ǿ
XIII
∞ **Ǿ** ∞…

Rhiann shook dirt on his shoes and concentrated. In an instant, Rhiann returned to the slopes of Mt. Airie.

The Tree Shepherd communicated, "Back so soon! You robbed the forests of Sagain of a treasure. One should not use Magick to injure creatures of Nature and Magick. You are shameless!"

Rhiann Klarje winced upon hearing the telepathic message and replied, "No, no, my friend. I respect the forest and the treasures of Sagain. I have saved the silver maple tree and toot and see scroll plant. They sit now on a hillock in the midst of a lovely vale. But it's unguarded. I have enlisted the aid of natural barriers to protect it, and done what I can with my Magick, but the trees stand vulnerably. I intend to take a companion from this stand of trees."

CHAPTER 43

The purplanana tree...
Persuading the Tree Shepherd

The Tree Shepherd commented out loud, "I can't say I'm glad to see you again, sorcerer."

Rhiann answered, "Planting the toot and see scroll tree in the Green Vale took only a moment. I had to wait for the waters from a ground spring to spray the tree with water. As an aside, he waters refreshed me."

The Tree Shepherd inquired sardonically, "What more do you intend to take from the forest?"

Rhiann Klarje asked, "Over a hundred purplanana trees stand in this wood! I plan to take one. I hoped you'd help me avoid the phase spiders. I don't have to touch the tree, but I'm going to place a slow spell on the spiders so they won't nefariously bite an unsuspecting denizen of the simple world that will become the purplanana's new home. The gray light is soothing, Tree Shepherd. The gentle spray of the rainbow waters baths the area on the little knoll. The circle of trees needs a shepherd. Have you considered my offer?"

The great green tree answered, again aloud, "I've tended these forests on the slopes of Mount Airie since the time of the great light and devastation that was the dawn of Magick, sorcerer. I find the rays of the distant suns comforting. I can't see myself any other place."

"A Slow Spell enhanced by Permanence will retard the movement of our little friends without harming them. I'll take a purplanana tree now," the sorcerer replied unhappily.

"Time. How long will you be away?" the green giant asked.

"A while," the sorcerer answered evasively. "Thought I might take a bit of nourishment first. I have a bit of Maranna's treacle and some wafers given me by the Allotter. Will you share?"

"I'll make do with the suns' rays, the waters from the skies, and the nutrients of this good soil upon which we stand, sorcerer," the Tree Shepherd answered.

"Oh, don't be so austere. Extend one of your shallow roots. Maranna's molasses are beyond compare," Rhiann chided.

The Tree Shepherd reluctantly lifted a sinuous root from the ground and stretched it toward the sorcerer. Rhiann placed a bit of the treacle upon the root. The great green tree withdrew the root. The sorcerer detected a bit of satisfaction from the silent ruminations emanating from his huge woody companion.

Rhiann Klarje extended his staff, dropped a bit of the treacle on the staff, and uttered an incantation. An aura covered a nearby purplanana tree. Several little phase spiders blurred and then scurried into the sanctuary of their webs. The sorcerer then traced a circle around the little tree and repeated the Dig, Shrink, and Translocation incantations. Then he and the purplanana tree disappeared and left the Tree Shepherd alone on the slope of Mt. Airie.

Rhiann arrived in Green Vale and placed the purplanana bush in its new home. The circle now had eight occupants.

The purplanana bush…

Ǿ ∞ Ǿ

IV

∞ Ǿ ∞…

Rhiann studied the growing circle of plants. He needed the shepherd. He took soil from Iyaca's garden at Harmony House. It was time to call for reinforcements. In an instance he stood by Iyaca and Maranna. His friends wore glum faces.

Iyaca said, "Thynna's armies are advancing into the desert. A great battle is imminent."

Rhiann said, "It was predictable. Maranna, I need your help."

A humming bee approached and buzzed around her as Maranna flew in slow circles over gorgeous plains. The Tri-delta Grasslands, one of Sagain's natural beauties, filled the large area between the ranges of mountains containing Roaring Gap in the north and towering Mt. Airie in the south. Herds of grazing animals such as Blue Nus, Phi Gamms, and Red Machis flourished in the area. The Tri-delta was so named because three rivers, the Eastern Sticks, the Red River, and Green River converged to form the East River at the foot of Solitary Mountain. The East River continued on to the Rivers' Eye where it joined Lovills River. The confluence of the great rivers created the impassible Dead Man's Rapids that flowed beyond the Rivers Eye and ultimately reached the Eastern Sea. The grasses were multi-hued but mostly auburns and violets. The waters flowing in the Red River were…white and milky. Tributaries that ran through great forests of bovine trees fed into the Red River as it coursed through the lands and the milky saps of the trees trickled into the rivulets. The waters of the Green River were…green. The sources of Green River were the Green Mountains that surrounded Greensborough. Green grasses flourished near Greensborough. Maranna enjoyed the panorama, but now the time had come to seek out the cantankerous Tree Shepherd. Rhiann had run into a brick wall in his negotiations with the ancient tree herder and asked the siren to try to persuade him. Maranna evaded a three-eyed Roc hunter and watched the beast snare one of its favorite prey, not surprisingly a Roc. Rocs liked to feast on purplanana fruits, and the Tree Shepherd tended a large stand of purplananas on the slopes of Mount Airie. Perhaps that's where he'd be. His limited teleportation ability still made him a bit hard to catch up with. Maranna flew over Mount Airie's lower slopes and crossed an ugly, denuded area. Several men with large axes hacked away at priceless ancient redwoods and green oaks that had stood since the dawn of Magick. Maranna couldn't resist flying near the men, cloaking herself with invisibility to cheat them of the chance to gaze upon her beauty, and singing a lament. The lumberjacks put down their axes and sobbed incessantly.

The green giant looked sadly at the simple green bush that was once the silver-fluted fruit bearing tree and its two remaining companions. The Tree Shepherd heard the distant, incessant chopping of woodsmen's axes. Then, blessed silence! The chopping stopped. At least for a while the assault on his beloved growths was interrupted. The gentle fluttering of wings distracted him. Wyverns, dragons of many ilks, Manticores, rocs, griffons, Pegasi, and Cloudmares regularly flew over Mount Airie. A pleasing fragrance filled the air. Only on rare occasions had the Tree Shepherd beheld sirens. The siren glided gracefully to a point just beyond the reach of his lower branches and stared at the massive tree. Long orange-red hair fell disheveled across her chest and down her back. Each long hair bristled with radiance and life. Large feathered wings sprouted from the small of her back and rose above her svelte figure. She attempted to disguise the presence of the long full brushy tail that extended behind her. The wondrous, extraordinary female smiled demurely. When she spoke her melodious voice warmed the Tree Shepherd's every branch and root.

"Be comforted, great one. You have served our world long and well. I've watched from your time as a sapling. Now your skills are needed anew," the winged female's voice purred.

The silkiness of her voice blended her words into a soothing tone. The Tree Shepherd would have uprooted and walked over the ledge of Mount Airie's tallest cliff had she asked! Instead the ancient tree herder summoned strength, resisted her beguiling smile, and said, "I assume you've cast lots with the traveling sorcerer, winsome wench!"

"Do you speak of NET?" she queried.

"NET? I know him as Rhiann," the Tree Shepherd followed.

The temptress replied coyly, "NET is, to most, the nameless enchanter of Thynna, old fellow. He seldom reveals his name. You are privileged."

The green giant grumbled, "Nothing is privileged about my dealings with the sorcerer! Your seductive manner is wasted on me, siren. I am privileged to safeguard what remains of my grove. The sorcerer's robbed me of three of my charges. I can't stand against his spells."

The female quickly responded, "Rhiann means well. He won't harm you and your trees."

The Tree Shepherd shook his upper branches, stomped the ground with an exposed root, and said, "I'll have no part of his mischief. If you'll be gone, I have work to do."

The siren asked, "May I sing you a song?"

The beleaguered Tree Shepherd responded, "Somehow I know you are going to sing regardless of my reply."

The winged female sang. Fatigue had accumulated from ages of toil and overwhelmed the towering tree spirit. For the first time in his long existence his burdens left him and he slept. The Tree Shepherd awakened on a hillock in the midst of a circular green vale. The Tree Shepherd assumed a height of sixty feet. This great height afforded a view of the surrounding area. He stood on top of a knoll that was an island of greenness. Great expanses of red, yellow, and orange foliage expanded in all directions beyond the vale. At the fringe of the circular vale the red and orange foliage changed to deep green. Taller trees and bushes rimmed the entire roughly circular area, but a valley filled with short shrubby plants made up the greatest part of the surrounding green vale. The hill sat in the center of the circular vale. Bright green plush grass covered a rim that extended several paces. At the edge of the green moss, the terrain inclined gently at about fifteen degrees for thirty paces and reached the floor. The floor of the circular island of greenness extended several hundred paces, rose gently in several areas, and circled the central knoll. A grassy upslope began where the floor ended and extended fifty or so paces to the top of the central hill. Many small rivulets coursed through the landscape. A gentle breeze crisscrossed the warm valley. The odd sky overhead had some blueness intermingled with the ever-present amber light.

Shrubby plants filled the hillsides and the floor of the Vale. The plants did not grow in rows. Instead the plants were arbitrarily set in the gently rolling terrain. None grew on the central hill. Very few other plants intermingled with the plants.

Above him the Tree Shepherd saw an amber sky. The light was the cumulative effect of three suns, a small bright yellow rapidly moving sun, a dark unmoving spiral, and an equally odd vague gray light source that flickered just above the horizon. Parallan... World of Three Suns...

The Tree Shepherd looked about him. He now assumed a height of fourteen feet. On top of the hillock, he and eight other trees surrounded a central spring.

Thirteen places were prepared in the circle. The Gem Bush from Thynna, great green oak from Greensborough, snowberry bush from the Hanging Gardens, Sick Amore from Andalusia, Jellybean bush from

Artemis, silver maple, toot and see scroll, and purplanana trees occupied eight positions. He filled a ninth. Four awaited occupants. The Tree Shepherd sighed. No one resisted the Siren's song.

The Tree Shepherd…

Ǿ ∞ Ǿ
VII
∞ **Ǿ** ∞…

CHAPTER 44

The Pear Tree...

Of the gathering of the pear tree...

The pear tree was collected from the ancient Kingdom of Dardania, which was named after the pear. The name Dardania means literally "Pearland." The traveling sorcerer liked the word pyriform, which means pear-like and also enjoyed pears, though not as much as he relished apples. NET searched long for exactly the right plant. This tree he had chosen was precisely thirteen feet tall and bore thirteen fruits, which were rounded at their end and smaller toward the stem. When in bloom, the tree bore pink blooms. In some distant past, it must have been related to the bluerose and other rose plants. Once the pear tree was in place, only three places remained unoccupied. The pear tree never grew taller and always bore thirteen fruits.

The pear tree...

$$Ø \infty Ø$$
$$II$$
$$\infty \, Ø \, \infty...$$

The sorcerer greeted the Tree Shepherd but did not tarry and was again quickly away. Time passed. Once the odd gray sun drew near the Green Vale and bathed the world with intense gray light. Then the sorcerer returned.

CHAPTER 45

The L'orange Tree

The l'orange tree caught the traveling sorcerer's eye during a visit to a primitive world of little Magick and a single sun. A grove of the large trees grew on the slopes of an icy peak in an area called the Iron Mountains. Giants of all sorts lived in the rugged mountain range, which was quite inhospitable to the folk of the simple world Donothor. Giants were not the sharpest knives in the drawer. Giants were ordinarily solitary creatures, but communities of the great creatures existed in the great expanses of the Iron Mountains. Giants didn't usually care for other giants. Rivalries between tribes and individuals of the same tribe prevented cooperation. The Iron Mountains provided the perfect habitat for the great beings. Many beasts inhabited the mountains. Diverse creatures thrived in the wide variation of climacteric conditions. Thermal belts warmed by volcanic activity favored plant growth.

Red Giants, the most aggressive of the tribes of giants, favored warm stamping grounds and enjoyed heat! Their great forges created immense weapons and armors. They were fond of flesh and treasure. Treasure to a Red Giant might be a pretty but worthless rock, priceless diamond, or bejeweled chalice. Red Giants understood nothing of Magick. Most giants were as "un-Magick" as a people could be. The Red Giants preyed on the great gap in the northern range of the Iron Mountains. Only giants, large groups of ogres, and the foolhardy risked the perilous journey through the pap connecting the lands of the East and Donothor, which lay to the west of the mountains. Rarely a Light Sorceress or a dragon traversed the gap. Red Giants came by the name because they lived in Red Mountain. Red Giants were taller than Ice

Giants and had dark hides and hair. Pygmy gray dragons sometimes accompanied red giants. The pygmy dragons served roles similar to familiars. Ice Giants preferred cold but tolerated more temperate areas. Ice Giants had bluish hide, gray beards, and body hair. Their favorite prey was the mastoangus herds of the icy Iron Mountain plateau. The mastoangus ate plants that preferred cold and flourished on the icy plateau. The white grasses contained phlouride and clearosyll. Phlouride and clearosyll aided by the sun's rays and nutrients from the icy turf sustained plant life. Creatures that ate the white grasses had very strong teeth and clear skin! Ice Giants also preyed on enormous giant ice slugs that were numerous throughout the mountain ranges. Ice slugs averaged twenty-five feet in length and survived by digesting stone and the iron that gave the mountains their name. They resembled relatives that resided in the deep dark places of the world. Ice Giants located and followed the slugs by locating their excrement. The boneless slugs squeezed into crevices, reached the ore deposits, digested the iron, and passed the iron as gold. Rumors existed that gold was valuable in other lands. In the Iron Mountains of Donothor the metal was just slug droppings and had no value. The digestive juices of the great slugs were highly acidic and corrosive. Many giants suffered burns and lost weapons due to the saliva of the slugs. Giant ice slugs spat saliva up to one hundred feet. Giant ice slug was good eating- if you were an Ice Giant! Rhiann Klarje studied the creatures in the mountains with interest. The Hinderburgh giants allied with the Council of Thynna were most like red giants.

Ornery Ice Giants cultivated the odd L'orange trees, which produced luscious fruits from ice and sunlight. The plants had deep blue leaves. Regardless of the ambient temperature, ice always covered the leaves. The Ice Giants chipped off the ice to induce the plants to produce more fruit. If left alone, the large trees always produced a consistent number of delicious fruits. The orange smooth-skinned fruits rivaled pumpkins in size. Gathering the tree was tricky. The large ice giants guarded the trees tenaciously. Rhiann produced simple Fire Spells. The Fire Spells dissuaded the big beasts long enough to allow the sorcerer to make off with the l'orange tree in the usual manner. He arrived in Green Vale during an amber period. The tree made a nice addition to the circle of the Thirttene friends.

When the l'orange tree was planted, eleven stood in the circle. The sorcerer again disappeared.

The l'orange tree...

Ǿ ∞ Ǿ
XI
∞ **Ǿ** ∞...

CHAPTER 46

The Rainbow Luck Tree, aka
The Cherry Bomb Bush...

Only three rainbow luck trees grew in all of Sagain. One of these grew in the Hanging Gardens, cultivated by the Old Ones. Two others grew on a rocky slope among garnetberry bushes in the mountains to the east. Garnetberry bushes flourished and bore deep red berries that were about the length of an inchworm in diameter. The flavor of the crunchy berries exploded on the tongue. Garnetberries were the favorites of many denizens of Sagain, including Pegasi and displacer bears, also called mountain airy bears. The rare mountain airy bears inhabited mountainous regions and had the ability to apparently vanish into thin air. Actually they were very good chameleons...and displacers. The beasts had deceptive intelligence and natural ability of Magick that always made them appear to be three feet to the right, left, front, or rear of their actual position. The displacer bears, as the airy bears were often called, were akin to the infamous six-legged panthers with horny-ridged tentacles growing out of their shoulders that lived in the deep swamps and made survival there very difficult.

Sometimes called the rainbow bush, luck tree, and cherry bomb tree, the unusual trees were thirteen feet tall and covered by small, cherry-sized fruit that was either red, green, blue, black, white, or polychromatic (multiple colors). The unripe fruit of the tree was translucent. The rainbow bush always had thirteen unripe fruits and thirteen of each color. If one of the colored berries was picked, a translucent fruit appeared in its place and one of the existing clear fruits changed to the color of the fruit that was picked. The clear fruits contained no seeds. Old Plants were long-living and poorly understood. The rainbow luck tree never grew taller.

The red berries were called cherry bombs. If picked before allowed to ripen, it'd blow up in one's hand. If allowed to ripen, the fruits were edible. The Magick of the tree allowed only one of each type per person per lifetime. If you eat one of the red berries after it ripens, you will feel hot; eating the white berry will make you feel cold; you will taste mint if you eat a green one; eating the black berry will create a slight burning sensation beneath your skin; devouring the blue berry will give you a little shock; finally, eating the chromatic fruit will give brilliant hues to your skin. All the effects will be brief. Nothing happens if you eat a second of the same color. A lingering and valuable benefit of eating the berries of the Rainbow Luck Bush is resistance to the effects of the breath of the dragon of the same color as the berry that you eat. If picked after ripening and dried, the red berries exploded when thrown. If picked at the wrong time, the red berries exploded immediately. The rainbow bush produced cherry bombs only once each season.

Rhiann Klarje arrived on the mountainside and interrupted the supper of a mountain airy bear. After a tricky battle, the sorcerer bested the wily beast and prepared one of the two rainbow luck trees for Translocation. Before removing the tree, the Nameless Enchanter of Thynna placed Magick to protect the remaining tree so that only the Magick of a Wish Spell could transplant, destroy, or graft the tree. He then cast a hallucinatory terrain spell on the area to make the entire area appear as a stony outcropping. Only the most discerning Pegasi, mountain airy bears, and sorcerers discovered the location of the remaining rainbow luck tree.

NET transplanted the rainbow luck tree on the hillock in Green Vale. Now twelve trees stood in the circle and overlooked the idyllic vale. The geyser erupted regularly and bathed the Tree Shepherd with invigorating waters. Once again the sorcerer looked toward the Tree Shepherd. On this occasion he spoke, "I look forward to this sojourn. Soon this labor will be finished. Please tend my...our flock."

Then he was away.

The Rainbow luck bush...

Ǿ ∞ Ǿ

VI

∞ Ǿ ∞...

CHAPTER 47

The Apple Tree...

The Traveler's Tome recorded a place called Carroll County in the cloud shrouded beautiful blue world. Translocation had carried Rhiann Klarje to the lands of the third planet from an unremarkable little sun. The little planet sat in the sun's Goldilocks's zone, and Nature expressed many climacteric variations. The sorcerer enjoyed the blue-greenness of the mountains. Locals referred to the mountains as the Blue Ridge. Names of passages through the mountains intrigued the sorcerer. He particularly liked Fancy Gap, Orchard Gap, Wards Gap, and Low Gap. Rhiann Klarje explored widely in the area and investigated a mountain called Sugarloaf. He anticipated finding a Jellybean Bush in a place so named, but he found only green trees and foliage. Enterprising gentlemen named Ralph and Arthur had established an orchard in thermal belts and grew luscious fruits called apples. The traveler found numerous varieties of the delicious fruit. Ralph's son Sam and Arthur's son Garnet had nurtured the growth and the orchard flourished. NET returned to the foothills of the Blue Ridge Mountains. The orchard in Virginia filled a special place in Rhiann's heart. He traveled there right after learning his Uncle Mayard had died. Watching the orchardist warmed Rhiann's heart and lifted his spirits.

Garnet brushed back another bead of sweat from his brow. Half a century of trudging up and down the hillsides of the thriving Virginia orchard had not dulled his vision. Garnet had followed and widened his father's footsteps. The gentle Virginian still outworked younger men. Today he carried a ladder thrice his height on his shoulder and walked alone toward another tree to thin apples. His efforts maintained the apple trees' health. The small deciduous apple tree was a species of the rose family that reached 10 to 39 feet tall and had broad densely twiggy crowns. The leaves were alternately arranged simple ovals with an acute tip, serrated margin, and slightly downy underside. Blossoms appeared simultaneously with the budding of the leaves. The flowers were white with a pink tinged color that gradually faded, with five petals, one to one and a half inches in diameter. The fruit matured in autumn and was typically 2 to 5 inches in diameter. The center of the fruit contained five carpels arranged in a five-point star, each carpel containing one to three seeds. Garnet knew every tree in the orchard.

Rhiann enjoyed his visits to the simple blue world. This orchard became one of his favorite places. He enjoyed the industrious people going about their tasks. If only he could carry the Virginians' work ethic to the sorcerers of Thynna! The sorcerer remained inconspicuous during his visits. The blue world was Nature's domain. Rhiann saw Magick in Nature and marveled at the simple farmer's skill in tending his grove. Garnet's skills rivaled the most veteran tree herders on Sagain, and he performed the tasks without the benefit of Magick. The orchardist placed his ladder against a bearing tree. The small canine that followed Garnet threw his ears back and looked directly toward Rhiann. The sorcerer was discovered. Garnet descended the ladder and looked toward the young visitor.

The dog barked but obediently stopped when Garnet patted his head.

"Hullo," Garnet said cheerfully.

"Hello!" Rhiann managed.

Garnet continued, "I'm Garnet. Are you looking for the pack house?"

Rhiann answered, "No…no, I'd like to talk to you. My name is… NET. I've watched you tending the trees. I admire your great dedication. It looks like hard work. Are you a Tree Shepherd?"

The orchardist replied, "I'm not a shepherd. We don't have any sheep. Some of the neighbors still have cows. I had to give mine up. Too much work to do in the orchard! NET? You've an odd name. Can't say I've heard such. I just work the land and enjoy the orchard. Hard work doesn't hurt a man! I'd rather work here for two full days than take a trip to Boone."

Rhiann said, "So…you don't like to travel."

Garnet replied, "Can't say I do. Have you traveled far?"

The sorcerer continued, "Yes…I'm not from these parts. What are local people commonly named?"

Garnet lifted back his worn cap a bit and again wiped his brow and followed, "That's a might peculiar question. Have heard folks named Archer, Fisher, Hunter, and Bowman. But not 'Net'."

Rhiann felt a bit uncomfortable and continued, "NET is my, what do you say, cognomen? My mother named me Rhiann. You have a fine beast. What's his name?"

Garnet quizzically asked, "Cognomen? Beast? You talk a might funny, young fellow."

Rhiann searched for words. His Comprehend Languages Spell was a bit weak on vernacular. After a few awkward moments he managed, "Nickname! NET is my nickname! It's what my friends call me. The beast… the four-legged creature beside you. I can't understand his tongue."

Garnet chuckled, "That's funny. His name is Drum. He's a pretty good dog. If a man wanted to go hunting, Drum's always done a good job, but he doesn't talk much."

NET, hoping to build rapport with the seemingly gentile man, replied, "Is the hunting good around here?"

Garnet sighed and answered, "Pretty good. It's been a little dry. I saw a few rabbits."

NET continued, "Do you have cheethras, invisibears, and mountain airy bears, rocs?"

Garnet answered, "Uh, no. Might see a bear. Doubt there'd be one in town, uh, in Mount Airy. Foxes, coons, deer, and ducks are more common."

The orchardist stared quizzically at the sorcerer.

Rhiann studied the trees. "Garnet, some of the trees have differing leaves. Is that Magick?"

Now Garnet really laughed, "You *aren't* from around here are you? Must be a city fellow! That's grafting. We grow several kinds of fruit in these orchards."

Rhiann Klarje rubbed the cherry-red birthmark on his chin and asked, "Garnet. I was wondering…might I have one of these trees?"

Garnet chuckled briefly and then answered, "I suppose a man could use a backhoe to dig one up."

NET continued, "I'm serious."

Garnet scratched his head and said, "You must have a truck nearby to haul it. Sam won't mind. I'll call Joe. He'll bring the backhoe."

The traveler said, "I…I won't need a backhoe…or any other digging implements… only your permission."

The comment perplexed the kind orchardist. Garnet answered, "I suppose… I don't see how…"

Rhiann Klarje said, "Thank you. I'll leave the ground undisturbed."

The robed gangly young man scurried around the base of the apple tree with a little shovel, scooped up morsels of dirt, placed the soil in a tiny bucket, and uttered what sounded like a child's limerick.

Garnet advised, "You'll never move any dirt with those little tools. The roots go deep."

The sorcerer completed the Dig Spell. Blue light flashed through the orchard. Garnet and Drum were alone. The young man and apple tree had disappeared. Green grass grew over the site where the missing tree had stood. Garnet scratched his head, looked at Drum, and said, "Nobody's going to believe us, Drum. We may as well finish the thinning."

The Tree Shepherd sensed the aura of the spell. Rhiann appeared on the hillock. A new tree sat in the prepared ground.

"I'm not familiar with the new tree. Where in Sagain did you find it?" the Tree Shepherd asked.

"It's an apple tree. It's not from Sagain. It's from…Virginia," Rhiann answered evasively. About the height of three Drelves or thirteen feet, the first tree bore red luscious unfamiliar fruits. Varying in size and shape, one hundred and sixty-nine fruits grew on the tree. Typical for plants in the Green Vale, the tree had green leaves. The tree's light pink blooms brought to mind the common bluerose plants. An apple tree from Virginia filled the thirteenth place. The circle was complete.

The Apple Tree

Ǿ ∞ Ǿ

I

∞ Ǿ ∞

The circle now contained thirteen trees. Rhiann chatted briefly with the Tree Shepherd. The playful tree sprite emerged from her green oak home and broke out her full repertoire of charms. Rhiann politely declined her advances and began the process of scattering dirt from Harmony House on his boots. He concentrated on the cottage and was back in an instant. The emptiness of the cottage caused him consternation, but soon Iyaca, Maranna, Nona, Mors, Decima, and the Cloudmares Urra, Syrrth, and Shyrra returned to Harmony House.

Nona said, "Are your tasks complete?"

Rhiann said, "No."

Maranna followed, "But you said the Apple tree was the thirteenth occupant of your circle. What more have you to do?"

Rhiann said, "My Uncle Mayard had another request. There was something more of Sagain that he wanted saved."

Nona asked, "What? Haven't you, haven't we risked enough?"

Rhiann said, "You."

Nona quizzically asked, "Us!"

Rhiann said, "The Three Sisters are one of Sagain's treasures. Uncle Mayard's requests included finding a new home for you My Uncle sensed Thynna's aggression. He asked me to carry you away from Sagain. Thynna's legions are too many. There's a place for you in the blue world. You need only promise to not interfere in the course of the citizens of the simple world."

Nona said, "That's not happening. We must defend our home. General Chiron has thrice met Thynna's armies in the deserts north of the Hanging Gardens and thrice defeated them. At great cost of life. The Council of Thynna has again amassed an enormous force, and our scouts tell us its ranks are bolstered by Hinderburgh Giants. Donovan has sent a legion of Gnomes and Dwarves to shore up our defenses. No, Rhiann, we won't take the easy way out. We plan to stand with our defenders. In fact, we must return now to the Gardens. It's been an honor to help you fulfill Mayard's requests. This last one... carrying us away from the Gardens we love just can't occur. Sisters, we must take our leave."

Decima briefly held Rhiann's hand and kissed his cheek. She said, "Finish your other work, Rhiann. Sagain needs you... more than I do."

Nona, Mors, Decima, and the Cloudmares departed and left Rhiann, Iyaca Vassi, and Maranna by Harmony House's cozy hearth. Rhiann stared into the fire. Maranna moved to his side and wrapped her velvety left wing around his shoulders. Iyaca Vassi took a piece of vellum and started to write.

'The Gathering of the Thirttene Friends.'
"Of the Nameless Enchanter of Thynna and the Gathering of the Thirttene Friends." Respectfully written by the hand of Iyaca Vassi…

CHAPTER 48

The Thirttene Friends

In Green Vale the rays of the approaching Gray Sun bathed the new arrivals. Auras surrounded the thirteen trees. The geyser in the fountain at the top the hillock erupted and bathed the circle of trees with rainbow waters. The shy Dryad that lived within its thick bark left the green oak and sat on the Tree Shepherd's branches.

The dryad said, "It's nice to be among friends. I feel at home."

The mighty Tree Shepherd silently communicated to the voluptuous little sprite, "Yes, among Thirttene friends and we are home."

The Tree Shepherd looked around the circle.

The Apple Tree…

The Pear Tree…

The Snowberry bush… one hundred and sixty-nine white berries covered the Snowberry Bush from the Hanging Gardens.

The purplanana tree from his old grove on Mount Airie, saved from the woodsmen's axes… the tree had thirteen elongated purple fruits that were about six inchworms' lengths long. Several intricate webs intertwined in its branches. The little black spiders were nestled in their webs.

The large green oak…the large tree was commonplace to Sagain and most worlds. It fit into the circle well. The large forty-foot-tall oak bore no fruit.

The Rainbow Luck Tree or cherry bomb bush…small cherry-sized fruits covered the thirteen-foot-tall tree adjacent to the oak. The little fruits were red, green, blue, black, white, and chromatic (multiple colors). The little green tree bore thirteen fruits of each variety.

Himself...he projected an image that was fourteen feet tall and fruitless.

The jellybean bush...the odd plant bore one hundred and sixty-nine speckled berries.

The gem bush...the little shrubby growth had clusters of thirteen gems of thirteen colors.

The Silver Maple from his grove...oddly the silver maple had thirteen green leaves and innumerable leaves of silver.

The l'orange tree... the thirty-nine-foot-tall tree that bore thirteen huge orange fruits. Its leaves were deep blue green. Even though the temperature was comfortable, thin slivers of ice covered the leaves of the orange tree.

The Sick Amore...the twelfth tree bore thirteen heart-shaped fruits. According to legend, ingestion of its fruit was the equivalent of imbibing a love potion. Some thought the bittersweet fruit was poisoned. One who consumed the fruit might become intoxicated, lose reason, and long for more.

Finally, the thirteen feet tall "toot and see scroll" tree taken from his grove on Mount Airie...the tree had thirteen branches, a trunk with a diameter of thirteen inches, leaves divided by thirteen veins, and thirteen fruits.

The Tree Shepherd's innate sense of time told him the little yellow sun traversed the sky in sixteen hours. After 60 cycles the little sun withdrew to a nadir and darker skies prevailed for 15 cycles. Gentle orange-skinned visitors to the Green Vale marveled at the new arrivals and called the little sun Meries and referred to the 15-cycle time as Dark Periods. Every eight cycles, 600 of the 16-hour days, the orange-skinned folk called Drelves came to the Vale and harvested tubers from the roots of the plants they called enhancing plants. The orange-skinned folk were true friends of the forest. The Tree Shepherd asked the flirtatious Dryad to refrain from interacting with the forest people. Between the harvest times, small numbers of the Drelves tended the plants.

When Meries drew high in the sky, the little star bathed the World of the Three Suns with amber light, warmed the world, and imparted beautiful yellow and orange hues to the skies of Parallan. The second sun was called Orpheus. Rather than a round bright spot, the dark sun Orpheus was akin to a large dark unmoving spiraling defect in the sky. Giant Orpheus gave little light and controlled the movement of Meries. The third sun was called Andreas. Andreas, the Gray Wanderer, appeared in the sky irregularly. Oft times Andreas came into view as a gray speck on the horizon. From time to time the wanderer left the skies altogether. Every now and then the gray sun wobbled a bit closer. The gray rays of Andreas strengthened the Tree Shepherd and his charges.

The Thirttene Friends…

$$Ø \infty Ø \text{ I} \infty Ø \infty$$

The Apple Tree…

$$Ø \infty Ø \text{ II} \infty Ø \infty$$

The pear tree…

$$Ø \infty Ø \text{ III} \infty Ø \infty$$

The snowberry bush…

$$Ø\infty Ø \text{ IV} \infty Ø \infty$$

The purplanana bush…

$$Ø \infty Ø \text{ V} \infty Ø \infty…$$

The tree Sprite's home, the great green oak…

$$Ø \infty Ø \text{ VI} \infty Ø \infty…$$

The Rainbow luck bush…

$$Ø \infty Ø \text{ VII} \infty Ø \infty…$$

The Tree Shepherd…

$$Ø \infty Ø \text{ VIII} \infty Ø \infty…$$

The Jellybean bush…

Ø ∞ Ø IX ∞ Ø ∞…

The gem bush…

Ø ∞ Ø X ∞ Ø ∞…

The silver maple…

Ø ∞ Ø XI ∞ Ø ∞…

The l'orange tree…

Ø ∞ Ø XII ∞ Ø ∞…

The Sick Amore…

Ø ∞ Ø XIII ∞ Ø ∞…

The toot and see scroll tree…

Collectively, the Thirttene Friends.

Ø ∞ Ø
I, II, III, IV, V, VI, VII, VIII, IX, X, XI, XII, XIII
∞ Ø ∞

The Thirttene Friends

Ø ∞ Ø
I, II, III, IV, V, VI, VII, VIII, IX, X, XI, XII, XIII
∞ Ø ∞

CHAPTER 49

Rhiann's Legacy

The wayfaring sorcerer Rhiann Klarje traveled often, immersed his being in his tasks, established the Circle of Thirttene Friends in Green Vale on the World of the Three Suns, reproduced Sagain's Seven Wonders of the Veldt on the blue cloud-covered world, later constructed Stone Circles modeled after those on the blue world outside Thynna's walls, salvaged and secured artifacts of Magick, and protected of the Source of Magick. Rhiann Klarje created a chamber of Magick to carry others on his journeys. Such travel required rare exotic materials, including shypoke eggshells. NET made many trips to the blue world, the World of the Three Suns, and Donothor. On one occasion Maranna and her sisters Lorelei and Serena accompanied the sorcerer. Maranna spent time in a beautiful wood in a land of snow and water and particularly enjoyed places called fjords. Lorelei stayed at a place on a roaring river, which the people of the land named for her. Serena remained in a place called Thermopile, where she sang to sailors. NET could not persuade Lorelei and Serena to return, but Maranna returned with him to Sagain. Iyaca Vassi had completed the tome detailing the gathering of the thirttene trees in the world of the three suns. Rhiann made ready and traveled to Green Vale. He arrived during a gentle rain shower. The Gray Wanderer filled the sky and bathed the world with grayness. NET presented Iyaca's writing to the Tree Shepherd. The Dryad playfully teased him.

The great tree said aloud, "I resisted your request to come to this place, Sorcerer. I'll never really trusted sorcerers, but you've brought me and my charges to a wondrous place. Please thank the siren for her song. I'll look forward to your visits."

NET replied, "Knowing you are watching over this growth reassures me. The Drelves are deserving stewards for these treasures. Lady of the Tree, are you comfortable in Green Vale?"

The Dryad answered, "Well, yes, sorcerer. I've found many friends. Just one thing… please bring the handsome Gnome Donovan when you come back. I'd still like to show him the inside of my tree."

Rhiann sprinkled some soil from the garden at Harmony House on his boots, uttered a simple phrase, and disappeared. He arrived at Harmony House and found Venla Faxxine and Maranna in full battle regalia.

Maranna solemnly said, "It begins. The host of Thynna nears the Hanging Gardens. We were just leaving."

Rhiann sighed and said, "I'll go with you."

He rode upon Venla's broad shoulders.

The sorcerers of Thynna had great powers of persuasion and promised prodigious bounty. The Alliance of Thynna challenged the Three Sisters and their allies at the Hanging Gardens in the Veldt in the great battle of ancient times. The Sisters and their allies resisted the effects of Magick, but the physical power of the giants, ferocity of the wild men, and sheer numbers of the armies the Alliance of Thynna ultimately overwhelmed the trio's force. Just when the Three Sisters faced their doom, NET used his powerful spell and whisked away them, certain of their allies, and exceptional artifacts of the Hanging Gardens. The Three Sisters committed to continue NET's work and not interfere in the affairs of their new world. They carried with them the Old Language and schematics of the Seven Wonders. In microcosm the ancient culture of Sagain lived on.

The Trio entered the legend and lore of the blue world and indirectly affected those who trusted in fate rather than work to meet their ends. Some will always cast their fate to the wind and foolishly trust in the 'fates.' In this the Spinner, the Allotter, and the Unturning were held blameless. They avowed not to use their devices.

An exhausted Rhiann Klarje returned to Harmony House. Iyaca worked diligently on the chronicle of the wandering sorcerer's deeds. Maranna insisted Rhiann delay further travels and rest at the cottage. Mayard Klarje's fears had come to pass. The siren confirmed that Thynna's host razed the Hanging Gardens to the ground. The Council ordered the land be made infertile. Old Ones suffered immeasurable losses. The defenders of the Hanging Gardens neither asked for nor received quarter. For the most part only the wide inhospitable expanses of the Veldt defended the other wonders from Thynna's armies. The Amazons were a notable exception. The womanly warriors routed a force from Thynna in the desert as it approached the sacred Temple of the Huntress Artemis. Maranna wrapped her soft left wing around Rhiann and pulled him to her. He fell asleep before she began her song. The siren and Iyaca helped him to bed and left him to catch up on needed rest. Fitful slept kept dreams away for a time. Then he dreamed of time spent with his Great Uncle Mayard and his friend Donovan. His mind's tired eyes looked upon the beauty of the Hanging Gardens. Then...

Wisps...
Threads...
Threads of Magick...
Threads of fate...
Threads of time...
Threads connecting worlds ...
Dreams connecting worlds ...
Dreams of Magick...
The Magick of Dreams...
Magick connecting dreams...
Magick connecting worlds...
Grayness...

Grayness entered his dreams.

Rhiann's late Uncle's face appeared in his dream and his mind retraced a memory... he talked with his Uncle in the Hanging Gardens...

Mayard said, "I'm going to bequeath an artifact to you that my grandfather passed to me. He received it after a visit from Grayness."

Mayard reached into his raiment and produced a small nondescript gray stone.

A single rune appeared on the rock and persisted for thirteen heartbeats.

Ω

Then the single letter faded, and three runes appeared on the surface of the rock, which briefly emitted gray light.

$$\acute{Ø} \, \infty \, \acute{Ø}$$

The runes faded after 21 heartbeats and the single rune reappeared. The pattern repeated three times. Three runes appeared on the stones surface.

$$\acute{Ø} \, \infty \, \acute{Ø}$$

Mayard said, "This is an Omega Stone. It's priceless. You must hold it precious. Keep it with you at all times. It seeks its fellows. It came to our ancestor after a dream. I don't know exactly what it does. It gives me a sense of direction. Nona held it and it made her feel stronger."

The dreaming Rhiann took the little rock and held the stone in his hand. A single rune appeared on the rock and persisted for thirteen heartbeats.

$$\Omega$$

Then the single letter faded, and three runes appeared on the surface of the rock, which briefly emitted gray light.

$$\acute{Ø} \, \infty \, \acute{Ø}$$

The runes faded after 21 heartbeats and the single rune reappeared. The pattern repeated three times.

The stone warmed, softened, and meld to his flesh. He released the little rock and it resumed its shape. Rhiann said, "It feels good in my hand. It gives me a sense of protection, but I don't feel stronger. Nor do I get a sense of direction."

Mayard said, "The runes always follow the same pattern. It gives different holders different feelings. Different strokes for different folks."

Rhiann said, "Are you sure it's safe?"

Mayard continued, "It passed along the Klarje family line to me. Cydney Klarje received the stone after a dream. Keep it safe. In all the years I carried it, it's only reacted like you witnessed and given different feelings to those who hold it. One day you'll learn its purpose."

Shapeless Grayness replaced Mayard's face and communicated, "Treasure this Omega Stone. It marks your location to its fellows and is their patriarch. Through it you can share the gifts of the Bloodstone. Carry the stone and three Windward Staves to a Stone Circle. Circles augment the power of Grayness. The patriarch will share its life's blood."

Grayness faded. Images of Caye Klarje and the playgrounds of Thynna drifted into Rhiann's mind's sleeping eye. Then the pleasant touch of Maranna and Decima touched his cognizance. Then redness entered...

Wisps...
Threads...
Threads of Magick...
Threads of fate...
Threads of time...
Threads connecting worlds ...
Dreams connecting worlds ...
Dreams of Magick...
The Magick of Dreams...
Magick connecting dreams...
Magick connecting worlds...
Dream raiders...
Elf pressure...
Albtraum...
Albträume, elf dreams, nightmares...

Redness entered his dreams. A foreboding voice simply said, "I feel your waves of the sea of Magick. I feel you, shaman. You can't you're your path from me."

Blueness filled his dreaming mind and Rhiann entered a time of dreamless sleep. When Rhiann awakened the Omega Stone rested beside him.

EPILOGUE

The leaders of Vydaelia and their allies gathered around the First Wandmaker Yannuvia. Yannuvia studied an odd parchment and its strange seal. The seal was made of a hardened blue substance. Lettering was etched or burned into the blue material.

Ǿ ∞ Ǿ

∞ **Ǿ**∞ **XIII** ∞ **Ǿ**∞

Ǿ ∞ Ǿ

Yannuvia, four-armed Carcharian Bluuch, Mender Fisher, Duoth leader *Mose14*, and Ranger Jonna carried Omega Stones. The beautiful sea elf Piara, Yannuvia's greenish look-alike Clouse, gray elf Commandant Inyra, and she-Drelve Kirrie wore amulets with Sibling Stones. Those four small purplish artifacts mimicked the effects of Omega Stones. The presence of the four Sibling Stones activated *Read Magick*.

Yannuvia touched the Knock Wand to the seal and muttered **"Cow vine cool ledge."** The seal crumbled. A hologram of the runes remained where the seal had been. The ghostly runes rose into the air and flickered an odd reddish color above the Spellweaver-Wandmaker. Yannuvia unrolled the parchment, touched it with the red and blue-tipped Master Wand, and said, **"Hairy True Man."**

Yannuvia began, "The scroll is titled 'the Gathering of the Thirttene Friends.' The Tree Shepherd of Green Vale credits authorship to Iyaca Vassi. The chronicle recounts the deeds of the Nameless Enchanter of Thynna."

Albträume

Ǿ ∞ Ǿ

Ǿ ∞ Ǿ
I, II, III, IV, V, VI, VII, VIII, IX, X, XI, XII, XIII
∞ Ǿ ∞

The Thirttene Friends

Ǿ ∞ Ǿ
I, II, III, IV, V, VI, VII, VIII, IX, X, XI, XII, XIII
∞ Ǿ ∞

Printed in the United States
by Baker & Taylor Publisher Services